The
Anarchists'
Convention

Also by John Sayles

The Anarchists' Convention

Stories

JOHN SAYLES

HarperPerennial

A Division of HarperCollinsPublishers

"At the Anarchists' Convention," "Hoop," "Breed," "Golden State," and "I-80 Nebraska, m.490–m.205" appeared in *The Atlantic;* "Children of the Silver Screen" appeared in *Quest/79.*

A hardcover edition of this book was published in 1979 by Little, Brown & Co. It is here reprinted by arrangement with Little, Brown & Co.

First HarperPerennial edition published 1992.

Designed by Susan Windheim

LIBRARY OF CONGRESS CATALOG CARD NUMBER 91-58466

ISBN 0-06-097476-1

92 93 94 95 96 RRD 10 9 8 7 6 5 4 3 2 1

Contents

Home for Wayfarers

THEY ALWAYS HAVE the Career Girls sit together. At least they do at New England Life and at Hub Mail usually and at the First Boston Savings and Trust and here at the Home for Wayfarers.

"Maybe it's so we don't infect the regular help," says Chickie da Costa. "Or maybe it's so we don't find out what they're gettin paid for the same jawb."

Nina has a desk by the window, looking down on the parking lot and the grounds beyond it.

The Home for Wayfarers
Sincerely Thanks

_____

For the Gift of _____ Dollars

Nina writes the name from the donation letter and fills in the amount given. The thank-you card has an owl on it, a drawing by one of the children. She addresses an envelope by hand, stuffs the card in, puts it on the pile for Deke to pick up.

Nina listens to the others talk as she works. The Home is

one of the best jobs Career Girls has sent her on. The supervisor is nice and the food is supposed to be good in the cafeteria. Most of the others have worked together here and there, and the two South Boston girls, Mary and Kathleen, are best friends.

"You do your work here," says Chickie da Costa, "there's no prawblems. Some places they're breathin down your neck the whole day."

"Like banks," says Barbara, squiggling improvements onto the picture of the owl. "Banks they're always on your fuckin case. Scared you'll mess up their precious computer cods."

Gwen clears her throat. Gwen clears her throat whenever someone swears, but they don't seem to notice. Gwen is in some kind of religious group.

Nina pulls another letter from her pile. Mr. and Mrs. George C. Papanicholau. There is barely room on the card.

"You're pretty fast," says Chickie da Costa. "The other girl we had, she couldn't write."

"She could write," says Kathleen, "only you couldn't read it. Not even the numbers."

"That's okay for filin, or if they got you on a machine, but for this stuff, where it's goin out for public scrutiny and all — no way. They had to send her back to Career Girls." Chickie looks over Nina's shoulder. "But you, you got nice handwriting."

"Thank you." It's the first she's said since she introduced herself. "It isn't that hard."

"For you it's not hod, but for some people, you'd be surprised."

Deke comes to collect another batch of letters. He wears a body shirt open four buttons and has a nice tan. He's dark, with white white teeth. He smiles at them, flashing all thirty-two as he approaches.

"Hi girls," he says. "Got some more work for me?"

Kathleen pushes forward her stack of completed letters.

"Kind of pokey this morning."

He wears turquoise rings on all the fingers of his left hand.

"He wore his pants any tighter," says Chickie when he's gone, "he'd be bleedin out the ears."

"He thinks we're gettin all agitated over here," says Barbara. "He thinks we're over here creamin in our draws."

Kathleen and Mary giggle and Nina smiles. Gwen clears her throat.

"He joins Career Girls he thinks he's gonna clean up," says Barbara. "I worked with him over to this clearinghouse, they sent out all this stuff — electric bidet kits, whir-pool attachments for your tub, plastic bedpans — all this medical stuff. Deke was there packing boxes. You said two kind words to him he's on your case the rest of the day, hangin around."

"I sawr him over to Lucifer the other night."

"You're kiddin."

"Tryin to put the moves on every girl in the place."

"So'd you go home with him?"

Kathleen gives Mary a knuckle-punch in the shoulder. "Wise guy."

"Did you see him dance?"

"Yeah, he shakes his ass a lot. Thinks he's Gawd's gift to women."

"Some gift," says Chickie. "Tell Gawd he shouldn't of bawthered."

Barbara is in the bathroom when the supervisor comes over.

"How's it going, girls?"

"Just fine, Miss McCurdy. We're cuttin it down to size."

"Is Barbara okay?" Miss McCurdy is in her fifties. She wears glasses hung by a ribbon around her neck.

"She'll be fine, Miss McCurdy. It's her period or something."

Miss McCurdy frowns. "She doesn't look well. She doesn't look like she gets her rest."

"She gets loaded in there, Bobra," whispers Chickie when the supervisor is gone. "Every morning she goes in there, smokes a joint. Then after lunch another one. You want to see handwriting, catch hers by the end of the day."

"So how'd the interview go?" asked Robin. "Was she nice?"

Nina looked at the print on the wall, trying to remember who had bought it. "Uhm, there was a note downstairs that said she'd already found a roommate. So I didn't meet her."

"Oh." Robin was sitting on the footstool in the center of the room, watching Nina collect her belongings.

"Do you remember," asked Nina, "which of us this belongs to?"

"The Cassatt? I think we bought it together when we were setting up here. At the Coop. Why, do you want it?"

"Well —"

"The only thing is, since we painted over the wallpaper, it gets a lot of sun there — there'll be a patch left."

Nina lifted the corner of the print, saw the different shade underneath.

"Didn't take long, did it?"

"No. It wasn't up that long. But take it if you want it, I can get something else that size, or maybe bigger —"

"No, no —"

Hummer came back from the Square with more beer. He said hi to Nina and went into Robin's room.

That was how it had started, Hummer going into Robin's room, Robin joining him, hushed voices. Nina sitting alone on the couch, waiting a bit, then finding something to do. Hummer moving in. The tension always there, spilling over now and then into something overt. Confrontations.

"The M. C. Eschers are mine," said Robin. "Both of them, I'm pretty sure. And that one with all the animals, the lion and the lamb and all that, that one's yours. You had it at school I remember."

Nina picked up the throw pillows she'd made, then put them back down.

"No sense in taking these," she said. "They're meant to go with this couch."

"When you find where you're going to be, maybe you'll need them."

"Wherever that is."

"I told Mrs. Malaparte about the change in the lease."

"What did she say?"

Robin shrugged. "She didn't seem to care. As long as Hummer doesn't keep his bike on the landing."

"And what's it called again?"

"The Family of God." Gwen is very mysterious about her group. She doesn't volunteer anything, but Chickie keeps after her.

"I never heard of it."

"We don't prostyletize."

"I should hope not. And they do everything for you?"

"We do everything for each other."

"You give them all your money?"

"We don't have property separate from each other."

"Not even a toothbrush?"

Gwen doesn't answer.

"I know a guy went into the Moonies," says Barbara. "He doesn't get to have any prawperty either. But then he never had any in the first place."

"Is that where you shave your head?" asks Kathleen.

"Those are the Hare Krishnas," says Nina.

Chickie looks at her. "You know about that stuff?"

"No. Not much."

"I worked with a girl," says Mary, "was a Scientologist."

"That's right, she was," says Kathleen. "Over at the brewery where we were filing."

"And what do they believe in? Besides plasterin the trolley with their pamphlets?"

"I don't know, but she used to give them a regular pot of her paycheck."

"And I thought the Catholics were bad," says Chickie, "with the collection plate under your nose every time you turn around. You don't keep anything for yourself, to buy yourself clothes or something?"

Gwen shakes her head. "The Family buys our clothes for us."

"You're kiddin. They pick them out and all?"

"Clothes aren't important."

Chickie laughs. "Tell that to the gang in Filene's Basement. Clothes ont impawtant."

"At the house we all wear plain white robes."

"Like in a choir."

"Sort of."

"You all live together?"

"There's more than one house."

"And you all eat together?"

"Yes. And when I go out working they pack me a lunch."

"Jeez."

"My mother packs my lunch," says Mary, "on the jawbs where the food is lousy." Mary and Kathleen both live with their mothers.

"And is there somebody who's like, you know, the big cheese? The center of the whole outfit?"

"We believe in God —"

"No, not *Him*, I mean somebody real, somebody *liv*ing."

"The Family is the center of everything. We do things as a Family."

"And you pray together I bet. I seen you with your eyes closed here —"

"I'm meditating."

"Oh. You're into that too." Chickie shakes her head, skeptical. "I don't know, Gwen. The living together I could handle, if you got enough room, and the eating and the singing and all that. But I'd never let them pick my clothes out. Never."

Rummaging through her desk for another pen, Nina finds an old photograph. A large, very old photograph lining one of the drawers. Three rows of girls in baggy middy blouses and ankle-length skirts. It has a sepia cast to it but hasn't faded much. The girls are in their early teens, and many of them are pregnant. A bunch in the back row are trying to hold in laughter, covering their faces, turning their heads to the side. Somebody made a wisecrack.

What a nice way, thinks Nina. Surrounded by friends in the same situation. She shows it to the others and puts it up on the wall by her desk.

"Unwed mothers," says Kathleen. "They told us how after the Civil War there were all these kids walking around with no place to go, and a lot of the girls got into trouble. So the society ladies in Boston stotted this place up. At least that's what they told us."

"They got all kinds now," says Mary. "Little boys and girls. You'll see in the cafeteria."

"Now that's what you get," says Chickie da Costa studying the photograph, "you let other people pick your clothes out."

Deke comes over and smiles at them.

"Hey girls," he says. "You're falling behind."

Deke's job is to take the stuffed envelopes, seal them and run them through the postage meter. Somehow he barely manages to stay ahead of them.

"That's right," says Barbara. "We got no time to talk to you."

Barbara has drawn teeth on an owl, is writing a name in the blank, letter by letter, taking her time.

Deke looks at Nina. "You're new here."

"That's right."

Deke smiles at her, stands looking down at her work.

"You're pretty."

Chickie snorts. Mary and Kathleen giggle.

Nina fills out a card. Mr. and Mrs. Frank Capadilupo.

"My name's Deke. I don't think we've met."

"I'm Nina," she says without looking up. Chickie groans.

"Would you like to have lunch with me?"

He's sitting on her desk now, blocking the light from the window.

"Look," says Nina, sighing, staring up at him, "don't waste your time. You're not half as sharp as you like to think you are. Forget it, okay?"

Chickie snorts and the Southie girls cover their faces.

Deke fingers the medallion that hangs against his chest. He shrugs, stands.

"You girls got more work for me?"

2F DESIRE 3RD F, SPACIOUS ROOM, BACK BAY, NON-
SMOKER, MUST LIKE CATS, $80 MO. PLUS UTIL. CALL
FOR INTERVIEW.

It was a very nice apartment. It was on Commonwealth, on the top floor, and the living room got a lot of sun late in the day. One of the cats played with an old tennis ball in a square patch of sun broken by the outline of the hanging coleus plants.

"What's that like," asked Melanie, "temporary work?"

Nina shrugged. "Mostly filing, some typing if you're fast enough. They send you around to different offices that have some big job they need out in a hurry. Or else it's just cheaper for them to hire temps. They don't have to pay any benefits."

"I worked for a while in an office," says Alissa. Alissa had long, straight blond hair. Melanie had black hair just growing out from a frizzy permanent. "It was the pits."

Alissa was still in school, and Melanie was out but taking classes.

"I take one at Joy of Movement," she said. "And an acting workshop and then there's this woman I do Tai Chi with."

"It gets pretty low-key around here," said Alissa. "I think you can always tell by the cats in a house. If the cats are all hyper, running around chewing things and not using their box, then you've got problems in the house."

"Where have you been living?"

"In Cambridge," said Nina. There were drawings from Lewis Carroll up on the walls. There were bayberry candles — Nina could smell them though they weren't lit. "My roommate's boyfriend moved in and there just wasn't enough space."

"All my classes are at night," said Melanie, "and a lot of the time Alissa stays over with this guy Greg. We wouldn't be in each other's way much of the time."

"We don't do any big number with eating," said Alissa. "The refrigerator and the oven work fine. We leave notes to make sure the cats get fed."

"You'd probably have to have a phone, wouldn't you? For them to tell you where to go in the morning."

"You don't have one?" Nina had noticed the jack sticking out of the wall when she came in.

"You could have it in your room."

"We're not here a lot of the time, but it's good to have a sort of base of operations. You'd usually have the nights to yourself." Another cat was sleeping in Alissa's lap. "If you wanted to have somebody stay over that's fine, as long as things stay pretty low-key."

"I may be moving to Vermont," said Melanie. "But I don't know. I've got friends up there. They've got this farm, and it's you know, like a group effort but people come and go. I don't know, I've heard it's real cold up there."

"If Melanie was to move," said Alissa, stroking the cat's head, "I'd take her room and you could move into mine. You'd have a window then."

There is a small table in the cafeteria set aside for the Career Girls. Miss McCurdy takes her lunch at her desk back up in the office. At the long tables there are counselors with bunches of grade-school kids. Eating, laughing, playing with each other.

"I thought of going to secretarial school," says Mary, "but it costs an om and a leg." Mary and Kathleen want to be hired for permanent jobs at one of the big insurance companies.

"I could get up fifty more words a minute, they'd send me out for typing and I'd get hired in no time. That's what most of the girls do, they find a place they like and do a good jawb and get asked to stay on permanent."

"Yeah, that's prawbly the smottest way," says Chickie. "Why should Career Girls make all the money and we do all the work?"

"Did you ever think of getting together," says Nina, "and trying to get a bigger cut of what the employer pays out?"

"What, like a union? Never work. The regular employees, the secretaries, they don't even have one. How you gonna get temps, they don't know each other, they don't work the same place from day to day, how you gonna get them together?"

"We have a lot in common."

"Sure, we're all stupid, workin for peanuts. We should get on regular, like Mary says."

"In the Family," says Gwen, "we aren't allowed to have full-time jobs."

"That figures."

"If you got more schooling," says Kathleen, "they give you a better jawb. Whether your typing's good or not. My cousin, she went to Boston State two years, she walked into a hawspital looking for a receptionist jawb and they made her head clerk in accounting. She gets holidays, paid vacation, health insurance —"

"I went to Nawtheastern one semester," says Barbara. "But I quit. I couldn't see it, out on the fuckin Green Line every day to sit in a classroom. My girlfriend dropped out and then I quit."

"Where'd you go to college?" Chickie is looking at Nina. Nina hadn't said anything about going to school. "BU?"

"No."

"Where then?"

"Bard."

"Bod, what's Bod? I never heard of it."

"It's in New York."

"You from there?"

"Connecticut."

"From Connecticut and went to school in New York. What, you moved? What'd you take there, what'd you major in?"

"English."

"You should be a teacher."

"I tried it. Substituting. I didn't like it."

Chickie snorts. "Substituting isn't the same thing. Substitutes, it was tawture what we used to put them through. They know about that at Career Girls? The English?"

"I suppose."

"Prawbly doesn't cut a whole lot in office work, does it? Well, you got nice handwriting, anyway."

Nina eats and watches the kids. They are crowded around the tables, arms brushing, spearing forkfuls of cake from each other's trays, jostling, teasing. She spots a couple she'd like to take home with her, little curlyheads with bright eyes. The counselors talk among themselves over the children's heads.

"I think it's a bad jawb," says Chickie da Costa. "The minute I heard it on the radio I smelled a rat. Somebody bought em that podden."

The big item in the morning news is Governor Dukakis officially pardoning Sacco and Vanzetti, clearing their names in the record books.

"How do you know?"

"Hey, those Mafia, they get in trouble, the big cheeses down in Prawvidence bail em out."

"They aren't Mafias," says Barbara. "It said they're political."

"Mafia, politicians, it's the same bunch. Dukawkis is in the bag."

"They're dead," says Nina. "They were anarchists who were accused of a robbery. The evidence wasn't any good but they were electrocuted anyway."

"They're dead already?"

"They died in nineteen twenty. But they weren't cleared officially till today."

"Huh." Chickie shakes her head. "Lotta good it does em now."

"What's that?" Kathleen is looking at Gwen's lunch.

"Pork."

"Oh."

"You ought to try some of this," says Chickie. "It's real good. And they don't chodge us for seconds."

"No thank you."

"They packed that for you, the Family?"

"Food isn't important."

"Right." Chickie nudges Nina under the table, rolls her eyes. "Food's not impawtant. I hope my stomach's listening. And you, you're not eatin Bobra?"

"I don't have much of an appetite today."

Barbara excuses herself to go to the bathroom.

"She doesn't look good," says Mary.

"She suppawts her boyfriend," says Chickie. "A real loser. I seen them together she comes to Career Girls for her check."

"She looks tired."

"She's wrecked so much of the time, she can't hold a jawb. That's why she does this stuff. Idiot work."

"And he doesn't have a jawb?"

"Not that you'd notice. I asked her. I was thinkin of moving in with my boyfriend. But both of us would be bringin it home, we'd split the rent. We want to go to the Bahamas."

"What's there, the Bahamas?"

"Real nice beaches, hotels, trawpical forests. He's been once before."

"With somebody else?"

"Won't tell me." Chickie makes a face. "That's one of the reasons I'm not movin in, there's too much stuff he doesn't tell me."

"You think she's smoking a joint in there?"

"I wouldn't be surprised, Mary. Personally, I can't see it. Makes the time drag, makes the day go longer."

"Speaking of which, here comes Lover-Boy."

"Spare me. Are you guys done?"

Deke walks toward them with his lunch, flashing his smile, singing. He sings along with his radio all day. As he sits the Career Girls all stand and take their trays to the waste barrel.

The houses were set hundreds of feet back from the meandering road, some of them completely out of sight behind stone walls and giant elms. The lawns were left shaggy but not overgrown. The stone walls were carved into flat planes, into long rectangles and rounded pillars, as if the Yankee masons wanted to do in stone what Europeans did in shrubbery.

Two granite statues had once flanked the entrance to the driveway, a lion and a lioness looking haughtily across the gravel to each other. The lion's paw had rested on a small globe which disappeared one night, neatly separated as if it had spun away under its own power. The lion disappeared soon after, leaving only the marble base. Mother supposed it was fraternity boys back from Easter vacation, that it had turned up in some New Haven dormitory, painted and scrawled with graffiti. When Nina was little she imagined that it had risen of its own and run off to search for the missing ball. That it had made itself mortal by sheer will-power, every day growing warmer to the touch, thawing from the inside out, till it had walked away one night, stiffly, proudly, leaving little piles of rock dust for tracks.

The lioness stayed, but didn't look as sure of itself.

Redboy was sleeping on the empty pedestal when Nina drove in, the big Irish setter Mr. Worth had brought when he moved in with Mother. Redboy had an enormous head and snored when he slept.

It was a large colonial house, white with black shutters and shingles. Only the name on the box had changed since Nina lived there.

Nina ate shrimp salad with her mother in the sun-room.

"You're moving out?"

"We decided it was best. There isn't room enough for three."

"Do you like him?"

"Hummer? No, not much."

"Robin's parents won't be happy."

"They're never happy."

"And how is your friend Meredith?"

Nina hadn't heard from Meredith for over a year.

"Okay, I guess. Still in med school."

"And little Sara?"

"She went back to California."

"And the one I thought was so lovely, the Jewish girl —"

"She got married."

"Oh."

Mr. Worth wasn't there. Nina usually managed to time it so he'd be off on business.

"They were such nice girls. Do you see any of your other friends in Boston?"

"Most of them are down in the City. Boston is a two-year town, three at most. They do their time and then move to New York."

"Oh."

Her mother nodded for a long moment.

"Gloria Fortner died."

Nina tried to remember which one she was.

"The second this year. One of our most faithful classmates."

Mother devoted herself to reunions. Smith, class of '43. It was an obsession, getting the girls together. Mother bombarded them with newsletters, with old pictures, with birth and death announcements, with arrangements for the next get-together. She made tours of the East, New York to Philadelphia to Boston, catching old classmates at home and staying on for a few days.

"I'm trying to get a contingent together for the service. It's in Branford."

"People are busy, Mother —"

"It seems they have less and less time as they get older. With me it's the opposite."

"Maybe if you left a little more time between reunions, Mother, people would have a chance to recover, to get nostalgic again."

"It isn't nostalgia," said Mother. "It's *friend*ship."

Mr. Worth was converting Nina's old room into an office.

"Your father felt I needed a better environment for my work. I have so much correspondence." Mother touched her arm. "I hope you don't mind."

"I don't live here anymore," said Nina. "Mr. Worth does."

"I'm sorry. Your *step*father."

"I think it will make a nice office. The light is good in the morning."

"Every year there seems to be more paperwork," said Mother. "And every year fewer of the girls seem to have the time."

Redboy had been digging up the garden again. Nina helped her mother replant the oxalis.

"Muffy Chandler's daughter just moved to Boston."

Mother always knew someone, some classmate, whose daughter was moving to Boston.

"It sounds like she's having her troubles. Drifting."

"You mean like me."

"I didn't say that. I didn't say you were drifting." Mother frowned under her sun hat. "I meant that she doesn't know what she wants to do with her life either. And she's very independent."

They worked quietly for a while.

"Your stepfather wants to dig a swimming pool back here."

"Uh-huh."

"More for entertaining than for swimming. With a patio. He doesn't swim."

Redboy was there, snuffling over the dirt clods they'd piled. Mother shook her head.

"They're so sweet-tempered and handsome," she said. "But so stupid."

"Do you shoot guns?"

"Everything but. The whole basic-training thing."

"My oldest sister was in," says Kathleen. "She had a great time there for a while."

Chickie makes a face. "The service? How can you have a good time, the service, they're always givin you awders all the time?"

"It's not so bad. You just don't take it serious. And there's

all the other girls there. There was times, my sister, her barracks was just like a slumber potty."

"And they pay for your education," says Mary.

"So what rank did your sister get to be?"

"Oh, she got tired of it so she got pregnant."

"They let you out for that?"

"If you're not married they do."

Chickie snorts. "Beats a note from your mother."

Whenever Miss McCurdy passes she eyes the photograph
Nina put up on the wall. Whenever Nina looks to the back of
the room Deke is watching her, smiling.

Mr. and Mrs. Samuel Rivkin. Two hundred dollars.

Nina is the fastest, along with Chickie. Then Mary and
Kathleen, then Gwen, who seems to be meditating more
often as the day wears on, and then Barbara. Barbara isn't
drawing anymore. She goes to the bathroom.

"She's not gonna work like the rest of us," says Kathleen,
"she should go home."

"She's got prawblems." Chickie can talk and work steadily
at the same time. "Hey, it's like that gospel lesson in church,
where the guys who worked all day got paid the same as the
guys who only came for the last hour. I mean, she's not makin
you work any hodder. It's beween her and the employer."

Nina tries to wait till Barbara comes back but can't hold
out.

Barbara is leaning over the sink, her face drained pale.

"It isn't gonna come. It's over a week now."

"Your period?"

"My stomach feels like shit but there's no dischodge."

"It might be something else."

"I'll kill the fucker," says Barbara. "I'll break his fuckin
head."

If it was Chickie or one of the South Boston girls Nina

would have put her arm around her. But Barbara stands there with her fists clenched, cursing into the sink.

"Don't tell nobody, okay?" she says. "They find out they'll send me home. I need the hours."

Nina comes back to her desk alone.

"Get a couple good hits in there?" asks Chickie, and nudges her in the ribs.

Mr. and Mrs. Vernon Dahlhart, twenty-five dollars.

Deke comes over to ask Barbara if she's all right. She tells him to fuck off. He says she should get more sleep.

Mr. and Mrs. Warren Friedrich, ten dollars.

Miss McCurdy finally comes over and just stands looking at the photograph on the wall.

"I'm sorry," says Nina, "does that bother you?"

"I'm not used to having something up there. And that picture —"

"It looks really old."

Miss McCurdy sits back on Nina's desk, upset, shaking her head. "Times have certainly changed."

"They look like my yearbook field-hawkey picture," says Chickie da Costa, "only puffier."

"When I was a little girl in Philadelphia," says Miss McCurdy, "the sisters used to march us all over to this place, a home for unwed mothers. Wayward girls, they called them then. And we had this poem we'd recite about Saint Catherine. She must have been the patron saint of wayward girls."

Miss McCurdy strains to remember.

> Saint Catherine,
> Saint Catherine,

she says,

> O lend me your aid,
> And grant that I may never
> Be an old maid.

A husband, Saint Catherine.
A good one, Saint Catherine.
But anyone better than
No one, Saint Catherine.

A husband, Saint Catherine.
Good, Saint Catherine.
Handsome, Saint Catherine.
Soon, Saint Catherine.

Miss McCurdy shakes her head, wipes her glasses.

"You must of been real pawpular with that," says Chickie da Costa. "Must of brung the house down."

Nina takes the picture off the wall and slips it under her pile of letters.

"Thank you," says Miss McCurdy. "I don't know what bothers me about it. Just fussy about the office, I guess, like to keep things in place."

"Personally," says Chickie after she's gone, "I was in that condition, I would of told em to go piss up a rope. Sisters and all."

Gwen clears her throat. Barbara goes to the bathroom.

Nina addresses letters, fills out thank-you cards. It's better work than cross-checking figures at a bank, or personalizing form letters for an insurance company or filing financial aid at BU. It's better than folding electric blankets for new-account bonuses. It's better than being a receptionist for anybody. And the food is good in the cafeteria.

Deke plays his radio in the rear of the office, relentless top-forty disco, and Chickie and Mary and Kathleen talk on.

Every time Nina finishes a letter from the pile she uncovers more of the girls in the picture. Some of them have their arms around each other, some hold hands. There are some real beauties with clear, sharp eyes. Their hair is long, braided. Nina thinks of them putting each other's hair in braids every morning.

Ms. Colleen Walsh. Ten dollars.

A few minutes before quitting time, Nina sees Deke hugging a woman in the parking lot. A woman in her forties, with a tan and a trim, tennis-player's body. Deke hugs her, kisses her on the lips. They walk away hand in hand.

"So," says Nina, "Deke's got himself a sponsor. No wonder he's so cocky."

Chickie looks out the window. "That's his mother. She picks him up."

"Every day?"

"Uh-huh."

"His mother."

"Whatta you want?" says Chickie, shrugging. "He's a retod."

"Oh."

"What, we'd give him all that gas he was nawmal? She has him go out on simple jawbs. She's friends with the big cheese at Career Girls."

Miss McCurdy lets them go a little early, signing their time slips. They all take the Green Line back toward the city, but only Mary and Kathleen end up in the same seat.

Nina takes the photograph with her. She plans to put it up on the wall in her bedroom, wherever that turns out to be. Nina looks at the photograph in her lap as they rattle through Brookline. She wonders what the girls in the back row were laughing about.

At the
Anarchists' Convention

SOPHIE CALLS TO ASK am I going by the Anarchists'
Convention this year. The year before last I'm
missing because Brickman, may he rest in peace,
was on the Committee and we were feuding. I
think about the Soviet dissidents, but there was always something so it's hard to say. Then last year he was just cooling in
the grave and it would have looked bad.

"There's Leo Gold," they would have said, "come to gloat
over Brickman."

So I tell Sophie maybe, depending on my hip. Rainy days
it's torture, there isn't a position it doesn't throb. Rainy days
and Election Nights.

But Sophie won't hear no, she's still got the iron, Sophie.
Knows I won't be caught dead on the Senior Shuttle so she
arranges a cab and says, "But Leo, don't you want to see
me?"

Been using that one for over fifty years.

Worked again.

We used to have it at the New Yorker Hotel before the
Korean and his Jesus children moved in. You see them on the
streets peddling flowers, big smiles, cheeks glowing like Hit-
ler Youth. High on the Opiate of the People. Used to be the

New Yorker had its dopers, its musicians, its sad sacks and marginal types. We felt at home there.

So this year the Committee books us with the chain that our religious friends from Utah own, their showpiece there on Central Park South. Which kicks off the annual difficulties.

"That's the bunch killed Joe Hill," comes the cry.

"Corporate holdings to rival the Pope," they say, and we're off to the races.

Personally, I think we should have it where we did the year the doormen were on strike, should rent the Union Hall in Brooklyn. But who listens to me?

So right off the bat there's Pinkstaff working up a petition and Weiss organizing a counter-Committee. Always with the factions and splinter groups those two, whatever drove man to split the atom is the engine that rules their lives. Not divide and conquer but divide and subdivide.

First thing in the lobby we've got Weiss passing a handout on Brigham Young and the Mountain Meadow Massacre.

"Leo Gold! I thought you were dead!"

"It's a matter of days. You never learned to spell, Weiss."

"What, spelling?"

I point to the handout. "Who's this Norman? 'Norman Hierarchy,' 'Norman Elders.' And all this capitalization, it's cheap theatrics."

Weiss has to put on his glasses. "That's not spelling," he says, "that's typing. Spelling I'm fine, but these new machines — my granddaughter bought an electric."

"It's nice she lets you use it."

"She doesn't know. I sneak when she's at school."

Next there's the placard in the lobby — WELCOME ANARCHISTS and the caricature of Bakunin, complete with sizzling bomb in hand. That Gross can still hold a pen is such a miracle we have to indulge his alleged sense of humor every year. A malicious man, Gross, like all cartoonists. Grinning, watching the hotel lackeys stew in their little brown uniforms, wondering is it a joke or not. Personally, I think it's in bad taste, the bomb-throwing bit. It's the enemy's job to ridicule, not ours. But who asks me?

They've set us loose in something called the Elizabethan Room and it's a sorry sight. A half-hundred old crackpots tiptoeing across the carpet, wondering how they got past the velvet ropes and into the exhibit. That old fascination with the enemy's lair, they fit like fresh kishke on a silk sheet. Some woman I don't know is pinning everyone with name tags. Immediately the ashtrays are full of them, pins bent by palsied fingers. Name tags at the Anarchists' Convention.

Pearl is here, and Bill Kinney in a fog and Lou Randolph and Pinkstaff and Fine, and Diamond tottering around flashing his new store-boughts at everyone. Personally, wearing dentures I would try to keep my mouth shut. But then I always did.

"Leo, we thought we'd lost you," they say.

"Not a word, it's two years."

"Thought you went just after Brickman, rest his soul."

"So you haven't quit yet, Leo."

I tell them it's a matter of hours and look for Sophie. She's by Baker, the Committee Chairman this year. Always the Committee Chairman, he's the only one with such a streak of masochism. Sophie's by Baker and there's no sign of her Mr. Gillis.

There's another one makes the hip act up. Two or three times I've seen the man since he set up housekeeping with Sophie, and every time I'm in pain. Like an allergy, only bone-deep. It's not just he's CP from the word go — we all had our fling with the Party, and they have their point of view. But Gillis is the sort that didn't hop off of Joe Stalin's bandwagon till after it nose-dived into the sewer. The deal with Berlin wasn't enough for Gillis, or the Purges, no, nor any of the other tidbits that started coming out from reliable sources. Not till the Party announced officially that Joe was off the Sainted list did Gillis catch a whiff. And him with Sophie now.

Maybe he's a good cook.

She lights up when she sees me. That smile, after all these years, that smile and my knees are water. She hasn't gone the Mother Jones route, Sophie, no shawls and spectacles, she's nobody's granny on a candy box. She's thin, a strong thin, not like Diamond, and her eyes, they still stop your breath from across the room. Always there was such a crowd, such a crowd around Sophie. And always she made each one think *he* was at the head of the line.

"Leo, you came! I was afraid you'd be shy again." She hugs me, tells Baker I'm like a brother.

Sophie who always rallied us after a beating, who bound our wounds, who built our pride back up from shambles and never faltered a step. The iron she had! In Portland they're shaving her head, but no wig for Sophie, she wore it like a badge. And the fire! Toe-to-toe with a fat Biloxi deputy, head-to-head with a Hoboken wharf boss, starting a near-riot from her soapbox in Columbus Circle, but shaping it, turning it, stampeding all that anger and energy in the right direction.

Still the iron, still the fire, and still it's Leo you're like a brother.

Baker is smiling his little pained smile, looking for some-one to apologize to, Blum is telling jokes, Vic Lewis has an aluminum walker after his stroke and old Mrs. Axelrod, who knew Emma Goldman from the Garment Workers, is dozing in her chair. Somebody must be in charge of bringing the old woman, with her mind the way it is, because she never misses. She's our museum piece, our link to the past.

Not that the rest of us qualify for the New Left.

Bud Odum is in one corner trying to work up a singalong. Fifteen years younger than most here, a celebrity, still with the denim open at the chest and the Greek sailor cap. The voice is shot though. With Harriet Foote and old Lieber joining they sound like the look-for-the-Union-label folks on television. Determined but slightly off-key. The younger kids aren't so big on Bud anymore, and the Hootenanny Generation is grown, with other fish to fry.

Kids. The room is crawling with little Barnard girls and their tape recorders, pestering people for "oral history." A pair camp by Mrs. Axelrod, clicking on whenever she starts awake and mutters some Yiddish. Sophie, who speaks, says she's raving about the harness-eyes breaking and shackles bouncing on the floor, some shirt-factory tangle in her mind. Gems, they think they're getting, oral-history gems.

There are starting to be Rebeccas again, the little Barnard girls, and Sarahs and Esthers, after decades of Carol, Sally and Debbie. The one who tapes me is a Raisele, which was my mother's name.

"We're trying to preserve it," she says with a sweet smile for an old man.

"What, Yiddish? I don't speak."

"No," she says. "Anarchism. The memories of anarchism. Now that it's served its dialectical purpose."

"You're a determinist."

She gives me a look. They think we never opened a book. I don't tell her I've written a few, it wouldn't make an impression. If it isn't on tape or film it doesn't register. Put my name in the computer, you'll draw a blank.

"Raisele," I say. "That's a pretty name."

"I learned it from an exchange student. I used to be Jody."

Dinner is called and there's confusion, there's jostling, everyone wants near the platform. The ears aren't what they used to be. There is a seating plan, with place cards set out, but nobody looks. Place cards at the Anarchists' Convention? I manage to squeeze in next to Sophie.

First on the agenda is fruit cup, then speeches, then dinner, then more speeches. Carmen Marcovicci wants us to go get our own fruit cup. It makes her uneasy, she says, being waited on. People want, they should get up and get it them-selves.

A couple minutes of mumble-grumble, then someone points out that we'd be putting the two hotel lackeys in charge of the meal out of a job. It's agreed, they'll serve. You could always reason with Carmen.

Then Harriet Foote questions the grapes in the fruit cup. The boycott is over, we tell her, grapes are fine. In fact grapes were always fine — it was the labor situation that was no good, not the *fruit*.

"Well I'm not eating *mine*," she says, blood pressure climbing toward the danger point, "it would be disloyal."

The Wrath of the People. That's what Brickman used to call it in his articles, in his harangues, in his three-hour walk-ing diatribes. Harriet still has it, and Carmen and Weiss and Sophie and Bill Kinney on his clear days and Brickman had it to the end. It's a wonderful quality, but when you're over seventy and haven't eaten since breakfast it has its drawbacks.

Baker speaks first, apologizing for the site and the hour and the weather and the Hundred Years' War. He congratulates the long travelers — Odum from L.A., Kinney from Mon-tana, Pappas from Chicago, Mrs. Axelrod all the way in from Yonkers. He apologizes that our next scheduled speaker, Mikey Dolan, won't be with us. He apologizes for not having time to prepare a eulogy, but it was so sudden —

More mumble-grumble, this being the first we've heard about Mikey. Sophie is crying, but she's not the sort you offer your shoulder or reach for the Kleenex. *If steel had tears,* Brickman used to say. They had their battles, Brickman and Sophie, those two years together. '37 and '38. Neither of them known as a compromiser, both with healthy throwing arms, once a month there's a knock and it's Sophie come to borrow more plates. I worked for money at the moviehouse, I always had plates.

The worst was when you wouldn't see either of them for a

week. Phil Rapf was living below them then and you'd see him in Washington Square, eight o'clock in the morning. Phil who'd sleep through the Revolution itself if it came before noon.

"I can't take it," he'd say. "They're at it already. In the morning, in the noontime, at night. At least when they're fighting the plaster doesn't fall."

Less than two years it lasted. But of all of them, before and after, it was Brickman left his mark on her. That hurts.

Bud Odum is up next, his Wisconsin accent creeping toward Oklahoma, twanging on about "good red-blooded American men and women" and I get a terrible feeling he's going to break into "The Ballad of Bob LaFollette," when war breaks out at the far end of the table. In the initial shuffle Allie Zaitz was sitting down next to Fritz Groh and it's fifteen minutes before the shock of recognition. Allie has lost all his hair from the X-ray treatments, and Fritz never had any. More than ever they're looking like twins.

"*You,*" says Allie, "you from the Dockworkers!"

"And you from that yellow rag. They haven't put you away from civilized people?"

"They let *you* in here? You an *an*archist?"

"In the fullest definition of the word. Which you wouldn't know. What was that coloring book you wrote for?"

At the top of their voices, in the manner of old Lefties. What, old — in the manner we've always had, damn the decibels and full speed ahead. Baker would apologize but he's not near enough to the microphone, and Bud Odum is just laughing. There's still something genuine about the boy, Greek sailor cap and all.

"Who let this crank in here? We've been infiltrated!"

"Point of order! Point of order!"

What Allie is thinking with point of order I don't know, but the lady from the name tags gets them separated, gives each a Barnard girl to record their spewings about the other.

Something Fritz said at a meeting, something Allie wrote about it, centuries ago. We don't forget.

Bud gets going again and it seems that last year they weren't prepared with Brickman's eulogy, so Bud will do the honors now. I feel eyes swiveling, a little muttered chorus of "Leoleoleo" goes through the room. Sophie knew, of course, and conned me into what she thought would be good for me. Once again.

First Bud goes into what a fighter Brickman was, tells how he took on Union City, New Jersey, single-handed, about the time he organized an entire truckload of scabs with one speech, turning them around right under the company's nose. He can still rouse an audience, Bud, even with the pipes gone, and soon they're popping up around the table with memories. Little Pappas, who we never thought would survive the beating he took one May Day scuffle, little one-eyed, broken-nosed Pappas stands and tells of Brickman saving the mimeograph machine when they burned our office on 27th Street. And Sam Karnes, ghost-pale, like the years in prison bleached even his blood, is standing, shaky, with the word on Brickman's last days. Tubes running out of him, fluids dripping into him, still Brickman agitates with the hospital orderlies, organizes with the cleaning staff. Then Sophie takes the floor, talking about spirit, how Brickman had it, how Brickman was it, spirit of our cause, more spirit sometimes than judgment, and again I feel the eyes, hear the Leoleoleo and there I am on my feet.

"We had our troubles," I say, "Brickman and I. But always I knew his heart was in the right place."

Applause, tears, and I sit down. It's a sentimental moment. Of course, it isn't true. If Brickman had a heart it was a well-kept secret. He was a machine, an express train flying the black flag. But it's a sentimental moment, the words come out.

Everybody is making nice then, the old friendly juices

flowing, and Baker has to bring up business. A master of tact, a genius of timing. A vote — do we elect next year's Committee before dinner or after?

"Why spoil dinner?" says one camp.

"Nobody will be left awake after," says the other. "Let's get it out of the way."

They always started small, the rifts. A title, a phrase, a point of procedure. The Chicago Fire began with a spark.

It pulls the scab off, the old animosities, the bickerings, come back to the surface. One whole section of the table splits off into a violent debate over the merits of syndicalism, another forms a faction for elections *dur*ing dinner, Weiss wrestles Baker for the microphone and Sophie shakes her head sadly.

"Why, why, why? Always they argue," she says, "always they fight."

I could answer, I devoted half of one of my studies to it, but who asks?

While the argument heats another little girl comes over with used-to-be-Jody.

"She says you're Leo Gold."

"I confess."

"*The* Leo Gold?"

"There's another?"

"I read *Anarchism and the Will to Love*."

My one turkey, and she's read it. "So you're the one."

"I didn't realize you were still alive."

"It's a matter of seconds."

I'm feeling low. Veins are standing out in temples, old hearts straining, distemper epidemic. And the sound, familiar, but with a new, futile edge.

I've never been detached enough to recognize the sound so exactly before. It's a raw-throated sound, a grating, insistent sound, a sound born out of all the insults swallowed, the battles lost, out of all the smothered dreams and desires.

Three thousand collective years of frustration in the room, turning inward, a *can*cer of frustration. It's the sound of parents brawling each other because they can't feed their kids, the sound of prisoners preying on each other because the guards are out of reach, the sound of a terribly deep despair. No quiet desperation for us, not while we have a voice left. Over an hour it lasts, the sniping, the shouting, the accusations and countercharges. I want to eat. I want to go home. I want to cry.

And then the hotel manager walks in.

Brown blazer, twenty-dollar haircut and a smile from here to Salt Lake City. A huddle at the platform. Baker and Mr. Manager bowing and scraping at each other, Bud Odum looking grim, Weiss turning colors. Sophie and I go up, followed by half the congregation. Nobody trusts to hear it secondhand. I can sense the sweat breaking under that blazer when he sees us coming, toothless, gnarled, suspicious by habit. Ringing around him, the Anarchists' Convention.

"A terrible mistake," he says.

"All my fault," he says.

"I'm awfully sorry," he says, "but you'll have to move."

Seems the Rotary Club, the Rotary Club from Sioux Falls, had booked this room b*e*fore us. Someone misread the calendar. They're out in the lobby, eyeballing Bakunin, impatient, full of gin and boosterism.

"We have a nice room, a smaller room," coos the manager, "we can set you up there in a jiffy. Much less drafty than this room, I'm sure the older folks would feel more comfortable."

"I think it stinks," says Rosenthal, every year the Committee Treasurer. "We paid cash, the room is ours."

Rosenthal doesn't believe in checks. "The less the Wall Street Boys handle your money," he says, "the cleaner it is." Who better to be Treasurer than a man who thinks gold is filth?

"That must be it," says Sophie to the manager. "You've got

your cash from us, money in the bank, you don't have to worry. The Rotary, they can cancel a check, so you're scared. And maybe there's a little extra on the side they give you, a little folding green to clear out the riffraff?"

Sophie has him blushing, but he's going to the wire anyhow. Like Frick in the Homestead Strike, shot, stomped and stabbed by Alexander Berkman, they patch him up and he finishes his day at the office. A gold star from Carnegie. Capitalism's finest hour.

"You'll have to move," says the manager, dreams of corporate glory in his eyes, the smile hanging on to his face by its fingernails, "it's the only way."

"Never," says Weiss.

"Out of the question," says Sophie.

"Fuck off," says Pappas.

Pappas saw his father lynched. Pappas did three hard ones in Leavenworth. Pappas lost an eye, a lung and his profile to a mob in Chicago. He says it with conviction.

"Pardon?" A note of warning from Mr. Manager.

"He says to fuck off," says Fritz Groh.

"You heard him," echoes Allie Zaitz.

"If you people won't cooperate," huffs the manager, condescension rolling down like a thick mist, "I'll have to call in the police."

It zings through the room like the twinge of a single nerve.

"Police! They're sending the police!" cries Pinkstaff.

"Go limp!" cries Vic Lewis, knuckles white with excitement on his walker. "Make em drag us out!"

"Mind the shuttles, mind the shuttles!" cries old Mrs. Axelrod in Yiddish, sitting straight up in her chair.

Allie Zaitz is on the phone to a newspaper friend, the Barnard girls are taping everything in sight, Sophie is organizing us into squads and only Baker holding Weiss bodily allows Mr. Manager to escape the room in one piece. We're the Anarchists' Convention!

Nobody bickers, nobody stalls or debates or splinters. We manage to turn the long table around by the door as a kind of barricade, stack the chairs together in a second line of defense and crate Mrs. Axelrod back out of harm's way. I stay close by Sophie, and once, lugging the table, she turns and gives me that smile. Like a shot of adrenaline, I feel fifty again. Sophie, Sophie, it was always so good, just to be at your side!

And when the manager returns with his two befuddled street cops to find us standing together, arms linked, the lame held up out of their wheelchairs, the deaf joining from memory as Bud Odum leads us in "We Shall Not Be Moved," my hand in Sophie's, sweaty-palmed at her touch like the old days, I look at him in his brown blazer and think *Brickman*, I think, *my God if Brickman was here we'd show this bastard the Wrath of the People!*

Schiffman's Ape

THE GIBBONS CONTINUE to feed while the leopard shakes the young pig to death. The leopard is in its black phase, it holds the pig's haunch in its jaws, patient, giving it an occasional violent jerk, then resting. The muscles in its neck and shoulders are bunched tightly, it breathes in steady rhythm. Gibbons swarm the trees for the climbing vines of purple grape, small, bright yellow birds flit after insects under the forest canopy, and on a branch directly above the leopard, a male Schiffman's ape sits picking lice from its chest. Even the pig, in shock, seems to stare at some distant objective.

Squatting in the underbrush some thirty yards downwind, a bearded man watches breathlessly, taking notes.

"I've seen it."

Lisa is boiling river water on the little cooking fire when Warden reaches the clearing. His eyes are wide with excitement, the Bolex bounces and twists on its strap around his neck as he rushes to her.

"I've seen it!"

"Oh my God. Where?"

"Other side of the river, just down from the ford."

"How many?"

"Just one. That leopard we heard last night had a pig, I stopped to shoot some film, and there it was. Just *sit*ting there, in a tree. Schiffman's ape. Hurry, let's pack it up and get back over there."

"You're sure, honey?"

"Positive. We've found it. Hurry now."

They hug quickly and begin stuffing equipment into their backpacks. Twice Warden repacks an item Lisa has put in at a bad angle. The water is dumped, fire doused and spread, and they are off ducking low branches and hanging vines, stumbling along the overgrown path to the river. Lisa is beaming, chattering questions, and Warden reminds her to keep her voice down. When the path is wide enough to permit it they hold hands.

June 3 — First sighting of ape. Full-grown male on west bank of river. No sign of others. Ape is almost as large as a chimpanzee, with the chimp's large, expressive facial area, but is extremely woolly and long-armed like the gibbon. Re-sighted ape further north of ford. L. is beside herself, like a schoolgirl. Followed ape till dark when it settled high in a lodge tree.

Schiffman was a public-relations man hired by an oil company to put out a line on their new drilling offshore from the island. He came on location to film a commercial about the environmental-impact study the company had paid for, but the terrain around the Holiday Inn where the drillers stayed wasn't wild enough for his purposes. He took his crew inland to the old temple in the forest and it was near there that the first footage of the ape was shot. It was just another monkey to them, some nice local color, but a New York editor who'd worked on the Jane Goodall specials for the network picked up on it and screened the film for a primates man at Columbia. A new species, possibly an addition to the select club of the great apes. Schiffman exploited the hell out of it for the oil company and the inevitable scientific controversy arose. Various experts and skeptics studied the film, the Bigfoot and Loch Ness legends were resurrected, and Schiffman was linked forever with the new primate in the popular imagination.

Warden and Lisa were on the island, at the Holiday Inn, when the story broke, just off a plane from the States. They were funded and equipped for a three-month field study of the island's dominant gibbon population, the *Hylobates lar*. A telegram from Warden's department caught them just in time with their new objective. They had a jump on the rest of the scientific world.

Schiffman's ape (*eremites hirsutus*): a large, tailless Old World primate of the family Pongidae (disputed), found only in the Indonesian rain forests.

They had a departmental romance, Warden an associate professor and Lisa a graduate student. Part of her grant was met by caring for the laboratory animals, and their first meetings were in between cages by the night monkeys. Warden was doing three hours of behavioral observation a day and often Lisa would come and talk to him by the one-way glass as he watched the monkeys and scribbled onto his clipboard. She was very shy and at first they talked only monkeys. She had a tendency to humanize the animals' behavior, to anthropomorphize, that both annoyed and amused him. Lisa had nicknames for all the animals, even the lower forms, the rabbits and hamsters and white rats. She called all the crickets Jiminy. She talked softly to the animals as she handled them, as she fed them and watered them and injected them with massive doses of carcinogens. She thought the night monkeys were cute, especially the babies.

Warden had her in both his graduate-level courses. She was quiet but a very good student. He had noticed her right away, not so much for her face, plain and pale, but for her bottom. She had the most fantastic bottom, the kind Warden liked best, with a pronounced lordosis like the !Ko tribeswomen of the African bush that made it ride high and stick out invitingly. A black behind on a blond girl. Once or twice she had walked ahead of him on the campus and he had followed, past his destination, watching her bottom move in her pants. When Warden daydreamed about the girls in his classes, Lisa and her bottom were well up on his list.

Their first personal talks by the cages were about a boy she was seeing, an undergraduate, a star soccer player. It came out that the boy had problems with impotence, that Lisa held herself at fault. Warden drew on his experience to advise her. He advised her and his advice became reassurance and his reassurance, late one night on the floor between the rhesus and the scurrying lemurs, became demonstration.

It was an incredible semester. Warden and Lisa were at each other in between classes, before and after his observation periods, overnight and all weekend long. More than once the janitor found him asleep by the night monkeys, notes spilling from his lap. Warden lost so much sleep his boundaries began to blur, he would find himself reaching to squeeze Lisa's bottom out in public or when she came up at the end of class. She slept on her stomach, and he loved to pull the covers up so her cheeks were exposed, loved to knead and jiggle them while she mumbled nonsense through her dreams. She loved sleeping with him, he could tell, loved that he knew what to do and did it, loved just listening to him talk in class or in bed, hearing all the things he knew. It was an incredible semester and somehow his work didn't suffer.

Behavioral Observation — Platyrrhine (night) monkey
(Aotes trivirgatus)

Lab study — Adult male C and adult female P in 6'x4' cage.

2:03 a.m.   Male and female approach each other at center of cage. Social sniffing. Female lifts tail slightly as male sniffs her genital area.

2:05   Mutual grooming behavior, highly agitated.

2:07   Male mounts female from rear. Copulation, apparently successful. Three or four pelvic thrusts, ejaculation occurring on the last, long thrust, the lower part of the male's body quivering for a moment. Male dismounts.

2:10   Resume mutual grooming.

2:12   Male mounts female from rear, copulation, apparently successful. Dismounts.

2:14   Male and female run to opposite ends of cage. Male licks his genitals.

2:16   Male, uttering kiss-squeaks, approaches female. Mounts from side. Unsuccessful copulation. Dismounts.

2:19   Male climbs side of cage, uttering short barks. Drops behind female, who assumes submissive posture. Male mounts from rear, copulation, apparently successful. Dismounts. Mounts again immediately, copulation, apparently successful.

2:23   Mutual grooming behavior.

2:25–4:00 Repeated mountings and copulations, all apparently successful. Female remained receptive throughout. Mutual grooming behavior grew more and more perfunctory.

The ape is feeding on grapes in a vine-clogged tree. It eats slowly, methodically working its way from cluster to cluster. Suddenly the tree is alive with a group of gibbons. It is a family unit — adult male, mother with infant, two subadult females. The smaller gibbons try to scare the Schiffman's away. They feed in an exaggerated frenzy, swinging from branch to branch with breakneck speed, jamming grapes into their mouths, making extraloud chomping noises. Schiffman's ape ignores them. The gibbons swing faster, wilder, there seems to be a dozen of them buzzing through the tree.

"Look at him. He's not budging." Distant whispering, trading looks through the binoculars.

"It's only a display. This must be part of their usual range."

"Do you think it travels alone?"

"Seems like it. Could be like the orangutan, lone males are fairly common. Or maybe something has driven it a lot closer to the temple."

"Or maybe," says Lisa, "he just got lonely."

Warden shoots her a hard look.

"Sorry."

"Hopefully he'll lead us to others. We've got to figure out the bonding patterns."

"He's so *woolly*. More than the gibbons even. And those *arms* —"

"Travels mostly by brachiation, we can assume that right now. Glad I packed all those lens filters, we'll be shooting directly against the sky most of the time."

"What shall we name him?"

"Alpha. It's our first subject."

"No, I mean a *real* name."

Warden smiles indulgently. "Sure. Why not. Uhm — how about Esau?"

"Esau?"

"From the Old Testament. 'Esau was an hairy man.' "

"I like it."

The gibbons slow, begin to feed regularly. Esau isn't moving.

There is a story that the people of the Indonesian lowlands tell about the orangutan, the 'man of the forest.' It takes place when all creatures, including men, had just been formed and sat in the forest waiting for the Creator to give them their natures. The Creator came down from the mountain and told them to gather round. To the bird He gave flight and song, to the leopard He gave strength and savagery, to the python stealth and cold-bloodedness. There were two men at that time, twin brothers named Simang and Jaru. By the time the Creator got to them He had run out of natures. So He said to them, "You will be complex creatures, I will let you choose one aspect from the natures of each of the other creatures. But you must choose together and agree on everything."

At first Simang and Jaru were in close agreement. They chose stealth from the python, strength from the leopard, quickness from the lizard, hot-bloodedness from the boar, and caution from the rodent. But when they considered the bird, Simang wanted its flight and Jaru wanted its song.

"With flight," said Simang, "I will soar in the air above all the other creatures, even the birds, and with my strength and cunning I will rule over them."

"But with song," said Jaru, "all the other creatures will hear what we have in our hearts and minds, and we will be understood."

They argued, and suddenly, with the strength of the leopard, Simang attacked Jaru and spilled his hot blood. The Creator intervened just in time to prevent a murder. He was very angry.

"For this act," he said to Simang, "you and your race will part from Jaru and his race, and you will be outcasts. You will soar in the air but never really fly, and will rule over only what you can reach with your long, grasping arms."

"Jaru, you and your race will be masters of the earth, but whenever you meet the descendants of Simang or the other creatures, you will sing, but none will understand."

From that day Simang and his race dwelt in the forest, separate from other men, and were the loneliest of creatures.

Lisa wakes first and crawls out from the little pup-tent. She is naked, a shocking white against the rich, rich green of the rain-forest vegetation. Lisa has never seen such greens; being surrounded by them makes her feel a bit surreal, like she is living in a painting by Gauguin. She stands and stretches her body, sweat evaporating beneath her arms and breasts in the cool morning air. A gray mist hangs close to the ground, the insects aren't flying yet. Early sunlight filters through the canopy in visible rays, it splashes off the tree bark, dapples the leaves. Lisa smiles just looking at it, feeling it — the rich green ferns, the mist, the slanting rays, drinkable air, small yellow birds flitting silently, like butterflies, under the canopy. She hugs herself, runs her hands through her hair. She looks to the top of Esau's lodge tree, fifty yards distant, but can't see him.

Lisa pulls on her still-damp underpants, tugs on the two pairs of thick hiking socks, all the while scanning the trees for the ape. She pulls a sleeveless undershirt over her head, struggles into her fatigue pants and jacket. The cloth is dry but stiff with sweat, her skin begins to itch immediately. She works the leather of her heavy waterproof boots till she can jam her feet into them, fingers aching as she pulls the laces tight. Lisa wraps her thick utility belt around her waist, straps on her watch. She smears bug repellant on her face, neck and arms. She uncases the binoculars and looks into the treetops through them.

Warden crawls out of the tent, sleepy-eyed, and makes a passing grab at her bottom. He feels only the extra notepads in her back pocket. He is spotted with dried, grayish dabs of zinc-oxide ointment covering his skin eruptions. He squats and begins to tinker with the backpacks. Lisa moves away from the tent, searching above with the glasses.

Flummmph!

A stream of urine and loose, yellowish feces cascades onto Lisa from above. Esau hoots, shakes the branch he hangs from violently, then swings off with the sun at his back.

"Oh. Oh shit. Oh my God. Oh —"

Lisa is splattered, the binoculars dripping, she grimaces and looks down her front.

"Oh my God. Oh look, it's, look, all in my *hair* —"

Warden pokes at a splat of feces with a stick. "Mostly fructivorous," he says. "But probably some insects and birds' eggs. Got to get his protein somewhere."

June 10 — Subject ape's reaction to the presence of L. and me is what we expected. Since we began following him night and day, ape has remained in trees, traveling by brachiation and feeding on fruit and bark in the treetops. Ape expresses aggression towards us in various manners of display:

1. Staring — Ape will cease brachiation and stare at us, body rigid.

2. Hitting away — Fanning the air in a shooing gesture towards us.

3. Attacking — Directed rush falling just short of contact with us, hair erect, movement exaggerated and jerky.

4. Threat sounds — These often accompany the other three displays:
   a. Kiss-squeaks
   b. Raspberry
   c. Loud and repetitive 'lork' noises
   d. Exaggerated chomping
   e. 'Ahoor' howls
   f. Barks
   g. Grumphs
   h. Combinations of these

So far subject is the only Schiffman's we've come in contact with. Ape travels and feeds within a range bordered by the river that is overlapped by the ranges of at least two bands of gibbons. Ape begins feeding around 7 a.m., continues for roughly two hours, then rests for two to three hours in a tree. Feeding and brachiation then resume until sundown. Ape does not travel at night, sleeps high in a favored lodge tree. Covers 4,000 to 20,000 feet in a day. Hopefully ape will soon be fully habituated to our presence, and our observation will have no effect on his behavior.

The ape is swinging away, silhouetted in the sun, zigging and zagging rapidly through the forest canopy. Warden struggles below, hacking wearily with the machete, now and then switching it to his left hand for a few strokes. Lisa offers to take the point for a bit, but no, he says, she can't cut fast enough, they'd lose him. Sweat stinging his eyes, tramping over the swampy, root-tangled section of forest, Warden grinds his teeth and tries to keep the ape in sight, tries to transfer all his resentment for it into his machete stroke. It won't keep still. Warden is sucking wind through his ears, the vegetation glows phosphorescent green before him, throbbing in and out of focus, a bright scarlet edge outlining its form. He is dizzy, he can't feel his legs. He glances back at Lisa. Her GI shirt is soaked, she moves in his wake with solemn concentration. Warden stumbles, stops.

"What's the matter?"

"You've got to rest, Lisa. I don't like your color."

"I'm all right. I can go on."

"I can't have you collapsing on me." Warden tries to gulp air as silently as possible. "He's not going to come down and help me carry you back to camp."

"I can go on."

"We can catch up with him later. If you could see the way your eyes look, all —"

"Honey, what's that on your *arm?*"

It is a green leech, fat as a little finger. A shudder runs through Warden, he fights not to cry out.

"Get it off me, quick! The grease, where's the *grease,* dammit!"

Lisa pulls the tube of thick grease from her back pocket, looking at the pulsing leech as if it were a specimen on a glass slide. She seems to be taking her time.

"Come on, come *on!*"

Lisa squeezes the tube till the leech is completely covered. She scans the treetops, waiting. The ape has stopped and is feeding just up ahead.

"He sure likes his privacy."

"Privacy is a human concept, Lisa. Only a human concept. He's afraid. When he stops being afraid he'll stop running. How are you doing?"

"Huh?"

"Have you got your wind back yet?"

"I said I was all right. You sure you don't want me to do the machete for a while?"

Warden realizes he is still gripping the machete tightly, his knuckles squeezed white. "Is that thing ready yet?"

Lisa flicks the glob of grease and insect off his arm with her finger. "Maybe," she says, "the less we press him the less he'll run. He's got to eat sometime."

Warden begins to contradict her, then holds still. Eating wasn't only a human concept.

By the second semester they were together Lisa was comfortable with her position in between the faculty and the student body. It was all right for Warden to bring her to get-togethers among the younger faculty, and the men would gather around her whenever she came. But Warden decided he didn't like parties much anymore. Lisa refused to give up her student friends, which put him in an awkward position, and she had grown a little too familiar with the department staff. Not that Warden wanted her creeping around in awe of his colleagues, it was just — appearances, maybe, just an uneasy feeling he got about how quickly she had adapted to the role of faculty girlfriend.

There were some rough moments. Over spring break Lisa went home and while she was there slept with an old high-school friend. Nothing important, she told Warden, just one of those things. He didn't like to see her acting so cold-blooded about it when he knew something must be disturbing her pretty badly to pull a stunt like that on him. And shortly after that he got involved in a thing with a woman in the Psych Department, nothing really, nothing worth telling Lisa about.

Psych was feuding with Biology again and the Environmentalists wanted their own department. There was pressure from every direction, and Warden felt vaguely irritated much of the time. He had to get tough with Lisa in her studies, she'd been slipping. "If you're ever going to amount to anything," he told her, "anything more than just another good-looking lab assistant, you'd better get on the stick right now." She worked hard, he had to admit that, it left her very little time for parties or her other friends and she wasn't able to go home for midsemester break. The time with just each other was good, Warden felt, they needed it.

Some rough times. He had a long article to write, two survey courses to hold down, plus the strain of having to truck out to the zoo three times a week to do observation for his department head's book on the group dynamics of baboons. It wore at his patience and there were a lot of arguments with Lisa. He had her soccer star in class, her ex-boyfriend, who was something of a bust academically. Once, grading a really awful paper the boy had done on sexual dysfunction in captive animals, Warden very nearly wrote "You should talk" on it. That was the kind of mood he was usually in. It was a wonder he and Lisa survived the semester intact.

Behavioral Observation—Hamadryas Baboon
(Papio hamadryas)

Municipal zoo population of twenty-two animals in free-ranging enclosure.

1:12 p.m.   Dominant male, Rufus, approaches estrous female Nini with stiff-legged display, canines bared. Nini presents genitals in submissive posture. Rufus mounts, copulatory thrusts.

1:14   Subadult male, Dobbs, approaches estrous female Cocoa, sniffs genital area. Attempts to mount. Dominant male Rufus dismounts from Nini, rushes at Dobbs with attack display. Dobbs crouches in submissive posture, Rufus makes brief mounting display on Dobbs, then mounts Cocoa. Pelvic thrusts.

1:18   Subadult male Dobbs approaches estrous female Sheena, genital sniffing. Sheena presents, Dobbs mounts. Copulatory behavior till Rufus rushes over from Cocoa, toppling Dobbs from Sheena's back and driving him away with bites to the neck and shoulder. Sheena remains frozen in submissive posture, back arched and genitals presented. Dobbs climbs to top of tire apparatus, screaming, and sits with year-old males. Rufus returns, stiff-legged, and mounts Sheena. Violent copulatory thrusting, watching Dobbs all the while.

Esau climbs a tree that hangs out over the rushing water very close to camp. Half the tree's roots are exposed, river current pulling it farther from the bank each day. The branches stretch far out over the middle of the river. Esau climbs out on the farthest and thinnest of these for a thick cluster of grapes that hangs on its end. He feeds suspended over the churning white water, a fall would sweep him over jagged rocks and a ten-foot drop-off just downstream. The branch groans under his weight, sags, supported mainly by the climbing grapevines that tie it in with higher, sturdier branches.

Warden and Lisa watch from a spot on the bank several yards upriver. Warden catches his breath silently each time the ape shifts its grip. He thinks of how difficult it was to find the subject, of the uncertainty of finding others in the area. He thinks about the limits of their grant provisions, of their time, thinks of all the data they've already collected. To intervene would be directly contrary to their purpose and methodology, but still — the ape hangs by one arm over the torrent, pulling handfuls of grapes loose.

This was an opportunity to be more than a footnote in some other professor's research, a chance for Warden to be listed in the tables of contents with all the great field pioneers, with Yerkes and Schaller and DeVore and C. R. Carpenter. Weren't scientists always interfering with marginal species, helping to preserve them so they might be studied? What could be more marginal than Schiffman's ape, its only known specimen currently hanging on the brink of extinction? It wouldn't really be interfering, it would be — preservation, yes, preservation in the interests of science, it would be —

A vine pops and the branch sinks down a notch.

"Esau!" calls Lisa, up and waving her arms, "Esau watch out!"

The ape immediately swings back up the branch and takes off away from them, soaring from tree to tree. Warden gives Lisa a stern look.

"I'm sorry, honey," she says. "The river's so high, that branch, it scared me. I was afraid for him."

Warden sighs wearily.

"I couldn't help it."

Warden gives her a little pat on the cheek, smiles forgivingly. "I understand, baby."

June 18 — Subject, Esau, descended to the ground for the first time in our presence today, to drink from the river. He drinks by dipping his hand in the water and then sucking from the thick hairs on the back of it. Subject, Esau, remained on ground after that and L. and I were careful to keep a good distance away. He is becoming habituated, and apparently Schiffman's ape does a good deal of his traveling and feeding on the ground. Contrary to my first impression, he does exhibit knuckle-walking when not in an agitated state. Esau has not yet crossed the river to the temple side, indicating that the original sighting by the film crew was either a stroke of luck or of a different member of the species.

Darkness.

—— —— ——

"Careful, honey, the tent pole."
"Don't worry about the tent pole. Are you wet enough?"
"I don't know. It hurt a little the last time."

—— —— ——

—— —— ——

—— —— ——

"Do you think he's watching?"
"Jesus, Lisa, we're inside the tent, it's pitch-black outside, what could he see?"
"He can hear."
"I'll try to be quiet."

—— —— ——

—— —— ——

"Honey, I'm so *sticky*. This heat —"
"You'll get used to it. It doesn't bother me that you're sticky."

—— —— ——

"Oh God."
"What now?"
"I can't remember if I took my pill."
"Take an extra tomorrow. That works with your kind, doesn't it?"

"I get it mixed up with the Atabrine and all the salt tablets."

"Take an extra tomorrow, it'll be fine."

— — —

— — —

"Careful."

— — —

— — —

— — —

"I think something's biting me."

"Oh Christ."

"Well it's not *my* fault. What's wrong, honey?"

"Forget it. Just forget it."

"Please, don't turn your b—"

"Forget it."

Darkness, and silence.

Summer vacation proved to be a watershed in their relationship. The application to have Lisa hired as a research assistant didn't come through — there was no pretense she could use to stay at the university, no way she could afford it alone. Lisa didn't seem as disappointed as Warden expected. He'd never realized she could hide her feelings so well. She said she thought she could survive three months at home, without him. One summer apart wouldn't change things between them if they were really good for each other. The day before exams started Warden asked her to marry him.

Lisa was stunned. She had never considered it. None of the people they knew were getting married, it seemed such a gesture of — of com*mit*ment for somebody to make to her. She had never thought in terms of marriage, the idea excited her. She said yes and for a period they were back to humping like rabbits whenever they met.

Her parents were ecstatic. "We'd given up on her," said her beaming dad to Warden at the reception. "We'd given her up to science." He nudged Warden and nodded to where Lisa and her mother were weeping and hugging. "I should have known nature would come through. Girls will be girls."

"They tell me you work with animals," said an uncle, a very red-faced and liquid uncle.

"Primates."

"What's that?"

"Monkeys."

"Oh."

"And man. Right now I'm running experiments on chimpanzees."

"I see. Now which are they? I know King Kong was a gorilla."

"Like in Tarzan. Cheetah was a chimpanzee."

"Hah! Right, old Cheetah. Me Tarzan, you Jane. So," he clapped Warden on the back, "you gonna carry our little girl off into the jungle?"

Behavioral Observation — Chimpanzee (Pan troglodytes)
Subject — Young male, Zipperdee

Experiment   Zipperdee was placed in a large room barren except for a 3'x3'x3' steel cage in the center of the floor. Inside the cage was a small box painted bright blue, with bright chrome handles on the closed lid. Opening the lid triggered a mechanism that shut the cage door, trapping the animal in the cramped quarters. The box was empty. The animal was left in the cage for fifteen minutes after trapping himself, then taken to a neutral room for five minutes while a box of a different color was installed. The experiment was then repeated, eight trials in all.

Results   Zipperdee continued to trap himself by opening the lid to look in the box, despite his obvious dislike for being closely confined. Learning did take place — with each successive trial he took longer to approach the painted box, often trying to reach through the bars to lift the lid. But when this failed his curiosity always prevailed and he ended up entering the cage. Once trapped he shook the bars and made characteristic distress noises, and repeatedly turned to open the lid as if to be reassured there was still nothing within the box. As Zipperdee was known to retain complex maze and machine-operation procedures for as long as a week, this was surely not a failure of memory. The experiment was repeated with Tom-Tom, another young male, this time without changing the color of the box between trials. Again the subject trapped himself repeatedly.

Esau is traveling on the ground, walking unhurriedly, with Warden and Lisa following. He appears to be constantly sulking, his head hanging down from his shoulder blades as he moves. He stops, lifts his nose in the air. His hair fluffs a bit, half-erect. The muscles in his arms tense.

Three apes, Schiffman's apes, appear in the clearing ahead. Warden and Lisa grab hands, holding tight.

There is an adult male, same size as Esau, an adult female, and a younger, smaller female. Esau's hair is standing up straight. The three walk toward him warily. The adult male sniffs at Esau's hindquarters loudly, almost snorting. The two females stand in front of him, rigid, their faces inches from his. Esau is so stiff he is trembling slightly.

The male begins to hoot, tears a hunk of fern from the underbrush and shakes it. Esau turns to face him and the females both begin to throw bits of ground-debris at him. Esau lowers his head and bolts up a tree, the other Schiffman's all chattering and making empty-handed throwing gestures at him. The male sees Warden then, gives out a high yip, and they are all swinging away through the trees.

Warden and Lisa watch until the three disappear. They look at each other, turn, and trudge after Esau.

July 5 — Esau's social behavior may or may not tell us much about the bonding patterns of Schiffman's ape. From the behavior observed so far I would postulate that the species travels singly or in extremely small groups, much like the orangutan. Their favored food materials are widely dispersed. Intraspecies contacts have been much more tense than those with the gibbons or smaller monkeys in the area. L. thinks Esau might be an isolated case. More data, based on a wider variety of subjects, are needed.

"Well, you're in a wonderful mood."

"Don't start, Lisa."

"*I* didn't start a damn thing. You started it when you banged out of the tent this morning."

"I should feel like a million dollars? I'm hot, I'm wet, I'm dirty and I'm going to stay that way for a long time. I've got crotch rot halfway down to my knees, I can't spread my legs without it burning —"

"So do I."

"I hadn't noticed the difference."

"What's that supposed to mean?"

Warden turns away from her. Esau is on the ground about a hundred feet away, poking under the bark of a fallen log for grubs.

"I wish you'd walk further from the tent before you do your business," he said.

"I can't always *make* it that far, I *told* you that. I can't control it."

"Stop eating the damn grapes, then. That's what's doing it, you're up in the tree eating grapes with Esau. Going native on me."

"I'm not up in the tree with Esau. And I get sick of dried food."

"We're here to *watch* the animal, not to *em*pathize with him. It's not very objective."

"What's not objective?"

"Your whole attitude. Just look at your half of the observation notes, it's obvious. We'll have to go over it all when we get back."

"And what about yours?"

"Mine is fine. If you want me to give you a refresher course I'd be happy to."

"Oh Christ."

"Where are you going?"

She keeps walking, away from Warden and Esau.

"Lisa." She doesn't respond. He calls. "Not near the tent, Lisa."

Lisa stops, takes a huge breath, then screams at the top of her lungs. Screams over and over. Warden looks to see if Esau has been scared off. The ape stands looking back at him, and their eyes meet, thinks Warden, with some measure of understanding.

Behavioral Observation — Schiffman's ape (eremites hirsutus)
Field study — Adult male Esau, adult female with dependent infant.

Warden writes frantically, pad against thigh, not taking his eyes off the scene before him. He's glad Lisa is back at the tent. He flicks a glance at his watch —

5:48 p.m. Esau encounters female Schiffman's carrying infant on her back, feeding on ground. She stiffens, hair erect, as he descends and sits several feet to the left of her.

5:49 Female exhibits staring threat-display. Esau approaches slowly. Female emits warning squeaks. They stare at each other, bodies rigid, for a full minute. Esau stands bipedally, extends arms to full width and utters booming 'grumph' sound. Female exhibits 'waving away' display.

5:51   Esau rushes female, who bites at him, then flees uttering distress shrieks, the infant clinging to her back screaming. Esau chases, nipping at her haunches, catching her after several yards. The infant is knocked to the ground. Esau, penis erect, attempts to mount the female from the side. She claws and bites him off, turns and faces him in attack display, teeth bared. Esau picks the infant up and waves it over his head in threat display, apparently unaware it is not a branch. Female jumps at him, grappling and biting, and infant is dropped again, still screaming. Esau holds female's head under arm and mounts her from side again, pelvis half over her shoulders, and begins thrusting. Female breaks free, grabs infant, and scurries up a tree. Esau follows and female swings away. He pursues, but lighter female, even with infant clinging to her, outdistances him.

5:54   Esau gives up pursuit. It begins to rain, a steady, heavy downpour typical of this time of day. Esau sits hunched on a low branch in the rain and begins to masturbate, manual stroking method, a mournful look on his

Warden pauses, breathing excitedly, shielding the pad from the rain with his body, and tries to think of a more scientific word than *mournful*.

July 20 — Esau seems more depressed lately, something weighing on him. He spends more time sleeping in the daytime, staring off into space, going through the motions of feeding near the boundaries of the other Schiffman's' range. I now have his total confidence; my presence, rather than an irritant, often seems to have a calming effect on him.

The rainy season is on us and we are slowed by the humidity.

Warden empties the backpacks, dropping each item heavily onto the ground directly behind Lisa. Lisa sits and writes in her logbook, frowning in concentration. Neither speaks. Warden gathers the canteens, letting them clatter together loudly. He kicks through the equipment spread on the ground till he finds the compass. Lisa writes. Warden struggles to load himself up, then pauses and watches her from behind. He blinks sweat from his eyes. He squats down beside her.

"Lisa?"

She doesn't look up from her log.

"I've been thinking. Maybe when we get back, when this is under control, it would be a good time to have that baby we talked about."

Lisa looks up and stares, stares at Warden as if he's the strangest thing she's ever seen. He sighs, rises to go.

"I should be back from the temple by six," he says, voice flat now. "Remember what I said about your observation notes. Objectivity."

She doesn't watch him walk away.

Everything was the same, being married, and everything was different. That was what Lisa always said to her friends and it drove Warden up the wall. He'd make a disgusted face and she'd turn to him and say that she knew what she meant, she just couldn't put it in words. Which was even worse. Warden was at her constantly for her irrational thinking, though he liked it that she relied on him to make most of the decisions. And when Lisa did make a hard choice by herself, she did it with a coldness and finality that scared him.

But it was her stubbornness when she was being irrational that bothered him the most, her stubbornness when they disagreed about something. Her irrationality seemed to surface most often in disagreements.

It was the same as before they were married, but with something added, something more at stake.

Being a faculty wife was hard on her, Warden could tell that. It prompted him to apply for the field study. They both invested a lot of hope in the possibility of being funded, and the first year of their marriage came to seem like a lingering disease that only the grant could cure.

Somehow living together was more expensive than living separately had been, and Lisa had to go back to her job caring for the lab animals. They spent long, silent evenings at home, reading, studying, just sitting. Lisa called Warden at his office every day after the department's mail had arrived, to check if there was any word. Gibbons were Lisa's favorite primate, she was thrilled at the prospect of studying them in the field. Gibbons formed long-lasting pair bonds, they were affectionate and peaceful with each other, there were few differences in secondary sex characteristics and the females generally shared leadership and guarding roles with the males. They hadn't been studied at all thoroughly, the research would be important. Often Warden and Lisa would catch each other staring into space, and they would sigh, and one or the other would say, "If only the grant would come through."

Lisa came home one night upset by the gerbils. The gerbils had started eating each other, they had been put in smaller cages usually reserved for the white rats, in order to make room for a new shipment of specimens. There had been seven incidences of cannibalism in one week. Lisa came home upset and there sat Warden clutching the letter of approval from the Foundation. She cried for an hour.

Warden is returning on the temple side of the river, walking upstream to the ford. He sees Lisa first, sitting on the far bank by the overhanging tree, writing in her log book. He shades his eye and squints up at the grape-laden branch for Esau. The branch is gone.

Esau clings to it in the middle of the river, the remnants snagged on a rock, rapidly breaking away. Clusters of grapes tear loose and churn downstream, bursting apart against shoals. Warden looks to his wife.

The rope is in their camp, only a few yards behind her, the bamboo pole is there, she has the machete to cut branches or vines. Esau is only six feet from the bank. The water roars past him. Warden could call and ask her to intervene, to stop her observation and save the ape. He could ask her.

Lisa looks across the water at Warden, looks at him without expression. She goes back to her writing.

Gibbons feed from the trees along the bank, swinging by their long arms. Small, bright yellow birds flit after insects beneath the forest canopy. A wild pig roots along the side of the pathway just upstream. The bearded man stands motionless and watches the woman across the river. The woman writes slowly, in a flowing script. Schiffman's ape grimaces, lips drawn back over his gums as he strains to lift his chin above the rushing water. The branch shifts.

The 7-10 Split

IF YOU DON'T HAVE your own shoes they rent you a pair for fifty cents. None of us are any big athletes, we meet at the lanes once a week, Thursday night. But some of us have our own shoes. Bobbi for instance, she got a pair cause the rented shoes have their size on the heel in a red leather number and Bobbi doesn't want everybody seeing how big her feet are. She's real conscious of things like that, real conscious of her appearance, like you'd expect a hairdresser to be.

We play two teams, four girls each, and take up a pair of lanes. It's Bobbi and Janey and Blanche and me against Rose Teta, Pat and Vi, and Evelyn Chambers. We've worked it out over the years so the sides are pretty even. A lot of the time the result comes down to whether I been on days at the Home or if Blanche is having problems with her corns. She's on her feet all day at the State Office Building cafeteria and sometimes the corns act up. I figure that I roll around 175 if I'm on graveyard but drop down to 140 if I already done my shift in the morning. Janey works with me at the Home and doesn't seem to mind either which way, but she's the youngest of us.

"Mae," she always says to me, "it's all in your head. If you let yourself *think* you're tired, you'll *be* tired. All in your head."

That might be so for her, but you get my age and a lot of what used to be in your head goes directly to your legs.

And Janey is just one of those people was born with a lot of *pep*. Night shift at the Home, in between bed checks when all the aides and nurses are sitting around the station moaning about how little sleep they got during the day, Janey is always working like crazy on her macrame plant-hangers. She sells them to some hippie store downtown for the extra income. She's a regular little Christmas elf, Janey, her hands never stop moving. It's a wonder to me how she keeps her looks, what with the lack of rest and the load she's been saddled with, the hand she's been dealt in life. She's both mother and father to her little retarded boy, Scooter, and still she keeps her sweet disposition. We always send her up to the desk when the pinspotter jams, cause Al, who runs the lanes and is real slow to fix things, is sweet on her. You can tell because he takes his earplugs out when she talks to him. Al won't do that for just anybody. Of course he's married and kind of greasy-looking, but you take your compliments where you can.

It's a real good bunch though, and we have a lot of fun. Rose Teta and Vi work together at the Woolworth's and are like sisters, always borrowing each other's clothes and kidding around. They ought to be on TV, those two. The other night, the last time we played, they started in on Bobbi before we even got on the boards. Bobbi owns a real heavy ball, a sixteen-pounder. It's this milky-blue marbled thing, real feminine-looking like everything Bobbi has. Only last week it's at the shop having the finger holes redrilled, so she has to find one off the rack at the lanes. At Al's the lighter ones, for women and children, are red, and the heavier ones the men men use are black. Bobbie is over checking on the black ones when Rose and Vi start up about there she goes handling the

men's balls again, and when she blushes and pretends she
doesn't hear they go on about her having her holes drilled.
Bobbi hates anything vulgar, or at least she makes like she
does, so she always keeps Pat in between her and the Woolworth's girls when we sit on the bench. Pat is a real serious
Catholic, and though she laughs at Rose and Vi she never
does it out loud. Pat's gonna pop a seam some day, laughing
so hard with her hand clapped over her mouth.

It was just after the men's-balls business with Bobbi that
Evelyn walked in and give us the news. We could tell right
off something was wrong — she wasn't carrying her ball bag
and she looked real tired, didn't have any makeup on. She
walks in and says, "I'm sorry I didn't call you, girls, but I
just now come to my decision. I won't be playing Thursdays
anymore, I'm joining the Seniors' League."

You could of heard a pin drop. Evelyn is the oldest of us,
true, and her hair has mostly gone gray, but she's one of the
liveliest women I know. She and Janey always used to make
fun of the Seniors' League, all the little kids' games they do
and how they give out a trophy every time you turn around.
Used to say the Seniors' was for people who had given up,
that they set the handicaps so high all you had to do to average 200 was to write your name on the scorecard.

Well, we all wanted to know her reasons and tried to talk
her out of it. Since she retired from the State last year, bowling was the only time any of us got to see Evelyn and we
didn't want to lose her. She's one of those women makes you
feel all right about getting older, at least till this Seniors'
business come up. We tried every argument we could think
of but she'd made up her mind. She nodded down the alley at
the AMF machine clacking the pins into place and she says,
"I'm the only one here remembers when they used to be a
boy behind there, setting them up by hand. You give him a
tip at the end of the night, like a golf caddy. I remember
when Al had all his teeth, when the hot dogs here had beef in

them. I'm the only one here remembers a lot of things and it's time I quit kidding myself and act my age. You girls can get on without me."

Then she said her good-byes to each of us and walked out, tired-looking and smaller than I'd remembered her. Wasn't a dry eye in the house.

But, like they say, life must go on. We evened the sides up by having either me or Blanche sit out every other game and keep score. While we were putting on our shoes we tried to figure out who we could get to replace Evelyn and even up the teams again. June Hundley's name was mentioned, and Edie McIntyre and Lorraine DeFillippo. Of course Bobbi had some objection to each of them, but that's just how she is so we didn't listen. Janey didn't say a word all the while, she seemed real depressed.

Janey and Evelyn were really tight. In one way it's hard to figure since there's so much age difference between them, but then again it makes sense. They've both had a real hard row to hoe, Evelyn's husband dying and Janey's running off. And they both had a child with mental problems. Evelyn had her Buddy, who was Mongoloid and lived till he was twenty-seven. She kept him at home the whole while, even when he got big and hard to manage, and loved him like she would a normal child. Never gave up on him. To his dying day Evelyn was trying to teach Buddy to read, used to sit with him for hours with travel brochures. Buddy liked all the color pictures.

And Janey always puts me in mind of that poor Terry on *General Hospital,* or any of the nice ones on the daytime stories who are always going blind or having their men stolen or losing their memories. Just one thing after another — as if having Scooter wasn't enough trouble in one lifetime. Janey has to bring Scooter on Thursdays cause there isn't a baby-sitter who could handle him. Al allows it cause like I said, he's sweet on her. There's no keeping Scooter still, he's ten years old, real stocky and wild-eyed, like a little animal out of control. At the Home they'd keep him full of Valium and he'd be in a fog all day, but Janey won't let the school use drugs on him. Says he's at least entitled to his own sensations, and from what I seen from my patients I agree with her. Scooter is all over the lanes, dancing down the gutters, picking the balls up, drawing on score sheets, playing all the pinball and safari-shoot games in the back even when there's no coin in them. Scooter moves faster than those flippers and bumpers ever could, even pinball must seem like a slow game to him. The only thing he does that Al won't stand for is when he goes to the popcorn machine and laps his tongue on the chute where it comes out. He likes the salt and doesn't understand how he might be putting people off their appetite.

Anyhow, you could just look at Janey and tell she was feeling low. She's usually got a lot of color in her cheeks, it glows when she smiles and sets off nice against her hair. Natural blond, not bottled like Bobbi's is. Well, after Evelyn left she was all pale, no color to her at all, and when we started bowling she didn't have the little bounce in her approach like she usually does. One of the things that's fun is watching the different styles the girls bowl. Like I said, Janey usually comes up to the line really bouncy, up on her toes, and lays the ball down so smooth it's almost silent. You're surprised when you hear the pins crash. Rose and Vi both muscle it down the alley, they're as hard on the boards as they are on the pins, and when they miss a spare clean the ball cracks against the back wall so hard it makes you wince. But when they're in the pocket you should see those pins fly, like an explosion. Bobbi uses that heavy ball and can let it go a lot slower — she always freezes in a picture pose on her follow-through, her arm pointing at the headpin, her back leg up in the air, and her head cocked to the side. She looks like a bowling trophy — sometime we'll have her bronzed while she's waiting for her ball to connect. Pat plays by those little arrows on the boards behind the foul line, she doesn't even look at the pins. She's like a machine — same starting spot, same four-and-a-half steps, same little kneeling dip as she lets go, like she's genuflecting. Blanche has this awful hook to her ball, some kind of funny hitch she does with her elbow on her backswing. She has to stand way over to the right to have a shot at the pocket and sometimes when she's tired she'll lay one right in the gutter on her first ball. She gets a lot of action when she connects with that spin, though she leaves the 10-pin over on the right corner a lot and it's hard for her to pick up.

I'm a lefty, so the lanes are grooved in my favor, but I don't know what I look like. The girls say I charge the line too fast and foul sometimes but I'm not really aware of it.

The other thing with Janey's style is the 7-10 split. It's the hardest to pick up, the two pins standing on opposite sides of the lane, and because Janey throws a real straight ball she sees it a lot. Most people settle for an open frame, hit one or the other of the pins solid and forget about trying to convert, but Janey always tries to pick it up. You have to shade the outside of one of the pins perfectly so it either slides directly over to take out the other or bangs off the back wall and nails it on the rebound. Even the pros don't make it very often and there's always a good chance you'll throw a gutter ball and end up missing both pins. But Janey always goes for it, even if we're in a tight game and that one sure pin could make the difference. That's just how she plays it. It drives Bobbi nuts, whenever Janey leaves a 7-10 Bobbi moans and rolls her eyes.

Of course Bobbi is a little competitive with Janey, they're the closest in age and both still on the market. Bobbi is always saying in that high breathy voice of hers that's so surprising coming from such a — well, such a *big* woman — she's always saying, "I just can't under*stand* why Janey doesn't have a man after her. What with all her nice qualities." Like it's some fault of Janey's — like working split shifts at a nursing home and taking care of a kid who makes motorcycle sounds and bounces off the walls all day leaves you much time to go looking for a husband.

Not that Janey doesn't try. She gets herself out to functions at the PNA and the Sons of Italy Hall and Ladies' Nite at Barney's when they let you in free to dance. The trouble is, she's got standards, Janey. Nothing unreasonable, but considering what's available in the way of unattached men, having any standards at all seems crazy. Janey won't have any truck with the married ones or the drinkers, which cuts the field in half to start with. And what's left isn't nothing to set your heart going pitter-pat. When I think of what Janey's up against it makes me appreciate my Earl and the boys, though they're no bargain most of the time. Janey's not getting any younger, of course, and any man interested in her has got to buy Scooter in the same package and that's a lot to ask. But Janey hasn't given up. "There's always an outside chance, Mae," she says. "And even if nothing works out, look at Evelyn. All that she's been through, and she hasn't let it beat her. Nope, you got to keep trying, there's always an outside chance." Like with her 7-10 splits, always trying to pick them up.

But she never made a one of them. All the times she's tried, she's never hit it just right, never got the 7-10 spare. Not a one.

Anyhow, last Thursday after Evelyn left we got into our first string and Janey started out awful. Honey, it was just pitiful to see. None of the girls were really up to form, but Janey was the worst, no bounce in her approach, just walked up flat-footed and dropped the ball with a big thud onto the boards. Turned away from the pins almost before she seen what the ball left, with this pinched look on her face that showed up all the wrinkles she's starting to get. Leaving three, four pins in a cluster on her first ball, then missing the spares. The teams were all out of balance without Evelyn, *we* were all out of balance. Blanche's hook was even worse than usual and Pat couldn't seem to find the right arrows on the boards and I couldn't for the life of me keep behind that foul line. Everyone was real quiet, Rose and Vi weren't joking like always, and the noise of the lanes took over.

Usually I like it, the girls all talking and laughing, that strange bright light all around you, the rumbling and crashing. It reminds me of the Rip Van Winkle story they told in school when I was a girl, how the dwarfs bowling on the green were the cause of thunder and lightning. It's exciting, kind of. But that night with Evelyn gone and the girls so quiet it scared me. The pins sounded real hollow when they were hit, the sound of the bowling balls on the wood was hollow too, sounded like we were the only people left in the lanes. It gave me the creeps and I tried to concentrate on keeping score.

Scooter was drawing all over the score sheet like he always does, making his motorcycle revving noise, but we've gotten used to reading through his scribble and I didn't pay it no mind. All of a sudden Janey reaches over and smacks his hand, real hard. It was like a gunshot, Pat near jumped out of her seat. Usually Janey is the most patient person in the world, she'll explain to Scooter for the millionth time why he shouldn't lick the popcorn chute while she steers him away from it real gentle. I remember how upset she got when she first come to the Home and saw how some of the girls would slap a patient who was mean or just difficult. She always offered to take those patients off their hands, and found some calmer way to deal with them.

But here she'd just smacked Scooter like she really meant it and for once his engine stalled, and he just stood and stared at her like the rest of us did. Then Bobbi's ball finally reached the pocket and broke the spell, Scooter zoomed away and we all found something else to look at.

It put me in mind of when Evelyn's husband Boyd had his stroke and come to the Home for his last days. It was right when they'd moved Janey to the men's ward to help me with the heavy lifting cause the orderlies were so useless. Evelyn would come every night after work and sit by Boyd, and in between checks Janey would go in to keep her company. Boyd was awake a lot of the time but wasn't much company, as he'd had the kind where your motor control goes and all he could say was "ob-bob-bob-bob" or something like that. What impressed Janey most was how Evelyn kept planning this trip to Florida they'd set up before the stroke, as if the rehabilitation was going to make a miracle and Boyd would ever get to leave the Home. She'd ask him questions about what they'd bring or where they'd visit and he'd answer by nodding. Kept him alive for a good six months, planning that trip. "How bout this Parrot Jungle, Boyd," I'd hear when I'd walk by the room to answer a bell, "would you like to stop there?" Then she'd wait for a nod. Janey would come out of that room with a light in her eyes, it was something to see. And honey, three weeks after Boyd went out, didn't Evelyn go and take her Buddy down to Florida all by herself, stopped in every place they'd planned together and sent us all postcards.

Anyhow, the night went on. Sometimes it can get to be work, the bowling, and by the fourth string everybody was looking half dead. Dropping the ball instead of rolling it, bumping it against their legs on the backswing, waving their thumb blisters over the little air vent on the return rack — a real bunch of stiffs. Almost no one was talking and Bobbi had taken out her little mirror and was playing with her hair, a sure sign that she's in a nasty mood. We'd had a few lucky strikes but no one had hit for a double or a turkey and there were open frames all over the place. Everybody was down twenty to forty points from their average and we'd only ordered one round of Cokes and beers. Usually we keep Al hopping cause talking and yelling gets us so thirsty. When I felt how heavy my legs were I remembered I still had to pull my eleven-to-seven shift, had to get urine samples from all the diabetics on the ward and help with old Sipperly's tube-feeding, I started feeling very old, like *I* should be joining the Seniors', not Evelyn.

Then in the eighth frame Janey laid one right on the nose of the headpin, first time she hit the pocket square all night, and there it stood. The 7-10 split. Sort of taunting, like a gap-toothed grin staring at her. It was real quiet in the lanes then, the way it goes sometimes, like a break in the storm. Janey stood looking at it with her hands on her hips while her ball came back in slow motion. She picked it up and got her feet set and then held still for the longest time, concentrating. She was going for it, we could tell she was going to try to make it and we all held our breaths.

Janey stepped to the line with a little bounce and rolled the ball smooth and light, rolled it on the very edge of the right-hand gutter with just the slightest bit of reverse English on it and it teetered on the edge all the way down, then faded at the end just barely nipping the 10, sliding it across to tip the 7-pin as it went down, tilting that 7 on its edge and if we'd had the breath we'd of blown it over but then the bastard righted itself, *right*ed and began to wobble, wobbled a little Charlie Chaplin walk across the wood and plopped flat on its back into the gutter.

Well, we all set up a whoop and Janey turned to us with this little hopeful smile on her face, cheeks all glowing again like a little girl who just done her First Communion coming back down the aisle looking to her folks for approval and even Bobbi, who was up next, even Bobbi give her a big hug while little Scooter drew *X*'s all over the score sheet.

The Cabinetmaker

LAURA'S WINDOW HELD a three-bridge view, but only a section of the Bay, jutting out from Oakland, was visible. You couldn't see San Francisco at all.

Michael had his plans spread on the living-room rug, he knelt studying them. He heard voices under the window, then the cans banging.

"Tyrone! Ty-*rone!* Gotta be gentle wif them thangs. You wake the princess up."

"An she turn me into a hoptoad?"

"Naw, man, you that already. All cover wif warts."

"Then why I want to be quiet for?"

The banging of the cans as they took them down the driveway to the truck. Two huge black men with long underwear showing under their shirts. When they turned back, cans booming louder, empty now, one caught sight of Michael. The man flashed his teeth and waved up to the window.

"Say hey, little white-fokes. Hope you warm an cozy up there."

Thinking Michael couldn't hear through the glass. Or maybe knowing that he could.

"Ax him to bring the princess down," said the other. "So's we can look at her nice little boodie."

"Bite your tongue, Tyrone. They hear you talk like that they stick you in the *com*-pactor. They use you for *land*fill, chump."

They went under his sight then, whanging the cans back into place. Michael wanted to shout to them, to tell them he only worked there. Just the hired help. He lived on the Flats like they did.

Or maybe they were from Oakland.

There was a little plaster burro by the side of the driveway that one of them managed to knock over as they left.

"Oooops. I tromped the donkey."

"Dammit, Tyrone, caint you do nothin but de-*stroy*?"

Michael brought his plans into the kitchen, laid them on his workbench. He always kept two sets, one for himself and a simplified version to show the clients. They liked to think they knew what you were going to do.

The framework of the base and wall cabinets was up. One section of counter top was finished, a big slab of butcher block. A friend of Laura's who was into crafts was going to do the rest. After Michael was gone.

She can hear him rustling paper downstairs while she looks at the prints from last night. Still under the covers, taking them one by one from the night table. It isn't him. Not yet. Something hasn't emerged, though she's sure that it's there on the film. She'll have to do some more printing, fiddle with the exposure, the contrast. To make him come out.

Laura pulls herself out of bed, tired. She waited till midnight to go down to the darkroom, not knowing if he would come over or not.

He was on his knees measuring when Laura came down, padding over the newspapers that covered the floor. She was wearing what the garbage men had wanted to see her in.

"Good morning, Michael."

"Morning."

Laura came down nowadays without putting her little bit of makeup on, came down with sleep in her eyes and pillow creases still on her face. In the beginning Michael had heard her fiddling in the upstairs bathroom for a good half hour before she made an appearance yawning and stretching as if she'd just tumbled out of bed.

Laura put a pot of coffee on the hot plate he'd rigged for her till they brought the gas stove, came over and kissed the back of his neck.

"You sleep okay?" she asked.

"Fine."

"I missed you."

"Mmn." Michael measured the drawer slots front and rear in case they weren't square. He'd already fastened the shelf standards. He accounted for the thickness of the metal guide and wrote a figure down.

"How's it coming?"

"It's coming fine. Gonna look really nice."

"How long do you think you'll be on it?"

She asked that almost every morning lately.

"Oh — four, five days."

Laura yawned for real. "Gotta get the kids up," she said, and crinkled out over the newspaper.

Aaron is up already, bouncing on his mattress.

"Is Mike here, is Mike here?"

It's always such a treat for them when he comes. Boys. She never figured on having boys.

"It's Michael, not Mike," says Laura. "He's downstairs working."

"When did he come?"

So nosey lately, even with all the precautions.

"Early this morning, like always. Now get your brother up and help him find his clothes. It's getting late."

There is a big glossy print of David on the wall between their beds. The one she blew up and retouched for grain. His Daddy face.

"And what are you smirking at?" she mutters to it as she leaves the room.

The first morning Michael put her up against the bare wall. The kitchen was stripped but for the old linoleum. The linoleum showed where everything had been. The breakfast nook, the pegboard wall, the cantilevered peninsula with the built-in electric range — all that early-sixties plastic and Formica the former owner had gone in for. The kitchen was empty.

"Face the wall," he said.

"Now reach up, slowly, very slowly, as high as you can. Hold it there. Don't go up on your toes. Okay, relax. Now flex your elbow and reach, slowly, as high as it's comfortable. Don't stretch."

She was wearing a tie-dyed sleeveless undershirt. Michael watched the muscles in her back move.

"Drop your hands and make like you're mixing something in a bowl on the counter. Put some muscle into it. Drop to where they're most comfortable."

She was tall. He'd make the counter height forty inches, maybe forty-two. He'd drop a section lower for her to work with long-handled spoons and mixers.

"Now turn and face me, Laura. Spread your arms out to your sides. Wide. Wider. That's nice."

He could tell she was trying to move gracefully. She tensed some when he measured her, when he laid the cloth tape softly on the inside of her arm, when he moved behind and ran it up her back. It was the right kind of tension. He could have asked her height and figured it all from that, but it was nice to see them move. To make them move for you that way.

"Aaaaaron! Isaaaac! Hurry up and get dressed, it's time to go! And don't flush the toilet!"

Laura poured herself coffee. She knew not to offer any. Michael had given up telling her how bad the caffeine was for her. Something she held on to from back East.

"Damn." Laura kicked at the plastic trash-baskets, half of them full of wood scrap. "They came, didn't they?"

"With the morning serenade."

"I always forget about it Wednesday night."

She separated the organic from the trash from the bottles and cans and lugged them all out to the metal cans.

They came from back East mostly, or the Midwest. Laura was from New Jersey and the last one, Diana, was from Kansas City. Kansas or Missouri, he forgot which. They came and bought houses and did things to them.

"Fog again," she said, shivering when she came in. "All they have here is fog. It's supposed to be sunny."

Michael shrugged. "It's different in Redondo. The fog burns off around noon and then it's real nice. It doesn't get clammy like up here."

"I'd like to see it sometime."

He could stretch the work to the full five, maybe six days if he wanted. Laura had lost track, she'd already paid him for the job. He busted a clutch on his van trying to go straight up Marin and had asked for an advance.

Aaron and Isaac came down, Isaac carrying his clothes, tottering to keep up with his older brother. Michael put the clothes on while Laura made lunches. The kids liked Michael, he brought a hunk of four-by-four and times when Laura wasn't having one of her migraines he'd give them each a hammer and let them bang nails into it. Just whale away. That way he didn't have to talk to them so much.

"Aaron," said Laura, "have you been trading lunches?"

"No."

"Are you sure?"

"Uh-huh."

"Then how come I find cake crumbs in your lunch box? I don't give you cake."

Aaron thought hard for a possible explanation, then gave up and shrugged. "I don't know."

"Don't be trading lunches. I want you to have what I give you and I don't want you getting anything else on the side."

Aaron mumbled something about nobody wanting to trade for his lunches anyway.

Laura ignored him and chopped an apple in half. The vein in her temple was starting up.

Tad had put Michael on to the job. He knew Tad from Redondo, from when he was heavy into surfing and went as Mike. Tad still called him Mike.

"Got a new lady on the table, Mike. She needs some cabinetwork." Tad did massage, acupressure and rolfing. Laura went to him for her migraines.

"Lives in the Hills, just divorced."

"Nice?"

"Very nice. Lady has a lot of tension in her abdomen, lower back, back of her neck. You know how that is."

Tad claimed to be able to tell the amount of a person's sexual activity from where their muscle tension lay.

"Yeah, I know."

"I'd take a whack at her myself, but I got my hands full right now. Lotsa ladies on the table. You know how that is."

Michael got his jobs through the Berkeley grapevine. He knew Tad, he knew a guy who had a gardening service, knew a guy worked in a day-care outfit, knew a guy who remodeled bathrooms. If someone needed cabinetwork they'd recommend Michael. Satisfied customers passed him on to friends.

"What'd I tell you?" said Tad the next time they met.

"Very nice."

"I'll soften her up for you in our sessions. Old Magic Fingers."

"You're a sport."

"Go for it, buddy."

Laura cleans up the lunch makings. He's good with them, Michael, but not obsessive. David was obsessive. They would have turned out just like him — spoiled, hypersensitive to criticism, insensitive to others. He's good with them, Michael, not on their case all the time. And for them to see him at his work, that steady, quiet crafting . . .

Michael went into the living room, sat on the couch to check his measurements against his stock list. He saw Aaron and Isaac leaving. Isaac bent to right the plaster burro, it was nearly as heavy as he was. Aaron opened his lunch box and unwrapped his sandwich. He pulled the sprouts from it and threw them into the jungle of succulents around the mailbox. The day-care panel truck came, and then the little bus to take Aaron to first grade.

When the bus had pulled away Laura sat by him and kissed him. Lots of tongue in it this time, a kiss that made Michael want to pull her down on the couch or floor with him. But Laura bounced away, reassured, muttering about errands she had to take care of.

She always did that when they'd spent a night apart, waited till the kids were gone then jumped on him. Sometimes it would be several times in a day, every time she came back from an outing. Like a nervous base runner, Michael thought, tagging up and leading off, tagging up and leading off. She didn't like to make it in the morning anymore, though, so Michael didn't let it get him excited.

Laura shivers in the darkroom. She holds strips of negative up to the light. It was a long time learning before she could tell anything from a negative, could see potential before it was laid on paper. He's there, she can see him in the pictures from the day at the beach. It's only a matter of bringing him out, separating him from the sand and sea a little more. More detail, more definition. Add some exposure time, maybe a moment longer in the solution. She looks again at the prints from last night. They look *like* him, but there's something indistinct. Something missing. Maybe a little burning-in around the face, and then get the brushes out — but no. Try a few more prints before you start retouching things.

The first time they had to take a shower, to brush sawdust from their hair and scrub the newsprint off each other. It was a huge old house, and when the kids had gone they would chase each other around it, stopping to make love wherever they made a catch.

Leading to that were a lot of carpentry lessons. She would come down and watch him work, silent, playing the mouse.

"You want to see how I do this?"

"Sure. I mean if I'm not in your way. I'd love to."

"Here, take hold of this."

She acted afraid of the tools. He knew she'd hung the plants and pictures in the living room, had gotten the yard back under control herself, had put the bird feeders up. But she acted afraid of the tools.

"I clamp this in tight here and you just lay it on that notch and draw it back to you. Nice and easy."

He'd come around her then, pressing lightly against her back, breathing hot on her neck, guiding her arm.

"Nice and easy. Back and forth. That's it."

It always reminded him of planing rough wood. You take your time, you don't push. Each thin layer would slice away clean, the grain exposed, the wood taking shape. Don't push. Let the tool do the work.

After the first time, the very next morning, she wasn't interested anymore. No more lessons, no more lengthy explanations on the couch about the relative costs and qualities of wood, plywood and hardboard.

"Oh," she said that morning, and from then on, "whatever you think will look best."

Laura hurries up the stairs to beat Michael to the phone. Sometimes he forgets and answers. Her mother, God, her mother would grill her for an hour.

Laura was on the phone when Michael came back into the kitchen. There was a phone in the living room and one in her bedroom upstairs but since he had worked there Laura always used the one in the kitchen. Except to talk to her shrink.

Michael looked in a catalog for hinges. She wanted the hinges visible, wanted brass.

"No, David, I'm not a kidnapper. When you signed the papers it said nothing about limiting where I could live. They like it out here, the schools are wonderful. No, I'm not warping their minds, David. If anything's warped it's genetic."

She was talking to her husband. She always ended up yelling at him. It was the only time she could show anger, she said — over the phone. In the waning days of their marriage she used to run from the dinner table to a pay booth down the block and call to express anger at her husband. The counselor had suggested it.

"What? The what? Jumper cables? I think they're in the trunk. What? No, I won't send them. No, I won't, that's ridiculous. Buy yourself a new set, David. They're not a West Coast phenomenon, they sell them in New Jersey. What? No, I don't drive the kids around on the freeways. That's Los Angeles, freeways. Here we have hills. And fog. Yes, they dress warm, they dress as warm as necessary. I'm not an idiot, you know. I'm not retarded. I fix them meals, keep them warm, pay bills, all on my own. What? If you start talking money, David, I'm gonna bang the phone in your ear."

She was yelling now. It took less time to get her yelling at David lately. A lot was coming out. Tad said the tension in her neck was breaking up. She had finally taken everything with *Laura Feingold-Muntz* written on it and blacked out the *Muntz*.

"You do that, David, you do that. And don't forget to tell the lawyer about the jumper cables."

Michael picked out a swaged-butt hinge from the catalog. He started marking where the doorframes would have to be mortised. Laura banged the receiver down and swore at David. She couldn't yet bring herself to swear at him on the phone. She dialed another number, waited. That would be her mother. Laura called her mother in New Jersey every other week, usually right after a call with David. They would talk for an hour. Laura called a sister in Boston and one in Miami. She had a thing about her family, Laura, but Michael never pressed her on it.

The mother wasn't home. Laura dialed another number.

Michael decided he'd cut the mortises right then. They looked like intricate work, made a good impression. He might be able to stretch the job a whole week. He dug through his tools looking for his wood chisel.

"Yes, she explained the different kinds for me. She gave me a booklet."

Laura had asked for some doctor Michael hadn't heard her talk to before.

"I've decided on the Copper-7. No, I've never had one before."

Michael stopped rooting through the toolbox.

"I discussed that with the nurse. Yes. Yes, as soon as possible."

When Laura got off the phone she sat and watched while Michael found the wood chisel. He turned to face the doorframe of one of the base cabinets.

"Those are really dangerous," he said.

"Huh?"

"IUD's. They're bad news."

"The pill makes me sick."

"Oh."

"I get all swollen around my neck. Same thing with my sister. It's an allergy. And you remember the smell I get when I react with the diaphragm jelly."

"Uh-huh."

"And I know how you hate putting those things on."

"Yuh." Actually he didn't mind those things at all, Laura did. She got goose bumps looking at them. In the waning days of their marriage David had gotten heavy into rubber goods.

"I mean I know the dangers. I'll keep having it checked once it's in."

Michael tapped the butt of the chisel with his mallet.

"It's your body."

"That's right. It's my choice. And I really want something permanent."

She went upstairs and Michael could hear her faintly, talking with her shrink.

"He's somebody — he's — really *spe*cial. That's all I can say."

Dr. Meyer is suspicious. He always hits you with a half-minute of dead air when he's suspicious. "Special?"

"For instance, I'm changing my birth control. Most guys would just be thinking of themselves, of their own pleasure. Michael is really concerned about *me*, though. I'm not used to that."

Almost a full minute of dead air. Laura jerks a knot in the cord, begins to pull it apart.

"Let's talk about David," says Dr. Meyer.

If he cut the mortises and stained all the framework this morning...

It was still warm in Redondo. And Big Sur. He knew a guy ran a store in Big Sur.

And a lady who had a house in Carmel.

Laura came down. She borrowed one of his heavy wrenches to smash garden snails on the sidewalk. Often after talking to David or her shrink Laura went out after snails.

She was in the garden a long time. Michael finished the mortises, put on his dust goggles and hooked the power sander up. He liked the buzz of the sander, he could get inside it and think.

The last one, Diana, had been a major hassle. Phone calls, nighttime visits, holding his check up so he'd have to come in person. Wanting to hash everything over again and again. She could talk a thing to death, talk it past death, Diana. She was an analyzer. She had a collection of every stuffed animal she'd ever owned, dozens and dozens of them, and she still remembered all their names.

The van would make it fine if he skipped the coast road and stuck on 101. And if he decided on Big Sur or Carmel he could cut over before Salinas. The sanding went smoothly, he switched to a finer-grained paper.

"You're sanding already," said Laura through her nose when she came back in. Sawdust was another thing she was allergic to. She had only told him that yesterday, when he tried to wrestle her onto the floor again. "Doesn't that mean you're almost done?"

"Not really. There's a lot left to do."

She heated soup she had made for their lunch. She had put too much barley in it. Michael ate slowly, quietly. Laura finished quick and watched him. It was how she made love.

"Do you know what you'll do after this job?"

"Nope."

"Nothing lined up?"

"Uh-uhn."

He pressed the back of his spoon against the barley to squeeze some liquid out.

"Are you ahead of your rent and all?"

She had offered before to put him up for a while, to move his stuff in. He'd been having a landlord hassle.

"No, I'm all set. Something will turn up when this is finished."

"Listen, have you ever done any big remodeling? I mean like knocking out walls?"

She had talked about letting each of the boys have his own room. It was a big job, a long job.

"No."

"You think you'd like to try it?"

"Maybe. Someday."

Laura made him a cheese-and-sprout sandwich to go with his soup. He didn't ask but she got impatient watching and had to do something with her hands. She was a nervous lady. All that caffeine.

"Are you going to come over tonight? The kids will be in bed by eight."

The doctor had given her an appointment for Monday. He had a cancellation, so she wouldn't have to wait so long.

Michael told her maybe, that he had a little side-job he might have to check on.

Laura sits on her bed changing her shirt. When the walls are being knocked out she'll fix up their beds in the playroom downstairs. Yes, they'd like that. And it will be good for Michael to have a major job. To design it himself, to have the whole upstairs to play with. And maybe then he could put the darkroom in shape, maybe build a little studio like she had in New York for her retouching work.

And they could use her bed. No more making it on the couch downstairs in hushed tones like high-school kids. Aaron and Isaac could get used to having Michael stay over, but they wouldn't be able to hear.

When she left, Michael dumped the rest of his lunch in the organic-trash basket and covered it with coffee grounds from her Melitta. Laura took a half-hour to dress for the Co-op. She wore jeans and a white-cotton Indian shirt. She looked great.

The front right tire on his van was looking pretty bald. And the spare wasn't much better.

"I'm gonna buy everything on my list," she announced, "no matter what their damn signs say. They're always warning you off the lettuce or the mangoes or whatever it is you want. I wish they'd sell it or not sell it and shut up about whether it's good for you or not."

She hugged Michael before she left. Rubbed herself up against him, more like a promise than a good-bye.

"I've got to stop by the butcher. But we should have an hour before they bring Isaac home."

Michael watched from the living room as she wound her old Fiat down the hill and into the fog.

Laura downshifts, leans into the corners. The driving is more fun out here. And having a yard, even with all the fog. She likes the way the houses hang on to the hills, the way the plants grow whether you fuss with them or not. The way everything seems to take care of itself. Berkeley is easy. Like Michael. Like Michael compared to David. David with his intensity, his hang-ups, his world view.

"You got to float with the current," Michael always says. "Just float with it and you're bound to stay on the surface."

You had to watch out for the undertow. Michael went up to her room. She had made the bed with two pillows. That was new, she used to keep the other in the bathroom linen closet. There was a picture of him, wedged into the frame of her dresser mirror, an Instamatic she'd taken when he dropped by for Isaac's birthday. A picture of him and Aaron and Isaac. That was new, too.

The van wasn't that bad. He'd just put on new shocks. He knew a guy ran a car clinic, let him use the tools and bay for free.

He could pick up the hardware on his way home, bring the stain along. If he worked late . . .

Michael dusted the cabinet frames and swept up. He laid fresh newspaper around them. He got the bucket of special stain from his van, the one-coat penetrating stuff from his last job. Diana had asked for it. He'd have to pick up more to do the drawers and doors at home. It cost an arm and a leg but it was quicker than two days of shellacking and one for satin varnish.

He got his brushes out, started laying it on.

If he worked late tonight he could stain the doors and drawers too, and put the hardware on. All but the hinges. Laura was getting a permanent filling in her root canal tomorrow morning, then seeing her bankers in the afternoon. The move out had left a lot of financial loose ends. If Michael could hustle his butt . . .

The lady in Carmel ran a pretty loose ship. He had built

her a studio. And he knew a lot of people in Big Sur. It would be good to get down there, lay low for a while. Coast.

Laura picks through the avocados, trying to find a perfect one. She smiles. Tomorrow morning she'll get him. Catch him poring over the plans in the kitchen, thinking he's the only one up. She loves to see his face that way, all serious, like a boy pretending to build a rocket ship. Tiptoe down the stairs, across the living room. It won't need retouching. No, it will be him, there in the kitchen with their plans. She'll lean slowly into the kitchen doorway and snap! She'll have him.

She'd come in tomorrow and it would be finished. He'd leave a note. She'd already paid him, that was good. He'd put the drawers together at home tonight, with lip fronts so he wouldn't have to cut rabbet joints. He'd pick the hardware up and put that on. It would look really good, she'd come in and there it would be, all done. It was a nice set, one of the best he'd ever built. And he wouldn't bill her for the stain.

Old Spanish Days

I

F A PATROL CAR or the Immigration came along there would be no one to look at but him. Amado hurries up State Street to work. It's always so empty, the shops not open yet, nothing moving. Jesús has been stopped, just walking, twice in the last month. But Jesús tries to look tough. And Jesús has his Green Card.

There are banners stretched across State for the Old Spanish Days parade. The other lavaplatos say that on Cinco de Mayo only the Mexicans celebrate, but for Old Spanish Days the whole town comes out.

Amado crosses the street to avoid the Fremont House. The old Anglos gone to drink are up and out at dawn, and sometimes they follow him and say crazy things he can't understand. They have their own tongue, the drunks, just like the ones in Durango.

The Fremont is the only brick building left on State. An earthquake took the others long ago, and when the Anglos rebuilt they decided to copy the original Californio settlement. Everything is adobe, or made to look like it. Stein's Drugstore, The Meating Place, the Great Lengths beauty parlor, Fat's Chow Mein, all the real-estate and travel agencies, the surf-and-turf restaurants. There aren't any Mexican restaurants on State, they're mostly wooden buildings across the freeway, on the East Side.

OLD SPANISH DAYS 1978

says the huge green-white-and-red banner above Amado —

¡VIVA LA FIESTA!

A patrol car eases up the deserted street. Amado makes a tunnel with his eyes, walks stiffly into it.

Beginning at eight o'clock at the Sambo's restaurant downtown, comes the squawk from the sound truck cruising the West Side, *the Old Spanish Days Fiesta Costume Breakfast. Enjoy huevos rancheros, hot chorizo and other authentic favorites. Costume competition commences in the parking lot starting at ten-thirty. Viva la Fiesta!*

"Qué pasa, nano?"
Luis stands outside the Golden Calf waiting for him, smiling and holding the brooms. Luis is younger than Amado, maybe seventeen, but has been up for three years and tries to act older. They sweep the empty parking lot.
"You hear what happen to Ortega?" Luis always sweeps too fast, raising a lot of dust. He does everything too fast, Luis.
"La Placa. They got him."
Amado had been there, waiting in the back of the car in front of the liquor store when the fight started. If the cop hadn't been right around the corner it would have been nothing. Amado saw him first and yelled, and the driver, who was illegal too, screeched away.
"I hear they pull him in," says Luis.
"That's right."

"I wonder what they do to him?"

Amado shrugs. "We should have gone to Rubio's. I told them we should." He wants to remind Luis that he was there.

"Rubio charges more."

"Maybe. But you go down lower State at night, you just ask for trouble."

When the parking lot is done they vacuum the dining rooms and the bar. It's Amado's favorite time at work, the restaurant all to themselves like they own it, like the soft, red carpet and cane furniture and leather bar-counter belong to them. The liquor and food are kept locked till Mr. Charles comes, so all they can do is pretend. Luis sits at a corner table in the bar and snaps his fingers for service till Amado comes over and gooses him under the arm with the vacuum. Sometimes they find money customers have dropped, but the night shift gets most of that.

. . . La Misa del Presidente, at the Old Mission at eleven o'clock. Benediction by the Mission padres and the finals of the Miss Spirit of the Old Spanish Days contest. Admission free. Viva la Fiesta!

"Put lettuce in box," says Mr. Charles. "Put box in walk-in."

He always talks that way to them, Mr. Charles, even to Jesús, who can sound like an Anglo.

"Then do chicken. Then do eggs," says Mr. Charles. He stands checking the produce off as it comes in from the delivery vans. "Armando do too. Armando help."

After correcting him the first dozen times, Amado has given up. It's like he's deaf to whatever they say, blind to the fact that they know where all the produce goes already. He calls Luis "Ruiz" and Ramiro "Ramirez."

"Your shift forgot to put the roast beef in yesterday," he

says to Motown, the black cook. "We had to eighty-six the French dip."

"I'll have Ross put one in this morning."

"See that you do," says Mr. Charles. He talks regular English to Motown but never looks at him.

Amado and Luis transfers heads of lettuce from bags into plastic containers and lug them into the walk-in. Mr. Charles comes in the early morning to check the deliveries and then leaves till dinner. The night people get him all shift. Mr. Charles gets nervous if he sees anyone standing still and can invent new jobs on the spot.

"Take meat to freezer," he says when the butcher's truck arrives. "Then get old bottles, put in box, we send back. Mucho work today, hurry, hurry, mucho work!"

. . . at the Beef and Brew, 1631 State Street, the annual Lions' Club Enchilada Luncheon. Guests in costume admitted half price. And on Embarcadero del Mar this afternoon, do your Old Spanish Days shopping at El Mercado, the Old World open market. All items are muy autentico and the price is right. Viva la Fiesta!

"Estoy ren*d*ido!"

Jesús blows in a little after eight. He's the senior lavaplato and Motown is in charge of the time cards so it's all right.

"All last night I'm out with mi ruca," Jesús says. "Too much bullshit. Din get any sleep."

"Which one was it?" Luis always wants to hear.

"Patty. The blond. She gonna wear me out, put me in the grave before my time. Good mornin, campesino!" He ruffles Amado's hair.

Amado tries to ignore him.

"I see you wearin shoes today, man. That's real progress. They not gonna believe it when you go home, tell em about paved roads and hot water an evrythin."

Amado has been up almost a year, used to live right in the city of Durango, can order a meal and read his pay slips in English, but still Jesús picks on him. Of course Parrando is newer and Jesús picks on him too, and he picks on Luis for being nervous and on Rudy for being fat and Motown for being black and Chow for being Chinese and old and on Ross for being stupid. Jesús picks on everybody he's bigger or louder than, which is just about everybody.

> *La mujer con el pelo negro*
> *Inflamando mi corazón,*
> *Su manera desahogado*
> *Despertando mi pasión —*

Jesús sings with a mariachi group in town, sings high and piercing and full of emotion. Even in rush times, with the radio on full blast and the dishwasher going and the disposal grinding and the cooks and waiters shouting threats at each other, Jesús can make you wince with his voice.

"I'm singin tonight," he says. "First at the courthouse and then at the Steak-and-Grape and then at the Museum for the Daughters of the Golden West."

"Bunch of old ladies."

"Hey, they pay us good, Luis. You come by an see how it's done."

"When you at the courthouse," says Amado, "sing a song for Ortega."

Jesús makes a face. "That's true, then, huh? They got him up there?"

"That's true," says Amado. "I saw him catch."

"Pendejo. He should of known better. You can fight over on Castillo or Monte Perdido and they don bother you. But lower State, watch out man. Too much bullshit, this town."

"Well they got him."

Jesús scowls.

"How come you not singin at the Park?" asks Luis. "That's where evrybody gonna be."

"Cause they got some shitkickers from down South, Luis, that's why. Probly some neighbors of Amado's."

"Charles say Luis got to stay late today," says Amado. "Cause of Ortega's not here. Cause of Old Spanish Day."

"Old Spanish Days," says Jesús. "Too much bullshit."

. . . Women's Club announces La Merienda, their annual Old Spanish Days party. And for your evenings, don't forget El Baile del Mar, nightly dancing under the stars in the El Encanto Restaurant parking lot. Viva la Fiesta!

"Platos!"

Steam, clatter and curses, the cry goes up and Amado hustles plates across the line to Motown. Lunchtime. Motown grilling a ham-and-cheese, old Chow scowling over an omelette and Ross, the big, slow Anglo, making a mess of the prep work.

"Platos! Más platos! Let's *go!*"

Motown whipping his spatula in, under, flip! onto the plate and under the lights.

"Skip!" he yells out to the floor. "Yours!"

Jesús peeling and de-veining shrimp, telling what the smell reminds him of just loud enough so the two Anglo salad girls can hear as they shred coleslaw nearby. Luis wrestling pots clean at the deep sink, Whitney, Skip and Ernesto careening in with loads of plates and silverware, shouting out their orders, sweating, and Ross's radio nasal, blasting —

Drivin southbound out of Oxnard,
Now how can I explain
The vision of sweet loveliness
Out in the passing lane?

She has a four-speed stickshift,
A set of radial tires,
And all the specs and extras
That every man desires —

"Ham-and-swiss omelette, hold the peppers, side of fries!" Whitney, the black maricón, glides in with a trayful. Amado at the wash counter — separate the silver and the plates, soak the silver, scrape the plates, then spray — he wears a layer of trash liner under his shirt against the wet, bounces the spray off into the long sink. He loads plates onto the rack, slides it into the washer, flicks it on with a buzz —

And as we pass Tarzana,
It's settled in my mind,
The way she drives it's clear that she's
Romantically inclined.

"Dumb fucker!" screams Motown at Ross. "Where's the cheese? I'm all out here!"

They all tease Ross, it's hard not to, but only Motown screams at him. And Ross is the only one he screams at.

"Idiot, grate some up, hurry!"

"Sauté pan!" shouts Chow to Luis. "Gimme sauté pan!"

The old, sour Chinese watching the eggs in front of him, holding his hand out for a clean pan —

"Mi mariquita!" Jesús gooses Whitney on his way through, then makes a move for one of the salad girls —

"Avo-bacon burger, side of fries, BLT on toasted whole wheat, Garden Harvest," starts Skip from the window —

"Hands off!" cries Jennifer, swatting by reflex —

"— and one side of mayo!"

"— *guajira, one-sida-mayo,*" sings Jesús to "Guantanamera." "*One-sida-maaaaaaaayo!*"

"The bacon, Ross, the bacon!"

Her ruby lips, her slender hips,
Her long and golden hair.
Her velvet-lined interior,
Equipped with fact-ry air.

The hungry look she gives me,
The seed of lust has sowed.
My Vega and her GTO,
A romance of the road.

Amado dumping the silver, sorting it, knives, spoons, forks, into the plastic drainers, onto the rack, pushing the silver in, the plates out, hot wash of steam billowing. Steam, clatter, curses and smells — egg-sulfur, garlic, charcoal, grease, sizzling deep fat, even, shouts Jesús in his crude L.A. Spanish, Chow's middle-aged alky breath —

I have the inclination,
And boys, I've got the time,
But I also have three little kids
And a wife in Anaheim.

Meat sizzling on the grill, eggs sliding in the pan, vegetables chopped and torn, fries bubbling, orders thrown together, snatched away, then hurtling back at Amado, scraping the plates, meat, egg, vegetable, grease, into the barrel with the side of his hand. Steam, clatter, cursing, smells —

Yes the exit ramp's approaching now,
And so we have to part.
The San Diego Freeway
Is stealing my heart.

"Platos! Let's go! PLATOS!"

... for the kiddies, La Fiesta Pequeña, followed by Carnivál!
The popular Old Spanish Days extravaganza tomorrow at
noon at La Playa Stadium. Viva la Fiesta!

In the lull after lunch-rush they eat. Jesús and Motown
have their hamburguesas, Jesús drinking a raw-egg chaser for
virility. Ross just picks, not hungry after eating his mistakes
all morning, and Chow drinks a beer. Amado, Luis and Ernesto heat up a panful of beef and peppers, warming their
tortillas over a burner. Skip orders a vegetarian omelette that
Chow cooks extra greasy for spite and the salad girls take
some carrots to chew out at the bar. Jesús turns Ross's radio
off.

"Too much bullshit, that station," he says. "Too much
cuacha."

Parrando and Rudy Peña look in, dressed sharp, already a
little high on their day off.

"Viva la Fiesta!" calls Rudy. "Viva la nalga!"

"Estoy bombo," grins Parrando, and blushes, pleased with
himself. Parrando is up only a month, they call him El Cañón
because he has such a big one.

"They got the floats all line up," says Rudy. "All them
little girls ready to march. Ay de mi!" He smacks his lips.

"We decorate Parrando's chile," says Jesús, "put it in the
parade, it wins first prize. All the ladies want to ride on it."

Parrando blushes again.

"At the Park they have Los Babies playin tonight," says
Rudy. "They do it for real at the Park. All the women be
there, get all hot. Even Luis get laid."

"I got to work tonight, double shiff."

"Why for?"

"Cause they get Ortega."

Rudy stops smiling.

"I heard that," says Motown from the other side of the
line. "Got his ass busted. That's too bad."

"I thin they send him back." Luis eats so fast the meat squirts out of his tortilla onto the floor. "They check his paper, give him to La Migra. La Migra take him back down."

"Gachos gavachos," mutters Jesús.

"If Mr. Charles would put in a word he might be okay," says Motown. "Or even the boss, if he found out. Aint no chance of that, though."

"Pinche jefe," says Jesús. "Pinche Mr. Charles."

"Old Ortega, up in the slammer. That's too bad."

"It's okay maybe, he goes back," says Amado. "He don like it here, is too fast. Ortega belong down South, nice an slow. Like Parrando." Parrando giggles, not understanding but hearing his name.

"An not like you, huh?" Jesús flicks a cherry tomato at Amado. "Half here an half there. Ni aquí ni allá."

"Just the same, it can't be any picnic," says Motown, up to start the soup for dinner, "sittin up in the slammer."

Rudy and Parrando leave, quiet now, and the salad girls return from the bar. Motown is bummed out, starts to sing —

The high sheriff said to Stagolee,

— staring moody into the pot —

"Boy, why don't you run?"
"Well I don't run, white fokes,
When I got my forty-one."

And the rest of the verses while they ease back into work, putting things into shape for the dinner shift. The way Motown tells it, Stagolee is so tough the noose can't crack his neck, so the sheriff has to get Billy Lyons's widow to poison him to death. Amado likes it when Motown sings. He does the glasses that have piled up —

> *Stagolee took that pitchfork,*
> *Laid it on the shelf,*
> *Said, "Jump back devil,*
> *I'monna rule Hell my bad old self!"*

Motown singing sets Jesús off, wailing, serenading the salad girls with the tragedy of the outlaw Heraclio Bernál —

> *Vuela, vuela, palomita,*
> *Encarámante a aquel nopal,*
> *Di que diez mil pesos ofrecen*
> *Por la vida de Bernál.*

High and sweet, trying to catch their eyes. Jennifer scowls, thinking the verses must be something dirty, and Sheri deals with Jesús the way she always does, pretending he's not there —

> *Y lloran todas las muchachas*
> *Del mineral de Mapamí,*
> *"Ya matarón a Bernál,*
> *Ya no lo verán aquí."*

High and sweet he sings, slicing mushrooms for the Veal Bonne Femme. And Ross, thinking he's been challenged, blurts out with

> *Twas a dirty little coward who shot Mr. Howard*
> *And laid Jesse James in his grave —*

but can't remember the rest.

> *. . . all you wranglers out there, the Competición de Vaqueros Rodeo and Stock Horse Exhibition at the Earl War-*

*ren Showgrounds Arena. Three nights of rumble-tumble
action! And today at five, the Mayor's La Fiesta Hour, by
invitation only. Viva la Fiesta!*

Amado rubs his teeth clean with a slice of lime and salt.
Jesús tells him it's time to clean the bathrooms.

"I do it yesterday. Is for Luis."

"Cabrón, Luis is busy. Go on an do it."

"No. I do it yesterday. We take turn." Every day Amado
tries to win a little ground back from Jesús. He'll glare back
at an insult or not laugh at a joke. If his English was better it
would be much easier. Jesús always teases in English.

"Shoot fingers for it," calls Motown from the range. "I
don't want to hear you bitchin at each other again."

Amado loses. He always does. It's an American game, the
fingers, he doesn't have a talent for it yet.

Amado is in a stall in the men's room, scouring the bowl,
when Luis ducks his head in to whisper.

"Stay in there, nano! The cops come, they askin bout Ortega. They checkin for Green Card."

Amado locks the stall door, squats upon the lid so his feet
don't show under, tries to breathe silently.

If only they had waited till quitting time, till his paycheck,
he could have sent another money order home.

If only he had started the ladies' room first, he'd be safe.

If only Mr. Charles or the jefe would put in for him, he
could get his Green Card.

If only Ortega had listened and gone to Rubio's.

Amado squats, listening hard for five long minutes. His
knees ache. Someone comes in, uses the sink. Amado waits till
the hand dryer is blowing to gasp for breath. The person
leaves. More minutes. Then Luis, quietly —

"Come out, Amado. They go now."

*. . . come all, to the El Desfile Historico, Old Spanish Days
historic parade! Better find a place early, you won't want to
miss a moment. Viva la Fiesta!*

Mrs. Lopert hands the pay slips out. They always fantasize
about what she does in her little office alone all day. When
Parrando punched the wrong time card and had to spend ten
minutes in with her straightening it out, Jesús greeted him
back in the kitchen with fire extinguisher in hand.

"We were comin in after you, nano, and use this to get her
off. Those old ones, they grab on, sometimes they don't
wanna let go."

Amado thinks that she drinks all day and it makes him sad
to look at her.

"What you gonna do with your pay, man?"

Amado shrugs. If he says he sends it home they laugh.

"Some I save. Some I spen."

He saves to visit at Christmas. He misses his mother and
father, his little sisters. It costs two hundred to be smuggled
back through La Migra. It costs nothing but the bus fare to
go down.

*. . . MacEvoy, please report to the reviewing stand. Will
Donald MacEvoy please report to the reviewing stand, your
mother is looking for you. Viva la Fiesta!*

They stand in front of the Peaches Bargain Boutique,
Rudy, Parrando, Amado, Rafael Torres and Angél from the
busboys, stand together on the curb watching the parade,
surrounded by Anglos. Anglos in sun hats and sunglasses,
with nose cream and Kodaks and folding chairs. They stand
apart with their arms folded across their chests, joking in
Spanish, running down all the floats, all the tourists and
marchers, and no one around them knows, no one under-
stands.

First there are Marines, hard-heeling down the center of State, eyes front, each supporting a flag. Then a little girl in a white linen dress, like for First Communion, tossing flower petals from a basket.

Ladies and gentlemen, our lovely Little Miss Spirit of the Old Spanish Days, Cynthia Louise Bottoms! Viva la Fiesta!

An Old Spanish Days powder wagon, with four outriders in shining black-and-silver charro uniforms. Angél recognizes Mr. Lomax from the liquor store, who called the police about the fight. He looks younger on horseback, bald-patch under a broad, black hat.

Ladies and gentlemen, El Presidente de la Fiesta and his family, Mayor Thomas J. Kelso! Let's have an Old Spanish Days round of applause! Viva la Fiesta!

A group of families comes next on horse and mule, dressed as Anglo pioneers escorting a covered wagon. Then more local ranchers on their horses, leathery husbands and wives in matching spangled outfits.

"Roys Roger!" cries Parrando. "Hopsalong Cossity!"

The marching bands come then, and Rudy leads the hissing and clucking at the baton girls in their sparkling pink tights, leads in teasing Parrando when the littlest ones, with their spit curls and spots of rouge and their mothers trailing on the sidelines, pass by.

"That's your speed, Parrando," they say in Spanish. "You have to start small and work your way up."

"Parrando's stick is taller than the girls," says Angél. "He'd scare them away."

"A gift like that to such a baby," says Rudy, shaking his head sadly. "If I had one like his I'd retire and let the women take care of me."

"How bout two inches for an amigo, Parrando? You got plenty to spare."

Parrando blushes, and Amado envies him a little. He never has to act hard, Parrando, the others accepted him after the first time he changed his pants in the laundry room.

A drum corps of black boys, whaling away in perfect time, marching tight and sharp, and then a float with a flamenco dancer, a Chicana. They cheer.

A colorful member of our Old Spanish Days celebration, Margarita Estrada will appear nightly at the Noches de los Estrellas pageant, under the stars on the Long Pier.

The County Sheriff's posse follows, and the Old Spanish Days Fire-Hose Cart and Engine Crew Bucket Brigade, the German Club float, the Town Assessor dressed as a Chumash Indian chief, the Elks Drum and Bugle Corps, and then, three flatbeds long, hung with paper lanterns, aglow with bougainvillea, camellias and hibiscus, fluttering with black lace fans, rustling with red and orange and yellow petticoats, comes the Native Daughters of the Golden West float and Mounted Honor Guard.

"Chingao!" says Angél.

The women offer bare, white shoulders to the sun, their hair piled high with combs, they smile and wave and click their castanets at the crowds lining State Street —

Old Spanish Days would not be complete without an evocation of the grace and splendor the Castilian Dons and Doñas preserved in their journey to the New World. This foundation of European culture has survived through the years to become our treasured heritage. Viva la Fiesta! Long live the Old Spanish Days!

— across Pedregosa, across Cota and Gutierrez and Salsipuedes, across Sabado Tarde Street to slow for pictures in front of the Peaches Bargain Boutique. Amado sees Mrs. Winters, who taught the night-school English class he was too tired to keep up with, dressed in scarlet. Little blond boys in white peon suits hold the trains of the longer dresses, while high-school boys in red sashes and bolero jackets mime playing instruments to a tape of a mariachi band. The women work their fans, click their castanets and wave to the flashing cameras, a beauty mark on every cheek.

At the very end come the low-riders.

After the last Spanish couple, the last pioneer family, the last child in pinned organdy strapped sidesaddle on a burro, come the low-riders.

"Chingao!" cries Angél. "Low-riders!"

The Bronze Eagles rolling down the center of State, four abreast, dozens of them, looking bad. Jacking their front ends up and down, Chevys, Dodges, old shiny Fords, pumping their lifts in violent spurts, whush! whush! whush! flashing axle then letting it drop, nose to the pavement. Amado cheers with the others, whistles, stomps, and they hear their countrymen scattered up and down the street. The Anglos have started to leave, chairs folded, cameras capped — they look back uncertainly, check their parade lists.

The Bronze Eagles rolling slow on State, four abreast, hissing, jerking, followed by a pair of poker-faced motorcycle cops wearing mirror-lensed shades.

"Viva la Fiesta!" cries Rudy. "Viva los low-riders!"

> *Twas there that I met her, my dark Señorita,*
> *Black silken hair hanging down to her waist.*
> *Her name was Lupita, she danced in a tavern,*
> *A flash of her eyes and my youthful heart raced.*

They have to pass by the Anglo block parties to get to Murieta Park. Lanterns strung, warm red light, people sitting or standing to the sides of the dance area, politely clapping time for the fast numbers. At one the old Anglos, the pensioners and retirees, are milling about to "Spanish Eyes." At the next middle-aged Anglos hop to a swing band playing "Rose of San Antone," and at the next, slightly younger Anglos slow-dance to an Italian singing "There is a Rose in Spanish Harlem." Amado, Rudy and Parrando skirt the parties, look for friends beneath the streetlights. They try to keep their bottle out of sight.

"Estoy bombo," grins Parrando. Parrando is weaving, smiling at everything, liquid. Rudy wants to ditch him and find girls but Amado is afraid he'll pass out somewhere and be arrested.

"Take it easy, hijo," he says to Parrando in Spanish. "In this town if you lay down on the walk, there isn't a neighbor to throw a blanket on you."

Parrando weaves.

They hear it way back on Milpitas Street, carrying in the night air, welcoming. When they're a block away they see the banks of field lights beaming over the rooftops. Murieta Park, and everybody is there. The warm-up group for Los Babies is set up on the pitcher's mound, guitars, woodblock, congas throbbing, amplifiers cranked up full letting the whole town know about it. Dancers dance wherever they are, children chase across the infield, groups of boys and groups of girls cluster on opposite foul lines, then break off in twos and threes to cruise by each other. Farmworkers in straw Stetsons, already loaded, wander happily through it all while others huddle around bottles, getting there. People sing along with the music in the key that suits them, while others sing totally different songs, shouting out to the black beyond the field lights. There are booths for food and drink, tables for this cause and that, a blanket spread by home plate for sleepy kids too heavy for their parents' arms.

A patrol car glides along the four sides of the Park, never leaving, never stopping.

> *Cuatro palomitas blancas*
> *Sentadas en un alero.*
> *Unas a las otras dicen,*
> *"No hay amor como el primero."*

"Viva la Fiesta!" cries Rudy. "Viva la Raza!"

Amado, wine-high, gives a whoop. For the first time in so long he feels at home outside of the kitchen. He stretches his arms out wide, throws his head back and yelps to the sky. Parrando joins him, howling like a pair of coyotes, howling at the top of their lungs.

"'Tas lucas," says Rudy, smiling but looking at them warily.

They meet Jesús and his Anglo girl. She isn't as pretty as Jesús has described, but she's just as blond, sun-and-seawater blond like Skip at work. When she smiles in greeting her gums show. Jesús rolls his eyes and tells them in Spanish what he's going to do to her, and how he'll come back later and find another, a Chicana.

"One for the belly," he says in Spanish, "and one for the soul."

Jesús sees Ramiro and Mendez and some others he knows who work at the Country Club and he takes his girl to show her off.

> *Mi amor, siempre libre,*
> *Siempre silvestre,*
> *Digame con un beso.*
> *Me sonrie, amor.*
> *Tus ojos prometen*
> *Mientra ta boca aguarda.*

Rudy sees a girl he knows from the junior high school, walking with two friends. They wear high-waisted, bottom-hugging pants, long sweater-coats. Rudy's girl has streaks of red in her hair.

"This is my friend Amado Cruz," he says. "And that is Parrando."

Parrando waves in their direction.

Rudy is very smooth, Amado is glad to be with him. He pairs them up right away. Amado gets Celia, who is pretty. With a good shape at thirteen, brown and thin like Nalda Perez back home. Nalda a mother already. Parrando is left with the heavy, Indian-looking one. She doesn't seem pleased.

Celia has her black hair in a braid for the Fiesta, and a flower behind one ear. Under her sweater-coat she wears a white camisole top, with a small golden cross around her neck. When Amado talks to her in Spanish she doesn't understand.

"I used to know some," she says. "From my grandmother."

Amado struggles with the words as they walk, his stomach tight now.

"Is like Cinco de Mayo," he says, "like Cinco de Mayo down South."

"Yeah, we have that up here too, Cinco de Mayo. The Chicano Caucus puts it on. We have that and the Fourth of July. Lots of fireworks."

"Qué?"

"Fireworks. Boom-boom-boom," she mimes an explosion in the sky.

There is a rumbling, a roar, and a pair of low-riders screech onto the street beside them, front hubs running inches from the ground. They hop the curb, drop even lower —Skreeeeeeek! a shower of sparks from their plated bottoms, a cheer from the crowd in the Park, and then they cut hard and thunder away with the patrol car yowling after them.

Amado watches after, their sound fading slowly. "I save my

pay," he says to Celia. "I buy one. A low-rider. I give you a drive."

Celia says that would be nice.

> *Quiero dormir en tus brazos,*
> *Cara a cara.*
> *Quiero tus labios, ta ternura.*
> *Cuando los brazos mi tengo,*
> *Yo tengo en bronce*
> *Toda mi alma.*

The wine finished, Rudy gone off with his girl, Celia and the little one home to their mothers and the field lights shut down for the night. Amado steering Parrando, lost, but somewhere near the ocean. He hears the surf. He hears others still loose in the night, distant shouts, curses, glass shattering. The night hot, still charged with Fiesta but scary now. Amado thinks they're still on the West Side, he looks out for the train tracks — "If you ever get lost, campesino," Jesús always says, "go find the ocean, take a left turn, an just keep *walk*in."

"Estoy *bomb*o." Parrando's eyes are nearly shut now, he moves in a daze. "Stoy muy borracho."

"You ever drin before this, Parrando?"

"Nunca," smiles Parrando. "De ningún modo."

Surf breaking close by, the backs of hotels rising, then —

"Viva la Fiesta!" cries Parrando when he sees the floats.

"*Chist!*" hisses Amado. Parrando covers his mouth, giggling.

The floats are unattended, moonlit in the beach parking lot. Crowded together they seem like a small amusement park, towers and banners and platforms, pennants flapping in the night air. Parrando darts in among them, tearing at crepe and flowers, tosses the bits over his head.

"Viva la Fiesta! Viva Ol Hispanish Day!" he yips.

Amado catches him on the Native Daughters of the Golden West float, tackling him in a tangle of hibiscus, bowling over a trellis. Parrando giggles, agrees to come along quietly, but first he has to pee. Amado has to also, they turn back to back, count five and let go, like duelists.

Amado is tapped and tucked when Parrando is just getting going. Amado stares, it really is huge. Parrando irrigates the bougainvillea, the hibiscus, the camellias, splatters the papier-mâché wall of the Old Spanish Days hacienda and is baptizing the throne of La Reina de la Fiesta when a strobe light flashes across his back and a loudspeaker crackles —

"STAY RIGHT WHERE YOU ARE."

Amado is off, sprinting into the dark, hurdling driftwood, the beach-sand slowing his flight like a bad dream, and dreamlike, the thought keeps touching his mind — *wait till I tell them in the kitchen*. Parrando startled in the light, fumbling to stuff it all back in, reeling away with it still out, flapping — Even Jesús, who never laughs at the jokes of others, even Jesús would be laughing.

Amado sprawls into a runoff ditch behind the bathhouse, legs rubbery, wind sucking in through his ears. He swallows his wheezing, tries to hear them. Surf breaking. Others still loose in the night, cursing, crying, shattering glass. Amado will get overtime for a few days if they catch Parrando, both he and Luis doing double shift till someone's brother or cousin just up comes to fill the opening. Parrando will be better off down South.

A spotlight plays across the sand, catches the breaking tips of waves. Amado squats in the ditch, presses tight to the wall. Maybe he'll see his family before Christmas.

Bad Dogs

BRIAN WAS MIXING Pest Killer for the dogs when Serena scratched on the cage door.

"Hello in there."

It was weird seeing her at the kennel, it was like the one time his mother had come to high school with the news about the old man. His mother in her old coat standing next to Jimmy Mahon's locker. It made him uneasy.

"I came to see the puppies."

"Right." Brian put the bucket aside and came out of the grooming cage. Serena stood back beneath the new sign Mr. Pettit had sprung for.

BAD DOGS

it said, above a black silhouette of a bad-looking Doberman wearing a spiked collar —

ATTACK DOGS FOR RENT

PUPPIES FOR SALE

STUD SERVICE

"BAD DOGS MAKE GOOD BUSINESS"

Brian didn't feel right kissing her, not in public and all, and he'd just seen her seventh period. He stuck his hands in his pockets and smiled and nodded toward the whelping cage.

"Over this way."

He walked close by her, though, in case Lovell was watching.

"Oh *look* at them!"

Women were like that with the puppies. Brian liked to watch them squatting down and making faces and laughing.

"They're only two weeks," he said. "They'll get even fatter."

"She looks exhausted."

Ilse lay on her side, dully watching two puppies tugging at her nipples while the others bumped and tumbled over each other at the water dish.

"She's a little old for it. Pettit's thinking of getting a new brood bitch."

"And what will happen to her?"

Pettit and Lovell were always making fun of people who were sentimental about the animals. Brian looked around, shrugged.

"Maybe somebody will want her for a pet."

The puppies were like fat sausages, ears uncropped, flopping.

"They don't look like Dobermans at all," said Serena. "It's a shame they'll be taught to be mean."

"Oh they aren't mean. High-strung, you know, but not — well, a few of them." Brian pointed to the cage where Wotan sat, neck stiff, ears erect, staring out through the mesh. "Him."

Serena gave a little shiver.

"Pettit uses him for the downtown merchants. The guys who keep a twelve-gauge under the counter."

Ilse yipped and pushed a little one away from her.

"They're such nice puppies."

"Yeah," said Lovell, appearing to stare at Serena's chest

and wink to Brian, "they sure is." He gave her his big, dimply smile.

"Lovell Keyes," said Brian. "This is Serena."

"You're real pretty, Serena."

Wham! He could just do that, Lovell, come right out with those and not sound ridiculous. Black guys could get away with it. Serena blushed.

"You Brian's old lady, huh?"

Serena uhmmed for a moment, not knowing what Brian wanted her to say —

"Yeah," said Brian.

Lovell shook his head, smiled. "What a waste."

Serena watched the puppies for a little while longer, then Brian showed her the guard dogs, showed her Loki and Siegfried and Gunther and Hagen, showed her the different cages and the exercise chute and the quarters where Thor lay sleeping after his second meal. As soon as she left, Lovell was next to him.

"Not bad, McNeil."

Brian shrugged.

"You gettin any?"

"No."

"Why not?"

Brian shrugged.

"Fine little bitch like that," Lovell shook his head sadly, "what a waste."

Brian had looked through Serena DiLallo for the first month of school. Looked through her and two other kids in the row to Mrs. Peletier at the board going over their *vocabulaire*. She would have stayed that way, the back of a head, out of focus, if Brian hadn't heard Russ Palumbo talking about her in study hall.

Palumbo was a fat kid who played football — tackle or guard or something dull like that — who was always flipping his wallet open to flash the foil-wrapped Trojan at you and saying he was from the FBI.

"Federal Bureau of Intercourse," he would say, and then try to goose you. A major asshole.

In junior high Palumbo had a vague but widespread reputation, having to do with an incident Brian had only heard the punch line of. "But it's stuck, Russ, it's stuck!" That one line, squeaked from the back of a classroom, had done in more substitute teachers than any combination of pen dropping, barnyard noises and pretended coughing fits.

Palumbo sat behind Brian in study hall, where Brian usually put his head in his arms and tried to sleep. Sometimes he actually could, but usually Palumbo kept him awake, telling dumb jokes to the kid across the aisle. Brian didn't know the name of the kid across the aisle, the kid didn't play any sport. Brian never saw him anywhere else in school, not in the halls or in gym or in wood shop or even at assemblies where everybody had to go. Brian sometimes wondered if they just kept him in study hall all day, sitting by the window laughing soundlessly at a new dumb-joker each period. He never had a gym bag or a book or even a pencil with him, he just traced the sayings and pictures scratched on his desk over and over with his finger, as if practicing for the time when he'd be given something to write with.

And when Mr. Crozier was deep in reading or out of the room, the kid across the aisle would pull the old heavy curtain away from the window and blow his nose in it.

"Debbie Moffat," Palumbo would say to the kid across the aisle.

"Really?"

"Really," Palumbo would nod solemnly. "I know the guy."

"Just one?"

"Hey, she's not a pig. She's been had, but she's not hooked on it. Not like some of them. Jo-Ann Testa."

"*Really?*"

"Yup."

"But she's a cheerleader."

Palumbo would sigh patiently. "Don't make no never mind. You know those flying splits they do?"

"Yeah?"

"Well that breaks it. Once it's broken, they figure no guy's gonna believe em anyway, so why not?"

"Jeez. Who else?"

"Serena DiLallo."

"You're kidding."

Brian shifted his head in his arms. It was a rotten way to sleep, always with your nose in your armpits. Palumbo must be bullshitting, she wasn't the type at all.

"I'm not saying she has, I'm just saying she would. It wouldn't be hard."

"*It* would be hard," said the kid across the aisle, "but *she* would be easy."

Palumbo didn't laugh. He didn't like it when the kid across the aisle tried to make jokes.

"This is true," Palumbo would say and nod solemnly again. "I'd say her pants could be gotten into without much effort at all."

"How can you tell?"

Yeah, thought Brian, how can you tell? With his eyes closed Palumbo and the kid across the aisle were like a radio show, one of those insomniac call-in things he'd got when reception was bad for the Knicks' game.

"You just watch her, watch the way she acts. I wouldn't mind gettin into those pants myself." Palumbo would lean back and smack his belly. "Mmmm-*mmmmmnh!*" he'd say. "Finger-lickin good."

Serena DiLallo and her pants stayed in Brian's mind. He had never thought of her. Every year at the beginning of school there seemed to be dozens of girls he liked in his classes, but after the first week all the good ones were snapped up. It was like that Oklahoma land rush thing in History class, he suspected the guys who got girls of some kind of cheating, some gun-jumping or secret knowledge. He'd never even considered Serena DiLallo and now it was probably already too late. He'd see her tomorrow in the halls with some jerkoff and word would circulate that her pants had been gotten into.

He had never thought of that expression before. It made him think of actually being in them with her, two legs through each leg, bellies touching, the nylon stretched to bust —

When the bell rang Brian had to do a Groucho Marx walk to get out the door without looking like a hat rack.

In French the next day he could no longer look through her to the board. He watched her hair brushing against her bare arms. When she bent to look in her book he could see how thin her neck was. He wondered about what Palumbo had said — she seemed awful quiet. She seemed like she probably took books home from the library and read them, books that weren't assigned. She didn't have a bunch of girlfriends she hung with or turn and laugh too hard when somebody made a crack like a lot of them did.

But once she had smiled at Brian in the hall and asked if he was getting ready for basketball season. Girls didn't come up and ask you questions for no reason.

Brian sat half listening to the class *répéter,* moving his lips, and imagined that he was reaching forward and stroking Serena's thin neck, rubbing his hand softly against the down on her cheek. Or kissing the backs of her legs. He did that sometimes, imagined with different girls. It alternated with his other favorite daydream, the execution. Sitting at the very back of Humanities class he'd give himself ten shots. He'd figure out what order to get them in — who might try to rush him, who was close to the door and might run, Mr. Wojicki, and always three or four left for the prettiest, most stuck-up girls in the class. He would stare at the backs of their heads and think, "You first, then you, then you, and then you just as you turn around —" Serena had never figured in either daydream before.

If he was Lovell Keyes he could just come out with it, straight on and sugary — "Hey, sweet thang," Lovell would say, "I gots my *eye* on you."

If he was Danny Naccaratto and could dance like they did on TV he could ask her to a dance.

If he was Tim Dougherty he could offer her a ride home in his GTO with the rabbit-fur dashboard.

Even if he was Russ Palumbo he could flash his rubber and see if she knew what it was.

Out of the fog he heard Mrs. Peletier ask if anybody knew what Bouviers des Flandres were. There was the half-minute of silence that followed any of Mrs. Peletier's questions.

"*Ils sont un type de chien*," said Brian. He felt Serena turn to look at him. "*Un type trés féroce.*"

It was Mr. Pettit's dream to have nothing but Bouviers, to cater to the country-estate crowd. If only their name were different.

"It sounds kind of faggy. People hear Doberman pinscher, German shepherd, they think Nazis, right, black leather and spike collars. Bouviers could eat them other two for breakfast, but people think French, they think poodle. It's an educational problem."

"*Eh bien*," cooed Mrs. Peletier, "*as-tu un Bouvier?*"

"*Non*," said Brian, "*mais je travail avec les chiens. Avec les chiens féroces.*"

Mrs. Peletier said it was *trés intéressant* and then the bell rang.

"You're really lucky." It was Serena, talking to him.

"Huh?"

"To get a job working with animals."

"Oh. Yeah. I guess I am."

"I like dogs best."

Brian said yeah, meaning so did he, though he could take them or leave them. The old man had hated dogs, so Brian never had one as a little kid. He was allowed to have a turtle once, but all it did was sleep.

"I have a dog named Spencer," she said. Brian didn't know where they were walking, but they were doing it next to each other, down the hall. "He's a fox terrier."

"They're nice."

"He's got a really fantastic personality."

She stopped in front of a Home Ec room, girls hurrying in with dress patterns. She had her back to the wall, books held to her chest, smiling up at him. Brian asked her if she'd like to go to a football game with him sometime. She said she would. She said she'd like to visit where he worked sometime. He said she could. The bell rang and released them. He took his time getting downstairs and stared coolly at Mr. Crozier as he walked in late to study hall. It was something he had been working on.

They went to the football game together and held hands and he put his arm around her. It was so cold and their clothes were so bulky. He explained the game.

He started walking to school with her in the morning and in the halls during lunch period. They did a lot of walking. They talked some, but afterward Brian could never remember what it had been about. They necked through a movie on a Saturday. That was nice, Brian discovered they really did get excited just like guys, the way he had always heard but never really believed. Serena seemed very — very understanding. That was it, that was why they never talked much, because they understood all they had to about each other. Or maybe they were both just quiet.

Work was a drag now that he had Serena to be with instead. It was cold and the dogs weren't getting enough exercise and were all on edge. And Brian had the worst jobs because he was low man. Lovell did a little feeding and the exercising and helped run Discipline Class and took care of Thor. He spent most of his time with Thor, brushing the stud dog over and over, talking to it, feeding it his special meals of beef and liver and eggs and cottage cheese. Mr. Pettit just sat in his little carpeted office with his feet up on his desk, taking phone calls. He wore white shoes.

"These shoes," Mr. Pettit would often say, "are the symbol of my success. I started out where you are, McNeil, but those days are long gone. I have stepped," he would say, "in my last pile of dogshit."

The worst job was caring for Wotan. Wotan was old and scarred and mean, a holdover from Mr. Pettit's shitkicker days. One eye was blind, the lid torn off in a fight, the white ball staring at you even when the dog was asleep. Sometimes Wotan would ignore his meal, sniffing haughtily, walking to the rear of his cage to sulk. Brian would put the bowl in the next cage, in front of Loki, and then Wotan would roar and leap at the wire mesh till Brian gave it back. He'd gulp the food down without a chew, his good eye darting warily from Brian to Loki and back.

"That one," Mr. Pettit always said, "that one you never turn your back on."

Brian had to plant Wotan at the switchyard at night. After his old man had died the railroad went to dogs to patrol the yard, over heavy union flak. Dogs were cheaper, and though they might fall asleep they'd never drink on the job. Brian would wear the gloves and keep Wotan muzzled till he was tied to his post. The voice, the deep, steady, authoritative voice Mr. Pettit taught him had little effect on Wotan. You muscled him into place, hooked him up, slipped the muzzle off and got away quick. Brian was glad it was Lovell who had to collect Wotan in the morning.

"I never like it in the morning anyhow," Lovell would say.

"You got to give him a couple hours, recharge the batteries."

Lovell was crazy for women, of any size, shape or age, and would talk for hours about the stable of them he was going to put together someday.

"This here's my trainin grounds," he would say. "This where I learn the fund*amen*tals. Watch old Thor, watch the bitches, and I know the *prin*ciple of the whole thang, y'dig?"

Brian had been walking around with Serena for a couple weeks before she came to look at the puppies.

"You gettin any?"

Lovell asked so abruptly, before Serena was even out of sight, that Brian didn't think to lie.

"Why not?"

The way Lovell said it made it sound like an oversight, like it had slipped his mind when the chance came along. Why not? Why wasn't he getting any? He shrugged, not knowing.

When he asked Serena she didn't seem to know either. They were down a block from her house pressing together just out of range of the streetlight. Serena had her arms under Brian's sweatshirt and he had his under her parka and their breathing frosted the air like a freight train chuffing into the station.

"I don't know. I never really thought about it."

"Don't you think we should?"

"I, uhm, I —"

"I'd really like to." Brian looked her straight in the eye the way he'd seen Lovell do it with the ladies in Discipline Class. The way Mr. Pettit taught him to look at the puppies when they were messing up, staring till they curled their tails under and flattened their ears and whined for forgiveness. Serena avoided his eyes, looking around at the street as if to say, "But where?" and Brian tightened his hold on her.

"It would be nice," he said. "Someplace warm, where we could be alone."

"Okay," said Serena. She didn't sound too ecstatic.

"When?" Brian pressed against her harder.

"Uhm — Saturday. My parents will be out Saturday."

Brian gave her the look again and Serena looked back, one of those solemn-faced ones he figured were looks of understanding and then she just about sprinted to her house. She'd agreed. She'd said yes, out loud and right to him. It was all set. It was all he could do when he got home to keep from calling and telling her not to forget.

Brian went to the Hibernian to stock up. Lovell probably could have gotten him some but he was embarrassed to ask, just as he was embarrassed to ask in a drugstore. He remembered the machine in the men's room at the Hibernian from when he used to collect the old man there. The machine sold combs and Kleenex and latex spiders and the last slot on the left gave you rubbers, even though the little window was empty. He got through the bar, pockets bulging with five dollars' worth of quarters, without any of the old man's cronies noticing him. But he was still feeding the dispenser when Slim Teeter sloshed in. Slim only had one kidney left and was a beer drinker from way back, so the men's room was his second home.

"Calm yourself, boy," he said, "calm yourself. It isn't a slot machine."

Then he peed for three full minutes.

Discipline Class was held Friday nights in the second tier of a five-tier parking garage. Wind whipped and whistled through the hollow concrete shell, the women wore their heavy coats. They were all women except for the little man with the big Alsatian who screamed his commands no matter how many times Mr. Pettit advised him not to. Mr. Pettit sat at one end of the tier in a director's chair, loudspeaker in his hand, while Brian and Lovell ran around assisting the women with their dogs. Mr. Pettit would give a command and then women would repeat it to their dogs and the dogs would look up at them in confusion and the women would look at Brian and Lovell for help. They did the Stay Command and the Recall on Leash, Heeling on Leash, the Long Sit on Leash, the Long Down on Leash and shaking hands. Mr. Pettit hated the idea of the dogs shaking hands but the women all insisted so he included it. There were poodles and Afghans and terriers and schnauzers and Samoyeds and a really stupid Irish setter and a pair of golden-retriever puppies and the Alsatian, which skulked and hung its head even when the guy who owned it wasn't screaming.

I think she's confused, they would say, or I think Harlan feels intimidated, or whoops, they would say, we've had another little accident. There was even one lady who kept complaining that her Afghan was bored.

"That again?" she would moan. "But Mitzi's be*yond* that, she needs a *chal*lenge."

Brian wanted to tell the lady that Mitzi would need six weeks' training to learn to lift her leg, much less anything challenging, but the lady was under forty and had all her teeth so Lovell never let him near her.

"What they want most in the world," Lovell would say, looking the woman deep in the eyes, "is someone to *obey*. They got someone they can look up to, they can count on, they can per*form* for, then they be in harmony with their natural *state*. You give em too much leash, make them think for theirselfs, they'll be just miserable."

Brian figured half the women were impressed by Lovell and half couldn't stand him, but since both groups just tightened up and listened when he'd come over and guide their hands it was hard to tell which felt what.

After Discipline Mr. Pettit held a small class for attack training. Two men with Dobermans came to this, and the guy with the Alsatian, and a very old woman with an Airedale named Boo stayed over. The woman lived alone in a large house and wanted a dog that would attack intruders but wouldn't scare her. Boo was terrified of the other dogs and spent most of his time watching them and wetting the concrete. Mr. Pettit gave Brian personal charge of Boo's training.

For the attack session Mr. Pettit would come out of his chair and join him. He'd trot out his command voice, his firm, controlled voice that left no doubts or questions. It would get stronger as the night went on, as Brian put on the gloves and padding and the dogs took running, snarling leaps at his throat. Lovell would stand back listening to Mr. Pettit and shake his head slowly.

"I *know* that tone," he would mutter to Brian, a sad smile on his face. "Every nigger in America heard that tone sometime. Make you feel just like a whupped dog."

Afterward, everyone else gone, it was Brian's job to clean up. Part of the deal with the parking garage. He would scoop and squeegee under the yellow fluorescent lights, the night wind howling through the ramps, and sing at the top of his lungs to keep the heebie-jeebies away. But they always got to him, the feeling that the wind outside was blowing everything into space, that when he stepped out there would be nothing left but black and cold and not a living soul who knew or cared that he existed. They got Brian just before midnight and not even thinking about Serena and her promise could warm him up.

On Saturday afternoon Serena said her parents weren't going to be away after all.

"We'll find someplace else."

"My mother is home on Saturdays," said Brian. "Even

when she's not, there's Mrs. Casilli downstairs, and her we could use for guard duty at Bad Dogs. No way." Brian shook his head and looked at Serena accusingly.

"I'm sorry," she said. "I'll try to think of something."

They went to a movie and she let him feel her breasts even though there were junior high kids all around snickering and lobbing popcorn at them. When he lost interest in those she put his hand between her legs. This was a new wrinkle. Brian got excited about the whole deal again and whispered to her that they'd find a place. The movie was almost over before his wrist got too tired.

They held hands and walked around the downtown. They looked in store windows, at Laundromats and diners, beauty parlors and real-state offices as if one of them would offer a place to lie down. They didn't talk except if Brian would ask her more questions.

"You have any friends who have cars?"

"No. Do you?"

"Do you have any cousins or anything whose families are out of town?"

"No. Do you?"

They went through the park but it was cold and the trees were too bare to hide them from view. It was nicknamed Salt-and-Pepper Park because all the interracial couples met there. A couple times Brian thought he saw Lovell in a parked car, talking up some woman.

"One time," said Brian, "our class went to the World's Fair for a field trip on this old bus without a bathroom on it and we drove back so late all the comfort stations were closed. Everybody had been eating all kinds of junk all day long and they had to sit and squirm for over two hundred miles."

"What it reminds me of," said Serena as they walked past the reptile house, boarded up till spring, "is Mary and Joseph in Bethlehem. No room at the inn."

"Yuh." He wished she would keep religion out of it.

They walked all the way down to the river, watched the birds bobbing for garbage awhile, then turned back. Serena seemed to have given up thinking and was a lot cheerier.

"I'm really sorry," she said, "I really thought they'd be away. Maybe some other time."

"Yuh."

"Are you mad at me?"

"Nope."

He didn't say another word to her till they had walked to within a block of her house.

"Can you get out after dinner?"

"I think so. Why?"

"I know a place we can go to."

"Oh," said Serena. "Good."

Their eyes were used to the dark by the time they reached the yard. Brian went ahead, talking firmly in the voice till the growling stopped. It was Loki, wagging his tail and jumping with delight when he recognized Brian. Brian had the dog sniff Serena thoroughly and she gave it some brownies she had made. The door to the watch shack came open with a kick.

There was a small black wood-stove, a hot plate, a cot and some rough blankets, a few canvas folding chairs. The yard workers used it to warm up between shunts in the winter. The cot was left over from the old man.

Brian unfolded the cot and dusted everything off and shook the blankets out while Serena sat and watched him with her hands clamped between her knees. It was freezing inside. Serena undressed beneath the blankets, the cot creaking and rattling, while Brian turned his back and tried to think himself stiff so he could get the damn thing on.

It went okay. Nothing got stuck. There wasn't room to lie side by side on the cot so Brian pulled up a chair and sat holding Serena's hand. He wasn't sure he remembered what any of it felt like. From time to time he lifted the blanket and looked under at Serena's body and they'd smile at each other. Understanding smiles. She was all goose-pimply from the cold and her breasts weren't half the size of Knockers Nieman's, who everybody laughed at in the showers after gym. Of course, Knockers was all fat, he even had fat toes and fingers. Serena's ribs and hipbones showed.

"Will you come in again?" she said. "I'm cold."

This time Brian did what he could to make it last, he took note of how everything felt, how it smelled and sounded and tasted, so he wouldn't wake the next day and feel like he was still a virgin.

The woman who owned Boo decided he would come along quicker if he were boarded at Bad Dogs and trained daily. He became Brian's main responsibility.

"If you can't teach him to attack," said Mr. Pettit, "at least get him to quit wagging his damn tail at everybody."

The idea was that Brian would train the dog to obey him and that obedience would then be transferred to his owner. It was the lady's idea, not Mr. Pettit's.

"Sit," Brian would say, and rap the dog on the croup. Boo would sit.

"Good dog, Boo," Brian would say, and Boo would jump up and wag his tail with pleasure.

"No, *sit*, Boo," he would say, and rap again, and Boo would sit again, looking up at Brian with his head slightly lowered, yawning nervously. "That's right, Boo, good dog."

Boo would whuff and jump up against him.

"No, Boo, sit. Sit."

They went to the shack together on nights when there was a football game or dance Serena could tell her parents she was going to. They liked to know where she was.

"I'm going out, Ma," Brian would say halfway down the

stairs to the front door, and she would say okay from wherever she was and when he got home she would make noises from her bedroom so he'd know she heard him come in.

They'd meet in front of old St. Patrick's school. The only hassle was if they were using Wotan on guard that night. Brian would have to lay the voice on him full force and if necessary threaten to hit him. The dog would stand aside, anger humming deep in its chest.

Serena would hurry her clothes off and get under the covers and shiver till Brian was ready. They didn't talk much in between, Brian could never think of anything that didn't sound obvious or cornball. If he didn't feel a certain way about her he wouldn't be there, would he? She understood that, he could tell.

They tried a couple different ways he had heard of but the cot was too small and too shaky so mostly it was the regular way. It always got them warm. Once he asked if he was big enough for her and she said she would fit whatever size he was, that's how women were. Brian wondered if it was true or if it was just Serena.

When basketball tryouts started he cut Boo down to one hour a day, after practice. It was a drag, but the insurance for the old man was still hung up and they needed the money. The railroad and the insurance company were claiming it was suicide, that passing out drunk in a boxcar headed for Michigan and freezing to death could be nothing but an intentional act. The caseworker said they were just trying to bully his mother into accepting a lower, out-of-court settlement. They were doing a pretty good job of it.

It was Barry Feingold, the manager, who clued Brian in. Brian was always the last one out of the locker room, and Feingold would sit by him while he dressed to talk about the team and things. Brian figured it was cause he didn't throw towels at Barry or call him names or because he was afraid to sit by the black kids on the team.

Feingold could never sit still on the locker bench, he rocked and squirmed and straddled, checked his watch to make sure it was still ticking and his wallet to make sure it was still there, pushed his glasses higher on the bridge of his nose and ran his hand through his curly yellow hair. He looked like a third-base coach giving steal signals.

"Do you know what I saw," Barry would say kicking his pile of wet towels, "in Coach's practice book?"

"What?" Brian would say in the disinterested style he was working on.

"I saw the first cut list," Barry would say and pause a second. "You're all right. You made it."

Brian would grunt and pull on a sock.

"Do you know," Barry would say playing with his clipboard, "what I heard Coach tell Mr. Fuqua today?"

"Nope."

"He told him you'd probably be one of his starters."

Brian would grunt and tuck in his shirt.

"Do you know," said Barry, staring at the ceiling because Brian was powdering his balls with Desenex, "what I heard in homeroom today?"

"Nope."

"I heard that Ditty Stack likes you."

Brian grunted. He slipped on his underpants. He shook some powder under his arms.

"Who said that?"

Barry got up and spun the dial on a combination lock. "Barbara Fazzone and this other girl were talking about who liked who and they said it. They said she likes you. And Barbara is her best friend, just about."

Brian grunted and pulled his pants on.

Brian didn't know Ditty Stack or any of her friends. She

was one of the ones who planned the dances and pep rallies, who were cheerleaders, who had parties at their homes, who rode down Central Avenue honking horns after football victories, who sat at the showcase table for lunch, the first table at the bottom of the cafeteria stairs, where nobody coming or going could miss them. Ditty had straight blond hair and real grown-up woman's breasts that swung and bounced and bobbled when she led the "Let's Go Offense" cheer.

"No cotton there," Russ Palumbo would say to the kid across the aisle in study hall, "those babies are the real McCoy. McCoys."

Russ Palumbo said a lot of other things about her, but with somebody as popular and hard to get close to as Ditty Stack you knew it was just guessing.

The last Brian had heard she was going with this guy who played fullback and who was an All-State wrestler. Though wrestling wasn't a popular sport.

In the cafeteria one day he heard giggling as he passed the showcase, and a voice whispered, "That's *him*. That's the one."

In study hall Russ Palumbo said, "McNeil, I heard Ditty Stack has the hots for you. You fart."

In the hall one day she passed him with some of her friends and smiled and said hi.

He had only been to the shack with Serena twice since basketball had started. There wasn't any football or dances for an excuse to get out and he was tired. Practice tired him out, and work. It was too cold to walk to school together, they caught different buses.

He wished he was Russ Palumbo and knew which girls would do what without having to go with them to find out.

Barbara Fazzone casually, almost accidentally fell into step beside Brian on his way to second-period class.

"I saw your name in the paper."

"Yuh."

There had been a preseason roundup article in the sports section the night before, and Coach had listed Brian as one of his starting five.

"Do you think we'll be good this year?"

"We'll be okay."

He knew Barbara a little, they had been in the same catechism Confirmation class.

"I can't wait till the season starts. I like it a lot better than football. You get to see everybody's face and it's not so hard to follow the ball."

"Yeah. I suppose it is."

"And then cheerleading is much better inside. You're much closer to the people."

"Uh-huh."

"Listen," she said, smiling and letting her arm brush his, teasing a little, "can I ask you a personal question?"

Brian shrugged. "I guess so," he said, then tried to think how he should answer it.

"What do you think of Ditty Stack?"

There were several things he thought of her, but he didn't know which one was right to say.

"I don't know her very well."

Barbara nodded seriously, filing it away. "I wonder if we'll win the league," she said.

"But," said Brian, "I'd probably like to get to know her better."

Barbara smiled. "Listen, don't tell anybody I said this, she'd kill me if she found out, but I think Ditty really likes you a lot."

"Oh."

"It's hard on her because she's so shy," said Barbara, "but she's really very friendly."

Brian had never thought of her as being shy. She did an awful good job covering it up.

"Uh-huh."

"And you know, if I were you, I wouldn't be afraid to just go right up to her and say that you'd like to get to know her."

Brian considered this.

"I bet that's all she's waiting for," said Barbara Fazzone. "And she's *such* a friendly girl."

When they were ten weeks old the Doberman puppies had their ears cropped. Mr. Pettit did it himself, examining each dog's head and then cutting a pair of cardboard patterns for each.

"You got to have an artistic sense," he told them. "You don't fit the right ears to the right dog they look like hell."

Brian held the puppies while Lovell gave them a shot of Nembutal in the abdomen. They wobbled around for ten or fifteen minutes, bumping into each other, while Brian prepared a strychnine solution as an antidote in case any didn't come up from the dose. When they fell out Mr. Pettit started cutting. He'd lay the cardboard pattern next to a floppy ear and clamp it on so the major blood vessels were shut off. He used a pair of serrated scissors for the cropping, drawing surprisingly little blood, and Lovell followed him up sewing the tips with catgut and a curved needle. Then Brian would take the clamps off and rig the ears up with tape and cardboard so they were held erect. Mr. Pettit had him do the cutting on the last one.

"What you got to be is *def*inite," said Mr. Pettit. "You don't want to worry the blades through and leave the tip all mangled. Just straight and clean and definite. Snip-snip, same as with anything else."

If the clamp hadn't slipped on the left one it would have gone fine.

Brian had the phone cord twisted around his free hand till the knuckles throbbed white.

"So anyways," he said, "I don't think we should see each other anymore."

She didn't live far away but the connection was lousy. Brian had to unwrap his hand and plug a finger in his ear to hear her.

"I don't understand," she said.

"It wouldn't be fair."

"What wouldn't be fair? Is something wrong?"

"I uhm — I'm going to be spending so much time with basketball, it wouldn't be fair to you."

"That doesn't bother me. Is that all?"

"I'd feel — uhm — I'd feel like I was losing you."

"What? I can't hear, there's something wrong with the phone —"

"I'd just be using you."

"I don't understand."

"I need more privacy."

"I won't call you up anymore if that's what you mean."

"Look, I really can't explain it, I just don't think we should see each other anymore."

"I don't understand."

"I'm sorry. It's my fault."

"Why? What's wrong, Brian?"

"It's just how I am. You know."

"I don't know. I never know what you're thinking."

It was as bad as he thought it would be. It was true though, he really didn't want to see her anymore. He didn't feel guilty either, which surprised him.

He spoke to her then in a firm, controlled voice, a voice that left no doubts or questions. And she did what she wanted, she said good-bye and hung up.

Lately he had noticed it — one of those things you overlook time after time, but the minute you see it you can't see anything else. Like the picture of Christ Russ Palumbo had that if you looked at it a certain way what you saw was a naked girl. Once you saw the girl it was hard to make out Christ in the picture again. Serena was mousy.

She was so small and skinny and she had mouse-brown hair and even her face reminded him a little of a mouse. And she burrowed. Whenever he looked at her undressing under the blankets in the watch shack he thought of a mouse burrowing. She was so timid with other people, so quiet and squeaky. He wondered why he hadn't noticed before they got together.

And she really didn't understand much of anything.

Brian was amazed at how easily it was to talk with Ditty Stack. It seemed like all you had to do was listen.

"Are you going to the dance after the game?" she'd say, and he would know she'd say yes if he asked her.

"I hate coming to school alone in the morning," she'd say, and he'd ask her where she lived, then offer to walk with her.

"I think that math homework is going to kill me," she would say, and he would suggest she copy his at lunch hour. He copied Barry Feingold's during first period, careful always to make a few mistakes.

"Where'd you get so smooth with girls?" she'd say, and he didn't know if he should laugh or not.

At times he had a hard time believing he was with her. He'd look over at her, sometimes touch her hair if she was in the mood where she wanted or would let him touch her in public. He liked to walk her past the huge trophy case by the gym, liked to see himself next to her in the reflection off the glass. Even then, at times, he would look and wonder, "What's she doing with *him?*"

"Hear you traded in for a new model," said Lovell at work. "You gettin the hang of it, McNeil. Got to change the menu if you gonna keep an appetite. Like m'man Thor."

Mr. Pettit made the dates but Lovell was in total control of

Thor's mating. Once or twice a week he'd work over somebody's brood bitch to prepare her, checking for fleas and lice,
checking that her discharge was clear enough and her parts
soft enough to make it all worthwhile.

"M'man Thor is got the life," he would say. "Eat an fuck,
eat an fuck, even got his own personal nigger waitin on him."

Lovell put together two extrarich meals a day for Thor,
supplementing them with wheat germ oil for vitamin E, and
egg whites "to give his spritz a little body."

Lovell didn't think much of the stock that was offered to
Thor, but Mr. Pettit wanted the cash. When another cow-
hocked, fish-mouthed, pig-eyed bitch would be brought in
Lovell would sigh and drag Brian over to look at what they'd
sunk to.

"What kind of litter you spect him to pump through *that?*"
he would say, and dig out his favorite passage in the breed-
ing book Mr. Pettit had given him.

" 'It is difficult enough, with all one's skill,' " he would
read, " 'to breed superior puppies from even a first-rate bitch.
But to clutter the world with inferior animals out of just any
old bitch is inexcusable.' " He would look to Pettit's office and
call, knowing he couldn't hear, "In-ex-*cus*able."

The mating was painful to watch, but Lovell insisted that
Brian join him when Thor was getting it on. The nipping
and yelping and nervous tension of the dogs was bad enough,
but more often than not they'd end in a lock, turning this
way and that till Thor was facing one direction and the bitch
the opposite, joined at the organs, whimpering.

"First she snarl to keep him away, then she won't let go,"
Lovell would say. "That's bitches all over."

The day before he was shot Lovell posed in the advertising
picture Mr. Pettit arranged. Mr. Pettit stood in the center in
his leisure suit and white shoes, hands folded awkwardly be-

fore him, flanked by Lovell and Brian on one knee, each holding a dog. Lovell was with Loki and Brian was with Wotan, holding him so his good eye was to the camera. The ad was in the paper the next day, on the same page where it said how Lovell had been shot by a Mr. Carter E. Green of Seventh Street. The article failed to mention Mrs. Cleo Green of the same address running into the street wrapped in a bedsheet, or the anatomical location of Lovell's wound. Mr. Pettit scraped dogshit from his work shoes and muttered that it was a typical nigger stunt to pull. Brian thought of visiting Lovell in the hospital but never got around to it.

Ditty Stack ran Brian ragged. She reminded him of Mr. Ricci, the JV coach. Mr. Ricci didn't believe in stopping to catch a breath between drills.

"You get your rest in bed," he would say. "Basketball is movement, basketball is action, you got to make it happen. You stand on your heels and they'll blow right over you."

Ditty lived like there was something chasing her, no sooner finishing one thing than she was thinking about the next. If Brian took her to the movies it was like a meal to her, down the hatch and forget about it. Sometimes she couldn't remember what they'd seen, couldn't tell you anything about it but maybe who the lead actress was. Ditty made plans for what they'd do, they did it, and she'd forget about it immediately. When Brian asked things about her before they'd started going together she said it was too far back to remember and not important anyways. Brian told her about himself and Serena one night, including personal things he hadn't meant to say. It made him feel funny. When he finished she told him she knew someone who could get tickets to see the Dead.

When they did it she seemed in a hurry to get her clothes back on. They went to the shack only once, a freezing night when Wotan was on duty. The dog crept out from a dark corner and stood blocking their way. A deep growl rumbled inside him, his black coat glistened in the moonlight.

"Wotan, sit!"

He held his head up and to the side to fix them with his good eye. He pulled his lip back to show his teeth.

"*Sit!*" Brian took a step forward and raised his hand. If he was alone he would have gone to get a board or a piece of iron. Ditty stood behind him, waiting.

Wotan didn't sit, but he moved slightly to the side, enough to let them slide by.

Ditty liked doing it well enough when they were inside but said the shack gave her the creeps. Brian hadn't even told her about the old man. He tried to explain how safe it was there, how no one would ever bother them, but she said the shack was out, it gave her the creeps. So the shack was out.

They didn't get to do it much. When the time and place were right she wasn't in the mood. When she was in the mood the time and place weren't right. He took her to parties she told him they had been invited to and introduced him to her friends. They did it in the bathroom at a party in Barbara Fazzone's house while Barbara's mother rattled the doorknob and asked if whoever was inside was all right. He took Ditty on double and triple movie dates she arranged. They did it in the back row of the Palace Theater during the eight o'clock show and got everything tucked back in just as the lights came up and the audience came streaming by. He took her out on joyriding double and triple dates in cars she borrowed from her girlfriends or from the boyfriends of her girlfriends. They did it in somebody's Falcon, sitting where she told him to park in front of an all-night Laundromat, where Brian could hear snow crunching under tires and feet of late-night laundry-doers. He went to dinner at her house and said thank you every time her parents moved and explained in detail why he hadn't yet applied to college though he himself didn't know the reason. And though Ditty had refused to use her house when her family was away or his place when his mother was out and Mrs. Casilli was at the chiropractor, refused because she said she'd feel guilty, although she wouldn't go to Brian's safe, cozy shack, she did it with him on her living-room couch a few minutes after she said be right up, Mom, and a few minutes before Brian called good night Mrs. Stack, Mr. Stack, slammed the door behind him and zipped his fly. That was the first time she ever made noises doing it.

Ditty cheered extra loud when Brian made one of his few, careful baskets, her straight blond hair flying, her real-McCoy breasts swaying and bouncing and bobbling. Once when they were horsing around in the shack Serena had pretended to be a cheerleader. Gimme an *F*, she yelled in a whisper, jumping up with Brian's undershirt over her little flat body. Brian gave her an *F*, gave her the *U-C-K* she asked for and they laughed and did it again. They had done it on the cot for hours with only an occasional lonely whine from Loki outside to hurry them.

"Sometimes it's too big," Ditty told Brian. "Not that it's that big, I mean you're not — you know. But sometimes the way I am and the way you are, it's too big. It hurts. Then other times, for some reason I'm all loose and it's too small. I mean it seems too small. I think it has to do with my period. That kind of thing usually does."

Brian wondered if people made do with whoever came along first or if they kept shopping around for a perfect fit. Or if there were other girls like Serena who would adjust to any size.

Brian spent French class trying not to look at the back of Serena's head. It meant staring at the ceiling a lot and Mrs. Peletier got on his case for daydreaming. Serena had made a friend, a heavy, red-haired girl who Brian remembered

vaguely from junior high. She had been good at making fart
noises with her hands. Serena and the red-haired girl were
always together, in the halls, in the cafeteria, up in the
bleachers at basketball games. He heard them talking and
laughing together. Serena wasn't so quiet. He wasn't jealous
exactly, it wasn't like she had found another guy and was
doing it. It was just that she seemed to be having such a good
time without him.

One lunch period Ditty whispered to Brian that she really
wanted to do it and led him out to the parking lot. She
picked a customized Chevy Impala, the old kind with the
huge manta-ray fins. Though there were roomier cars and
cars parked farther away from the windows of the school
Brian didn't argue. Ditty Stack wanted it in the parking lot
during lunch hour — Russ Palumbo on his best day never
dreamed up anything close to that. Brian had never felt bigger, he hoped it wasn't one of Ditty's tight days.

He had her panties off and was trying to twist around to
get his fly untangled when he saw someone coming, a boy
with car keys jingling in his fingers.

"What is it?" asked Ditty, on her back. Her head was
crammed down by the armrest, her legs bent and splayed
apart like a dog waiting to have its belly scratched.

The boy saw Brian, saw Ditty's feet sticking up in the air,
and stopped. The boy was an All-State wrestler, though
wrestling was not a popular sport. He had been fullback on
the football team. Brian remembered now that the boy
owned a customized Chevy Impala.

"What is it?"

"Nothing," said Brian. "Just a guy I know."

The boy turned and went back inside the school.

"Who is it?"

"Carter E. Green," said Brian.

"Carter who?"

Brian zipped up and reminded her there was only a few

minutes till fifth-period bell. He left the door open when he hopped out, Ditty gaping in confusion between her legs.

In the team picture for the yearbook, Brian's left arm is in a heavy bandage. He had just done the trick with Wotan's food dish, pretending to give it to Loki, and was reaching it back into Wotan's cage when the dog clamped ahold of his wrist. No snarl, no display, just a quick, silent pounce that brought Brian to his knees. Brian tried to command him to stop, but the voice wouldn't come, he couldn't work a sound past his throat. He banged on the cage with his free hand till Mr. Pettit came out. Wotan held on like a bulldog, blood running down his clamped jaws, looking Brian in the eye. He didn't listen to Mr. Pettit, not even when he shouted, and he chomped even harder when Pettit kicked him in the ribs. It took a double dose of Nembutal to put him out.

"You'd been inside the cage," said Mr. Pettit as he poured antiseptic on Brian's puncture wounds, "it would of been your throat."

Sometime later in the year, when Brian hadn't had a girl for months, Russ Palumbo approached him in metal shop.

"Wanna buy a balloon, kid?" he said, and flashed his wallet rubber. Brian ignored him.

"Listen, McNeil," said Russ Palumbo, "I hear that Ditty Stack is strictly a cockteaser."

Brian ignored him.

"That so? McNeil?"

"No, Russ," said Brian in the dry, disinterested style he had almost perfected, "she's not a cockteaser at all."

Palumbo's face brightened. "Yeah?"

"She's a cliff-hanger."

Thoroughly confused, Russ Palumbo walked away with a knowing laugh.

Hoop

RULE NUMBER ONE," Jockey would only have to
bend a little to line up his shots, "Never Show
Your Speed." Five-seven-two, corner pocket.
Jockey liked to punctuate his lectures with combination shots. Anybody at the Hibernian could tell you
Jockey Conn would pass up a half-dozen straight chippies for
a three-ball combination.

"You show your speed and they got you pegged. They
know just what you can do and what you can't do. They know
where to hurt you, Sport. Am I right?"

Brian liked the way Jockey would always call him Sport.
The old man always called him "boy," or, if he was really
gassed, "sonny."

"You pay attention to the Jockey now, boy," the old man
would call from the bar. "There's many a thing worth learning they don't teach at that school." And Slim Teeter would
say A-men. The old man and Slim would be trying to get in
as many cold ones as possible before five o'clock when the
prices went up. The bartender would usually be Sweeny, sitting over a racing form circling his picks. Sweeny never
played, he just picked and followed the results.

Preston laid five dollars next to Brian on the wooden bench. "There you go."

"Right. Nice game."

"Yuh."

Preston was a light-colored one, the kind the others called Chinaman. The kind the old man said made the best pimps. Preston wore a religious medal that sometimes hopped up and stung you when you played him.

"You almost took me," said Brian, but Preston was already gone around the corner. Five bucks was no little thing at the Children's Home.

"Not only do they ask for it, they beg for it." Three-seven-eleven, off the cushion and in. "And who are you to disappoint them?"

The word had gotten out about Brian and Condredge Holloway, the one from 13th Street Park that everybody called Boots. The word of how he had bet Boots on a one-on-one game and Boots had swallowed it. Everybody knew Boots was crazy, the white boy was on the varsity at school and, blood or not, Boots didn't even start for the Boys' Club. But Boots only lost it by three, he was close all the way and the white boy only came back to take it at the end. The word got out that maybe McNeil was only good as a team player, a pass-an-pick dude. One of Coach's boys.

"Hey! McNeil! Brian!" Practice had just broken up and he was heading down to the showers. Lucius pulled at his jersey from behind. "I hear you a gamblin man."

"Huh?"

"You an ole Boots. One-on-one game."

"Oh. Yuh. I almost blew it." He'd really have to work hard to make it look good with Lucius. Lucius gave away four or five inches and had almost missed the last cut.

"You want to try your luck again?"

"Against you?"

"Naw! Think I'm crazy like Boots?" Lucius had a chipped tooth up front that made him look like he was smiling more than he was. "You an my man Preston."

He could see Preston waiting beneath the far basket, dribbling a ball idly. "Preston's pretty good."

"You're a starter. He's only sixth man."

"He's taller than me."

"By a hair."

Brian sighed. It was a pretty fair nibble. "Okay. Fifty cents." Back into it easy, Jockey would say, never let them know you smell blood.

"Aw, man, make it a dollar. I mean Coach must think you better. He got you startin."

He sighed again and frowned. "Okay. A dollar."

Lucius smiled and gave a little laugh. Preston nodded to Brian and they started. Game to twenty-one, winner's outs.

Brian drove past but blew his first two shots. Just barely blew them. He only drove to the right. He got himself behind by four and settled there, matching points with Preston. There was only the three of them left in the gym, squeaking soles amplified, ball thumping back hollow from the empty bleachers. Echoes. It was nice, Brian calmed and played with Preston. He was down 16–12 when Lucius started laughing out loud.

"You are *done*, McNeil, kiss it good-bye."

Brian was on the outside, dribbling. "Game's not over yet."

"It is for you, man. Aint no way you win this one. No *way*. You *done* for, Jim."

Brian backed away from Preston a little, still bouncing the ball, and looked over to Lucius. "Done my ass."

"Oh-ho! Listen to him! Care to put some more coin on it?"

Brian made an elaborate thinking frown. "Yeah. Okay."

Preston waited with his hands on his hips, looking from Lucius to the white boy and back.

"Five dollars, Brian. Make it five. See what kind of balls you got."

He sighed and said okay and saw Preston cross himself. Preston had his right knee taped.

Lucius cracked up and did a little dance. "McNeil, buddy, your mouth just sign a check your ass can't cash." Lucius already had his money spent.

Brian shot from where he stood, shot easily as if throwing the ball away, and didn't blink when it swished.

"Sport, if God didn't want them gaffed, he wouldn't of made them fish. You don't take it, somebody else will." Jockey always ignored the sign on the wall and tried massé shots that barely missed. "Five hundred to one against. Anyhow, what I mean is, if you're gonna play for keeps you use everything you've got. An the most important thing you got is a sense of timing. Got to know when to coast and when to turn it on. Am I right? Got to hear Opportunity when she knocks."

"You listen to the Jockey," the old man would say, "that's very sound advice he's giving you. Opportunity will rise up but you have to take advantage of it. I missed my main chance and I'll regret it as long as I live." The old man would have his work jacket on, the one he had worn when he ran the day crew at the switching yard. He still wore it to keep the night watch over the deserted tracks.

"Op-por-tunity," Slim Teeter would declare from the pinball machine. "A-men." The pinball machine in the Hibernian was called the Riverboat Minstrel. Blackfaced jig-dancers goggled and grinned pink smiles full of watermelon seeds. Slim was a terrible machine player but liked the lights and the balls and the exercise. Slim said a man could drink all day as long as he got his exercise.

"You keep your eyes open, boy, opportunity is everywhere. Everywhere." The old man never turned, but talked to Brian by way of the mirror over the bar. "Twenty years on the railroad and never once did I ask myself where those loads, those trains, were heading. That's where it was, and I never went after it. Right under my nose and there I was, too blind to smell it."

"What your father means, Sport, is you go where the action is. You settle for what you got and life passes you by." Seven-ten combination, side pocket. "Right under your nose."

"Wasted my youth on a dead-end job. And youth, youth you never get back. Never."

"You were never wrong, McNeil," Slim would say, opening his eyes wide to signal a joke, "you were born with one foot on that rail and a beer bottle in your chubby little hand."

The old man would nod. "There's truth in that," he would say, and motion Sweeny for another cold one.

Brian shot from where he stood, shot easily as if throwing the ball away, and didn't blink when it swished.

Time was when he'd have called out "Goodwood!" or "Doosh!" or slapped himself five. Asphalt and chain-net days, pre-Coach days, when Hoop was the language you spoke, the language you thought in. When if you popped the chain it was a word on your tongue and you gave it voice.

Brian shot from where he stood and his tongue ached to call the swish in midair, ached for the days of Rudy and Fatback and Waterbug, for the games they put on. Rudy got rabbit legs, it would start. From his balls up he's all Rudy, but those pins got to come off some bunny. Brian would start it, Hoop-talking, Hoop-thinking, all of them would start it, playing their stories on tongue and asphalt. Rudy got rabbit legs, all thick an bulgy above the knee and stringy-like below it. And he pump the mothers mile-a-minute, hippity-hop, zippin round you ankles (Rudy short) and pushin that roundball up front, ball's a rabbit too. Rudy hop after it, fastest thing going cept maybe Humminbird White from down 13th Street Park and of course Waterbug. I mean Waterbug is *Waterbug*, you don't get faster. Rudy come bumpin and slidin up the middle, then jump out from the brier patch an lay it over the edge. Rudy go *up*. Little bit of a thing, no biggern a minute, up pawin round the rim. It was Rit, Big Wop, that got burned so he got to get back when his side gots the ball. Rudy start it back of the line and flip to Ernie. Ernie turns ass to the board and throw up that worthless hook he does, ball get lucky an hit high off the board stead of clearing the fence and go rolling down the street. Preston bring it down, throwin out his skinny arms and butt like somethin big gonna fall on him. Gets it back to Waterbug and we into it. Bug begins to work his show, hundred moves a second, talking to the asphalt with the ball, playin sounds down there and dancing to em. Brian flash open for a second but Waterbug busy, still working, he pass off when he get good an ready. Sees you when even you don't know you're open, got to be ready. The Bug he got eyes in his ears, back his head, man see you when you sleepin an know when you awake. Bug come down the right side till he throw one on a bounce to Rit, Big Wop put his underhand shitshot in. Ghinny is all ass and a yard wide, don't nobody get front of him when he's cuttin hard.

Screamin Winnie Wills starts in, his old high voice is always being coach and spectators, "Move the baw, move the baw, move the baw!" he go on like some old farm bird. Just a thing he does, like Preston wear that cross. Waterbug throw it to Winnie, shut him up for a second. Man can't talk with his mouth an the ball at the same time, he dribble hisself caught in the corner an heave it back out to Brian. Brian go left on Fatback, Back gives him that first step (Back like to rest on defense). B. push hard down the left baseline, slow a bit where it's sandy so he don't slide out, go up switch it to the right an let it go — ching! "Goodwood!" Old rusty-red net singin his song. Preston got it now, start in with his old back-up basketball, closin in slow, lookin back over his shoulder at the rim nown then, oh them nuns is done a number on this child's *style*. There's FUCK YOU in blue spray paint on the backboard from last Halloween, you puts the ball gainst the Y for a right-hand hook and gainst the C for lefty. Press put a right-hander smack on that Y but too hard, bound gets kicked out to Ernie at his spot, left corner the foul circle and it's in. Can't let the fat boy shoot from his spot, turn into a machine there. Rudy get halfway through the middle but Bug is tight with him so he dump it back to Fatback coolin his heels at the center line (Back like to get his rest on offense, too). That round middle-age gut bouncin once every two dribbles, he commence to workin on Brian. Stares at the ground under the man's feet, plays by the landmarks the ants leaves him. Halfway through a dribble he throw it up, straight up. Back's shot always got to make its mind whether to come down or go into orbit. Falls through the net without a sound. Shit a pickle. "Nice," he says. Back always say that when he hits one, nice. Ernie dribble in slow, the only speed he got, when Waterbug cop it right from under his legs. Man steal the pennies off a dead man's eyes he needed two cents. Bug zigs and zags till he got Rudy goin one way an hisself goin the other to ram in a jumper. But Winnie Wills fall down and cut hisself on the bottle glass, aint no big thing and he want to run home for surgery or somethin, can't but touch the dude an he fall apart. So Dukey Holcolmb come over from where he been foolin by the eight-foot basket an it starts up again, playin our show —

Rudy — Hoppin to the ball, rock forward then back then

forward then ba— then shoot forward pickin Bug off to lay
up a scoop but —

Rit — "Voit!!" say the Big Wop, waitin all along to cram
that Wilson sandwich down the man's throat —

Bug — Work a lightnin show past three men, offer Preston
a stuff but dump it back to Rit on a lay-up, good.

Rudy — Swipe the inbound pass, sees Ernie where Ernie
should be —

Ernie — Spotshot, good.

Back — No move, no dribble, just look at Brian's laces for a
second then let loose a skyball, freezes with his arm pointin
up —

Ball — Check out the stratosphere, gets lonely an come
down like a mortar shell off the rim, climb again, come down
to Brian —

Brian — Got the floor now, dribble an look around for
where to put in his two points' worth, walkin, talkin, signify-
ing in Hoop —

Brian shot and didn't blink when it swished. "Thirteen–
sixteen, my ball." He could see every step to his winning.
Businesslike, just push where Preston was weak and execute.
Execution, that was Coach's favorite word.

"Five of us there were, and only my poor brokenhearted
mother to take charge." The old man would be on his fifth or
sixth beer. It was usually somewhere in there that he'd get
sentimental and start being Irish.

"We were so poor I had to wear my brother's shoes for a
year when they were a full size too big for me. Stuffed with
newspaper."

Slim would wait a moment for the bells to quiet, for the
steel ball to run off the table. "We were so poor we had to
patch the soles of our shoes with cardboard."

"Shoes," Jockey Conn would say, squinting over the cue bridge. "Who had shoes?"

Brian peeled his practice uniform off and tucked the money in his Converse. Coach had given everybody who made the team a free pair. They were always called Converse instead of sneaker, the same way Theopolis Ruffin always said his father would pick him up in the Cadillac instead of the car. If you weren't on the team you wore Keds or Red Balls or the kind that were two bucks a pair mix'n'match from a bin in the supermarket. But if you made Coach's team you wore Converse All-Stars and nobody would steal them even if you didn't Magic Marker your name on the insteps. They were that easy to trace.

The others were already done with their showers and getting dressed. Brian listened to them yelling and snapping towels and shouting the dozens at each other over the locker rows. Trench warfare.

"Hey Dukey! Du-*key!*"

"Hey what?"

"Is it true what they say bout your mama?"

"Aw shit, man, don't start."

"It true she got some new furniture? Three beds and a cash register?" Laughter was invisible, scattered through the locker room.

"Man, you mama like a birthday cake. Everybody gets a piece."

"Yeah? You mama an me got one thing in common."

"What's that?"

"*You!*"

"Shit, Gregory's mama got the only pussy in town that makes change."

"So who wants change for a nickel?"

Brian ducked as somebody's jockstrap flew over the locker

top. Wire-stiff with old sweat, it skittered along the floor like an elastic tarantula.

"You mama like a cup of coffee, man. Hot, black, an waitin for the cream."

"Black? Who you callin black? Listen to the shit call the dog smelly. Your mama so black she got to drink buttermilk so she don't pee ink."

"Yeah, you mama, she lays for 'fays an screws with Jews."

"Ha. Hey Preston! Press-*tone*, you there?"

Preston usually played. Preston could cut with the best of them.

"Yeah. I'm here."

"Why aint we heard from you?"

"I don't have a mama. Remember?"

"A wasted youth. Only got as far as the tenth grade at St. Paddy's."

"A-men. St. Paddy's."

"It was a shame to see it fold."

"A-men."

"True, it was going down when the Eye-talians started moving in, but where else in fifty miles was there a high school half as good? And now that it's gone where can you send your boy for a Catholic education?" The old man would address the bar as if it was full, though there was only Teeter beside him, Sweeny at his horses, Jockey and Brian.

"Where, I ask you? Couldn't raise the money, they said. The people of the diocese just couldn't dig deep enough. But they'll pay for it in the end, they will. They'll pay through their teeth."

"Public school is free."

"Sweeny, you pay nothin, you get nothin. Public school! My boy here is at public school. A basketball player. Tell him, boy, on the starting five. How many white?" The old man's finger would jab at him from the mirror.

"Just me."

"There's your public school! Only one white boy on the floor. Oh, they'll pray they had St. Paddy's back, now that it's too late."

"You'll always have your coons in basketball." The eight ball would roll ever so slowly to thunk in the corner pocket. "Basketball is the coons' game."

The score reached 19–18, Preston's lead, Preston's ball. Lucius had gotten quiet. Preston drove and stopped to put up a short jumper. Brian had watched the same shot pass under his nose unmolested the whole game, but this time he slapped it from the air and recovered it back behind the line. When Preston came out to guard him he went left for the first time, hard and straight and fast. Preston could only turn to watch. 19 all.

The move was a drawn-out version of The Rocker, Water-bug's favorite. Waterbug had played ahead of Brian on the varsity for a while. Bug was Coach's playmaker, his hand on the floor. Bring the ball down the court, glance to the bench, raise his hand in fingers or call out a color to set the pattern. Coach had them playing the post-and-pick pattern basketball he had played when he was a student at the high school, back when there was no three-second rule and you had a center jump after each score. "The year they cut the bottom out the peach-basket" was the way Bug put it whenever they'd pass the trophy-case picture of Coach and his beefy Irish team-mates. "Man was a star the year they made the ball round." It was a drag-ass, ham-and-eggs kind of basketball but if you wanted to play for Coach that's what you played. And playing for Coach was the price for all the other things, for the names in the paper and the girls jumping round cheering your name, for satiny uniforms and Cons on your feet. For a chance to show your game off to the college recruiters. So

Waterbug set up Coach's patterns, called Number Two or Green Play and watched the team be run ragged by the run-and-gun pro style everyone else was using. Waterbug played ahead of Brian on the varsity, shooting four or five times a game and never from more than fifteen feet. For a while.

They'd lost the first three games of the year and were well on the way to losing the fourth. Brian had only seen action late in lost causes. Though he sat next to Coach, there was little chance he'd be called in before the outcome was decided. A minute man.

The other team knew all Coach's patterns by heart, Waterbug would get the first pass off and it would bog down. Late in the first half he called Number Four. But somewhere between the calling and the pass-off Bug saw an opening, the kind of half-step you thought about twice unless you were very fast. A risk. He faked and drove through for a lay-up. The next time down he interrupted the flow of the Green Play to throw in a thirty-footer. Coach wouldn't even allow them beyond twenty feet in practice. The others smelled it, felt something was up with Bug and took it off his hands. Theopolis Ruffin peeled back to steal the inbound pass, Perry Blaydes put a move on his man and threw in a double-pump hook shot. Waterbug led an improvised full-court press, zipping all over the floor giving instructions, pushing them on. "Stop an pop!" he yelled, "Run an gun! Shake your tailfeathers, children, let's get on the *case* here!" They were running loose and grinning, grinning on the basketball floor as if they were playing a game. They went into the locker room at halftime with a two-point lead.

Coach kicked chairs over. Coach threw chalk. Coach told them they weren't a bunch of sandlot kids anymore, they were a disciplined team and should act it. He told them not to let a few lucky buckets go to their heads, if he had to make substitutions he wouldn't hesitate. Waterbug sat through it all without speaking or looking up, sat and rubbed his legs with the baby oil they used so their legs wouldn't look all smoky. Jumpin Juice they called it.

"You've got to keep them under control," Coach said to Brian as they walked out for the second half. "They've got no self-discipline. That's why they're the sprinters and never the long-distance runners. Get yourself good and ready, son."

Waterbug went back to the patterns and tried to stick with them. He was poker-faced down the floor, raising fingers and passing off, dropping back to face the inevitable fast break from the other team. The game slowed, the crowd grew quiet. They went down by six points. It was Lucius who started.

"Hey Bug," he called out from the end of the bench, "lemme ast you a question. What ever happen to run an gun?"

"That's right, that's right." Dukey Holcolmb picked it up. "What ever became of stop an pop?"

"Scoot an shoot?"

"Jump an pump? Shake an bake?"

Most of the bench had picked it up, calling out as Waterbug dribbled the ball down the floor.

"Hey Bug," they called, "what ever become of slip an slide?"

"Float and flutter?"

"Style and pride?"

Waterbug stopped a good thirty-five feet out and picked up the ball. The crowded gym was still as everyone waited for him to raise a finger or call out a color. "Say now," one of them yelled into the silence, "what ever happened to *Waterbug?*"

They hardly saw the shot. That's how it was when he had a notion and he took it — like a snakebite. The ball swished and Brian felt Coach's hand on his neck.

"You go in there, son," he said, "and settle the boys down. Show me what you can do."

Brian crouched by the scorer's table, waiting for a whistle that would allow his substitution, and for a moment caught Waterbug's eye. Bug smiled and shook his head slowly.

Bug took the ball down the court and felt the ball alive in his hands. Felt the eyes of all the players and all the spectators on that ball and knew for now he had control of the game. He took the game and ran with it, feeling the pressure of Coach, the pressure of Brian, the pressure of all his careful, defensive games driving him forward through the snatching hands, felt it chasing him desperately around the floor. Bug listened hard for the rhythm of it, listened to the hard rubber kissing of sneaker soles on the floor, saw everything clearly written in feet, the distribution of weight, the leanings and balances, feints and retreats, and he was a half-step ahead of them all. He snaked through the other nine bodies to the basket, then left the crowd-roar hanging and dribbled past it and on out to open floor again. He teased the players with his ball, played the growing cheers and whoops of his audience in and out, in and out, handling the ball with breathless speed, offering it out for a dozen near-steals and snapping it back from the brink. He heard the crowd-sound building to a payoff and the tension for release building inside him and cut hard for the far corner, whipping away, back to the basket using up every bit of old asphalt flash-and-dazzle left to him, then jumping, turning, lofted a soft, slow, impudent shot as he flew out of bounds, a shot that said there's nothing you can do, there's nothing any of you can do about the Bug but watch and wait as it floated to be swallowed by the hoop.

People were laughing and clapping and slapping five in the stands and at first when he heard the buzzer Brian didn't want to move. But he trotted on and tapped Waterbug on the shoulder. "Have fun," said the Bug, "it's all yours."

Waterbug lasted another two weeks on the bench before he quit. He sat at the very far end, beyond Lucius. Brian saw him sometimes on the street in his P.F. Flyers and they would nod. Word was that Bug had picked up as a ringer for the local JCC team.

Brian took the ball back and went hard left again on Preston, then switched right for another lay-up. Preston's bandaged leg didn't plant when he had to change directions. 20–19. Brian faked right, went two long strides and stopped dead. Preston tried to dig in but the knee buckled. He knelt on the floor and saw the last point go in. 21, game.

"They'll always figure that it was luck, or cheating, or anything but the simple fact that you're better than they are and always will be." Thirteen-two-nine, off the cushion to kiss the five ball in. "Let em. Let em believe anything their hearts desire if it makes em feel better and keep coming back for more. But you've won, Sport, and that's the name of the game."

Brian was alone in the showers until Lucius and Preston came in and walked past him to the far end. Preston wore his medal in the shower. Preston had won the medal for getting a hundred on a test in Confirmation class. Brian and Preston and Lucius had played wall-ball against the chapel at St. Thomas after class every Wednesday, played until the nun from the Children's Home came and honked.

There wasn't much warm water left but Brian stayed under till the two had finished and walked past again. When he heard their locker doors slam he turned the shower off. He liked to be alone in the locker room sometimes, he liked the echoes he made. Like being in a church after everybody had gone. Brian dried himself on the way back to his locker. The five dollars were crumpled and sitting on his pants. His Converse All-Stars were gone. No idea who it could be, he would say. What can you expect from them, Coach would say, and order him a new pair.

"That's the way it is, Sport. The way to be a winner. You and me both know there's only one place that matters, and that's First Place. Am I right?"

At about quarter to five Sweeny would start clearing his throat and looking over to the pool table and making little dusting motions on the bar-top. Jockey would pay no attention. But at exactly five, without looking up at the clock, Jockey would sweep the balls into the pockets with his hand. He'd unscrew his cue into sections and put them in their leather sheath. He'd pull the green cap with the Hibernian insignia from his back pocket and jam it on his head. Sweeny would pass the push broom and the dustpan over the bar to him.

"Another day," Jockey would sigh, "another dollar."

Buffalo

BUFFALO.
　　Cleveland and Toledo.
　　On to Chicago. Gangsters sprawl, twitch and die, gunshot on the sidewalks. Cattle end their long western exodus and hang bleeding from hooks. Wind comes cutting off the Lake.

The country lay on the kitchen table, riddled with pinprick fissures, cake crumbs dwarfing the Rockies. As a boy Brian used the map for a dart board, closing his eyes, flicking. Wherever it hits is where I'll live. Flick — Vermillion, South Dakota. Maybe the best two out of five.

Peoria, Hannibal, Kansas City. Mail-order towns, jumping-off towns. Stock up the wagon and kiss the safe life good-bye. Brian was trying to write his mother a good-bye note. Nothing much to say, nothing that he really believed or that didn't sound sappy. Good-bye, I'm going west. Lighting out.

He had been as far west as Buffalo once, on a basketball trip. As far south as Jamestown on one school field trip, and to New York City after the World's Fair on another.

La Crosse, Albert Lea, Sioux Falls. Poor, one-blanket Indians building fires to survive till morning and the woolly black herds pushed back off the land they had covered like a robe. Sometimes it was hard to believe.

It had to be a note, not a letter. A last small word, something final. Like the boy in the Mexican War who drew a black bean — "Mother, in one half hour my doom will be finished on this earth." This wasn't a trip, a vacation, he wasn't off to CYO summer camp with her waving at the depot and name tags sewn on his underwear. He was leaving for good.

Dear Ma. Or better, just Ma. He wondered if there was still such a thing as Western Union. Like in the movies. As a boy he always thought of famous sayings coming by Western Union telegram.

DEAR SIRS STOP HAVE NOT YET BEGUN TO FIGHT STOP JPJ

He wondered if he should go north along the Lakes and through the Badlands or slide down south first. Roanoke, Knoxville, Chattanooga.

MA STOP KILLED ME A BAR TODAY AT THIS TREE STOP D BOONE

He heard creakings down the hall, his mother's insomnia. He tried not to rustle the country. She could never leave him alone if he stayed up late, she'd toss and turn and go to the bathroom and finally come out squinting and shivering and say oh, are you up?

They had never talked much, but only since the old man was gone was it so obvious. What had ever possessed them, at their age? His third-grade teacher on Open House night, complimenting them on their grandson's imagination.

He would leave her a note.

Ma — I wrote to school, the refund should be in the mail. I'm not going back.

He heard the toilet flush down the hall. The bathroom held her odors, he used to wait to use the ones at school in the morning.

Fort Scott, Wichita, Dodge City. Drunken cattlemen, crooked marshals, mannish whores. Kit Carson, Pueblo, Durango.

I am taking off and will send you postcards. Have enough money for now so don't worry.

Brian

He thought to mention he was heading west, but then where else was there for him to go? He thought to do his signature, the one he'd been working on, but then just printed it out like the rest of the message.

The light in the hall flicked on. He heard one of her sighs and pocketed the note.

Amarillo, Tucumcari —

"Oh, are you up?"

Her voice was moany with sleep. She squinted in the yellow kitchen-light and hugged herself with her arms. Thin blood, she always said, it ran in her family.

Santa Fe. Pony Express, stagecoaches, silver mines.

"You're reading the map?" It wasn't a question, she wasn't looking at him. She padded among the kitchen utensils as if she had come out searching for something lost, pushing at dishes and forks with one finger the way she always did.

"Would you like some hot cocoa? Help you sleep?"

"No thanks, Ma."

She got a pot and milk as if she hadn't heard. She never drank cocoa herself, it made her sick.

Your mama like a cup of coffee, he thought. *Hot, black, and waitin for the cream.* How safe the dozens had been for him to play, how far removed his mother was from cheatings and beatings. His mama never did anything. He watched her face over the stove and for an instant he felt bad.

"Think you could get some things at the market for me tomorrow?"

He had gone over every item, packing only what he couldn't survive without. The sleeping bag he'd bought cheap from a guy at school was out on the landing, along with the old man's boots. They had shared the same foot size.

"I don't think I'll be around tomorrow."

"You going somewhere?"

"I'm going away, sort of." He swiped cake crumbs off the map as he said it.

"Oh. Whereabouts?"

She stirred the milk a little. He could smell it now. Her spoon scraped gently against the sides of the saucepan and Brian held his head in his hands.

"I'm not really sure. I'll be gone awhile."

"You have enough money?" She frowned into the boiling milk.

"Yeah. Yeah, I've got plenty. No sweat for money."

"Will you be back before you're due at school?"

"I'm not going back."

The Coach would be the most upset about that. He was building his backcourt.

"Oh," said his mother, then, "We ought to talk about it."

"Yeah. We should. But I'm not going back."

She was silent for a while but for her kitchen sounds.

El Paso, Tucson, Yuma. Copper-colored desert. Old men with brown-paper skin, baking like lizards on rocks.

She slid a cup of hot cocoa in front of him, covering New Orleans and most of the Gulf.

"Help you sleep."

She washed the pot out as he wondered where he would hit the Coast. Where else was there to go?

She yawned and stared into the dish-filled sink. He could hear her mind working, trying to think of something else to say, to ask. He wondered if he should say the words to her now. Say good-bye. He kept his eyes on the map, elbows propped wide on either side of the country. She poked at a few things in the sink as if testing them for signs of life. The cocoa smoked and grew a skin.

Sacramento. Eureka —

She started as if from a dream, stared for a moment at the cup of warm milk that lay between them, and began to shuffle toward her bedroom.

"Well. Have a nice trip, Brian."

The hall light flicked off.

"Good night, Ma."

"Night."

It was hard to believe, sometimes. But at one time they had been right there. Along the Hudson. Up and down the valley. Syracuse, Elmira, Binghamton were the western frontier. They had been right there.

Buffalo.

Fission

TWO PUDDLES OF FLAB lifting and flopping down again. Feet. The toes were tiny and round, baby peas pushed into a mound of mashed potato. Mary Beth drove her old standard Chevy barefoot, shifting through the traffic flow on Interstate 80. They were surrounded by miles of flat, after-harvest cornfield. Mary Beth's cat, a huge, white female named Justine, slept on top of Brian's duffel bag in the backseat. The sun was nearly straight overhead.

"Not much to see out here, is there?" said Brian.

"Nope. Not a hell of a lot."

Mary Beth had picked him up just outside of Iowa City, going west. He had tried sleeping out the night before but it was too cold, mid-October, and he had shivered in his bag till daybreak. He hadn't eaten for two days, his stomach kept doing little fluttering things when he thought of it. He hadn't seen a mirror for a while and figured he must look pretty scruffy. He didn't get a single bite on the road till around ten o'clock when Mary Beth pulled up, two-hundred-plus pounds of her packed into an apricot-colored shift. "Hop in, honey," she said, "I'm goin your way."

There wasn't all that much room in the front seat. Mary

Beth had to spraddle her legs apart so her thighs didn't jam the steering wheel, and the squashed buttock closest to Brian spread out toward him, flowed against his hip. She felt like some thick, slow liquid sitting there, like warm molasses in a cloth sack. Brian got the impression, not so subtle, that she was coming on to him.

"Listen, honey," she said, "You're going to the West Coast, I can get you there in one ride." She had already told him she lived in San Francisco. "I got to stop down in Kansas City two-three days, then to Denver a little bit, but the people I know there can put you up no trouble and I'll be going straight on through to the Golden Gate. How bout it?"

He considered, then shrugged. "I think I'll take my chances on the road. You get back up on 80, maybe I'll still be out there, you can give me another ride. Thanks for the offer though."

"Well you just watch out for those Nebraska staties. They'll have your ass, honey."

"You hitched out here?"

She had a pretty face, Mary Beth, kind of Indian-looking. A pretty face floating on three chins.

"Honey," she said, "I used to *live* here."

"You're kidding."

"Daddy had a little place up the road a ways. Corn and hogs."

"You don't seem like you're from the Midwest."

"What's that supposed to mean?"

They passed a panel truck with a red, dripping steak painted on it and Brian's stomach did a triple-gainer. He wished he was sitting down to lunch somewhere. Or in the back getting some sleep with Justine. But he liked Mary Beth all right, she was the first woman who'd ever picked him up hitching. In fact she was the first woman he'd said more than hold-the-pickles-hold-the-lettuce to since he started hitching in New York.

"I just meant that I thought you were brought up in San Francisco," he said.

"People who don't understand make fun of farmers." Mary Beth braked a little to let a semi pass, her foot-flab spreading on the pedal. "Farmers aren't stupid. People who make fun don't know what goes into the life. Farmers, they got a lot of strange ideas about the rest of the world and from a distance it looks like they're just small-minded and dull but it's not like that."

"I don't suppose it is."

"The farm belonged to my grandfather and his father before that. He handed down a debt with the farm and it got a little bigger every year. You don't live so bad and you've got good to eat and a lot of money goes through your hands every year but none sticks. Mostly small farmers never clear out of debt. There's this big hole of loans and mortgages and federal land deals that you fall into and never get out of. My daddy worked the fields six days a week. On the seventh he fixed machinery.

"And it's just natural that from down in that hole a farmer can't see clear what's going on in the outside world. He thinks he's at the heart of the country and everybody should be watching him. He goes under and they don't *eat*. He can't be done without. That's where that farmer ego comes from, all that redneck pride. He's the backbone of the whole fucking nation, he thinks, with all the politicians and welfare chiselers feeding off his work just cause they outnumber him. Like locusts. So he trusts only himself and hard work and his fields. But they're not stupid, farmers. No way."

Brian nodded. "Then you liked it, even though it was hard?"

Mary Beth laughed. She had a great laugh, strong and throaty, that sent shock waves of flesh rippling all over her. "I *hate*d it, honey. Every damn second of it."

She put her hand on his knee, still laughing, and squeezed. It was nice.

"You ever been out here in the summer? When the corn is still up?"

"No. But they got corn in the East."

"Not like here they don't. Our house is — was — a good quarter-mile in from the main road. I had to walk out for the school bus every morning. Through all this corn. It was worst when the corn was high, way over my head when I was a little girl."

She paused and grinned a little to herself. "Young and short," she said. "I really wasn't ever what you'd call *little.*

"Anyhow, the corn was planted so the rows opened up to our quarter-mile of driveway. You know how from a distance, from the highway, you come at a cornfield from a certain angle and it's this solid block of stalks, then suddenly you're alongside and *zing!* those rows open up to you one after another, riffling by till the angle changes enough and it's all solid again?"

"Yeah," said Brian. "It's kind of neat."

"Well up close, right next to it, it's not so neat. The angle never changes. They just keep swinging open, one after another, and you're lost in them, under the tops of them, and you can't see the end of the road. Made me dizzy. Made me sick to my stomach sometimes, I'd stop and hang my head down toward my knees till it passed and then tried to walk with my eyes shut. But I knew they were still out there, I could see them behind my eyelids and it wasn't any better. Every morning before school, every evening after, to and from Bible class on Sundays. I still see those rows in my nightmares sometimes."

"Sounds like it's got a hold on you."

"Honey, my ears still perk up when the weather report comes over the news. There's a thunderstorm at night and I can't sleep. Mission and Fourth Street, nothing but peep shows and pawnshops, but some part of me is still worried about how the damn crop is doing."

Mary Beth wore at least a half-dozen rings, mostly turquoise and ivory. They gave the only hint that there were joints in her breakfast-sausage fingers. She wasn't wearing a bra. Brian could see her nipples standing out under her shift, the circle around them soaking through with sweat. His stomach started flipping when he looked at her breasts, he tried to avoid it. She was wet under her arms and in all her creases and the inside of the car had her sweet flesh smell. Brian could almost see the warmth coming off her, thick mammal waves of it wrapping him round the shoulders and neck, making him pleasantly sleepy, pleasantly horny.

Horny. It surprised him. Even with all the hitchhiker stories he'd been told, all the stuff Russ Palumbo used to whisper in study hall, it surprised him. About all the women out cruising for action. They pick you up, see, cause they know they'll never see you again. So they can do anything they want and not feel guilty. Palumbo was an asshole and full of it but he wasn't the only one with stories. Brian felt a little ashamed, a little left out, seventeen years old and he'd never been approached by a woman. No bored housewives, no nymphomaniacs, no sex-starved librarians. And here it was happening and he was surprised that he was a little excited. She was so *big*.

And she talked. In the road stories and in his daydreams the women never talked much. Mostly they clutched. They clutched and they clung and they pleaded and whimpered and moaned and panted and were ever so grateful afterward. Mary Beth had talked almost nonstop since he'd gotten into the car, mostly about personal things, things that made him uncomfortable. About her mother's funeral. About her hemorrhoids. She'd showed him the bruises on her arm and hip where her last boyfriend, a biker who did too much speed, had hit her in their parting fight. She was like an open wound, Mary Beth, all her hurt just kept pouring out and there always seemed to be more.

"Daddy wanted a boy," she said. "Wanted boys. He got me and that was it. Oh, Mama tried, Mama tried against doctor's orders and dropped a couple of things that would have been boys if they lasted a few more months. Little monsters. They had to take her works out then and I think she was relieved. It all went into me. Twelve pounds at birth and I just shot out from there.

"I always had to follow Daddy around after school and on weekends. It was like my punishment for being a girl. He didn't talk to me except to ask for the wrench I was holding or whatever and he didn't show me how to do anything. Didn't teach me the work. He just wanted me *there*. And I was so damn eager to please and afraid I'd do something wrong it makes me sick. When I remember my Daddy I mostly don't think of his face, I see the back of that sun-burned neck bent over some tractor or patch of crop. Don't be in my light, he'd always say when I came close for a look. Girl, you block out the sun."

It wasn't the talking alone that made Brian uneasy. People who picked you up usually wanted you to either entertain or to provide an audience. He was used to that. He got the feeling Mary Beth wanted more, and he didn't know if he had it to give.

"Mama, she went the other way. Just poured all her femininity into me. She was at her sewing machine every spare minute so's she could keep me dressed like a little storybook girl. Of course, I'd already busted out of the Junior Chubette department and was destined for bigger things. You can imagine how I looked. A heifer in organdy. I got a little older and she put me out on the block with the rest of the young girls, all groomed and curried at the school dances and the grange dances and the damn church dances. She'd drop me off in the car, happier than a pig in shit, and I'd just want to crawl under the sidewalk. All I remember about those dances is one or another of my string of first cousins slouching over with his hands in his pockets, mumbling, 'Let's go, Mary. It's my turn.' "

She belted out her laugh then, and Brian didn't know if he should join or not. He tried to smile sympathetically.

"Is your father still alive?"

"Yeah. He's a soil tester for the state. Lives up in Fort Dodge."

"He sold the farm, then."

"Lost it. Phagocytosis."

"Pardon?"

"It's a biological process, honey." Mary Beth swerved to avoid a woodchuck crossing the highway. "You've got a cell, right, and it reaches out with these arms of cytoplasm to surround a smaller cell or a solid particle. And once it's surrounded, inside the cell's membrane, it can be broken down by enzymes. It's a kind of eating."

"Oh."

"Daddy had a pretty small operation and he never really understood that if you didn't get bigger you didn't survive. So this big agribusiness outfit, the company that makes Justine's cat food but they own all kinds of stuff, they start buying out all the small farmers that surround Daddy. He's the only one who won't sell. Redneck pride. So once they're all around him they lay siege. For three years he sets a price for his crop, very small margin of profit, and they undersell him. They can afford to take a loss for a while, they've got the capital behind them, they've got the cat food and the dog chow and turkeys at Thanksgiving and who knows what else. They starve him out and the farm goes back to the bank. They'll wait till the price drops down some before they buy it from the bank. Phagocytosis."

"Where'd you get all that?" said Brian. "The cell stuff."

"You're looking at a former biology major. Parents sent me up to the Ag School in Ames, got me started in animal husbandry. I guess they didn't know what else to do with me since the marriage proposals hadn't exactly come flying in."

"You graduate?"

"Fraid not. Me and this girl who was my best friend transferred to the University of Iowa our junior year. Thought there had to be more to life than the good earth. The University already had a shady reputation in certain quarters, and while I was there it finally started to deserve it."

"When was that?"

" 'Sixty-nine. The campus action wasn't all that much compared to some places, but for Iowa it was a regular Sodom and Gomorrah."

"And your parents?"

"Daddy came to visit after I'd been there a month. Looked around and said come home with me now or don't come back at all. Maybe some kids were living together. Maybe there was a political slogan scratched on a wall. I don't know just what it was. But I wouldn't leave and he cut off the funds. Had to drop my classes but I stayed on in Iowa City. Got involved in some things." Mary Beth smiled. "You might say I switched from biology to chemistry."

"They disown you?"

"You got it. Complete with a we-shall-not-be-held-responsible notice in the local paper. Mama snuck a letter and some cookie-jar money past him once in a while, but that was when she'd already took sick. All I ever got from Daddy was the word through the grapevine that he thought I was just a big slut who'd never amount to a thing." Mary Beth shook her head and smiled. "Imagine that. A girl who's more popular on campus than the goddam homecoming queen. If only he could see me now."

"What do you do now?" asked Brian. "For a living?"

She had been hinting around at it for a while, talking

about all the business she'd done in Iowa City and all she had to do ahead of her. He'd been wanting to ask.

"I sell drugs, honey," said Mary Beth. "You're riding with the one and only Midwestern Connection." And laughed so loud the cat woke up.

The farmhouse was not nearly so run-down as he had imagined. Some high weeds around the porch, board windows, dust in the kitchen sink. Most of the furniture was still inside. The real decay was in the cornfields, the stalks bent and broken, tangling with each other. The rows that Mary Beth had talked about were overgrown into a solid jumble of vegetation.

"They can afford to plow it under and let the soil recover for a year or two," said Mary Beth. "Daddy couldn't."

She had brought a candle in from the car and found some more over the kitchen sink. It was a little spooky in the house, so unnaturally dark for the time of day, everything fuzzy with a layer of dust.

"Haven't been here since I was a sophomore in college. Seven-eight years. Surprised the bank hasn't changed the lock." Mary Beth handed Brian one of the candles she had lit. "Listen, honey, I think I want to poke around here a little bit. If you don't mind? I won't be too long, and then I can get you another hundred miles down the road. That okay?"

"No sweat."

"And what I thought was, since you said how you been up so long, it would be a chance for you to cop some z's. I'm sure they didn't move my bed from upstairs. Give you a chance to stretch out."

Mary Beth directed him to the bedroom then and headed off through the house. He could hear her bare feet, flap, flap, flap as she padded across the parlor.

The room was upstairs. Justine was already curled in the middle of the bed when he found it. He tossed her on the floor and lay down. There was a canopy over the bed and pictures of kittens with huge tear-shaped eyes on the wall. Brian kicked off his sneakers. The cat jumped beside him, was thrown off, jumped up again. Brian let her stay. He closed his eyes.

He felt like he was still moving, traveling over the highway at sixty. He flashed onto glimpses of whiteline zipping under, his stomach clenched for curves that never came. He started down a long slope, the back of his head floating, started coasting, coasting . . .

A twitch in his stomach brought him near to waking. The candle had gone out. Justine had left the bed. He thought he heard someone else in the room, breathing. He kept his eyes shut. He was lying on his belly with one hand across his heart and the other guarding his crotch. *Flap, flap, flap.* Mary Beth was standing by the bed watching him, he could smell her, feel her warmth. He waited. He felt his buttocks tighten automatically but managed to keep his breathing regular.

The bedsprings strained as she eased herself down beside him. She was stroking his hair, lightly, on the very edge of sensation. Allowing him to play possum if he wanted to. It was a road story coming true, she wanted him to make love to her. She wanted more than that, he figured, but she would settle for a roll in the dark and a wave good-bye on the highway. He breathed in her warmth and he got hard, knowing it would happen if he wanted it to. That he would be in control, she had come to him. He was set to open his eyes, to wake fully and roll over when a voice inside held him down. It reminded him of the way her feet flopped when she walked, remembered the rolls and puckers and dimples of her, remembered the way she looked sweating buckets through her thin shift. It was a Russ Palumbo voice, an after-school sneer in the hallway. Anybody want to fuck that, it said, hafta be deaf, dumb and blind. Woman escaped from the Hu*mane*

Society. The voice was as strong in him as the warnings from priests and nuns had once been, stronger. His cock backed down a bit, softened. Half-and-half, the kind he woke up with in the morning.

"Honey?" she whispered.

"Brian?"

He made his decision, let the voice make it, and stuck with it. Stuck with it even when she stroked his hair hard enough to make it an open question. He held himself still and the bed gave a mournful groan as it tilted back level and he heard her flap out of the room.

Brian's ass relaxed and he shifted onto his side. His erection nodded off like a man falling asleep.

There was Wheat Woman and then there was the Corn Queen. No talking, just vision and texture, knowing their names without hearing them. No tension or flirting, just a silent understanding of what was to happen.

Wheat Woman was first. She was dry. Her hair was cropped close to her skull, a tight-packed wool of small kernels that rasped when he brushed it against the grain with his hand. Her eyes were an unsettling flat gold with a large, black pupil. Staring, sunflower eyes. Her lips cracked as she opened her mouth, her tongue was sandpaper like a cat's when they kissed. She kept her eyes wide open. Her kiss stung him, no saliva or softness in it. Her breasts were hard kernels, the husks thick as fingernails. She moved closer. They clinched, both naked, her skin like burlap against his. She pulled him on top of her, gazing steadily out over his shoulder. He pushed himself in when she split her legs apart and she was dry and tight, like forcing his cock through a straw hat. She had his ass clutched in her stalky fingers and was jerking him hard in and out, pumping for moisture that never came, little puffs of fine chaff rising each time their hips clapped together. She was strong, a brittle strength that made him afraid to pull away lest he snap something. But his cock was scraped raw and she was still thrusting, threshing under him in a mechanical rhythm and he broke loose with a sound like falling through branches and she kept on bucking, eyes soulless as a shark's, with her knobby butt rapping the floor and her smile cracking to show a mouthful of brambles.

The Corn Queen came to soothe him. Her skin was taut and had a waxy yellow sheen. Her hair hung to her waist, albino corn silk that was cool as it slipped over his chest and belly. Her eyes were light green and when she bent to kiss him her lips stretched back over tiny white kernels of baby-corn teeth. Her tongue flowed down to comfort his dry throat while his own lolled in corn syrup, a long, drinking kiss of it. Her breasts hung down swollen, he squeezed one lightly and a honey-colored cream oozed from the tip. She smiled gently and straddled him. He reached between her legs and folded soft, green shucks back against her thighs, opening her, parted a tuft of corn silk and then she slipped herself down around him. She was wet, she was warm and more than slick. She rolled on him like oil, like there wasn't a hard bone in her body. His cock was swimming thickly, he couldn't feel the walls of her, the shape of her insides, only the warm syrup that poured out to butter their thighs and bellies, that flowed down and greased the floor beneath his cheeks till they were fucking in a puddle of her. It was too thick, too flowing, he didn't know if he was still hard in her and he was pressed helpless under her liquid weight, drowning in her and maybe he came but it was like spitting at the bottom of the ocean.

Honey.

Something about honey.

She was calling him, Mary Beth, calling up the stairs to see if he wanted to get up. Get up and eat.

Brian made some noise to tell her he was coming and rolled on his back. He had shot off in his pants. Wasted one, Russ Palumbo used to say. Got to dreaming pretty hot and heavy last night and I wasted one. Lot of nice pieces round here could of used it. Brian hadn't had a wet dream since he was sixteen and a virgin. He thought maybe they were supposed to stop once you'd joined the club.

He undressed and wiped himself off with his B.V.D.'s and put his pants back on. He threw the underwear beneath the bed. Give the movers a laugh when the bank sent them.

Mary Beth had found some canned food and had it going on the range, hash and baked beans and some cream-of-mushroom soup. She had brought bread in from the car and gotten an old toaster to work.

"They didn't bother to turn off all the juice," she said. "Just unscrewed the fuses."

She had changed from her shift into a bulky denim coverall. She was wearing work shoes. It was like her flesh itself had hardened while he was asleep. She sat him down and dished him out a plate and a bowl and spoke softly to him, almost like she was apologizing for something. It was all Brian could do to keep his stomach from climbing up his throat to meet the food halfway.

"You just chew on that for a while, honey, and then I got something special for our dessert," she said. "You let old Moby take care of you."

"Moby?"

She shrugged. "Mary Beth Dickson. The kids on the campuses where I do my, you know, business deals, they call me Moby Dickson. Had it since I was a girl. Sort of followed me around."

"Oh."

"Boys yelling 'Thar she blows!' in the hallways. What you call a literary allusion."

Justine yowled loudly from the front of the house and Mary Beth clonked off to see what was wrong. The toast popped up and Brian went and made himself a hash sandwich. He didn't know if there was anything he could say to

Mary Beth, anything that wouldn't make her feel worse. It's not that I don't find you attractive but — but what? Everything he could think of sounded like the line Angela Rizzo used to give him when he made any serious move on her. Sounded just as slight and just as false. He swallowed his food in big bites and felt each drop distinctly into his stomach.

"I slept like a rock," he said when she came back holding Justine. Maybe it would be better if she could think that he really hadn't known she was there. "Like a zombie. How long was I out for?"

"Couple hours," she said. "You've got plenty of daylight left for hitching." She crossed to the counter by the toaster and frowned. She dropped the cat.

"Oh shit."

"What's wrong?"

"Our dessert. The acid."

"What?"

"I had a couple squares of windowpane acid sitting here. I figured we both had a lot of flat country ahead of us, might be nice to put some wrinkles in it."

"Acid."

"Yeah. You know."

"I know. But what happened to it?"

"Justine must have gotten it, she's acting a little weird. But Christ, I figured the two of us would do a half-pane each and she ate four times that. It must have been her. You weren't over here were you?"

Brian looked at her. "I got the toast. I put it down on the counter to make a sandwich."

"Oh Christ. You think you might have picked it up on the toast?"

"I don't know, what's it do to you?"

"You never done it?"

Brian shook his head. It was one of those things that had

passed him by in school, like the Hong Kong flu had in the fifth grade.

"Oh, honey," said Mary Beth and took his hand, "I'm sorry."

He didn't know that they still made the stuff, there hadn't been anything on the news in years. "So it's me or Justine."

"Gonna be hard to tell right off if it's her. Cats are so spacy anyways. I don't really know what to do."

The idea kind of appealed to him. He wouldn't be responsible for anything, just stick his thumb out and let it carry him. "I think I should finish the beans," he said. "If I'm going places at least I'll have a full stomach."

Justine sat over the dash and stared at Brian for an hour and a half in the car. He stared back at her. Mary Beth drove and kept asking him how he felt. He didn't feel much different. A little nervous maybe. Still hungry. That was a strange one, still hungry.

"Some of it will hit you real quick," Mary Beth told him, "and then sometimes you get a batch that kind of sneaks up on you. You ate all that food, takes a while to digest — who knows? And then maybe it's just some weak stuff, I haven't tried any yet. How you feeling, honey?"

She drove him to the far side of Des Moines and turned south. She tried to talk him into coming with her to Kansas City. He got out of the Chevy and Justine hopped down into his seat.

"I'll be all right," he said, "you just watch your cat."

Mary Beth gave him an embarrassed smile.

"I'm sorry," he said.

"Honey," she said, "you got nothin at all to be sorry about. Nothin at all."

A careening, high-speed ride in the open back of a pickup truck got Brian past Omaha and well into Nebraska farmland, where he bogged down. There was a little confusion between the energy of the wind roaring around him and his own roaring energy, but he decided it was the food and the sleep. There was no sitar music, no psychedelic colors. A lot of road and a lot of harvested cornfields, but no surprising warps or wrinkles.

There was the pointilism though. He remembered the word from art class. The sky and the fields seemed to be made of millions of little separate dots of all different shades. Maybe it was the time of day, the purple dusk, or maybe there was pollen in the air. But field stayed field and sky stayed sky and the horizon line between them held steady. He felt the same, tired and dirty and impatient with the thinning traffic. It was twilight, more purple than he remembered, and he didn't feel like hitching anymore. He decided to bag it for the night.

There was a rise to the left of the road up ahead, he started for it planning to be well sheltered from the road's view. The field had been closely mown within the last day or so, it was jagged with stubble. Every few steps another field creature would unfreeze. Albino toads, tiny mice, snakes like shoestrings, dry-rasping grasshoppers, all scattering ahead of his path. They were a luminous violet in the twilight, they seemed confused by their recent uncovering. Brian skated his feet forward and went slowly. He eased down the far slope of the rise till he came to a patch of well-kept grass.

Green grass in the middle of a cornfield.

It was a level rectangle about the size of a large house foundation, cropped short as a putting green. It was a little strange but Brian was glad for a flat spot to lie.

He paused at the edge of the plot to watch what looked like a cross between a toad and a doormat hop away. Its back was scabbed from mower blades and half of one of its hind legs was missing. When it hopped it flew sideward and almost tipped on impact. It was trying to get away from Brian but could only flop in ever-widening circles around him. He was fascinated by the thing. Had never seen anything like it. He could watch it forever. The toad struggled through three revolutions before it became too dark to see and Brian moved to set up on the grass. He sat and unlaced his sneakers.

"WHERE HAVE YOU BEEN?"

A voice, deep and hollow, booming up out of the ground. Brian rolled into a crouch and strained to see which way he should take off.

"DON'T YOU PLAY GAMES WITH ME, YOUNG LADY."

Oh shit, thought Brian. It's taking hold. Taking hold with a vengeance.

"DERRY? IS THAT YOU? WHO IS THAT?"

A bank of light flicked on at ground level to his rear, soft blue lights like they used for outdoor Nativity scenes. Brian whirled to face them but could see nothing beyond.

"SPEAK TO THE LIGHT."

"What do you want me to say?" He felt a little ridiculous, talking alone in the middle of nowhere. "Listen, I'll leave if I'm trespassing or something."

"WHAT DO YOU WANT?"

"Nothing." He began to back off the grass, kicking his duffel bag behind him. "I don't want a thing."

"FREEZE!"

Brian froze.

"COME TO THE LIGHT."

Things were getting a little too Biblical for his comfort. There was no mistaking the authority behind the Voice, it meant business. He slowly approached the bank of blue lighting.

"WHAT IS YOUR NAME?"

"Brian McNeil."

"SPEAK DOWN."

"What?"

"SPEAK DOWN. INTO THE LIGHT."

"Brian McNeil."

"DO I KNOW YOU?"

"Jesus, I hope not." He could feel vibrations through his feet when the Voice spoke.

"WHAT ARE YOU DOING HERE?"

"I was hitchhiking. This looked like a good flat place to sleep out. I'll go somewhere else. I'm sorry, whoever you are."

It was silent for a while and Brian heard a faint crackling, like static. Bugs had discovered the lighting and were swarming around him.

"DO YOU LIKE CHINESE FOOD?"

Oh yes, it had taken hold all right. Brian had talked with more than a few acid dabblers and none had mentioned sound-and-light Christmas spectaculars. "Sure," he said, "but I haven't had any in a while."

"TAKE TWO STEPS FORWARD."

He stepped.

"NOW ONE TO THE LEFT."

Do the Hokey-Pokey, he thought. What is this?

"SEE THE ROPE?"

A short length of rope seemed to grow out of the ground.

"PULL IT."

Brian yanked and a yard-square flap of turf came up, the covering to a manhole shaft. A string of blue Christmas-tree bulbs lit the way down a bolted ladder. Brian couldn't see bottom.

"PULL THE LID BACK SHUT WHEN YOU COME DOWN," said the Voice, "AND TRY NOT TO LET ALL THE BUGS IN."

Brian considered a moment until the same feeling he'd had often on the road before swept him, the oh-well-what-the-hell feeling of being too tired and too bummed out to resist much of anything. He tied his laces and started down, thunking the cover over his head.

He heard metal sliding and a little more light filtered up the shaft. Several rungs down he saw that an airlock had opened and the hole widened into a small cement-walled room. There was nothing in the room but a steel vault-door beyond which Brian could hear an electrical cricketing. A bolt shot and the door pushed open. A hand clamped around Brian's arm.

"C'moan in."

The hand and the Voice's lack of volume startled him.

"Don't be skittish, I don't bite. I retreat."

"What?"

"Name's Ira Treat." Brian was pulled inside by a short man who looked to be around fifty. The man held his nose up in the air like a dog searching for a scent on the wind. He aimed his head at Brian when he spoke but it was clear that he couldn't see. "Welcome to the safest residential structure in the entire U.S. of A."

Everything inside seemed to be of shiny metal. Banks of fluorescent lights buzzed overhead and Brian had to shield his eyes.

"It's a bomb shelter?"

"It's my *home,* son. Where you headed?"

"California."

"Got people there?"

"Nope."

"You might want to reconsider. The Baja isn't so bad, and up toward Oregon, but the rest you're a sitting duck. They got that Vandenburg A.F.B. there and Fort Ord and the Presidio. Nope, California will go in the opening rounds. You hungry?"

Treat's eyeballs were barely visible under thick folds of flesh, as if they had burrowed deep to avoid the light. He wrinkled his nose when he spoke.

"A little," said Brian.

"Well you come right in and make yourself comfortable. This here is about as cozy as you're ever likely to get." He cocked an ear to the beeping and whining of the instruments farther into the room, frowning to concentrate. Didn't see a little girl up there dawdlin around the road, did you? My Derry is sposed to be back about now."

"Didn't see anyone."

"Choir practice or some such. Girl has got one sort of nonsense or the other keepin her at school all hours just about every night of the week. Sits down to dinner, grunts hello and she's off to bed. I just wave to her in passing. You go to school?"

"I used to."

"Drifter, huh? Sound pretty young, what are you, seventeen, eighteen? Good age to be a drifter, long as you stay clear of the primary strike areas."

Brian smiled at the word. "Drifter" was something they used to say on *Gunsmoke* on TV.

"You'll be staying for the night then. Gonna get cold."

"Oh. Uh, I left my bag and all up there. And if it's —"

"No trouble, no trouble. Not gonna rain, just get cold. Your bags are fine. C'moan, have a seat."

The room was a long tube, everything built in flush to the wall. All of it was gleaming metal, coppers and silvers and bronzes and golds, one entire wall of chrome-knobbed drawers opposite a wall of dials and instruments. Each instrument gave off its own steady sound reading. There was an electric-blue carpet and tubular frame furniture, each piece bolted to the floor. Treat sat Brian down on one of the couches.

"Looks like the inside of an atomic sub or something."

Treat snorted happily. "This isn't just any hole in the ground filled with gadgets," he said. "Oh no. This is *part* of me." He waved his arms to include the whole room. "Electronics, sonar, radar, all that technology is only an extension of the man who controls them. Shelter is what marks and protects the extremities of your body."

He waved at the wall of instruments. "My ears are twenty miles long. My temperature is fifty-eight degrees and falling exterior, a steady seventy-five interior. My skull can withstand a direct hit from any prenuclear warhead. My lungs can filter the bulkiest industrial waste or the tiniest subatomic particle. My stomach holds twenty years' supply of food and water. My excretions are solid cubes suitable for landfill or road construction. My skin will hold up against fire and ice. All I have to do is stay inside it. Chicken chow mein sound all right?"

"Fine."

Treat crossed to a panel of switches. He counted over and down and flicked one.

"*At the sound of the tone,*" said a woman's voice, "*the time will be eight twenty-seven — and ten seconds ——— BOOP! At the sound of —*"

He flicked it off. "Girl should be here any minute now. They got an activities bus drops them home. Might's well put the beans on."

Brian was having problems with the fluorescent lights. He seemed to be able to see the suspended gas molecules, to see the stream of electrons bolting through. He knew it was too small and too fast but he saw it just the same. He didn't even want to think about the dots on the carpet.

"At one time," said Treat, making his way to the wall of pullouts and appliances, "this area was lowest priority in the whole shootin match. All you had to worry about was the fallout and wind drift and all the secondary effects. So I sunk my money into a farm and built me a little civil-defense root cellar like the other folks around here had. The eyes were just beginning to dim a bit, doctors hadn't put the final word on them yet." He squatted and pulled out a huge drawer from the wall. Like a drawer in a morgue, filled with canned goods in compartments. Treat counted back and over, lifted one can, up and over and lifted another. He pushed the drawer shut with his foot.

"Then came the ironical part. The fellas in charge of dispersal at the Defense Department looked at a map and saw the same thing I did. Nothing here the other side would be interested in. So they laid in a slew of missile silos three miles down the road. Biological-testing station, it says on the fence, but I talked with some of the truckers bringing material in and it's nothing of the sort. Figured wherever I moved it'd be the same story, some damn thing drawing fire, so I made my stand here. Dug in."

The electric can-opener and stove were recessed into the wall, the empty cans went down a chute.

"Took three years to build and by the time they got around to the inside work my eyes were pert near gone, so I provided for it in the design. Everything fixed in its place. Not bad, huh? Made my bundle in aerospace after the War, circuitry design. Before all the federal money dried up. They'll be sorry though, the other side starts taking potshots from outer space and they'll wish they stayed behind the Program. Shortsighted sonsabitches." Treat groped in a utensil drawer for a spatula.

"Can I help with anything?" Brian wanted something to keep his mind off the dots. The mottles on the carpet were fluttering around like a cloud of moths.

"You just sit tight, young fella. Got everything I need at my fingertips." He pushed a pot against a lever and water streamed down to fill it. He laid it on a burner to boil.

"Talk to the people down to the school, up to town, you hear them laugh about the Mad Mole. That's what they've hung on me, 'the Mad Mole.' But when she finally hits the fan, and she's gonna one of these days, you'll see them swarming up top like locusts. Let us in, Mr. Treat, they'll say, save us. Save us. And I'll just flip on the loudspeaker and laugh

my head off. You heard the story bout the grasshopper and
the ant?"

"I think so. Yeah, the grasshopper never plans ahead or
something."

"Right. Well I'm the ant." He opened a smaller drawer
and pulled out a box of powdered milk. "I worked my tail off
and I saved and I saved and I bought a hunk of security for
myself and my little girl. Long as an ant stays in his network
in the ground he's all set, can't be touched. I worry about the
daughter when she's outside all day."

"They probably got drills and all," said Brian. "You know,
civil defense." It seemed very important to act straight with
Treat, to make a good impression. The weirder the old man
got the more important it seemed.

Treat snorted and palmed the excess from the top of a cup
of powdered milk.

"We used to have to face the wall and put our heads between our legs," said Brian, "close our eyes and cover our
ears." He wanted to do it right then and there. His legs felt
like they were tubular steel, bolted to the floor. He didn't
dare try to lift a foot for fear he wouldn't be able to. "When I
was little, first grade or so. A teacher would come by and tap
us when it was through. They tried ringing the bell but some
of the kids held their ears too tight to hear."

Treat shook his head. "That's all fine and dandy *if* you're
far enough away from the contact point and *if* you're warned
way in advance. See, first you've got your fireball flash, blind-
ing light. Three seconds later is your primary heat flash, a
little temperature rise and if you're lucky it won't fry you or
burn up all your oxygen. Then comes a shock wave tearing
buildings down and then is your radiation heat flash. You
survive everything else and that radiation will still get you in
a couple of hard weeks if you're not far enough from the
blast. Don't tell me about *drills*, young fella. When she's out
there at school it's like she's being held for ransom and every

new morning there's another kidnapping. Don't tell me about *drills*."

Brian was silent. He touched things. He was really there.

Treat was stirring the milk powder into a pitcher of water. He held his hand steady and his face composed, it was clear he hadn't been born blind. "You drink milk?"

"Not much. Sometimes."

"Real milk?"

"Yeah, I guess so. You know, homogenized."

"Ever hear of strontium 90?"

"Yeah. It was on a chemistry test."

"Got to be careful what you let into your body, son, what your let into your shelter. The enemy within is as dangerous as the fire from the sky."

"Yuh." The guy was a certified whacko. Brian noticed a full-length poster on a door at the end of the room. An adolescent rock star in a white leather jumpsuit.

"You're a pretty quiet young fella, aren't you? Got a lot on your mind I suppose."

"Yuh," said Brian. It felt now like blood was running from his left leg into pipes under the floor, through a complicated filter system and then pumped back up into his right leg. "I suppose."

"You kids, you don't talk so much, but you're deep thinkers. Maybe that's good, but it's hard to be around when you depend on your hearing. My little girl, my Derry, she's another deep thinker. Can't get two sentences out of her. But the gears are always turning in that head of hers, I can tell."

Treat perked his nose up as there was a short, deep note from the instrument panel.

"Must be her now."

There was another note, slightly higher.

"It's all done with pressure plates," he said. "You step in my periphery up there and I get a tone. The warmer you get, the closer to the trapdoor, the higher the tone gets."

The panel was working up toward a high C. Treat flipped a switch, went to the vault door and wrestled it open.

"C'moan in, honey, we got company."

The girl was a half-foot shorter than her father. She was small but not so young.

"Derry, this here is uh — Brian? Brian. Young fella this is my little girl."

She stepped into the room, wiggling her arm free of her father's grip and squinting against the bright. "Hey."

"Hey."

She was cute, maybe ninth-grade age, and wore a lot of makeup. Deep purple over her eyes, heavy on the liner.

"Choir practice get out late?"

"Yuh," she said and gave Brian an impy grin.

"Have a pretty good day in school?"

"Okay."

"Have any tests?"

"Nope."

"You have much homework?"

"Nope."

"You hungry?"

She peeked over to what was heating on the stove. "A little."

"Brian here is a drifter. He's headed for California."

"Oh."

"Well why don't you wash up for dinner, honey, and we'll get this show on the road."

"Sure."

"These kids," he said to Brian as she sauntered past him with a little smirk, "they don't talk. Deep thinkers, the lot of them, worriers and planners. You got to make allowances for it, hold up both ends of a conversation, pull teeth. And Derry," he shouted across the room, "how's about you clean that bedroom of yours a bit? Almost fell and broke my skull in there today, all them damn stuffed animals lyin around. You hear me?"

The deep thinker turned at her door and gave her father the finger.

Derry changed into gym shorts and a sleeveless T-shirt for dinner. There were wells in the table where the plates and glasses fit. Treat managed to dole out the chow mein and Minute Rice with a minimum of groping. He hooked his thumb over the lip of each glass as he poured the watery-looking milk and when the level reached it he stopped. He squeezed into his bolted seat, bowed his head and folded his hands for grace.

Brian copied the motion but averted his eyes from his plate. He couldn't handle it. Every grain of rice was a separate entity, he felt an urge to count them. Derry ignored her father and scooped Bosco into her milk.

"For the food on our table," he said, "and the roof over our head, we thank Thee, Lord."

Brian was very hungry but the food wouldn't stay quiet. The rice squeaked on his teeth like rubber boots over hard-packed snow, the water chestnuts were like splitting rails and the bamboo slivers were deafening. The food wouldn't stay quiet and wouldn't stay still and Derry's foot kept nudging his. Her legs weren't that long, it had to be intentional.

"They picked the Marines cause the Marines always had to go first, always got chewed up liberating the beachfront. Didn't tell us much, that's their way, let you rumor yourself so scared that the real thing isn't so bad when you finally come up against it. Hell, all we knew was what we'd heard the Haberdasher say on the radio, wasn't nobody knew the first thing about hydrogen bombs or what effect radiation would have on folks. Not even the scientists were so sure. Half the guys expected the islands to be run over with atomic Jap monsters, things with X-ray eyes that would glow in the dark. They gave us a hurry-up lesson in how to use the special equipment right there on the ship, kept warning us whatever you do, don't get contaminated. S'what they said, 'contaminated.' Same word the chaplains always used in their VD lectures.

"So the orders get passed down and they say Nagasaki, on Kyushu island, and be prepared for anything. Surrender was official already but who expects some Nip has just been H-bombed to listen to the news?"

A hunk of chicken plopped off Treat's fork and he bit down on bare metal. Derry giggled. A bean sprout whimpered as it slid down Brian's throat. Derry's foot brushed his ankle. He could feel her toes grasping to hold his pants-leg.

"It wasn't anything out of the usual," said Treat, "not at first. A big river valley and a port that had been bombed. A lot of the damage to the buildings was from conventional attacks before. Wasn't much left at the bottom of the valley, but as you rose up the sides vegetation went from black to brown to yellow to green. The burns on people were in that pattern too, mostly on one side of the body, darker and deeper the further down into the valley you went. Of course, the worst weren't even there to be seen. Pretty much vaporized, maybe their shadow burnt into the side of a building. Remember this one woman, she had been nursing her baby when the blast came. About halfway up the valley wall she was. One of her breasts was tanned a deep dark brown, the other white from where her baby's head soaked up most of the radiation."

Brian gagged on his milk and got some up his nose. Derry handed him the Bosco. Treat worked on his plate in a counterclockwise direction, tapping it lightly with fork tip to be sure he missed nothing.

"It was the weeks after, when we were administrating the island and classifying the doomed that it got rough. People's hair fell out. Women's — that long, black, beautiful hair pulled out by the handful, you'd see little girls like Derry here, barely high-school age, all bald and scabby-headed.

Kids' teeth crumbled like candy. Men grew breasts. People died of nosebleeds that wouldn't stop. People just starting to feel the poisoning would sit in the hospital waiting and see all the stages they were headed for sitting around them, meet relatives who they couldn't recognize but by voice. A lot of them blinded in the first flash got their sight back and wished they hadn't. Quite a few recovered and never let on, preferred to grope and bump and cry in the dark though there was nothing physically wrong with their eyes. Who knows, maybe they *didn't* see. And then the babies that were born — God. It was like Nature decided to review all the false starts and bad experiments she made on her way to evolving man. Things without arms, things without legs, two-headed things, legs or arms without anything else. One woman delivered up this big ball of teeth fused together, looked like a sea urchin. The ones who got vaporized, they were the lucky ones, them and the blind ones who didn't have to see it."

Treat almost tipped his glass putting it back into its table-well. He had a clot of rice on his neck. "You want to get the dessert, Derry?"

"Mnph."

"I feh I wuh." Chicken juice dribbled down her chin and she had to snake it with her tongue.

"You go get it and try waiting till you're done chewing before you speak. There's things you can get away with in front of me that you can't do in front of company."

She stuck her little red tongue out in front of both of them and went to the refrigerator.

"It's a chore raising her myself," whispered Treat to Brian. "Trying to keep her safe, teach her the right way. The wife passed on in 'sixty-four, Derry was only two. That's her on the door down there, back when we lived in Houston. I gave Derry a picture to send and have it blown up, so's she'd remember what her mother looked like."

Derry returned with three plastic tubs of Whip and Chill

pudding and some spoons and she blushed a little. Treat was pointing to the poster of the rock singer.

"I took that when we put the down payment on our first house. My first big NASA check signed right over to the realtors. But she was in seventh heaven."

Brian managed to say that she was a nice-looking woman.

"That was before the cancer got her. Thing called chronic granulocytic leukemia caught hold of her and wore her down for two hard years before she give up the ghost. Course it's a thin line between what was caused by the cancer and what was caused by the radiation therapy, but for the person in pain it don't matter which is the culprit. She was sick to her stomach every morning, upchucked two meals out of three, didn't have a spark of energy."

Derry vacantly spooned pudding into her mouth. Treat's voice had taken on a detached tone, like a senile parish priest reciting the financial report.

"Cancer," he said, "is when cells begin to divide out of control. In my wife's case it was too many white corpuscles being produced in her blood. It spreads, cancer does, with out-of-control cells affecting the neighboring cells and making them go crazy too.

"Nuclear fission is cancer on the level of the atom. Unstable elements are bombarded by free neutrons that cause the atoms to split into smaller atoms. The bonding energy of the original atom is released along with more free neutrons that make neighboring heavy atoms go crazy in a chain reaction. Out of control. So more energy is released. Seismic energy and heat energy and nuclear radiation. Buildings falling and fires and radiation sickness."

Derry sighed and closed her eyes.

"They gave her X-ray treatments. We can control it, they said, it kills off white corpuscles. She'd eat a sandwich and her gums would stain the bread pink. They took her female business out. There were hairs grew on her chest.

"We can control it, they say, we've harnessed the Dragon. Keep things even with the other side and nobody will dare make the first move. Or if they do it'll be a limited war. Limited.

"We've got the cancer under control, they told me, and then her bone marrow went wrong from all the X-ray exposure and they tried to draw it all out and replace it but her heart just quit. Had to keep it under control, they told me, it was her only hope."

Ira Treat laid his fork down on an empty plate.

Brian didn't know what he was expected to say. He had his own problems. His attention was drifting, not so much on to other subjects as out into the room in a very physical way. It was as if his mind were matter and that matter was diffusing into the air like some trace element, some gas. He was losing his bonding energy. He squeezed his head with his hands to push it all back in but the effect was a distant pressure, as if a light truck had driven over the shelter on the land's surface. Brian was grateful for the lead lining, the steel-reinforced concrete that surrounded him, that kept him from mingling with soil and sky.

Derry asked could she finish his Whip and Chill if he wasn't interested.

They sat in the living-room section of the main chamber. The fewer walls there were, the easier for Treat to keep an ear on his instruments. Derry rinsed what dishes there were and put them in the washer, then sprawled on a couch across from them to read a fan magazine while her father talked. Brian took to reciting Hail Marys and Our Fathers to try to keep an anchor on his mind.

"Do you know what 'BM' stands for?"

"Huh?"

"Ballistic missile. A big bullet. Didn't have such things till the very end of the Big One, when Germany got their V-1's and V-2's mailing out. We had bombers. Fat Man and Little Boy were delivered by manned crews, Nips had had a few Zeros in the right place and it would have been a different story on Hiroshima. But it wasn't long before both the Reds and us had BM's and push-button war was upon us. We had the real goods in the payload department to ourselves for a couple years, but Mrs. Rosenberg helped bring a speedy end to *that* situation."

Brian had only a vague idea of what the man was talking about. It all made him think of mushrooms. Mushrooms were the last thing he wanted to think about.

"Now, a ballistic missile is a quick draw, greased lightning compared to one of the old B-52's or the Tupelev-20 Bears the other side had. And there's no pilot error, a BM is a mechanical kamikaze. But in the early fifties it ran on liquid fuel that had to be mixed just before firing, it had to be launched from the surface. What we in the trade call a soft zone. Made folks think their own hardware could be totaled by a strike and they wouldn't get a shot off. So it was itchy-trigger-finger days, days of the Golfer and Dulles and brinks-manship. Everyone obsessed with getting their rockets into the air first, thought that would decide the whole ball game."

Liz & Dick, blared the cover of Derry's magazine. Sonny & Cher & Jackie & Burt & Dean & Frank & Elvis & Lucy & Liza & The Lennon Sisters. Derry lay on her stomach and slowly kicked her feet to the time of her loud gum-chewing. She munched and sucked and smacked and smiled over to Brian every now and then.

Our Father who art in Heaven, thought Brian, *hallowed be Thy name —*

"Then the boys in the lab come up with solid fuel. So all those missiles could be hardened, dug down into silos or onto submarines. Our Minuteman silos can take, oh, three-hundred-pounds-per-square-inch overpressure. This place can handle four hundred. Need an awful good shot with some heavy yield to crack that.

"Anyhow, the name of the game turned into something called 'assured destruction.' Say they launch a first strike against our missile sites, a counterforce strike. Assured destruction means we still have enough throw power and warheads left to inflict what they call 'unacceptable damage.' Now this is with both sides playing by the rules — no spasm war, where its countervalue strikes against cities instead of missiles. We can control it, they say, like always."

. . . blessed art Thou amongst women, and blessed is the fruit of Thy womb, Jesus. Holy Mary . . .

"Well, all this boiled down to the theory of mutual vulnerability. Neither group would fire first cause it was a sure thing both would be wiped out. That was supposed to be a comfort. Course it isn't the rocket boys down in their mountain bunkers who are mutually vulnerable, no, it's you and me and Ivan Doe over there on the other side. We're mutually vulnerable as you can get. Was about then, under the Harvard Man, that I planned this place."

There was a hole in the seat of Derry's too-tight gym shorts; a round, pink berry of flesh peeped through. Brian had started to smile back at her through the purplish fog that had come up in front of him. She would sigh and roll her eyes when her father started up again and Brian would answer with what he thought was a mildly sympathetic smile. He couldn't feel exactly what it was doing on his face though, it tended to get away from him.

"Nowadays things aren't so simple. You've got your anti-ballistic-missile system and your multiple warheads and better homing systems and you got computers speeding the whole thing up. There's still some conventional stuff, though. Our B-52's and F-111's shoot a missile called a Hounddog and the other side still has Bears and Mya Bisons that fire something called a Kangaroo and the yellow-peril folks there have even got a thing to deliver, an old TU-16 Badger, and the whole menagerie is there waiting to come down like a rain of toads."

Treat was up and pacing now, talking faster than ever, building for some kind of climax. The words were making less sense than ever to Brian; it sounded like a sin-blasting Bible sermon in some foreign but familiar language.

"Don't matter what delivers it, you set off your standard twenty-megaton payload and millions of people are going to feel it. That's a thousand times the force of the Fat Man we hit the Japs with. These days you got your thermonuclear reaction, fission-fusion-fission, where the fission generates the heat to set off the hydrogen isotope and deuterium fuses to form helium and enough destructive energy to parboil the state of Nebraska."

The fog was thicker now, it seemed to be falling down from the fluorescent lights, falling like snow in a paperweight. Treat was hoarse, his movements jerky. He was totally mind-fucked, thought Brian, but he seemed to know his stuff.

"And it's not just the two of us anymore. Britain and France, they got it and the yellow-peril folks are making great leaps forward. And the lab boys come up with a synthetic, plutonium. P-239, cheaper to make than U-235 and just about as effective. So we got the nuclear equivalent of the Saturday-night special and before you know it any young-punk nation looking to build a reputation will have their own bomb. It spreads, it excites the neighboring cells and you can't control it. And us mere *people* are left out in the rain. People aren't but a fart in a fire storm to them. They'll jacket a warhead with U-238 or cobalt to make it extra dirty, to really set those gamma rays whizzing. They've done studies on how long it would take the country to recover to a certain level after a full-scale war. They've decided what acceptable damage is and I don't accept it."

Treat slumped into a chair.

"The hell with them all."

Derry gathered her magazines and left the room. Brian switched to the Act of Contrition. The fog cleared a bit and he heard the instrument panel plainly again. Treat's head lolled back a little as if he were resting, breathing wide-mouthed like a fighter between rounds. He was very pale, his hair a thin white. The Mad Mole.

And I detest all my sins, thought Brian, *because of the loss of Heaven and the pain of Hell. But most of all —*

Derry scuffed back into the room. She was in a pink short nightgown and fuzzy slippers that had bunny faces on the toes and cottontails at the heel. She was trying hard to stick out what she had to stick. She looked like a sexy Easter duckling wiggling her tufted butt and breasts. She bounced over and plopped in her father's lap, never taking her eyes off Brian. It was like a toddler showing off a new lollipop, proud and possessive and more than a little taunting. Look what I've got and don't you wish you could get some? Treat kissed the top of her head.

"Night honey. Mr. McNeil is going to be out here on the couch so don't be too noisy in the morning. Gimme kiss."

She rolled her eyes and held her nose and gave him a peck on the cheek. Brian wanted to swat her.

"Night Daddy."

The girl hopped off her father's lap and tiptoed to Brian and kissed him. It was more like a meal than a kiss and he fought to keep his tongue rooted. She skipped away before he could react with much more than a gasp for air. Derry disappeared into her bedroom.

"The light of my life, that one," said Treat. "Worth her weight in gold."

He went on for a bit, running down like a tired phonograph, about the difficulty of judging superiority in the arms race, the relative merits of the Sentinel and Safeguard defense systems, the fallacy of deterrence. He tired and Brian drifted. Finally he pulled the couch out into a bed and showed Brian where the bathroom was.

"Have a safe night," he said, and retired to his room.

A loud fan clicked on with the bathroom light, a high-pitched hummer. The toilet bowl looked funny. Brian sat and saw directions pasted on the wall across from him. Close lid, pull lever and waste material will be thermally disposed. The other writing was even stranger. It was on the toilet paper, roughly three letters per sheet in red Magic Marker. *See you tonight,* it said, *Derry.* The message and Brian's waste material went out in a thermal hiss.

The pullout bed was comfortable enough but sleep was out of the question. There was the instrument panel noise to contend with, thoughts of what Derry was up to and a new wave of cellular dissipation. Brian remembered from his few real high-school drunks what a tricky business lying down was, that the ceiling tended to revolve in one direction and his stomach in another. But the concepts of stomach and ceiling weren't so definite, the action now wasn't revolution or rotation but Brownian movement. His molecules scattered softly outward till they met dense lead-and-steel molecules that bounced them back in. Sound was included in the deal now, the bleeping and whirrings of the instruments were solid particles pinging in the air-mix with him. Welcome to the oneness of being, thought Brian, and rolled on his front to try and hold some of himself in.

This went on for quite a while. He had a sense of being the room and everything in it. Not a good feeling. It occurred to him that maybe his thermally disposed wastes were vapor now and had dispersed to remingle with him. He felt himself, the room, tilt very slightly. He smelled, no, collided with odor molecules, of grape bubble gum. Derry was sitting on the edge of the bed.

Twice in the same day. Seventeen years of drought and then twice in the same day.

This time when his hair was brushed he turned and opened his eyes. She was a little brat. She was probably underage. But he felt a pressure to respond, felt it like the holiest Commandment. Thou shalt not turn it down. He tried to collect himself, to think himself hard, and wondered why it hadn't already happened. Compared to Mary Beth Derry was sex itself and yet he wasn't tingling down there. He tried to think dirty thoughts. He had to keep the Commandment, he couldn't waste another one.

Derry stuck her gum on the couch and began to nibble at his neck, she slid her warm, chubby hand slowly down his chest, across his belly and stroked the underside of his balls and all the wandering molecules of his consciousness came charging back like the Seventh Cavalry to an Indian massacre. She was re-forming all his boundaries with her mouth and fingers, showing him his edges.

"Um," she said, and "Nnnnh!" and all kinds of little skin-sucking noises. Derry made love like she ate dinner, fast and loud. She knew what she was doing, sort of, and did it with almost frantic enthusiasm. Her nightie was off and she slid under Brian's spread blankets and emerged squirming on top of him. His eyes had adjusted some to the dark now and he saw how brown her nipples were pointing out from her single-scoop breasts, chocolate-kiss nipples swollen hard in his palms and lips. Her tongue darted over him and he smelled the saccharine grape wherever it had been. She locked her legs around his thigh like a vise and humped and squirmed till it was slick with her wetness. Then she was down flat-tonguing the head of him, slow, tasting licks. All the molecules galloped to where the action was and it felt hard as steel, dense as lead and she bit it at the middle, gentle with her teeth. She was up and spraddled and aiming it, holding it with two hands, rubbing the head against her greased lips making excited little-girl sounds and he wanted to ask her to keep it a little quiet but she plunged down around him hot and tight, tight as white on rice and she bounced, bounced like a kid testing her new summer-camp mattress for spring and the bed crunched and Brian clutched at her little buns, squeezing to keep her from flying off. She was doing it by the book and it was a cheap drugstore-paperback and it came to him that she was more excited over some red-underlined passage she was imagining than about him, it came to him that she was making an awful lot of unnecessary noise and Treat might hear. But all that was a little distant. What was immediate was that the molecules in his cock were getting awfully crowded, more and more of them, denser and denser and fast neutrons were beginning to act up and he was approaching his critical mass which was scary and exciting at once, Derry bouncing, bouncing, smacking damp against his belly and thighs and if it blew now he didn't think it would ever stop, just keep coming and coming till he and Derry were a cloud of charged zygotes drifting in the atmosphere and it was pulling on him now, making wet-munching sounds and Derry was making a high giggle and Treat was bellowing.

"Derry!" he was bellowing, "Stay still Derry, I'll come and help you!"

Help her what? Derry lurched off and was away from the bed, still giggling hysterically. Brian rolled out on the floor onto his hands and knees. He strained to see through the dark. He heard rustling from the kitchen area and then saw Treat, saw him coming crouched and wary with a big iron skillet in his hand.

"Derry! You get clear of him Derry. I'll fix him."

"It wasn't me, Daddy," she sniffled from the door to the bathroom, "honest. It wasn't me."

"You go to your room, Derry. I'll take care of this."

Brian tried to crawl silently but his thighs made sticky sounds as they brushed, coated with Derry's goo. Treat made a rush and swung but slipped in mid-stroke on a bunny slipper and went down on his side. Brian leapfrogged the bed and grabbed his pants and sneakers. Treat growled and scrambled back into the darkness to block the vault door.

"Just you try, boy," he snarled, "just you try to get by me."

Brian felt something clinging at the back of his head. It was Derry's gum, tangled in his hair. He slipped quickly into his pants and heard Treat take a few steps forward in the long tube of darkness. He found the other bunny slipper with his foot and tossed it off to the left. Treat made a move, then stopped.

"Can't fool me, boy. I hear you breathe. I hear your heart beat. There's no way you can hide, I hear everything."

Brian felt no desire to explain. It was beyond explaining, out of control. He tied his sneakers together and looped them over his shoulder. He eased sideways on tiptoe, reached the storage wall and began to yank the morgue drawers out, tossing handfuls of canned goods onto the floor between him and the father. Treat came forward a bit and Brian scooted to the other wall, groped to turn on the water and the can opener and the solid-waste compacter and the electric blender, and trotted back to the bed. He could see Treat dimly now. The old man had his nose up in the air and his arms spread wide, listening for all he was worth and slowly backing out of sight to the vault door again.

"I'll wait you out, boy!" he shouted over the sound of the appliances. "I can wait a day or a week if I have to, but you better give up the idea of ever seeing sky again. You walked into your own grave, boy, and there won't be no rising again."

Brian picked up the blankets and spread them in his arms. If he could net Treat and wrap him he'd have a shot at that door. He heard Derry come out behind him and stand by the instrument panel. He crept forward with the blankets held ready, probing with his toes for food cans. He could hear Treat nervously tapping the skillet on the metal door. He crept within ten feet of the exit.

"I can smell you, young fella," hissed Treat. "I'm onna kill you."

Brian brought the blankets up high and collected his breath for his pounce and then everything cut dead. The water, the opener, the compacter, the blender, all the instruments peeping from the rear cut off stone silent and were replaced by a single high-piercing whistle. Treat's mouth popped wide open and the skillet clanged to the floor. Brian ducked and covered his head, the instinct of a hundred Hollywood war movies, but the bomb never fell. The whistle didn't deepen in pitch and Brian turned to see Derry giggling by the instrument panel, her hand on a lever and red light flashing over her face. Treat was running, falling on canned goods and smacking thigh and chest into the open morgue drawers and screaming something about spasms and the other side and the Dragon breaking loose. Brian was through the vault door and digging barefoot up the ladder with the bomb-whine chasing him, the airlock whanging shut beneath nearly chopping his legs and up, butting the trapdoor with head and shoulder to scramble to his duffel bag with the sneaker laces strangling him and Treat's voice roaring over the loudspeaker:

"YOU'LL FRY! YOU STAY UP THERE AND YOU BURN, BOY, YOU'LL LIGHT UP LIKE A MOTH IN A THOUSAND SUNS! YOU'LL BURN, BRIAN MC NEIL, YOUR EYES WILL MELT AND YOUR BRAIN WILL SIZZLE AND YOU'LL BURN IN HELL ON EARTH!"

Brian shouldered his bag and sprinted barefoot into the cold, purple night.

Breed

BRIAN WOKE on the lee side of a hill with a buffalo licking his face. At first he was only aware of the tongue, sticky and thick as a baby's arm, lapping down to sample his ears and cheeks. He had laid his sleeping bag out in the dark, snuggling it at the foot of what he took to be a drift fence, to have at least some shelter from the grit-blasting Wyoming wind. If it *was* still Wyoming; he hadn't been awake enough during the last part of the ride to look out for signs.

As he squirmed away from whatever the big thing mopping at his face was he glimpsed through half-sleep that each of the posts in the fence was painted a different color. Cherry red, lime green, lemon yellow. He was in a carny-colored corral with a live bull bison.

No.

He tried to go back under, thinking it was only the effects of the three-day power-hitch across the country from New Jersey, all that coffee and all those miles talking with strangers. But then the rich brown smell dawned on him and he knew. He knew. He had never seen a live buffalo before but he was sure this was what they smelled like. It smelled like The West.

The buffalo retreated a few steps when Brian sat up, fixing

him with swimming brown walleyes. There were bare patches worn in the wool of its flanks and hump, shiny black leather showing through. Its beard was sugared with dust and meal of some kind, and Brian could hear the flop of its tail chasing flies.

"Morning, Buffalo."

The animal snorted through its flat nose for an answer, made munching quivers with its jaw. Brian fingered matter from his eyes and peered out over the fence to where he remembered the road. There were cutout letters hung from a crossbar like the ranches he'd seen in southern Wyoming had. Brian read them backward. CODY SPRAGUE'S WILD WEST BUCKIN' BISON RIDE, it said, FOOD — GAS — SOUVENIRS. Brian didn't understand how he could have missed the sign and the flapping pennants strung from it, even in the dark. The buffalo licked its nose.

Brian pulled on his sweat-funky road clothes and packed his sleeping bag away. The buffalo had lowered its eyelids to half-mast, no longer interested. Brian stood and walked around it. A shifting cloud of tiny black flies shadowed its ass, an ass cracked and black as old inner-tube rubber. There was something not quite real about the thing, Brian felt as if stuffing or springs would pop out of the seams any moment. He eased his hands into the hump wool. Coarse and greasy, like a mat for scuffing your feet clean on. The buffalo didn't move but for the twitching of its rump skin as insects lit on it. Brian gave it a couple of gentle, open-palmed thumps on the side, feeling the solid weight like a great warm tree stump.

"Reach for the sky!"

Brian nearly jumped on the animal's back as a cold cylinder pressed the base of his neck.

"Take your mitts off my buffalo and turn around."

Brian turned himself around slowly and there was a little chicken-necked man pointing an empty Coke bottle level with his heart. "One false move and I'll fizz you to pieces."

The little man cackled, showing chipped brown teeth and goosing Brian with the bottle. "Scared the piss outta *you*, young fella. I seen you there this morning, laid out. Didn't figure I should bother to wake you till you woke yourself, but Ishmael, he thought you was a bag a meal. He's kind of slow, Ishmael."

The buffalo swung its head around to give the man a tentative whiff, then swung back. The man was wearing a fringed buckskin jacket so stained it looked freshly ripped off the buck. He had a wrinkle-ring every other inch of his long neck, a crooked beak of a nose, and dirty white hair that shot out in little clumps. Of the three of them the buffalo seemed to have had the best sleep.

Brian introduced himself and stated his business, which was to make his way to whatever passed for a major highway out here on the lone prairie. Thumbing from East Orange to the West Coast. He had gotten a bum steer from a drunken oil-rigger the other night and was dumped out here.

"Cody Sprague," said the little man, extending his hand. "I offer my condolences and the use of my privy. Usually don't open till nine or ten," he said, "but it don't seem to make a difference either whichway."

He led Brian across the road to where there was a metal outhouse and an orange-and-black painted shack about the size of a Tastee-Freeze.

"People don't want to come," he said, "they don't want to come. Just blow by on that Interstate. That's what you'll be wantin to get to, isn't but five miles or so down the way. They finished that last stretch a couple years back and made me obsolete. That's what they want me. Obsolete."

Sprague clucked away at Brian's elbow, trotting a little to stay close as if his visitor would bolt for freedom any second. He called through the door of the little Sani-Port as Brian went in to pee and change to fresh clothes.

"You got any idee what it costs to keep a full-grown Amer-

ican bison in top running condition? Not just a matter of set
im loose to graze, oh no, not when you've got a herd of one.
Got to protect your investment, the same with any small
businessman. Dropping like flies they are. That's an en-
dangered species, the small businessman. Anyhow, you don't
let him out there to graze. Don't know *what* he might pick
up. You got five hundred head, you can afford to lose a few to
poisnin, a few to varmint holes, a few to snakes and whatnot.
Don't make a dent. But me, I got everything I own riding on
Ishmael. He don't dine on nothin but the highest-protein
feed. He's eaten up all my savings and most of the last bank
loan I'm likely to get. You ever ridden a buffalo?"

"No," said Brian over the flushing inside, "I've never even
been on a horse."

"Then you got a treat coming, free a charge. You'll be my
icebreaker for the weekend, bring me luck. I'd offer you
breakfast, but confidentially speakin, the grill over here is
out of commission. They turned off my lectricity. You might
of noticed the lamp in there don't work. How they expect a
buffalo to keep up its health without lectricity I'll never
understand. It's that kind of thinking put the species on the
brink of extinction."

Brian came out with fresh clothes and his teeth finger-
brushed, and Cody Sprague hustled him back into the corral
with Ishmael.

"Is there a saddle or anything? Or do I just get on?"

"Well, I got a blanket I use for the little girls with bare
legs if it makes them nervous, but no, you don't need a thing.
Like sitting on a rug. Just don't climb up too high on the
hump is all, kind of unsteady there. Attaboy, hop aboard."

The buffalo didn't seem to mind, didn't seem to notice
Brian crawling up on its back. Instead it lifted its head
toward a bucket nailed to a post on the far side of the corral.

"How do I make him go?" asked Brian. There was no

natural seat on a buffalo's back, he dug his fingers deep in the wool and pressed his knees to its flanks.

"That's my job, making him go, you just sit tight." Sprague scooted out of the corral, then returned with a half-empty sack of meal. He poured some in the far bucket, then clanged it with a stone. Ishmael began to move. He was in no hurry.

"Ridem cowboy!" yelled Sprague.

Brian felt some movement under him, distantly, a vague roll of muscle and bone. He tried to imagine himself as an eight-year-old kid instead of seventeen, and that helped a little. He tried to look pleased as the animal reached the bucket and buried its nose in the feed.

"This part of the ride," said Cody apologetically, "is where I usually give them my little educational spiel about the history of the buffalo and how the Indians depended on it and all. Got it from the library up to Rapid. Got to have something to keep them entertained at the halfway point while he's cleaning out that bucket. You know the Indian used every part of the beast. Meat for food, hide for clothes and blankets, bone for tools, even the waste product, dried into buffalo chips, they used that for fuel. There was a real — real affinity between the buffalo and the Plains Indian. Their souls were tied together." He looked to Brian and waited.

"He sure is big." Brian threw a little extra enthusiasm into it. "I didn't realize they were this big."

Sprague spat on the ground, sighing, then looked up to see what was left in the bucket. "Pretty sorry attraction, that's what you mean, isn't it?"

"Well, I wouldn't say —"

"I mean isn't it? If he don't eat he don't move." Cody shook his head. "The kids, well, they pick up on it right away. Least they used to before that Interstate swept them all off. What kind of ride is it where the animal stops and chows down for five minutes at a time? Got so bad he'd commence to drool every time he seen a human under twelve years of age. Feed, that's all they understand. Won't mind kindness and he won't mind cruelty but you talk straight to his belly and oh Lord will he listen. That's how they got extincted in the first place, they seen their colleagues droppin all around them but they were too involved with feeding their faces to put two and two together. They'd rather be shot and scalped than miss the next mouthful. Plain stupid is all." He gave Ishmael a thump in the side. "You'd just as soon name a rock or a lump of clay as give a title to this old pile of gristle." He squatted slightly to look the buffalo in the face. "A damn sorry attraction, aren't you? A damn sorry fleabag of an attraction."

He straightened and hefted the meal. "Might as well be stuffed, I figure. Put him on wheels. The few people I get anymore all want to snip a tuft of wool offen him for a souvenir. I had to put a stop to it, wouldn't of been a thing left. Cody Sprague's Bald Buckin' Bison."

Ishmael lifted his head and flapped his tongue in the air a couple of times.

"Got to fill the other bucket now. He expects it. Took me the longest time to figure the right distance, long enough so it's two bits' worth of ride but not so long that the thoroughbred here thinks it's not worth the hike. The kids can tell though. I never been able to fool them. They feel left out of it, feel gypped. Um, if you don't mind, would you stay on him for the rest of the ride?" Cody was hustling across the corral toward another hanging bucket, with Ishmael swinging a liquid eye after him. "He needs the exercise."

Brian sat out the slow plod across the corral and slid off when it reached the bucket. He brushed his pants and got a stick to scrape his sneakers clean of the buffalo stool he'd stepped in. The rich brown smell was losing its charm.

"You'll be going now, I suppose," said Sprague coming up behind him.

"Uh, yeah. Guess so." It was a little creepy, the multi-colored corral in the middle of all that open range. "Thanks for the ride, though."

"Nothing to keep you here, Lord knows." He was forcing a smile. "S'almost nine now, business should pick up. Ought to build a fire, case anybody stops for a hot dog." He gave a weak cackle. "I could use it for part of my pitch — frankfurters cowboy style. Call em prairie dogs."

"Yuh."

"You'll be wantin that Interstate I suppose, get you out of here. Five miles or so north on the road and you'll smack right into it."

"Thanks." Brian shouldered his duffel bag. "Hope the trade improves for you."

"Oh, no worry, no worry. I'll make out. Oh, and here, take one of these." He fished an aluminum star from his pocket and presented it to Brian. "Souvenir for you and good advertising for me."

Deputy Sheriff, said the badge, *Issued at Cody Sprague's Wild West Buckin' Bison Ride.* There was a picture of a cowboy tossed high off the back of an angrily kicking buffalo. Brian pinned it on his shirt and Cody brightened a bit.

"Who knows," he said, "maybe today's the day. Maybe we'll get discovered by the tourist office today and be written up. You get your attraction in one of those guidebooks and you got a gold mine. Wall-to-wall customers, turn em away at the gate. I could save up an maybe afford an opposite number for Ishmael. Don't know if or what buffalo feel but I suppose everything gets lonely for its own kind, don't you?"

"I suppose."

"Say, I wasn't kidding about that fire. If you're hungry I could whip us up a late breakfast in no time. There's stock I got to use before it goes bad so it'd be on the house."

"I really got to get going. Sorry."

"Well, maybe you brought me luck. Yessir, maybe today will be the day."

Brian left him waving from the middle of the corral, buckskin fringes blowing in the quickening breeze. When he was out of sight around the bend he unpinned the aluminum star and tossed it away, it dug into his chest too much. Then the signs appeared, the backs of them first, then the messages as he passed by and looked behind. Every thousand yards there was another, starting with WHOA! HERE IT IS! and progressing to more distant warnings. When Brian got to FOR THE RIDE OF YOUR LIFE, STOP AT CODY SPRAGUE's he couldn't hold out anymore, he dropped his bag and trotted back to where he'd chucked the star. He found it without too much trouble and put it in his back pocket.

He went through the land of blue-green sage clumps, leaning into the wind whipping over low hills, walking alone. There weren't any cars or people. More sage, more hills, more wind, but no human trace but the road beneath him like a main street of some vanished civilization. Open range, there were no fences or water tanks. He looked at his Road Atlas and guessed that he was a little ways up into South Dakota, a little below the Bear in the Lodge River with the Rosebud Indian Reservation to the east and the Pine Ridge to the north. He tried to remember who it was he'd seen in the same situation. Randolph Scott? Audie Murphy? Brian checked the sun's position to reassure himself that he was heading in the right direction. There was nothing else to tell by. A patch of hill suddenly broke free into a butternut cluster of high-rumped antelope, springing away from him. He was in The West.

He had been walking on the road for over an hour when an old Ford pickup clattered to a halt next to him. A swarthy, smooth-faced man wearing a green John Deere cap stuck his head out.

"Who you workin for?" he called.

"Huh?"

"Who you workin for? Whose place you headed?"

"I'm not working for anybody," said Brian. "I'm trying to hitch west."

"Oh. I thought you were a hand. S'gonna give you a ride over to whatever outfit you're headed for."

Brian tried not to look too pleased. Thought he was a hand. "No, I'm just hitching. I was walking up to the Interstate."

"You got a hell of a walk. That's twenty miles up."

"But the guy said it was only five."

"What guy?"

"The old guy back there. He's got a buffalo."

"Sprague? You can't listen to him, son. A nice fella, but he's a little bit touched. Got a sign up on 90, says it's only five miles to his place. Figured nobody's gonna bother, they know the real story, and he's right. Guess he's started to believe his own publicity."

"Oh."

"But you hop in anyway. I'm goin up that area in a while." Brian tossed his duffel bag in the back and got in with the man. "J.C. Shangreau," he said, offering his hand. "I'll get you north surer than most anything else you're likely to catch on this road. If you don't mind a few side trips."

Brian had to kick a shotgun wrapped in burlap under the seat to make room for his legs. "Don't mind at all."

"Got to pick up some hands to help me work my horses." Shangreau had quite a few gold teeth in his mouth and very bloodshot eyes. "Got me a couple sections up there, I run seventy-five head. Gonna have ourselves a cuttin bee if I can roust out enough of these boys."

They turned off left on one of the access roads and began to pass clusters of small trailer houses propped on cinder block. Shangreau stopped at one, went to the door and talked a bit, then came back alone.

"Hasn't recovered from last night yet. Can't say as I have either. There was nothin to celebrate, cept it being another Friday, but I did a job of it. You know when your teeth feel rubbery in the morning?"

Brian wasn't used to adults asking him hangover questions. "Yeah."

"That's the kind of bag I got on. Rubber-toothed."

He stopped at another trailer with no luck. This one hadn't come home overnight.

"Hope he's feelin good now, cause there's an ambush waitin at home for him. I had a big one like that in the kitchen I'd think twice about carryin on. She'll just squeeze all the good time right out of that man."

"Many of these people around here Indian?" Brian asked it noncommittally, fishing. The drill-rigger the night before had gone on and on about how the Indians and the coyotes should have been wiped out long ago.

"Oh sure," said Shangreau, "most of em. Not many pure-bred though, things being what they are. Most of these boys I'm after is at least half or more Indian. You got your Ogalala around here, your Hunkpapa and the rest. I'm a good quarter Sioux myself. Old Jim Crow who we're headin after now is maybe seven-eighths, fifteen-sixteenths, something like that. It's hard to keep count. Jim has got three or four tribes to start with, his mother was part Flathead as I recall, and then he's got white and I wouldn't be surprised if one of them buffalo soldiers didn't slip in a little black blood way back when. But you won't see too many purebred, less we catch Bad Heart at home, and he's another story altogether. What are you?"

"Irish."

"Me too, a good quarter. Monaghans."

They came to a pair of trailer houses that had been butted up together. A dozen fat little children wearing glasses ran barefoot out front. An older fat boy with extrathick glasses and a silver-sprayed cowboy hat chased them, tossing a lasso at their legs. Brian got out of the pickup with Shangreau and a round, sad-looking man met them at the door to the first trailer.

"I see you're bright-eyed an bushy-tailed as everone else is this mornin," said J.C. "Them horses don't have much competition today, it looks like. Jim Crow, this here's Brian."

"Hey."

Jim Crow nodded. He was wearing nothing but flannel pajama bottoms and his belly hung over. His slant eyes and mournful expression made him kind of Mongoloid-looking.

"You know anyone else could join us? Couple of my possibilities crapped out on me."

"My brother-law's here from over the Rosebud. Sam. I'll ask him. And Raymond could come along. Raymond!"

The boy in the silver cowboy hat turned from where he had just cut a little sister out from the herd.

"You're coming along with us to work J.C.'s horses. Go tell your ma."

Raymond left the little sister to untie herself and ran off looking happy.

Sam was a little older and a little heavier than Jim Crow and had blue eyes. Brian sat in front between J.C. and Crow while Raymond and Sam were open in the back. Raymond's hat blew off almost immediately and they had to stop for him to run get it. His father told him to sit on it till they got to J.C.'s.

They stopped next at a lone trailer still on its wheels to pick up a young man called Jackson Blackroot. All the men got out and went to the door to try and catch a glimpse of Blackroot's new wife, who was supposed to be a looker. She obliged by coming out to say Hello boys and offer to make coffee. They turned it down, suddenly shy. She was dark and thin and reasonably pretty though Brian didn't see anything outstanding. Jackson was a friendly young guy with a big white smile who looked like an Italian. He shook Brian's hand and said he was pleased to meet him.

Bad Heart's trailer was alone too, a little box of a thing sitting on a hill. J.C. stopped out front and honked once.

"Be surprised if he's there," whispered Crow.

"If he is I be surprised if he shows himself."

They waited for a few minutes with the motor running and Shangreau had the pickup in gear when a short, pock-scarred man emerged from the trailer and hopped in the rear without a greeting.

It was a long bumpy way up to Shangreau's ranch and he did most of what little talking went on. The other men seemed to know each other and about each other but weren't particularly comfortable riding together.

"Brian," asked J.C., "you in any big hurry to get up there?"

Brian shrugged.

"I mean if you're not you might's well stop for lunch with us, look on when we work the horses. Hell, you can join the party if you're careful, can always use an extra hand when we're cutting."

"Sure." Brian was willing to follow just about anything at this point if there was food in it. He hadn't eaten since yesterday morning. He wondered exactly what cutting was going to be.

The J.C. Ranch wasn't much. A side-listing barn surrounded by a wood-and-wire corral and a medium-sized unpainted shack in a couple of thousand acres of dry-looking open range. The shack squatted on a wood platform, there was a gas tank and a hot water heater on the front porch. J.C. explained that this was the working house, they had another aluminum-sided place farther west on the property. There were wide cracks in the floorboard inside, blankets hung to separate the rooms. Shangreau's broad-faced wife grunted a hello and went back to pouring cornstarch into her stewpot. She had the biggest arms Brian had ever seen on a woman.

The men took turns washing their hands in a pail and sat around the kitchen table. Lunch was a tasteless boiled-beef-and-potato stew that the men loaded with salt and shoveled down. There was little talk at the table.

"Well now," said J.C., pushing back in his chair when everyone seemed finished, "let's get at them horses."

The men broke free into work. They readied their ropes and other gear while Brian and Raymond collected wood, old shack boards, and dead scrub for the branding fire. They built up the fire in a far corner of the corral, Jim Crow nursing it with a scuffed old hand-bellows. When there were bright orange coals at the bottom and the irons were all laid out, the men spread with ropes in hand, forming a rough circle around the narrow chute that led into the corral from the barn, what Shangreau called the squeezer.

"And now, pilgrim," he said waving Brian back a little, "you gonna see some *mas*culatin."

Raymond went up and started the first horse out through the squeezer and things began to happen fast, Brian struggling to keep up. The horse was not so huge, its back about chin-high to Brian, but it was thick and barrel-chested, its mottled gray sides working fast with suspicion. Raymond flapped his hat and clucked along the chute rail beside it till it was in the open and the men were swinging rope at its hooves, not picture-book lassoing but dropping open nooses on the ground and jerking up when it stepped in or near them. It took a while, plenty of near-misses and times when the horse kicked free or the rope just slipped away, and Bad Heart was closest to Brian cursing a constant chant low on his breath, fuckin horse, goddam horse, hold im, bust the fucker, and Raymond was in the corral trying to get his rope untangled and join the fun and Brian was hustling not to be trampled or roped.

"Bust im! Bust im!" J.C. was yelling and the stocky horse wheeled and crow-hopped but was met in every direction by another snapping rope. Finally Sam forefooted him cleanly and Jim jumped in quick to slip one over the head and jumped back to be clear as they hauled the animal crashing down onto its side.

"Choke im down! Choke im down!" yelled J.C. and they held its head into the ground with the rope while Bad Heart, cursing louder now and grimacing, wrestled its hind legs bent, one at a time, and strapped them back against its belly. They held it on its back now, writhing and lathered, eyes bugged hugely and nostrils wide, the men adding a rope here and there to help them muscle it still. Shangreau motioned Brian up with his head and handed him a rope end.

"Choke im," he said, "don't let him jerk. You let him jerk he's gonna hurt himself."

J.C. went to where the tools were laid out on a tarp and returned with a long, mean-looking jackknifey thing. The horse rested between spurts of resistance now, its huge chest heaving, playing out in flurries like a hooked fish. The men used the pauses to dig in their heels and get a stronger grip. J.C. waved the blade through the branding fire a few times, then knelt between the stallion's pinioned legs.

"Hold him tight, boys, they're comin off!"

The horse farted and screamed and shot a wad of snot into the blanket Bad Heart held its head with all at once, its spine arched clear off the ground and whumped back down, but J.C. had them in his fist and wouldn't be shook. He aimed and he hacked and blood covered his wrists till they cut free in his hands, a loose, sticky mess that he heaved into the far corner of the corral. He wasn't through. The horse rested quivering and Brian shifted the rope from where it had scored its image in his palms and J.C. brought what he had pointed out before as the masculator, a pair of hedge clippers that gripped at the end instead of cut.

"Ready?" he called, and when they were straining against the horse he worked the masculator inside and grabbed it onto what he wanted and yanked. There was blood spurting then, flecking the horse and the men and staining solid one leg of J.C.'s work pants. The rest was relatively easy, the branding and the tail-bobbing, the horse too drained to do much more than try to wave its head under Bad Heart's knee. With the smell of burnt flesh and fear around them, the men shortened their holds, worked in toward the horse, quiet now, Bad Heart's stream of abuse almost soothing. Each man grabbed a rope at some strategic point on the horse, J.C. taking over for Brian, and when each nodded that he was ready, they unlooped and jumped back in one quick motion. The horse lay still on its back for a moment, as if it had fallen asleep or died, then slowly rolled to its side and worked its legs underneath. It stood woozily at first, snorted and shook its head a few times, groin dripping thinly into the dirt, and then Raymond opened the corral gate to the range beyond and hat-flapped it out. It trotted a hundred yards off and began to graze.

"Forget he ever had em in a couple minutes," said J.C. He thumped Brian on the back, his hand sticking for a moment. "Gonna make a cowboy out of you in no time."

The men sat near each other, leaning on the corral slats, resting.

"What's it for?" Brian decided there was no cause to try to seem to know any more than he did. "Why can't you leave them like they are?"

"It's a matter of breed." J.C. was working a little piece of horse from the masculator jaws. "You leave them stallions be, they don't want a thing but fight and fuck all day long. You don't want your herd to inbreed. Let them inbreed and whatever it is strange in them comes to the surface, gets to be the rule rather than the exception."

Bad Heart sat alone across the corral from them, over by where the genitals had been thrown. Raymond tried to do tricks with his rope.

"Don't want em too wild," said Jackson Blackroot.

"Or too stunted and mean," said Sam. "Or too high-strung."

"And you don't want any candy-assed little lap ponies. Like I said, it's a matter of breed. We keep one, maybe two stallions isolated, and trade them between outfits to cross-breed. You stud my herd, I'll stud yours. What we want is what you call your hybrid vigor. Like all the different stock I've got in me. Irish and Indian and whatnot. Keeps one strain from takin over and going bad."

"But you do keep a stud horse?"

"Oh yeah. Now I know what you're thinking, these sod-pounders up here haven't heard of artificial insemination. We know all right, it's a matter of choice. I been up to county fairs and whatnot, seen the machines they got. The mechanical jack-off machine and the dock syringe and all that. If that's your modern rancher, well you can have him. If God meant beasts to fuck machines he would of given em batteries. It's like that ASPCA bunch, always on our backs about the modern rancher and the proper way to masculate. Now there isn't but one way to do it. Ours. Horses know they been *cut*."

Cutting and branding and bobbing took about a half-hour per horse. It was tense, hard work and Brian got numbed to where only the burnt-hair smell when the brand was seared on bothered him. He liked the shouting and sweating and the physical pull against the animals, and supposed the rest, the cutting and all, was necessary. They didn't seem to mind much after it was done.

The men seemed to loosen and touch more often as they got deeper into work, breaks between cuttings grew longer and more frequent. They sat on a little rise to the side of the corral passing dripping ice-chest beers and a bottle of Johnnie Walker J.C. had provided, gazing over at the string of fresh-cut geldings. Gimme a hit a that coffin varnish, they would say, and the bottle would be passed down, bloody hand to bloody hand, all of them half-shot with liquor but soon to work it off on the next horse.

"Must be some connection with their minds," said Sam. "Once you lop their balls off, whatever part of their mind that takes care of thinkin on the fillies must turn off too. So they don't even remember, don't even think like a stallion anymore. They forget the old ways."

"They turn into cows, is what. Just strong and dumb."

"But you got to do it," said J.C. "Otherwise you might's well let them run wild, run and fuck whenever they want, tear down all the fences and keep territory all to themselves. Nosir, it's got to be done."

The afternoon wore on in tugs and whinnies. Raymond forefooted a big roan all by himself and Brian caught a stray hoof in his thigh that spun him around. One of the horses, a little scab-colored animal, turned out to be a real bad one, kicking all red-eyed and salty, running at the men instead of away until Bad Heart up with a branding iron, swinging at its head and spitting oaths but only managing to herd it right on out of the half-open corral door. It scampered up the rise with the others, kicking its heels and snorting.

"Raymond, dammit!" yelled Jim Crow. "You sposed to latch that damn gate shut!"

"I *did!*" Raymond had the look of the falsely accused; he took his silver hat off to plead his innocence. "I closed it right after that last one."

"Then how'd it get open?"

"It wasn't me."

"Don't worry about it," said J.C. "We'll have to go catch him tomorra. He's a tricky sumbitch to bring in. Just a wrong-headed animal, is all. That's the one you give me," he said to Bad Heart, "pay back that·loan."

Bad Heart grunted.

It was turning to evening when they finished. A cloud of fat black flies gloated over the heap of testicles in the corner. Brian had a charley-horse limp where he'd been kicked. They sprawled on the rise and pulled their boots off, wiggled red, sick-looking toes in the air, and sucked down beer in gasping pulls. Still-warm sweat came tangy through their denim, they knocked shoulders and knees, compared injuries, and debated over who would be sorest in the morning. Bad Heart coiled the rope he had brought and lay down alone in the back of the pickup. They pondered on what they should do next.

"The way I see it," said Jim Crow, "it's a choice between more of Minnie's cooking and goin out for some serious drinking."

They were silent then, it was up to J.C. to pass the verdict on his wife's cooking.

"Sheeit," he said, "if that's all that's keepin us here let's roll. What's open?"

"Not much. Not much legal, anyways. There is that whatsisname's place, up to Interior."

"Then let's get on the stick. Brian, you a drinkin man?"

"I suppose."

"Well you will be after tonight. Interior, what's that, fifty mile or so? Should be able to get there afore dark and then it's every man for himself. No need to change but we'll have to go round and tell the women. Let's ride, fellas."

In the pickup they talked about horses and farm machinery and who used to be a bad hat when they were young and who was still capable of some orneriness on a full tank

and about drunks they'd had and horses they'd owned and
about poor old Roger DuPree whose woman had the roving
eye. They passed liquor front seat to truck-bed, taking careful, fair pulls of the remaining Johnnie Walker and the half-
bottle of Mogen David J.C. had stashed under the barn floor.
Brian closed one eye the way he did when he drank so they
wouldn't cross and Bad Heart carefully wiped the neck when
it was his turn. They banged over the yellow-brown land in
the long plains twilight, holding the bottles below sight-line
as they stopped at each trailer to say they wouldn't be out too
late. Raymond started to protest when it was time for him to
be left off, but Jim Crow said a few growling words and his
mournful face darkened even sadder — it would just *kill* him
if he had to smack the boy. Raymond didn't want a scene in
front of the guys and scooted off flapping the rump of an
imaginary mount with his silver hat. The liquor ran out and
Sam's belly began to rumble so they turned out of their way
to hunt some food.

They reached a little kitchen emporium just before it
closed up and J.C. sprang for a loaf of Wonder Bread and
some deviled-ham spread. The old woman in the store wore a
crucifix nearly half her size and wouldn't sell alcoholic bev-
erages. FOR PEACE OF MIND, said a faded sign over the door,
INVESTIGATE THE CATHOLIC FAITH.

"Sonsabitches damnwell ought to be investigated," said
Jim Crow. "Gotten so I can't but give a little peep of colorful
language around the house and she's off in the bedroom on
her knees mumbling an hour's worth of nonsense to save my
soul. What makes her think I'd trust that bunch with my soul
escapes me."

"Now they mean well enough, Jim, it's just they don't
understand Indian ways. Think they dealin with a bunch of
savages up here that haven't ever heard of religion. Think
that somebody's got to get theirselves nailed to a tree before
you got a religion."

"Fuck religion!" shouted Bad Heart from the back, and that ended the conversation.

A sudden rain hit them with a loud furious slap, drenching the men in the back instantly and smearing the windshield so thick that J.C. lost sight and the pickup sloughed sideways into the shoulder ditch. It only added to their spirits, rain soothing them where the sweat had caked itchy, not cold enough to soak through their layer of alcohol. It gave them a chance to show they didn't give a fart in a windstorm how the weather blew, to pile out and hunker down in the mud and slog and heave and be splattered by the tires when the pickup finally scrambled up onto the road. The flash downpour cut dead almost the moment the truck was free, just to make its point clear. J.C. spread a blanket over the hood and the men stood together at the side of the road waiting for Jackson Blackroot to slap them down a sandwich with his brand-new Bowie knife. The ham spread was a bit watery but nobody kicked, they hurried to stuff a little wadding down to soak up more liquor. They pulled wet jeans away from their skin and stomped their boots free of mud on the road pavement. J.C. came over to Brian.

"Don't you worry about the delay, son. We'll show you a real cowboy drunk soon enough."

"No rush."

"Damn right there's no rush. Got time to burn out here. Time grows on trees. Well, bushes anyway, we're a little short on trees. There isn't a picture show or a place with live music in some hundred miles, the Roman Church is about the only organization has regular meetings and you can have that. Isn't much cause for people to get together. Workin horses like we done is something though. A little excitement, even if it is work. Hell, it's better that it is work, you feel good about it even after it's over, not like a drunk where it takes a couple years of selective memory to make it into something you like to talk about."

"Doesn't seem so bad."

"Oh, there's worse, I'm sure. But I see you're passing through, not staying. Nobody lives here unless they were born here and can't hack it anywhere else. It's why most of the land around here was made into reservation, nobody else wanted it. Oh, the Badlands, up by Interior, they're striking to look at so the Park Service took them for the tourists, but the rest — hell, even the migrating birds don't come back anymore."

"Where you traveling to, Brian?" It was old Sam that asked.

"California."

He frowned. "You best be careful. That California is wild. Had a brother was killed there."

"I'll watch myself."

"I'd steer clear of it if it was me. They say it's wild."

J.C. laughed. "When was this brother killed, Sam?"

"Just around the start of the war. Got himself caught in something called the Zoot Suit Riots and that was all she wrote. Just plain wild."

"You know where I found Brian?" said J.C. "He was walkin up Six-Hat Road there by Petrie's, sayin he's gonna walk to the Innerstate. Seems he got his directions from old Cody Sprague there."

The men laughed. "Be better off gettin em from the buffalo," said Jackson Blackroot, "at least he's a native."

"Sprague isn't from around here?"

"He come out from some city back east, what was it, Philadelphia —?"

"Pittsburgh."

"Right. He come out from Pittsburgh on his vacation one summer and he sees all these roadside attractions up there on 90, the prairie-dog village, reptile farms, Wall Drug Store, all that, and he thinks he's found his calling. He worked in some factory all his life and always had something about bein' his own boss, owning his own business. So he takes his savings, which couldn't of been much, and buys himself two acres down on Six-Hat, the most worthless two acres in the whole state probly, and somewhere he gets ahold of that animal. Gonna build a dude ranch with the money he makes selling rides. Well it's been six, seven years now and I don't know how the hell he survives but he still hasn't got but them two acres and that animal."

"He's a nice old guy though," said J.C. "Talk your ear off, a little crazy, but a nice old guy."

"He's a character all right," said Jackson.

"He's an asshole." Bad Heart climbed into the rear of the pickup.

They had eaten all the bread and were talking about Sam's brother getting killed in Los Angeles when Jackson remembered something.

"Hey," he said, "what we gonna do about that wake they're having over there for Honda Joe? Suppose we ought to go?"

"Just slipped my mind," said J.C. "Live just five mile away from us, no way I can't make an appearance, and it slipped my mind. Listen, as long as there's all of us together and we got the truck —"

"I suppose we ought to go."

"Damn shame it is, young kid like that. Goes through all that Vietnam business with hardly a scratch, gets himself a Silver Star, then comes back to smash hisself up on a goddam motorsickle. Young kids like that seem bent on it. I remember I couldn't talk my brother out of his plan for all the world, nosir, he had to have his California."

"It wasn't this it would have been some other," said Jackson.

"If it wasn't the bike maybe he would of drunk himself to death like some others around here."

"No, I don't think so. Honda Joe was always in a hurry to get there."

"Well he got there all right. In a couple pieces maybe, but he got there."

"We ought to go look in on him, for his mother's sake. What say, fellas?"

"I never liked Honda Joe," said Bad Heart.

"Well then, dammit, you can stay in the truck."

"If there's one thing I can't stand," said Jim Crow very quietly when they were on their way to Honda Joe's wake, "it's a sulky Indian."

It was still twilight when they passed by the access road to J.C.'s place again. He didn't offer to drop Bad Heart home before they went on. They crossed Six-Hat Road, Brian was just able to make out one of Cody Sprague's signs to the right, and then a half-mile farther along they were stopped by a horse standing in the middle of the road, facing them.

J.C. turned on the headlights and they saw it was the scab-colored one that had escaped in the afternoon.

"The hell's he doin out here?" said J.C. He turned the engine off and got out quietly. He left the door open and walked slowly toward the horse, talking soft. "Good horse," he said, "nice horse. Come to papa. Attaboy."

The horse stood for a moment, nostrils wide open, then bolted off the road and out of sight. J.C. slammed back into the truck. Only Bad Heart dared laugh.

The trailer was alone and far away from the blacktops, far even from the oiled road that serviced most of the other places around. It sat as if run aground next to the dry streambed that cut through a gently sloping basin. Young men's cars, Pintos and Mavericks, Mustangs and Broncos, surrounded it, parked every which way. To the rear was an orderly block where the family men had pulled in their Jeeps and pickups. J.C. slipped in among these and the men eased out. They had sobered, what with the food and the surprise rain and the knowledge of the work cut out ahead of them. They shuffled and stuffed their hands in their pockets, waiting for J.C. to lead. The mud and blood had stiffened again on their clothes, they tried to get all their scratching done before they had to go in. Bad Heart stretched out in the rear, glaring out into space. J.C. sighed and fished under the seat, behind the shotgun, and came out with a pint of gin. "I was saving this for an emergency," he said, and tossed it to Bad Heart. "Entertain yourself."

They were met at the door by two dark old Indians wearing VFW hats. Evening, gentlemen, glad you could come. There was a visitor's book to sign and no place to sit, the trailer was crammed to its aluminum gills. There were nods and hullos from the men already inside, crop and stock and weather conversations to drift into, and woman-noise coming from back in the bedrooms. Drink was offered and declined, for the moment anyway. A knot of angry-looking young men leaned together against one wall, planning to make yet another wine run up to Interior and back. Suspicious eyes lingered on Brian, coming hardest and hairiest from the young men. Brian felt extra uncomfortable in his sun-lightened hair and three-day road stubble in the midst of all the smooth, dark people. He was glad for the stains of horse-cutting left on him, as if having shared that gave him some right of entry.

Mrs. Pierce was on them before they could get their bearings. She smelled of tears and Four Roses and clutched at their elbows like she was drowning.

"J.C.," she said, "you come, I knew you would. And Jim. Boys. I knew you'd all come, I knew everybody'd come for my Joey."

She closed one eye when she had to focus on somebody. She squinted up to Brian. "Do I know you?"

"This is Brian, Mrs. Pierce," said J.C. "He's been workin horses over to my place."

"Well Brian," she said sober-faced, talking slow as if explaining house rules to a new kid in the neighborhood, "you just make yourself at home. Joey had him a lot of white friends, he was in the Army."

The woman had straight black hair with streaks of iron gray, she stood up to Brian's shoulders, her face flat and unwrinkled. She could have been anywhere from thirty-five to fifty. She was beautiful. Brian told her not to worry about him.

"You come to stay a while, J.C.? You have something to drink? We got plenty, everybody brang for my Joey. We'll go right through the night into tomorrow with him. Will you stay, J.C.?"

"Well, now, Mrs. Pierce, we'd really like to, we all thought high of young Joseph there, but like I said we been workin horses all day and these boys are just all *in*. I promised their women I'd get them home early and in one piece. You know how it is."

The woman gave a little laugh. "Oh, I do, I surely do. We'll get him home in one piece, that's what the recruiters said, come onto Rosebud when we were over there. Make a man of him and send him back in better shape than when he left. Well, he's back, I suppose. Least I know where he is, not like some that are missing or buried over there. Don't figure anyone'll want to borrow him anymore." She stopped a moment and turned something over in her mind with great effort, then looked to J.C. again. "We're havin a service Tuesday over to the Roman. Appreciate it if you all could be there."

"We'll make every effort, Ma'am. And if there's anything you need help with in the coming weeks —"

"Oh no, J.C., save your help. Won't need it. After the service I'll just hitch up and drive on out of here. Go up north, I got people. I put two husbands and four sons in this country now and I'll be damned if it gets a drop more outen me. No, I'm to go up north."

"It's hard livin up there, Mrs. Pierce."

"Well it aint no bed a goddam roses down here neither, is it?"

The men hung on in the main room a bit more for courtesy, swapping small talk and trying to remember which of the wild Pierce boys had been responsible for which piece of mischief, trying to keep out of the way of the women, who seemed to know what they were there for. Mrs. Pierce weaved her way through the somber crowd assuring and being assured that her poor Joey was a good boy and would be sorely missed by all. Brian noticed she was wearing the boy's Silver Star on a chain around her neck.

It took a good hour to get through the crowd, the people didn't seem to see much of each other and there was a lot of catching up to do, but they were herded steadily, inevitably, toward the bedroom where they knew Honda Joe would be laid out. They shied and shuffled at the doorway a little, but there was no avoiding it. A steady, humming moan came from within, surrounded by other, soothing sounds. J.C. took a deep breath and led the way.

Whoever did the postmortem on Honda Joe must have learned the trade by mail. The corpse, tucked to the chin under an American flag, looked more like it should have been leaning against a stuffed pony at the Wall Drug Store than like something that had lived and breathed. The skin had a thick look to it and a sheen like new leather, and even under the flag you could tell everything hadn't been put back where it belonged. The men went past the Murphy bed on both sides, up on their toes as if someone was sleeping. They clasped their hands in front of them and tried to look properly mournful. Jackson Blackroot muttered a few words to the corpse. Brian took his turn and concentrated on a spot on the boy's hairline till he felt he'd put in his time. He was moving away when he heard the whooping from outside.

"Yee-haaaaa!" somebody was yelling. "Yipyip-yeeeeee!"

There was the sound of hooves then, and the whooping grew distant. The men emptied out into the night range to see what it was.

"Yeow! Yeow! Yeow!" called a voice over to the left. Someone was riding a horse out there in the pitch black, someone pretty loaded from the sound of him.

"Goddam Indians," grumbled one of the old men wearing a VFW hat. "Got no sense a dignity."

"Yee-hahaaaaa!" called the rider as a gray shape galloped by on the right.

"Sounds a bit like Bad Heart," said J.C. "Sounds a whole lot like him."

They went to J.C.'s pickup and Bad Heart was gone. There was some gear missing too, some rope, a bridle. They checked in the front. J.C.'s shotgun was still there but Jackson's Bowie knife was gone.

"He loses it I'll wring his goddam neck," said Jackson.

The men all got in their cars and pickups then and put their headlights on. The beams crisscrossed out across the little basin, making eerie pockets of dark and light.

"Yah-haaaaa!"

A horse and rider appeared at the far edge of the light, disappeared into shadow, then came into view again. It was Bad Heart, bareback on the little scab-colored stallion. It strained forward as if it were trying to race right out from under him. There was something tied with rope to its tail, dragging and flopping behind, kicking up dust that hung in the headlights' arc. Bad Heart whacked its ribs and kneed it straight for the dry streambed. It gathered and leaped, stretching out in the air, and landed in perfect stride on the far bank.

"Fucker can ride," said Jim Crow.

"Fucker could always ride," said J.C. "Nobody ever denied that. Like he's born on horseback."

Bad Heart lay close to the line of the stallion's back, seemed to flow with its every muscle. With the day's blood staining his old tan Levi's and the scabby red-brown of the horse it was hard to tell where one began and the other left off.

"Yee-yeeheeeeeeee!"

Bad Heart circled the trailer a few more times before a couple of the young men commandeered Jeeps and lit out after him. It was a good chase for a while, the Jeeps having more speed but the little stallion being able to cut and turn quicker. They honked and flicked their lights and kept Bad Heart pinned in view of the trailer but couldn't land him till he tried to make the horse jump the streambed one time too many. It just pulled up short and ducked its head, sending him flying over, tumbling through the air till he hit halfway up the opposite bank.

The horse trotted off out of all the lights and Bad Heart lay wailing.

He was pretty scraped up when they got to him, one side of his face all skinned and his left leg bent crooked from midway up the thigh. He cursed as they made a splint from a rake handle, cursed as they carried him in on a blanket, cursed when they laid him out on the Murphy bed next to Honda Joe.

"Wait'll the fucker wakes up in the mornin," he kept saying while they tried to calm him down. "Gonna have a big surprise. Wait'll he wakes up. Big fuckin surprise."

Jackson found his Bowie knife tucked in Bad Heart's boot when they pulled it off. The knife was bloody up to the hilt.

Brian went out with J.C. and Jackson to see about the horse. Everyone had turned their headlights off so J.C. got his flashlight from the pickup. They walked out in the dark a bit and then they heard whuffing up ahead and J.C. shined at it.

The stallion held its head up high, eyes shining back amber in the beam, bridle dangling, chest and sides lathered and heaving. It stood and looked at them as Jackson whispered his way up and took the bridle.

J.C. came up and took the Bowie knife from Jackson. He cut the rope free from the stallion's tail. Brian went back with him to see what had been dragging behind.

It was a blood-sticky hide. The hair coarse and greasy, like something you'd scuff your feet clean on. It had a sad, lonely smell. It smelled like The West.

J.C. played the light off away from it. "I suppose we best take this thing over, break the news to old Sprague. You wanna come along for the ride?"

"Sure."

"Spose we'll call it a night after that. Get you up to go in the morning." He turned the flashlight on the stallion limping a bit as it followed Jackson toward the trailer. "There isn't all that much to do in Interior anyways."

Golden State

THE MEXICANS TOOK Brian across the desert and over the mountains to the Coast in the black night. They sat in the front seat and spoke to each other in their language for the entire ride. Brian was relieved not to feel obligated to talk or to listen. Only the violent shaking of the old Comet kept him awake.

The Mexicans turned south when they hit 101 and Brian got out. The road was halfway down the western slope of a string of mountains. Trees blocked the view but he could hear the ocean in the distance. The Pacific. It was the warmest night he'd had on the trip; it would be easier to sleep out now and find his way to the water when it got light.

Brian started down through the woods, looking for a flat spot to lie, and stopped when he saw the word. It was barely visible over the treetops, glaring in blue neon. HAMBU. Brian spread his bag out and lay down. He had hitched a hard three thousand miles and in the morning he would be there. The hours of Spanish in the dark car, the steady ocean sound, the strange word in the sky — all made him feel like he was in a foreign country, an island in the South Seas maybe, or the coast of Africa.

"You can gain more knowledge in one crossing of the

map," Brian's father used to say, eyes swimming in an early-evening buzz, "than in four years at one of your so-called institutes of higher learning. Travel, travel is the greatest educator." The old man had missed the war, had made it over to Scranton once for a railworkers' convention and down to Atlantic City a few summers with the family. He did the rest of his traveling in front of the TV at the bar in the Hibernian. "When I was young I should have listened to my itchy feet," he'd say, "instead of another certain part of my anatomy. I chased the girls till your mother put salt on my tail, and then I wasn't a young man anymore."

Brian slept well, waking only to shift position in the bag, and whenever he sat up he could see the word shining in the night.

HAMBU.

The mountain blocked the rising sun but he woke automatically before dawn. It was cold; he hurried to dress and to get moving. The word was gone but the ocean sound was still there. He started down.

He saw telephone lines first, then broke into the open on a road. There was a drive-in hamburger stand under a huge sign. End of the word must have burned out.

The sun was up and casting long westward shadows by the time Brian walked down into the town. The streets were deserted, not even a delivery truck out, and the paper scattered everywhere made it even more forlorn. Election posters and handouts. Brian remembered that it was the day after. The faces of smiling candidates flapped around his sneakers as he walked. It was a small town with low, Spanishy architecture and all kinds of spiny green plants he had never seen before.

He came to a circular plaza and stopped to rest. There was a fountain statue in the center of it, surrounded by a high-walled moat. A pair of bronze-and-birdshit forty-niners panning for gold. The water wasn't running.

The moat walls came up to Brian's chest, the water still and clear. He could see coins shining up at him from the bottom, could see quarters and half-dollars among the pennies. He had a little over four dollars and one cinnamon doughnut left from his trip. There was no one around.

Brian took his jacket off and rolled up his sleeves. He pushed himself up and balanced at the pelvis on the edge of the wall, like he was on the parallel bars in gym. He bent down and dipped in as far as his arm would reach. The water was freezing cold, his hand didn't touch bottom.

He tied the strap of his duffel bag around his left leg for ballast, then swung his right over so that he was straddling the wall. He took his shirt off and leaned over sideways. Farther. The duffel bag was lifted clear off the ground and the water was up over his armpit and he still couldn't reach. The coins looked so near, looked like they were only a few feet below the surface. He gave one more effort and began to slip in, stopping himself only by digging in his nails and flailing with his wet arm. He managed to shift his balance back and flopped panting onto the street.

Brian put his shirt and jacket back on. He tossed a penny into the water and watched how long it took to hit bottom. The bottom of the moat went below the street level, the water was probably over his head inside. It was an illusion, the water magnified the coins so they looked closer. ETERNAL HOPE, said the plaque that lay at the forty-niners' feet.

The Pacific Ocean was green. He realized it was cold, late in the year and early in the day, but he had expected blues from the Pacific, pastel blues and turquoises and aquamarines like in the surfing movies or the picture of Balboa and the soldiers in his American History book.

"It's like nothing you've seen in your life," the old man used to say to Brian, shaking his head in wonder. "None of the freezing garbage-and-oil-fouled puddle you've got here, none of your miserable boardwalk rinky-tink. It's pure and clear and just slightly cool to the skin, breaking over the white-sand beaches of the Golden State. The mere sight of it could stop your heart with beauty," he'd say. "And the sun they've got, filling up the sky, toasting the air about you, that sun sets *into* it, warming your face as you look out over the water."

There were plastic benches behind a low stone wall, with steps leading down to the beach every hundred yards or so. There was a plain of sand strewn with a kind of seaweed Brian had never seen. Giant brown peapods, as long as Brian was tall. The beach was alive with reddish brown squirrels that twitched from spot to spot. Brian squatted at the edge of the water and waited for a wave to reach his hands. Up the beach a ways an old wooden pier stretched out into the ocean a good quarter-mile. Brian patted his face with seawater and returned to sit behind the wall. He watched the waves and ate his doughnut.

Two men were walking along the wall toward him. They were too far off to see any detail of their faces. One was a lot taller than the other. They came closer. Older men, both wearing canvas sneakers. Kind of rummy-looking.

"Mind if we siddown, young fella?"

Brian didn't see how he could refuse. They weren't going to shake any change out of him, though, and once they realized that they'd probably leave. He nodded to them. The tall one sat at the other end of the bench and the stocky one, a Chicano with an amazing crop of thick, black, wino hair, offered his hand.

"Pleasetomeeyou pleasetomeeyou berry please," he said and pumped Brian's hand like he was shaking an aerosol can. "You know Misser Horse? He own tot big buildin by the school, berryberry weltymon, I use to work por him ohyes tot not ri' Donnydonny?"

"Slow down, Cervantes," said the tall one. "Take your time."

"Ohyes, Donnydonny. Slowdown." He sat next to Brian, smiling with a set of beautiful white teeth.

"Don't think I recognize you," said the tall one. He had a small blue Navy bag that he was fishing his hand through. "You just get into town?"

"Yuh."

"My name is Daniel Boone," he said, "and the fella next to you is Cervantes. He don't make much sense no more but he's a helluva good man. What's your handle?"

There was no way he could top them, even if he made one up. "Brian McNeil."

"And where do you hail from?"

"East Orange."

"Oh yeah. I been there." He winked at Brian. "You thumbin?"

"Yuh."

"Thought so. I went on the road a while, I was your age. Till the war come."

Daniel Boone's white hair was still wet, combed sideways across his head. It looked like he had pressed his pants by folding them into a square and putting them under something heavy, they were covered with checkerboard creases. He wore a red flannel shirt and had metal teeth. They were aluminum or something, whenever he opened his mouth there was a flash.

"Say, Jersey," he said, "you haven't seen an old fella down here this morning, big old fighter's ears and a green overcoat? Can't really talk, just kind of grunts and gurgles?"

"Tot Stofey he grung he groang he is so har to unnerston ohyesohyes."

Brian said that he hadn't seen anyone.

"Funny, he's usually down here by now." Daniel frowned

and pulled a quart bottle of Thunderbird from his bag. "Maybe he decided to take his breakfast in bed. Care for a pull, young fella?"

It couldn't have been much after seven and Brian didn't like wine, but it was an occasion. He had just seen the Pacific for the first time, he had made it to California, and here was an alky offering instead of asking. He took a modest gulp.

His father never touched wine. "It's a sneaky, back-door way to drink," he'd say. "If you're going to bend an elbow don't be diddling around with any of your glorified fruit juice. Give me an honest glass of beer or some Irish whiskey, something to keep the fire going inside." The old man drank flat beer at breakfast, sheltered from the evening's chill at the Hibernian, and carried a pint bottle of fuel for his night watch at the freight yard. He had a difficult time staying warm.

"Speakin of bed," said Daniel, "where'd you put up for the night? Mountains?"

"Yuh."

"That's good. Town cops'll bust your ass you try to lay out on the beach. Me and Cervantes have been setting up in the dead-car pile back of the Earl Scheib body shop there. Had me a Cadillac last night. Best sleep I had in months."

Cervantes took a hit and passed the bottle back to Daniel. Both of them lipped the neck. Brian had tried to pour his directly to the back of his throat without touching glass.

"You wouldn't know I just come out of the hospital, would you?"

Daniel looked like his best move would be to check right back in, but Brian let it ride. "Nope."

"I mean, do I look like a dyin man? I just been in intensive care three months, fell down the stairs over to the Hotel Sutter and fractured my hip. Lost forty pounds up to the VA, drippin chemicals into my veins from a bottle. You believe it? Lemme tell you, New York, it was pretty much touch-and-go. Thought my number was up. They called my next of kin, my sister-in-law, and explained how I shouldn't never drink again or it'd kill me." He snuggled the bottle in his lap. "So here I am trying to commit hairy carey. Don't have the guts to jump off that pier, so I'm taking the slow boat." Daniel Boone smiled his metal smile.

"You know Misser Carey Misser Carey, he ron a boosher chop? Many many meats ohyesohyes."

"Not *that* Carey, Cervantes. Take it easy."

Brian could feel the sun on the back of his head now. It gave a golden edge to the wheeling gulls. Cervantes grinned next to him. For a wino he didn't smell bad at all, probably better than Brian with his road-funk. The ocean breeze, maybe.

"It blows through the palm trees," the old man used to say, swaying gently over a stein of beer or sitting in a booth as far from the jukebox as possible, "blows warm, so warm, and you can smell the fruit trees of the Polynesian islands in it. Sweet and warm." The old man smelled thickly sweet, smelled of oranges gone to mash. The watch shack he manned each night at the freight yard had originally been the stall where they held all the fruit that shipped in, in the days before the trucks took it over. The smell was part of the wood, it had gotten into the work jacket the old man always wore. When he walked into the Hibernian the regulars would wince and shake their heads. "Good Lord if it isn't McNeil," they used to say, "with our daily dose of vitamin C."

"You vote, young fella?" asked Daniel.

Brian shook his head. "Not old enough. I'm eighteen next month."

"Well, you didn't miss much. It's a bitch, Election Day, always has been. For starters, they don't let the liquor stores open till the polls close. So unless you scored a lot on Monday you got to go dry most of the day. And you can forget panhandlin, there's so many jokers out with pamphlets and flyers and buttons, vote this, vote that, send some thief to the state-house. Everybody just fixes their eyes straight ahead and clamps their hands shut in their pockets and won't stop for nothin. Poor scufflin wino don't have a chance, all that com-petition. Took us all day to make this little quart here and if Cervantes hadn't walked off with a six-pack of beer from the campaign headquarters in the Sutter it would have been an awful cold night."

Daniel sent the bottle down again. They seemed to be tak-ing smaller pulls to stretch out the little that was left. Brian didn't like what it did to the roof of his mouth. Cervantes took out a round tobacco tin and some papers and began to roll a cigarette. His fingers were the same color as the to-bacco. He worked quickly and didn't spill a flake.

A patrol car cruised up on the street behind them and stopped a couple hundred feet away. Daniel hid the Thun-derbird between his legs.

"You see who that is, Cervantes? That Price? I can't make him out with the sun off the windshield there."

"Doan know Donnydonny, the sun he big doan see."

"Price works mornings, usual. He'll pinch you for havin an open bottle in view. We shouldn't of thrown the bag away."

The car started up again, eased past and out of sight.

"Last time they had me up on the hill they were talking about Price. Man almost blasted him away with a shotgun. Fellas in the station said it wasn't for a bum shell we'd have a new bull rainin on our parade every morning."

Cervantes handed Daniel a cigarette and began to roll an-other.

"You do beautiful work, buddy. Just as neat as a tailor-made and twice as deadly."

"Tonkyou, Donnydonny, tonkyou."

Daniel turned to face Brian only when he had a question. The rest of the time he talked staring out over the ocean.

"I never messed with no shotgun," he said. "I'm a knife fighter. Killed three men with a knife, one at Iwo, two at Tarawa. Demolition. I'd go in before the beach assaults. You believe it?"

Daniel Boone looked down to Brian and he had to nod. It was possible, just barely possible.

"Brooklyn, my friend, I detect an air of misbelief. Well lookit here."

Daniel rose and pulled up his pants-leg. There was a round, reddish mark on his pale calf. "Punji stick," he said. He pulled up the front of his shirt. There were puckered scars on either side of his sagging belly. "Jap round," he said. "Got me from the side, went in here, came out there. Lots of blood but it didn't puncture my stomach." He turned to show another souvenir over his kidney. "Shrapnel. A short round from our own artillery. I called in the coordinates and some greenhorn laid one in behind me." Daniel tucked in his shirt and sat back down.

"We'd swim in, all you could carry was demolition equipment and a knife. Cut their throats, all three of em, didn't think a thing of it. Wouldn't figure I'd be such a long time doing away with myself, would you? Hairy carey."

"He got steaks an bacongs an sosage an rose-biff an —"

"Settle down, Cervantes, you'll drop your smoke all over."

"— an homborger Donnydonny."

"I can still outswim anybody in this town," said Daniel Boone. "I had asthma when I was a kid."

It was too obvious a setup, there was no way he'd ask what the connection was. Hitching across the country had left Brian tired of playing straight man.

Daniel leaned back and dragged reflectively on his cigarette. He sighed. He crossed his legs. He picked at his nose hair.

Cervantes smiled steadily, like a sideman in a country-western band. From time to time he would run his hand through his hair, still holding the lighted cigarette, and leave a streak of ash in it.

"So this fella from the neighborhood," said Daniel finally, "was like an uncle to me, he said he'd give me a five-dollar —" he screwed his eyes shut to think hard "— scholarship? To the Y?"

"Membership."

"Membership. See what the booze'll do to you? Give me a five-dollar membership to the Y if I'd promise to swim underwater every day, as far as I could go. Cured the asthma. God, I could swim. Still can, I bet."

Daniel looked like he'd drown in a footbath. Brian smiled. "Could you swim out to the end of that pier?"

"No sweat, Manhattan, no sweat."

"Ohyes Donnydonny, you con swim ober honrid, tree honrid bee-yon feets, m'hmn m'hmn Donnydonny yes you con."

"Three hundred billion feet is a lot of water, buddy. Don't get me in over my head." Daniel turned to Brian. "Say, Philly, you know what ESP is?"

Brian groaned inwardly. He had ridden with a half-dozen astrology freaks on the way out, including one guy who was convinced he was the reincarnation of Stephen Foster. Sang spirituals the entire Indiana Turnpike.

"I guess," said Brian. "Mind waves and all that stuff?"

"You believe it?"

He shrugged.

"I do," said Daniel Boone. "I got it."

Brian had figured as much. "What's it do to you?"

"Well, you see, most people only got three dimensions. You got ESP, then you got *four* dimensions. Brain power is your fourth dimension."

Daniel got up to spit over the wall. He looked out on the beach.

"Sumnabitch. Lookit all the squirrels."

"Yuh."

"No shit, Philly, there's thousands of em, see for yourself. This aint no DT's. DT's I get lizards. Never seen so many squirrels, not even in the park. Beach is just covered with em. Wonder what they're eatin?"

Daniel watched for another moment, then shook his head. "Shouldn't think about food. Haven't put nothin in the stomach for some time now. Hairy carey."

"Pork shop an chickens an libber an —"

"That's what the booze'll do to you, right there." Daniel turned to point at Cervantes, who grinned.

"Donnydonny, my gooboddy. We take care take care."

"Slow down, Cervantes. But he's the best goddam sumbitch around. Aintcha buddy?"

"Ohyes, Donnydonny."

Daniel sat back down. "Man I served with, was lost when we took a shell off Tarawa. Went overboard. He's been callin me ever since, callin from the dead. He's out there in the fourth dimension." Daniel dropped his head forward into his hands and sighed. "Jeez, I'm burnin up with a fever."

"Take a dreeng, Donnydonny. You torsty, yes?"

Daniel ignored his friend. "See, usually he comes in loud and clear, his voice callin to me from out there. But this mornin I can't seem to make him out, it's like he's callin from underwater. Gurgles."

"He drowned, didn't he?"

"I suppose. But he always talked clear before. I can't understand it." He rubbed his eyes and pulled a paperback book out of his bag.

"Say, Philly, you look this here over and then tell me if you believe it." He passed it across Cervantes to Brian. *Beyond the Mind,* by Dr. Milton Shopenhauer. Case histories and commentary. "Look it over and then tell me what you think." He eased his head back into his hands.

When he got really liquid, Brian's father heard freight trains. Steam-driven freights rolling across the plains, rolling through small towns thousands of miles away. "At first it's not even a sound," he'd say, chin lifted, eyes closed in concentration, "it's a slight movement, a thickening in the night air about your ears. Stronger then, a wind blowing far off, then deeper, and there's a tingling up your legs and it turns to water, streams of water gathering into a rushing river, cascading down and suddenly all around you, shaking you, like the engine is driving the blood through your veins and it's shaking you, taking you, taking you along with it wherever it's going and Lord God you want to go, you *want* to but you're rooted to the ground and the power rattles down through your body into your feet again, out of you, and the train tears off, tears away with that long, moaning wail and it's water, and it's wind, and it's a slight thickness in the air and then it's gone and left you, stranded in the still, cold night." It always gave Brian a shudder when the old man heard his trains. He'd keep his eyes closed for a long while, as if still listening, and sometimes he'd fall asleep like that, sitting chin up at the bar, listening.

Brian opened to the middle of the book. The usual amazing feats and astonished friends. A story about a shopkeeper in Belgium who had ESP and was examined by a lot of scientists and made the papers once or twice and then died, still minding the store. He was psychic but not too bright.

Daniel sighed and passed the Thunderbird down for last hits. When it came back to him he took care of the last drops and arced it over the wall.

"Wonder if I hit them squirrels."

"Hey, Daniel Boone." Brian figured he might as well get it over with.

"Huh?"

"I believe it."

"Huh?"

"The ESP. I believe it. But what good does it do you?"

Daniel smiled. "Pittsburgh, it's our link with the next world. I was an atheist till I tumbled onto the fact that I had it. I believe that when you die you go into the fourth dimension. Only a few people can use their brain power to break into it while they're still alive. Pioneers."

"Oh." It didn't exactly answer his question, but it would do.

"Hey," said Cervantes to Brian, "you know Misser Horse? Misser Horse he lib oberdere, berry big mon you know, lib in a cossle, noosepaper, berry big. I lob him berry much, he gib me chob ohyesohyes."

"Say, Cleveland," called Daniel, "you ever fight? You got a nice little built on you, fella your size."

"Nope. Not in a ring or anything."

Daniel shook his head. "That's why the game is finished, can't get a white kid to put on the gloves."

"Did you fight when you were a kid?"

"Sure. I had a couple bouts when I first come out here. Saw some pretty good people come up. I dropped Blinky DiPersio in the second round once, left hook and down he goes. I was heavyweight then, you believe it? S'what the sauce will make of you. Blinky, he gone on to fight some of the great ones. Those were hungry days, hungry fighters. But now, you can get by on welfare, why beat your brains out? It's dead." He shook his head as if his dog or grandmother had passed away. "Dead." He began a yawn that ended as a minor dry-heave.

"Cleveland," he said, "you wouldn't happen to have forty-three cents would you? We need forty-three cents to make us another quart."

It seemed like the sociable thing to do. Brian counted out his change and added it to what Daniel had given to Cervantes.

"That's real Christian of you, son. Any preferences?"

Brian said no and Cervantes headed off into town.

"Mostly I was a sparrin partner," said Daniel. "Worked with that fella I was lookin for earlier, Stuffy. He was California light-heavy champ, way back when, could have gone all the way if they'd known how to handle him. The drink done him in. Tradin too many punches might have softened his head some, but it was the drink, the drink that finished Stuffy." Daniel started coughing, his eyes bugging and the veins standing out on his forehead. He bent forward to catch his breath.

"Committin suicide."

"Maybe you ought to hang the bottle up for a while."

Daniel ignored the advice. "What you want to do, Cleveland, is thumb on down the road to Ventura. Gonna have a big fight card there Friday night. The fella that operates the concession will be hiring lots of people, you could get on easy. Tell him Daniel Boone sent you. They got Windmill White headlining the card, they'll need some extra hands."

Cervantes came back with another bottle of Thunderbird in a paper sack. Daniel opened it and passed it down. Brian swallowed hard. He wanted some of his forty-three cents out of it.

"If you're going to drink," the old man always used to say, nodding into life between the regulars who steered him home, "you might as well do the full job of it. Keep the edges off, keep the fire going inside. Put a few under the belt and it's a warm current I'm riding on, warms the blood, sets it traveling. Your blood sits still and you're a dead man." The old man put more and more drink between himself and the cold, slept later and later into the day, until in dead of winter he stumbled out from the watch shack to answer the siren moan of the midnight freight that always slowed as it rolled through the yard. They found him outside Chicago, stiff in the corner of an empty boxcar. It was the farthest west he'd ever been.

"Hey there."

Two men were standing behind the bench, grinning. Both had wiry, nervous bodies, bodies like TV bowlers. One had a big gap in his front teeth and a brush cut, complete with butch wax.

"Name's Pete," he said to Brian, winking and offering his hand.

The other man's grin ticked on and off his face. In fact his whole self was caught up in quivers and shakes. Both men wore short-sleeved cotton shirts and looked like they had slept in beds the night before.

"Mind if we join you?"

"Pete an Misser Miles Misser Miles!" Cervantes was beaming, excited to have more company. "Seedown goomorning seedown!"

They sat by Daniel at the other end. It was a four-man bench and things were a little cozy with five. Daniel made the formal introductions.

"This here is Sneaky Pete and Mr. Miles. That young fella on the other side of the bench is — what was it?"

"Oklahoma."

"Right. Oklahoma."

Brian traded nods with them.

"Hate to be b-blunt with you, Dan'l —" said Mr. Miles, his voice rattling inside him and escaping like the bleat of a cartoon lamb, "but you w-wunt have sumn to drink would you? I swear I'monna shake to pieces I don't get sumn under my belt."

Daniel upped with the quart. "Just one whiff in the air and they gather like sharks."

"Ah, you're my man." Mr. Miles closed his eyes and took it like medicine. "Gah-*dam* I needed that. Evy mornin this week I had these f-fuckin shakes. Chriseawmighty."

Sneaky Pete wasn't drinking.

"Misser Miles Misser Miles you nee a shabe you know you know, you goolookin honsome mon you use a shabe."

"I need more'n a shave, Cervantes. Christ, two tickets for driving while impaired this month, they tell me on the hill I get one m-more, drunk or no, it's my license." A shudder hit him in the breastbone. "Oh shit, I got em bad."

"Give him your makins, Cervantes," said Daniel. "A smoke'll calm him down. Roll yourself one, Miles."

"Hah! I couldn't roll down a hill this mornin, Dan'l, much less no cigarette."

"Roll one for Mr. Miles, buddy."

"Misser Miles? You lib up on the moanton, m'hmn ohyes, you got tot big ronch yes?"

"Hardly, Cervantes."

"Ohyes. Ri' nex to me, I got big ronch too m'hmn. I got seben-honrid-bee-yon heads of cottles."

Pete remarked that that was a lot of bull and Mr. Miles made the mistake of giggling, starting shudders through his body. The bag traveled up and down the bench once, skipping Pete. Cervantes gave Miles a cigarette. He had a hard time holding still for a light from Daniel and had to concentrate to keep it from slipping through his fingers. He choked on the first drag.

"Say, Oklahoma," called Daniel, "this your first time to the Coast?"

"Yuh."

"How you like it?"

"So far so good," said Brian.

Daniel laughed. "I remember when I first come out here, come for fame and fortune. I was gonna be the next Tarzan. Johnny Weissmuller had just turned in his water wings and I was all set to fill his moccasins."

"Give us your yell," asked Pete. "Your Tarzan yell."

"It's too early. I'd have the vice squad down on us. Yeah, I had all the qualifications. Big, good-lookin, could swim like a fish —"

"Didn't your teeth tend to rust?"

"I had my originals then, Pete, had my ivories. I had everything but the breaks."

"Then you switched to boxing," said Pete, "and you got em. Break your nose, break your jaw, break your —"

"One phone call, one photograph in the right hands and Maureen O'Sullivan would've been washin out my leopard-skin B.V.D.'s down by the river. Would've hit it big."

"Could you play-act, Dan'l?"

"Act, hell. For what? Me Tarzan, you Jane?"

"With me," said Sneaky Pete, "it was oranges. My older brother and me, we worked at this filling station, and he'd always be sending off for brochures about business opportunities out here. Used to hide from the boss down in the grease pit, read about our future. I remember the one that hooked us, can still see the picture in my head. Pretty girl standing under this tree just drippin with big fat oranges. 'Money does grow on trees,' it said, 'in the Golden State.' "

Pete laughed and scratched his scalp.

"So what happened?"

"What ever happens? We came, we saw, we got nowhere. My brother's been in and out of Folsom, if he takes another jolt it'll be a long one. To this day he can't stand anything to do with oranges. He'd get whattayoucallit, scurvy, before he'd even look at one.

"Yeah, it was oranges brung me out here."

They looked to Mr. Miles.

"I was born here," he said. "Just a little after my family come from Arkansas. My mother was eight months and counting when they piled everything on the Ford and started west. Nineteen thirty-one.

"Somebody told em they could eat in California."

Mr. Miles shivered as if the recollection chilled him.

"And how bout you, young fella?" called Daniel. "What's your excuse?"

Brian shrugged. "Where else is there to go?"

The men all laughed, Cervantes the hardest though he had no idea of what they were talking about.

"Sometimes," said Daniel Boone staring out over the water, "I get the feeling that if I concentrated, I could just drift on west, out across the ocean, past all the limits, into another dimension."

"More p-power to you, Dan'l. When you leavin?"

"Who could concentrate with a bunch of beach rummies around him? Sides, I got to take a piss."

"Well you better walk back to the bus station," said Pete, "cause I think that's Cramer in the squad car parked behind us and he'll bust you for exposure if you whizz over the wall. Mean bastard, that one."

"I tell you," said Daniel, creaking to his feet, "they wear a man down." He shook his head to clear it and headed into town.

"Old Dan'l," said Miles when he was out of earshot. "Man wasn't born, he was fer*ment*ed."

"Bet he's got the happiest body lice in town, though. Only fella I know can match him for alcoholic content is that old Stuffy."

"Stofey, he can no be fine," blurted Cervantes. "He no be here no there no anywhere this morning. He disappear tot Stofey."

"Oklahoma," said Pete, "you haven't seen an old wreck, looks like he used his head for a croquet mallet, big old green overcoat, smell'd gag a maggot? Talks like water going down a drain?"

"Nope. Who is he, anyways? Daniel asked after him too."

"Well, he's usually down here by now, this is his bench.

Just an old fighter gone to the bottle. He's sort of an institution down here."

"How'd he lose his speech?"

"It's sort of like what happened to our Mexican friend here, only in reverse. They both started out talkin normal, 45 rpm, and then when they burnt out their fuses Cervantes pushed up to 78 while Stuffy dropped to 33. If you could listen slow enough and deep enough you might be able to make out words when he talks. Mostly people just give him a nickel and pass on by. Or hold on to the nickel and cross the street."

"Man is all w-wino and a yard wide. Three generations of k-kids've had Stuffy pointed out to them for a bad example. Don't know what the town would do without him."

"Maybe they'd start pointin at you, Miles."

"Shit. Wouldn't be surprised, things keep up the way they been."

The patrol car screeched away.

"Bye-bye, Cramer. You going to work today?"

"Maybe yes maybe no. Got a h-half-hour to think about it. What about you?"

"Didn't you hear? I been laid off. Got daylight to burn."

"Any idea when they'll call you back?"

"Maybe Daniel can predict it for us. He hit you with that brain-wave stuff, Oklahoma?"

"Yuh. Said somebody was calling him from the dead."

Pete giggled. "He's probably picking up radio stations on those metal choppers of his."

"Things give me the h-heebie-jeebies."

Daniel came back, wearing a white apron and a broad grin.

"What he do over there, give you a job washin dishes?"

"Nah. I didn't quite make it to the facilities. And Sam, he wouldn't hold still for a hamburger, but I got him to give me this apron. Pissed all over my front." Daniel frowned. "And it's all your fault, Cervantes, you hadn't got that beer last night. It's the beer makes you piss."

"Ohyes Donnydonny ohyes m'hmn. Beers."

"Cramer went, huh?"

"He got tired of waiting for you to flash your ID there, Dan'l. Took off up the hill in a big hurry. Maybe he got an emergency call."

"Good riddance. I get bad brain waves from that cop."

"You still on that kick?"

"Pete, if you could concentrate —" Daniel closed his eyes and held his head with his fingertips "— I could put you in a deep trance."

"You hand him that b-bottle he can put himself in a deep trance."

Daniel's head slumped into his hands. "Six thousand comedians out of work."

"Just kiddin, Dan'l, there's sumn to it I bet. Weirdest thing ever happened to me was when I called up Roy Elrod and the phone didn't even ring, just old R-Roy started talking to me. Gimme the creeps."

Mr. Miles's shakes had calmed a bit but his eyes were still blinking like crazy.

"Will you look at that." Daniel stared at something between his feet. "Ant carryin a big boulder like that."

They all looked. Brian could just barely see a crumb of his cinnamon doughnut inching toward Cervantes.

"Ant can lift seven hundred pounds his weight."

"Seven hunnert times, you mean."

"S'what I said. A man was as strong as an ant he could lift that pier."

"You used to be a muscleman, Dan'l, what could you lift? Two hunnert, three hunnert pound?"

"Don't remind me. Move your foot, Cervantes, let'm go

straight through. Jesus, don't step on him, he's got enough troubles."

"Dan'l, I hate to say this, but I don't see no ant."

Pete winked down to Brian. "I think you're out in the whatchamacallit," he said. "Fifth dimension."

"Fourth dimension. And this aint no DT. DT's I get cockaroaches, not ants."

Daniel paled suddenly, he covered his eyes with his palms. "Jesus Christ, I'm a dead duck."

"You know Misser Horse? He own tot big buildin in the moanton, he berry big mon, I lob to work por him, lob him berry much."

"Cervantes, Hearst has been dead what — twenty years now? It don't really matter to him that you peddled newspapers once."

"Ohyes, noosepaper, berry big m'hmn m'hmn."

"A dead duck," said Daniel. "Aint gone near pussy in a year. A whole year."

"Maybe it's like me," said Pete. "I aint quit drinkin, I just laid off for a while."

"Nope. It's done with."

"Say Dan'l, whatever happened to the one they called Fat Lou? Haven't seen him round for ages."

"He's dead. They're all dead."

"I member that guy," said Pete. They were trying to change the subject, to get Daniel's mind off himself. "I member one night seeing him and Sparky, you know, the one with the neck brace, him and Sparky right here on these stairs goin down to the beach. Somehow they scraped enough together for a whole gallon of wine. Goin down these very steps, Sparky was holding it, when the bag tore and smash that gallon to smithereens. Whole gallon, didn't get a drop before it's broke. I seen Fat Lou just sit down and blubber like a baby."

"Never hold your wine by the bag, you got to keep your h-hand under it."

"No shit."

A man and a woman dressed in matching denim suits strolled self-consciously behind the bench. They turned to go down to the beach.

"Ought to put a sign up," muttered Pete. "No Trespassing —Winos Only."

"Aaaaaaaaaaugh!" Daniel clapped his hands over his ears and squeezed his eyes shut.

"What is it, Dan'l?"

"The gurgling," he said. "The voice. It won't stop."

Miles handed him the Thunderbird. "Relief is just a swallow away."

Daniel drank deeply, then threw his head back and stared up at the gulls.

"Yeah, I remember somethin like that happened to this b-buddy of mine." Miles exchanged a concerned look with Sneaky Pete. "Way back when. Vodka days, none a this wine shit, and my buddy had just turned twenty-one. Only liquor store in town was the old gray-bearded J-Jew, who even if you was toothless and wrinkled wanted to see ID. So my buddy goes in there and gets a fifth, slaps his card on the table and orders up like a man, and what does he d-do for his twenty-first birthday but drop it the minute he hits the sidewalk. His first legal bottle spread out on the pavement. He was strange in the head, this buddy, and he takes it for a sign from the Lord. N-never touched another drop."

"Hell of a note. And I thought my brother was crazy with his oranges."

"I'm a dead duck."

"I'll drink to that. Hand her over, Dan'l."

"Breakfast of Champions."

"No shit."

Cervantes fumbled the bag but recovered, giving Miles a big grin.

"You drop that wine an I'll drop you, Cervantes. Into the ocean with a rock tied around your neck."

"Ohyes m'hmn ohyes."

"Oh yes."

The bag moved from Mr. Miles to Daniel to Miles to Cervantes to Brian. Brian finished it.

"Don't chuck it, Nevada. Them squirrels."

Brian slid it under the bench, still in the bag.

"Tell you one thing," Pete cackled. "Now you can say, 'D. Boone killed him a bottle at this bench.' We'll put up a plaque."

"I'm finished. Hairy carey."

"You know Misser Carey? He got a boosher —"

"Shut up, Cervantes. I'monna lay out on the beach, get my strenth back." Daniel tried to get up but seemed tied to the bench. He fell back. He made it up on his third try; Pete and Mr. Miles tensed to catch him, but he straightened and swayed gently. Cervantes stood and grabbed the Navy bag.

Brian stuck the ESP paperback in it. "There's your book, Daniel. Thanks."

He looked down at Brian. "You believe it?"

"Sure, Daniel."

"I'll believe it, Dan'l, when you get down them steps in one piece."

Daniel got to the steps in a controlled lurch, with Cervantes wagging behind. He paused, took a deep breath, declared himself a dead duck, and started down.

"I'm worried about old Dan'l."

"Oh, he'll be all right."

"The thing is, Pete, I got this theory. You know how there always seems to be the same number of winos around? Like there's a steady figure? But you know they have to die, everybody dies. So my theory is that every time one taps out, that makes room for a new one. Somebody's got to fill the space."

"Now don't you worry, Miles. You're not as bad off as you think and Daniel's gonna perk up. He kept his mind out of that damn fifth dimension he'd feel a lot better."

Mr. Miles was shaking again, almost in tears. "I think I'm gonna lose my job," he said.

"Now come on, buddy, pull it together. Lookit there, he made it down to the beach as good as new. Now if your theory is right, there just isn't any room for a newcomer, is there? Daniel's gonna outlive us all. We can keep him up nights calling from the next world."

They were quiet then and Brian sat for a while, watching the waves and the gulls, enjoying his slight wine buzz. Now that he'd arrived he didn't know what to do. He was hungry. He asked the men about the fight in Ventura and they said yes, he'd probably be able to get on with the concession.

"Horace Greeley had the ticket," the old man used to say, winking through one of his playful periods. "Of course history tells us that he stayed home and sold it to somebody else. I don't believe the man ever saw the far side of the Mississippi. Oh, but I'm sure he told a fine story over a shot of rye, all full of nostalgia for what he'd never seen. Probably drummed up a great deal of business for the Union Pacific, too." The old man would peek at himself in the bar mirror then, and snort a little laugh. "They also serve who only sit and bullshit."

When Brian left, Sneaky Pete was dozing and Miles was shivering in the sun. He could see Daniel and Cervantes stretched out down on the beach. It was warm and nice and he liked the idea of getting a job with a fight card.

Brian walked back through town toward 101. It would be the quickest way down to Ventura. There was some kind of commotion in the center plaza when he got to it, dozens of people crowded around the forty-niners fountain. The water was on, cascading over bronzed boulders, streaming on down a sluice into the miners' pans, sparkling golden in the sun. There was a cop standing on the edge of the moat wall, hands supporting him from the crowd behind. He was fishing something from the water with a gaff, something very heavy hooked by wet, green cloth.

It was just getting warm when Brian reached the highway, only a little after eight. He had daylight to burn.

Tan

CON TINH TAN SITS in the waiting room. She avoids looking directly at the other patients. The Americans. She can see them partially reflected in the mirror that is the back pane of the fish tank. She can look past the underwater flash of lionfish, saltwater angels, yellow tangs, rock beauties, sea robins, past a ceramic replica of the Golden Gate Bridge, to watch the Americans, sitting and waiting.

There is music playing around Tan, music so quiet and without edge that sometimes it is like she is humming it to herself, though none of the songs are familiar. A single receptionist shuffles file cards at a desk. The window behind her overlooks the Golden Gate Park. The receptionist has large, blue eyes, made rounder and bluer with liner and shadow, made larger still by the tinted aviator glasses she wears. Tan wonders if the receptionist could ever keep a secret, could ever hide a fear behind such open, blue eyes.

Tan can see a small boy reflected from the fish tank, half obscured by a drowsy grouper, a small boy with a harness strapped around his head, cinching into his mouth. When he turns to talk with his mother his lips stretch far back over his

258 • JOHN SAYLES

gums and he looks like a small muzzled animal. He seems not to notice or care.

In 1963 Tan was thirteen and in the mornings would bicycle with her two younger brothers along the walls of Hue to the nuns' school. Her little sister Xuan went to grammar school closer to home, inside of the Citadel, and her older brother Quat crossed the river to go to high school. The nuns taught Tan poetry in Vietnamese, prayers in French, mathematics and history in English. She was a good student, which pleased Father very much. Your father expects you to do well in school, he would tell them at dinner. Only the educated person can save himself. Father never said what the person was saving himself from. Tan believed it was the lake of fire the nuns warned about, and she worked very hard.

Each night they faced the family altar to think about their ancestors, beginning with Mother. Then they'd say French prayers. All of Tan's ancestors, back as far as Father knew, had lived in Hue. But none lived and worked in the Citadel like Father did. Father had grown up with the Ngo family, had been a high-school friend of Ngo Dinh Diem. When Diem received the Mandate of Heaven he remembered his friend, and Father was given an important job in the city government. In Tan's house Diem was always spoken of in the same tones as the ancestors. They called him the Virgin Father and he was included in Tan's nightly prayers.

Tan liked mornings best, when she could take her time riding to school, surrounded by the high walls and the moats, the tiled roofs and gardens. She could look over the walls to see the mist rising off the Perfume River, could stop and rest by the Emperor's Gate and watch the city waking up. Hue was a walled garden.

The ride home was too hurried to enjoy. Tan was the eldest daughter, responsible for dinner and cleaning. It never bothered her. If she waited around school too long the boys' section would let out and they would tease her. Monkey. Tan had an extra pair of canine teeth that pushed her upper lip out and made her nose look fatter. Face like a monkey! the boys would cry and bicycle circles around her. Monkey-monkeymonkey.

But sometimes Tan would sit with the picture of Mother they kept on the altar and see the same teeth, the same lips and nose. It was her connection with Mother. It was her face.

Quat mostly stayed out with his friends from the high school. He came home just before dinner, tried not to get in an argument with Father, and then went out again. Father was a quiet and gentle man but Quat always managed to make him angry. Quat did well in school but didn't like the priests. Quat would speak against the priests or the government at dinner and Father would remind him where he was. They would begin to shout and Xuan would cry and then they would stop speaking to each other. Your father has work to do, Father would say to them, and move to his desk facing the far wall. Your brother is going out, Quat would say to them, and he would leave, grabbing a few last bites of food.

When they were younger Quat would sit with Tan in the walled garden behind the house and tell her stories. He told of the wars with the Chinese, and the one Tan liked best was about the Trung sisters who rose up to fight the invaders on elephant-back. She felt very safe and very peaceful, sitting inside the garden behind their house in the Citadel of the walled city of Hue. The stories Quat told were often bloody and terrible, but the Chinese had been defeated long ago.

Father arranged to have Tan's teeth taken care of. Their own dentist had said there was nothing to be done, but Father went to the Americans.

The Americans were there to fight the country people. The Virgin Father had allowed them to come. They lived in a place beyond the walls and across the river and weren't allowed to come into Hue. Tan had seen people who weren't Vietnamese, like the French priests, but she hadn't ever seen an American. She had heard stories, though, and was scared of them.

Father worked with the Americans sometimes. Sometimes he did favors for them and they returned the favors. He said they were very strange people, always laughing, like children. Father did some favors and arranged for an American dentist to work on Tan's extra teeth.

Father went with her the first time. The American was a young man who laughed and made faces for her, like a child. He was so big she didn't know how his fingers would ever fit in her mouth. He gave her shots till she could no longer feel any of her face but her eyes. She was too scared to make a sound or move. She felt that if she closed her eyes she might disappear. Though she studied English in school the American mostly used a kind of sign language with her. He slipped tongue sticks under his lip for fangs and made a deep monkey growl. Ugly. Then he yanked them out with a pair of pliers and smiled, showing all his white teeth. *Dep*. Pretty. That was what he was going to do to Tan.

Tan lay back and watched the huge fingers work over her and tried to keep her eyes open.

When she came home that first time her lip and gums were so swollen that she looked more like a monkey than ever and Father let her stay home from school for two days. Quat had an argument with Father about the Americans. But on the third day most of the swelling had gone down and Father was very pleased. He told Tan that she would go back to school, and that she would go back to the American for follow-up treatments.

She got used to eating and talking again and the boys no longer called her monkey. The nuns said it was wonderful. Tan was not so sure. Looking in a mirror, all she recognized were her eyes. The American had taken her face.

It was after the last visit to the American that Tan saw the bonze. He was trying to sit on the sidewalk just outside of the gate to the American compound. American soldiers were forcing him to move away and a crowd had gathered around. There were three or four other bonzes in the crowd, sunlight flashing off their shaven heads. Tan rode closer on her bicycle. The monks scared her, scared her even more than her Catholic nuns did. Father said that the Buddhists would never get ahead, would never move into the twentieth century, and that the monks were traitors to their people. The bonze who was trying to sit was very young, no older than Quat. Tan could see that he had let the nails on his little fingers grow long. The American soldiers pushed gently with the sides of their rifles and the bonze and the other Vietnamese moved across the bridge.

Tan followed, pedaling slowly. The crowd grew as the bonze walked through the edge of the city, they whispered and kept their eyes on him. He walked solemnly, looking straight ahead.

The bonze tried to sit in front of a huge pagoda. The people inside came out to watch but government soldiers roared up in a truck and began to push them away. The soldiers jabbed and threatened with the barrels of their rifles, and soon the bonze had to get up and move again.

He was crying a little. The crowd began to drop away. He no longer looked straight ahead, he wandered in a wide arc looking about for a place to sit. The section of town was familiar, he was leading Tan home.

He finally settled by the Emperor's Gate. He sat and began to pray and the crowd ringed around him. Three of the other monks sat to pray a few feet away from him, while another placed a metal gallon can at his feet like an offering. The bonze finished praying and dumped the contents of the can over himself. The crowd stepped back a few paces, and Tan held her breath against the fumes. The young man burst into flame.

Tan watched. No one in the crowd spoke. The bonze was the black center of a sheet of flame, he began to rock forward, began to fall, then straightened and held himself upright, still praying. The only sound was the burning. Tan watched and wondered if it was a sin to watch. She smelled him, meat burning now and not gasoline. He fell over stiffly on his side, a crisp sound like a log shifting in a cooking fire, and as if a spell had been broken sirens came to life and the crowd moved away. Tan pedaled home as fast as she could. She didn't tell what she had seen. She fixed dinner but couldn't eat, saying that her teeth hurt from the American.

Shortly after that the Virgin Father and his brother Nhu were murdered in Saigon. People shouted in the streets, honking horns and raising banners and the nuns kept Tan's class inside all day and told them stories of King Herod. Father was put in jail. He was a loyal friend of the Ngo family. Some government soldiers came during dinner and drove him away for questioning. Quat tried to stop them but Father told him to sit and finish his meal. He would be back after the questioning. He told them all to pray for him. The soldiers took Father away. Quat sat at Father's desk, facing the wall, and cried.

One of the office doors opens and a doctor walks into the waiting room. He nods to the boy in the face harness. The boy closes his mouth tightly and shakes his head. His mother whispers to him. He won't go. The doctor leans down next to him, talking in calm, fatherly tones. The boy's face turns red, he presses his knees together and clamps his fingers to the edge of his chair. The mother whispers through her teeth, the doctor takes hold of the boy's arm and squeezes. The boy goes with the doctor, looking to his mother like he'll never see her again.

The sergeant major darts after the Moorish idol, seeming to nip at its tail. They shoot through the tank in jumps and spurts till finally the bigger idol turns and chases the sergeant major all the way back under the shelter of the Golden Gate.

When Tan was sixteen she lived in the Phu Cam section of the right bank with Dr. Co, one of Mother's brothers. He didn't allow Tan and Quat and the other to call him Uncle. Always Dr. Co. He was older than Father. Father died in the jail from tuberculosis. A man came from the government and said that was what happened. Father was buried in the Catholic cemetery.

Most of the Catholics in Hue lived in Phu Cam. Dr. Co was political chief of their ward. He had eight children of his own and now five of his sister's to care for. The house was very crowded. Sometimes Tan rode her bicycle back into the center of town, to their old house in the Citadel. She would watch it from across the street until she saw someone moving around in it. Everything had to be sold or left behind, there wasn't even room for the family altar. Dr. Co kept Father's desk.

It wasn't good living with Dr. Co and his wife. Their children teased the younger brothers and Xuan all the time. Tan was the oldest girl and had to work hard in the house. Quat and Dr. Co hardly spoke to each other. Quat was going to Hue University with the money Father had put aside for him, money that Dr. Co thought should be used to run the combined family. Quat drove a taxi and brought some money home but it didn't seem to please Dr. Co. He said the university teachers were Communists. And that the Communists were responsible for Father's death. Quat spent much of his time with his friend Buu, who was working in the Struggle Movement. Dr. Co said the Struggle Movement was backed by the Communists, and that Quat or Buu or anyone else who got involved with the crazy Buddhists and their burnings and demonstrations would end in serious trouble. Quat never argued, he just walked away.

Tan went to the Dong Kanh girls' high school. She would ride along the river on Le Loi Street on school mornings, enjoying her freedom from the Co house. She did well in her studies and was considered one of the prettiest girls. The boys from Quoc Hoc would say things sometimes when she rode past but not in a mean way.

Dr. Co had late-night meetings at the house. All the children would be crowded into one room and Madame Co would go to sleep, but Tan had to serve the men. There were politicians from the ward and men who must have been doctors or worked at a hospital. They spent the night buying and selling medicines. Tan was tired at school the next day and she hated the way the men looked at her and made jokes when she brought them their food and drinks.

Tan tried to be obedient and agreeable in the Co house and tried to make sure everyone got enough to eat. Quat had his dinner out and the younger brothers could fight for themselves, but Xuan was small and thin and Tan had to save something out of her own bowl to give to her when the rest were sleeping. They would sit up and Tan would try to tell the stories Quat had told her, but the only one she could remember completely was about the Trung sisters. Xuan loved that one and always asked for it. Tan left off the last part, the part where the Chinese came back and the sisters had to drown themselves.

One day in the spring Tan and her classmates were let out of school early. People were milling in the streets, radios blasted news at every corner. Everyone had a different rumor about what was happening. Tan tried to bicycle home, but the way was too full of people. They were crowded around an old man carrying a radio and Quat's voice was coming from it.

Tan was excited and scared. Quat said that the Struggle

Movement was coming to fruit all over the country and that here in Hue the Buddhists and their friends had control of the city. Control that they meant to keep until their demands for reform were met. After each demand that Quat read, the people in the street cheered.

It was a strange kind of control. There weren't soldiers in the streets with guns like there had been after the Virgin Father was killed. The soldiers were all staying in their barracks in the Citadel. The city-government people were staying inside too, and there was no one guarding them. There were Buddhist flags flying everywhere. The Buddhists had the radio stations and the people in the streets. Tan had never seen so many people outside at once in her life.

The people in the streets were saying that they couldn't be beaten, the soldiers in the barracks were on their side and the Americans wouldn't dare interfere. The generals in Saigon would have to have elections, for none of them had the Mandate of Heaven.

In Phu Cam people were in the streets too, but they were much quieter. Trucks drove through with loudspeakers saying not to worry, they wouldn't be hurt. No one seemed to believe them.

There was a meeting at the Co house late that night. The doctor and his politician friends from the ward were there. Quat was there, and Buu, and several other people from the Struggle Movement, including two bonzes. They talked about peace, talked about how to avoid having people get hurt. Tan listened from the next room. Buu explained how the Buddhists had control of the city, how the First Division was staying neutral and the Americans were all hiding in their compound. He explained that it was important for the city officials to cooperate if they were going to avoid violence. That much of the violence might be directed at the city officials themselves. Dr. Co and his friends pledged to do anything they could to help in the difficult times ahead.

People waited to see what would happen. There were demonstrations but no government soldiers to break them up. Tan went to school, people went to their jobs, but there was a feeling of waiting, that no normal routine could be taken up till the demands were resolved one way or the other.

Quat started coming home for dinner. He talked openly about politics, about what he thought should be done to choose new leaders. Dr. Co hardly spoke. Quat talked constantly and in ways that were not right in front of one's uncle. It frightened Tan. Often at night now she could hear through the wall that Dr. Co was hitting his wife. Tan felt like she did after Confession, waiting to hear the Penance the Father would give her.

The rumors came first. Ky. Ky was coming to attack them. He was coming, closer, closer. It was hard to get reliable reports. They lived in a walled city and were afraid to travel far. They waited. They wondered if the Americans would let Ky come. One night when Quat was out Dr. Co said that Ky was a good man. He might not have the Mandate of Heaven but he knew how to get things done.

Buu brought the news that General Ky was in Da Nang, fighting the people there. So close. Ky's men were fighting the soldiers who had been stationed there, were shooting civilians in the streets and in the pagodas. The Americans had helped them transport the troops and weapons. Hue would be next.

Dr. Co didn't say anything. He went to bed. Madame Co looked relieved and said maybe the best thing would be to surrender. Quat and Buu talked late into the night. The only way to save it, to keep the Struggle Movement alive, was if Hue could present a united front against Ky. The Buddhists and the Catholics and the soldiers in the Citadel and the city-government people — all standing together.

School ended for Tan. Ky was coming, he had cut off food and supplies. Dr. Co brought home some bags of rice and boxes of medicine one night and hid them in the attic. They were for the siege, he said. When things got really tight he would ration them out to the people in his ward. He didn't tell Quat about them. Every day people said that Ky would come tomorrow. They waited. Rumors went around about the killing in Da Nang. But Da Nang was different, people said. Da Nang was crowded with refugees and Communists and Americans. The Americans walked around in the city like they owned it and dumped mountains of garbage alongside the roads. It was the kind of place you could expect a lot of killing. Ky would never dare to do the same thing in the Imperial City, would never march shooting into Hue.

A nun burned herself. Somebody burned the American library, and the American consulate. The leader of the Buddhists, Thich Tri Quang, told people to pray and be very holy. Buddhists planned to put their family altars out on the streets to stop Ky's tanks when he came. Everyone listened to the radio station. Quat spent most of his time there, and Tan heard his voice often.

One day Quat gave her a message to bring to Dr. Co. The doctor was gone when she reached home. She tried the house of one of his political friends. The friend's wife said he had left with Dr. Co, in a hurry. Tan tried the ward hall. No one was inside but an old man who said Dr. Co had been there with the other politicians but had left.

Tan rode into the center of Hue, to the city offices. There was no one but janitors in the City Clerk office and the District Court was empty. Tan went to the soldiers' barracks.

The soldiers were gone. The people in the streets in the Citadel said the soldiers had gotten into trucks and jeeps and driven northward out of town. Ky was to the south, in Da Nang.

Tan started back to the station. Thich Tri Quang was on the speakers telling people to stay off the streets. Ky was on his way and there was no one left to stop him. They had been

betrayed. Tri Quang told people not to resist, he didn't want
Buddhists killed like in Da Nang.

Before Tan reached the station the talking had stopped
and there was music playing. When she arrived there were
government soldiers standing guard at the entrance with
their rifles pointing out.

Dr. Co came home three nights later in a very good mood.
He said the traitors would be taught a lesson. He said that he
was glad that order had come back to Hue. He didn't mention what he was going to do with the supplies in the attic.
Quat didn't come home. Dr. Co said he must have run off to
join the Communists. He was lazy, he wanted other people to
do all the work, then come along and take it over. Dr. Co had
a lot to drink and said more about Quat. Quat was twenty
years old, he said, and yet without a wife or a job. He would
never amount to anything, never be able to take care of a
wife and twelve children, four of them orphans, like Dr. Co
did. When Dr. Co and Madame Co went to bed there was
noise, but not because he was beating her.

A week later a boy gave Tan a note from Buu. He had
hidden in a Catholic church when the soldiers came and now
he was going into the country. He had seen Quat captured by
the Ky soldiers and taken away for questioning. When Tan
went to the soldiers they said she should try the city police.
The city police had a record proving the existence of a Con
Tinh Quat, but had no idea of his whereabouts. He was
wanted for questioning.

Quat didn't come back. Sometimes late at night Tan and
the younger brothers and Xuan would sit facing each other
in a small circle and pray for him and cry. But quietly, so as
not to wake Dr. Co.

Tan sees a little girl watching her in the fish-tank mirror.
The girl is maybe five years old, sitting with her mother. One
side of her face is puckered with burnt skin, a nostril and the

corner of her lip eaten away. Her blond hair is tied up in pale blue ribbons. She smiles at Tan through the fish and plastic eelgrass and Tan smiles back. The little girl takes her fingers and folds her lids down to make thin eyeslits like Tan's. The mother looks up from her magazine and gives the girl a quick slap on the wrist.

Tan was eighteen. It was very early morning, only a few hours into the Year of the Monkey, when she was wakened by the popping. Close, a sporadic hollow popping and flashes like heat lightning in the sky. Dr. Co had just come back from a Tet party at the ward hall, he was still in his rumpled street clothes when he wandered out from his bedroom. It was monsoon season and had been drizzling on and off all night. Dr. Co held newspapers over his head and went out. He came back without the papers, hair plastered to his head, looking very pale. The Communists were attacking all over, he said — trying to take over the city. It would be best to stay in and wait for the Americans to come out of their compound and chase the Communists away.

They sat in the dark, no one sleeping, no one speaking, and listened to the popping. The sounds grew very close, the house shuddered a few times, and then they moved away. That was the Americans, said Dr. Co from the corner he was huddled in. When the ground shakes like that it is the Americans chasing Communists with their big guns.

At dawn Dr. Co and Tan went out to look. It was very quiet, raining lightly. Soldiers walked in the street carrying rifles — Vietnamese soldiers. They weren't the ones from the Citadel though. These men wore khaki uniforms and green-and-red armbands, and called to each other in the rapid dialect of northerners. Dr. Co hurried Tan back inside.

Dr. Co sent Madame Co and the young children to shelter at the Phu Cam Cathedral, a little ways across the railroad tracks. The soldiers wouldn't bother a woman and children.

Tan had to stay and help him gather their valuables. When it was dark they would try to reach the Cathedral.

Now and then Dr. Co had Tan peek into the street. There were people with rifles in everyday clothes, and the people with their hair in buns, the country people in black pajamas. The popping and explosions came from up by the American compound now, and from the walled city across the river. The Communists were in control of Phu Cam.

Dr. Co cursed the Saigon generals and the Americans. This was what came of declaring a truce with the Communists. Dr. Co gathered his papers and money and some of the medicines he had stored in the attic. Ever since the Struggle Movement failed, Dr. Co had been bringing home supplies and storing them in the attic. Things he said the Americans had given him. He put the medicines and a few cartons of cigarettes in his suitcases, but he left the American ham and beef upstairs.

In the early evening someone pounded on the door. Dr. Co told Tan to say he had gone to the hospital to treat casualties, and ran up into the attic. The pounding continued, someone yelled that they should come outside, that no one would be harmed. Dr. Co was called by name. Tan sat on the floor, too scared to answer the pounding. It stopped. After several quiet hours Dr. Co came down.

They tried to sneak out late at night. At the railroad tracks someone called for them to stop and searchlights came on. Dr. Co ran into the darkness and Tan tried to follow. The suitcase she'd been given was heavy and when she heard men close behind her she had to drop it and scurry away. Tan spent an hour squatting in the shelter of a small pagoda and then found her way home. Dr. Co slapped her for leaving the suitcase behind. How would the family eat, he asked, now that she had thrown all their money away? Tan saw no sign of the suitcase Dr. Co had been carrying.

They lay on mats in the children's room, several feet of darkness between them. They didn't speak for over an hour.

Neither slept. Then there was pounding on a door down the street. Voice shouting. Screaming, and a shot, very loud, very close, and a woman wailing on the street. Pounding on a door, closer. Dr. Co came over and lay by Tan, putting his arms around her. She couldn't tell which one of them was shaking so hard. Pounding right next door, more shots, more crying. Tan held her breath. She felt Dr. Co's heart beating against her back. The pounding came again, on the other side of the house. They had been passed over. The pounding moved on down the street.

Tan felt Dr. Co's breath hot on the back of her neck. He pushed his face through her hair and kissed her there. She was the one shaking now, she was sure of that. He rolled her onto her belly and pulled her clothes up. The northerners were near, she couldn't cry out. She couldn't think who she would cry to.

Tan felt crushed under his weight, the matting dug into her breasts. She tried to think of prayers. She was glad she didn't have to see his face. Tan bit her lip against the pain and he pushed into her from behind. That evening, frightened by the pounding, she had forgotten and not called him Dr. Co, had not even called him Uncle. Father, she had said, what will we do?

Dr. Co lay still on top of her when he had finished. He lay so still and so long that Tan thought he must have fallen asleep. But then he rolled off her and she groped her way to where she could wash herself. Tan sat shivering under her father's desk until dawn.

It rained heavily all morning and the fighting sounds were muffled. Dr. Co didn't meet her eyes or speak. When Tan looked out she saw a few of the country people riding by on bicycles. They didn't seem to notice how wet they were getting.

The pounding came in the afternoon. Dr. Co was called by name. He went up in the attic to hide. The people outside said they would start shooting if no one came out. Tan opened the door.

There were country people and a few people dressed in city clothes. They all wore red armbands. One was a girl who went to the Dong Kanh high school with Tan, a very pretty, popular girl. She wore a pair of pistols in her belt. Another of the people was Buu.

He looked much older. He held a clipboard in a hand with only one finger and a thumb on it. He pretended he didn't know Tan.

Buu asked where Dr. Co was. Tan said he had gone to the hospital. Buu said they knew that wasn't true. The people stood in the house, dripping, and told her not to be afraid, they were here to protect the Vietnamese from the Americans and the Saigon generals. Tan was too frightened to speak. Father, her uncle, the nuns in school — all had told of the terrible things that the Communists did to people.

Buu sat on the ladder leading to the attic and asked if they were hoarding meat in the house. Tan shook her head. Buu said he had learned about decay since he had been away from the city. If you lived too close to it you never noticed the smell, but any outsider could tell right off that things were rotten. Buu led the people up into the attic and they found Dr. Co hiding behind containers of American beef.

Dr. Co cried and pleaded. They bound his hands behind his back with wire, told him not to worry. They were only taking him for questioning. Buu told Tan to stay in the house until told what to do by the People's Army. The country people carried the meat out into the rain. Dr. Co didn't say good-bye.

Tan dressed in black and waited for night. There was no trouble at the railroad tracks and she reached the Phu Cam Cathedral. Women inside were wailing, beating their faces with their hands. There were no men. No men and almost no boys.

The Communists had come that morning, sobbed Madame Co, and had taken all the men and boys away. Just to a political meeting, they said, and then they would be brought back. They had taken Madame Co's four sons and Tan's two brothers. No one had returned. Xuan had volunteered to go for help to the government soldiers. She knew her way in the Citadel.

Tan told Madame Co her husband had gone to work at the hospital.

She started after Xuan in the morning. Rain beat down and there was fighting everywhere. She ran north toward the river, ducking between buildings when the fighting came close. She saw northern soldiers. She saw Americans. Loudspeakers said the People's Army was winning. A sound truck blared that the government soldiers were in control.

Tan was knocked to the pavement by an explosion. Her head hurt. She went on. Somebody shot at her. She felt the bullet pass, dove to the ground and cut her hands open. She stumbled onto a man lying dead in a puddle on the street. Tan crawled off him and ran for the river. The fight roared around her, trucks burning, houses burning, flames sizzling up to meet the rain. Tan saw blood running through the gutters with the rain. A flying piece of brick hit her, her side burning, and an old man fell in front of her, bleeding, tangled with his bicycle. It was the lake of fire the nuns had told of, it was the Day of Atonement. Her head hurt. Tan ran upright down the middle of the street, knowing only that she had to reach the river.

The bridge was gone. There was no way back to the Imperial City. Her head hurt. She had to get across. She held her head in her hands, tried to remember. She was the sister of — there was someone floating by in the water, facedown. She was the daughter of — the water was gray, its surface alive with rain. Glowing embers blew from the fires in the walled city and died as they landed on the water. She held her head and sat on the bank of the Perfume River, trying to remember who she was.

The air conditioner blows on Tan, her nipples stand up and hurt a little. She folds her arms across her breasts. They are so big, so hard, since the Chinese doctor did them. She is a tiny, thin woman with huge breasts. She wonders if they'll ever be small again, be soft. If she gives him her eyes maybe he'll let her have her body back.

There are pictures on the wall. Chins pushed back or strengthened, noses straightened and reduced, harelips mended. Oriental eyes made round. Before and After, say the pictures.

When Tan went back to the Co house it was full of government soldiers hiding from their commanding officer. They sat half-naked on the floor with their clothes hanging to dry, eating what was left of the food, cooking on a fire made from Father's desk. They called for Tan to come in and sleep with them. She ran. The Americans and Communists fought in the Bien Hoa suburb to the north. The Americans built a pontoon bridge and Tan crossed with thousands of other homeless people. The people said the Americans would feed them.

Tan wandered in the walled city, looking for Xuan, looking for food. Thousands wandered with her. The walls had crumbled under the bombing, half the houses were knocked down. People looted what they could before the soldiers came back. The soldiers had guns and took the best of everything.

The sun came out for one day and the bodies in the streets began to stink. Families, dressed in white for mourning, made circular graves for their dead in the red earth of the parks and school yards. The bodies were wrapped in black cloth, then in white, and buried in the mud. The Americans wrapped their dead in green plastic bags and left them on the curb for trucks to pick up.

Tan found Madame Co at a refugee center the government soldiers had set up. There was no food. Dr. Co had been found with his hands still bound behind his back, buried alive. There was no word of Madame Co's sons or Tan's brothers. No word of Xuan.

Tan wandered in the monsoon. Sometimes Americans would give her food. She was afraid to approach them alone, but joined groups of begging children. Tan found the men gave more if she talked like the little children. Hey, you, GI, she would call, you numba one. You give gell to eat, yes?

The Americans would smile if they weren't too tired and hand out a little food. People cooked what they could beg or steal right on the street, in water pots made from artillery shells.

The first time Tan saw Supply Sergeant Plunkett he was wrapped around a case of Army K-rations. He grinned at her as he hurried across the rubble, rattling his cans of beans and processed ham. Care for a bite? Tan was too hungry to be scared. His legs were so long that she had to run to keep up with him.

You, me, pom-pom, he said to her in the abandoned house they sheltered in. Boom-boom. Fuckee-fuckee?

He seemed very pleased when she didn't understand what he meant.

You vir-gen gell?

She told him she was.

Vay good. Me show you boom-boom. Then you eat. Beaucoup food.

He did what Dr. Co had done to her, but he looked her in the eyes afterward and smiled.

You no vir-gen now. You Plunkett gell.

Tan smiled back at him like she had learned from the

young children, smiled and said you numba-one GI. Numba-one boom-boom. Me eat now?

The Communists disappeared and bulldozers came to bury the walls and buildings that had been blown down. Tan went with Plunkett to Da Nang. He would give her money. If the Communists had taken her brothers and Xuan she would become wealthy enough to buy them back.

Plunkett set her up in a house on the edge of the sand flats in Da Nang, close to the refugee camps. There were four other girls who had American soldiers. Plunkett paid her rent and gave her money for food and clothes. She sewed most of it into a chair. It was nice having the other girls to talk to, there was a mama-san to keep the house and always enough food. Plunkett visited at least twice a week.

There was garbage everywhere in Da Nang, small mountains of it that little boys fought and played on. People in the camps sat all day waiting for food, crowded together like insects. There were girls on the streets, country girls who had sold eggs and produce in the market before the fighting. Buy me, buy me, they said. Me numba-one gell, suckee-suckee, six-hundred pi.

Plunkett would come to drink and for boom-boom. He liked how thin her body was, how her breasts barely stuck out. My little girl, he called her. He asked if she had a little sister he could meet. Tan said she had no sisters. He showed pictures of his little daughters back in America. Plunkett didn't like the name Tan, he called her Betsy. It was the same name as one of his daughters.

He smiled and laughed constantly, like a child. He said he didn't like her eyes. They looked like she was hiding something from him. You trick me, he would say. Alla time same-same. You Betsy unscrutable gell. He gave her money to have the round-eye operation like Madame Ky, like the other girls in the house. She sewed it in the chair.

Tan had been in Da Nang three months when the word

came about the men and boys taken from the Phu Cam Cathedral. Their bones were found buried together in the jungle a few miles from Hue. Most shot, some buried alive. Over four hundred men and boys. Plunkett gave Tan money to send to care for her brothers' bones.

Her belly grew. The other girls noticed first, then Plunkett. He was very angry and took her to his friend Dr. Yin.

Dr. Yin was Chinese and smelled of ammonia. Tan was terrified. Plunkett reassured her that Dr. Yin was an American, a soldier, and his friend. But Chinese was Chinese. Tan screamed and had to be given a shot when the young doctor approached her.

She was thin again then, but Plunkett didn't seem to like her so much. He brought her a Catholic-schoolgirl's uniform, like she had worn when she was little, and had her put it on for the boom-boom. Sometimes he made her bend over so he could hit her with his belt. He didn't smile or laugh so much anymore.

Plunkett left things at the apartment, medicines, food, sometimes guns. He ordered Tan not to touch them. She listened for hours to the American radio he had given her. She would lie in the dark at night twisting the dial back and forth, listening to all the different languages, all the voices blending into each other. She felt like she was floating, hearing everyone's private thoughts. When she woke the batteries would be dead and she'd be without radio till Plunkett came. He always had batteries with him.

Tan was twenty, had been in Da Nang two years, when she saw her sister on the street. Two Americans were walking with their Vietnamese girls. One of them was Xuan. She looked like all the other street girls, looked like she could take care of herself. Her American called her Sue-Anne. Tan followed, listening to her sister laugh at what the Americans were saying, and then let them walk out of sight. A moment later she thought better of it and tried to catch up, but Xuan had turned some corner and was gone.

Plunkett said he would send Tan to America. She would help him be a rich man. He explained that in America opium was used just like money, better than money. But government police would steal it from you, just like in Vietnam. It was hard to bring opium to America, but Tan could help him.

He took her back to his friend Dr. Yin. They explained how much just a little opium was worth if it was pure. She watched the doctor put it into the implants. They would be like a cyst, he said, like a thorn that the skin grows over. Harmless.

Tan lay on the slab and remembered all the stories Quat had told her. Dr. Yin put her under. She dreamed of riding a bicycle in a quiet, walled city.

When she woke her breasts felt mammoth, they jutted out stiffly from her body. The skin was stretched taut, the nipples pointing up and out. There was a scar in the crease beneath each breast, creases she had never had before. The breasts didn't feel a part of her. They belonged to Plunkett. He loved to grab them in bed. The future is in my hands, he would say, and smile like he used to.

He arranged for her to go to the American city of San Francisco. He would come later. Tan was afraid to tell him about the money she had hoarded, afraid he wouldn't understand. It was in piasters, and wouldn't be any good in America. It wasn't opium. The day before the plane took her, Tan ripped the money out of the chair and gave it to the other girls in the house.

It would be good in San Francisco, she thought. No one was fighting and there was always enough food.

A nurse, a young American girl, calls Tan into the office. She is seated in a leather reclining chair. Doctor is in the back washing his hands, says the nurse, I'm his assistant. The nurse asks Tan if she is sure she wants to go through with the eye operation, says she is a very pretty woman already. Tan says she wants to go ahead. The nurse leaves.

There are more pictures on the walls inside the office. Before and After pictures, profiles of breasts enlarged or made smaller. A picture of the doctor in Army fatigues sitting on a pile of sandbags. Tan closes her eyes, tries to steady her heartbeat.

Tan lived in a bad-smelling Mission Street hotel run by an old Thai man. The rent seemed high, but that was something the nuns hadn't taught about in English. Tan avoided talking to anyone, she took all her money with her if she went out and never walked more than a few blocks from the hotel. She waited for Plunkett.

A young brown-skinned woman with a little baby lived in the next room. Sometimes at night she would play her radio, slow, sad songs in Spanish to keep her baby from crying. Tan would lie in bed, listening through the wall, and think how nice it would be if she could be friends with the woman.

Tan waited. Her American money began to run out. She ate rice at a Vietnamese restaurant on Powell Street. On the sign out front was a map of Vietnam with the northern half painted red and the southern half painted green and all the major cities labeled. Young American men would come by with their girls and point to spots on the map, but very few came inside. Mr. Thuong, who ran the restaurant, would talk with Tan while she ate. He had come to America during the fighting between the French and the Communists. He seemed very kind, but Tan was careful not to tell much about herself. Her bill never came to what it said on the menu.

Tan waited in her room on Mission Street. She was afraid. Afraid of the Americans, afraid of being alone, afraid of being caught with the opium. They had searched her when she got to the Hawaii airport, a woman had put her hands up in Tan's private parts.

Plunkett wrote her a letter saying when he was coming. He wrote in the child-language he had used to talk with her. It was very hard to read. Tan went to the docks to meet him.

Passengers came off the big boat, but Plunkett was not among them. Tan asked a man from the boat, who took her to a policeman. The policeman said that Plunkett had been taken for questioning. He asked Tan's name and address and she gave him false ones. Plunkett never showed up at the hotel. Questioning meant the same thing in America that it did in Vietnam.

Mr. Thuong gave Tan a job at the restaurant when her money was gone. She made salads in the kitchen and tried to avoid the busboys and dishwashers, who were all Chinese. Mr. Thuong couldn't pay her much, she didn't have a Green Card, but if she ate at the restaurant she had enough to pay her rent.

One of the waitresses, a Korean girl named Kim, was friendly to her. Kim had another job, being a girl in a Chinese bar on Pacific Street. The Chinese men would come in a little drunk and Kim would sit by them and talk and they would buy her drinks. It made more money for the bar. The Chinese tried to do more and you could make extra. Kim let them touch her breasts. Kim said she was willing to sell her breasts but nothing beyond that. The girls in the bar were all Koreans and had American boyfriends or husbands. They had come over from their country with soldier husbands. Kim said it would pay much more than making salads, said the Chinese men would like Tan. She was small and delicate but had big breasts for them to touch.

Kim told her to have the round-eye operation. If she ever wanted to get an American boyfriend, to be able to become a citizen and get papers so she could have a nice job, she would have to have her eyes changed. That was how they wanted it. Tan said she was interested, but kept putting it off.

One morning Mr. Thuong came out from listening to the news and began to paint the bottom half of the Vietnam map red. There were tears in his eyes as he painted. At least, he said, it is all the same color now. It was that morning Tan decided for the operation.

Kim showed her the ad for the plastic surgeon in the yellow pages, a big ad with a picture of the doctor. Tan recognized his face.

Tan lies in the reclining chair wondering what he'll do. If he'll remember her. If he'll steal it from her or give her to the police. But one way or the other, she'll be free of it. The last of Vietnam locked inside her, next to her heart, will be gone.

The doctor comes in rubbing his hands on a towel. Tan catches her breath, tries to look calm. She wonders what she'll do when her eyes are round and unguarded.

Hello Tan, says Dr. Yin. I've been expecting you.

Children
of the Silver Screen

RAIN BLASTS THE STREET, each gray bullet bouncing up a half-foot from the pavement before it disintegrates. There is a loud, flat smacking from the posters on the wall. Black tears stream from Bogart's eyes, strings of ink dribble from his cigarette and gun. In the background a burro smears into desert sand.

Shine unlocks the glass doors though it is still early. He examines his reflection — forty, pleasant-looking but not handsome. Comic relief maybe, or the hero's older brother. He has always thought of himself as a sidekick, but never found a Duke Wayne to play Ward Bond to. The type that could never carry a picture alone.

The regulars start to trickle in, sniffing and dripping on the nearly bald red carpet, and Shine calls Gerald out to man the tickets. Gerald is deep into Eisenstein today, making change and tearing stubs without looking up, scowling intently at the book in his lap. "Montage," he mutters from time to time, nodding his head. "Montage."

They straggle past him, the buck-twenty-five matinee regulars, stomping their feet and blowing their noses, peeking back uneasily at the storm-slapped doors. Shine slides behind the candy counter and stations himself between gurgling tanks of orange and purple. He tries to guess what each will have, though there is not much to guess at with the regulars. Raisinets are a big mover, as are Black Crows and Chuckles, but the word has spread that the mr. Goodbars are past their prime.

The regulars mill beneath publicity pix of stars past and stars present, touring the lobby walls like penitents making the Stations of the Cross. A tall girl, made taller by the ruby-colored platforms she stands on, pops jawbreakers with her back teeth and wrinkles her nose at Carmen Miranda. The ruby is repeated on the girl's fingernails and wide, painted mouth, her polka-dot blouse is cinched in at the waist and puffed at the shoulders. Carmen Miranda smiles back, top-heavy with fruit, face frozen in a wink. Hard candy crunches, plastic jewelry clacks and the tall girl hums the opening to "Give Me a Band and a Bandanna." Catholic Prep boys, four of them, fidget and jostle in the middle of the floor and periodically bust out laughing at some enormous adolescent in-joke. A shifting, self-conscious island, they pace in their blue-nylon school jackets, flitting their eyes to the full-length lobby mirror with each pass and swiping furtively at the hair hanging wet on their foreheads. A very fat girl under an orange poncho drifts near the counter, sighing down into the glass, then tears herself away to stand by the water fountain. Her eyes never leave the bin of too-yellow popcorn. Two young men in tight, bright jean-suits sit on the black Nauga-hyde couch crossing their legs so their toes nuzzle between them, discussing triumphs and tragedies of the Great Ladies. Marvelous, they say — exquisite. It is all Marlene, Bette and Babs with them, Judy and Barbra and Joan and of course Poor Marilyn. They share a box of wintergreen Canada Mints and jiggle their matching two-tone saddle shoes. A thick-bodied old woman in tweeds enters, shaking droplets from her long, black umbrella. She sees Shine behind the counter and comes over to express her condolences.

"You've given us all a great deal of pleasure," she says, "I think you should know that we appreciate it."

They blow in, the Jujyfruits and Almond Joys, Junior Mints and Planters nuts, they grin and wince into bad Bogart impressions, they match wits naming the Magnificent Seven, or the Seven Dwarfs, or the seven major Golden Age studios. Dopey, they say, Warners and Universal. Steve McQueen and Charles Bronson, they say. Grumpy. A boy who looks like the Spirit of Che Guevera does a soggy soft-shoe in front of the men's-room door. The fat girl in the poncho tumbles for a box of popcorn, large, with a nickel's extra butter. A boy in a cape and a girl with a yellow slicker do a brief exchange from a Marx Brothers' picture and the young men on the couch roll their eyes and cluck their tongues. Old Pudge comes out from the projectionist's booth and nods to Shine. The lobby empties into the theater.

Shine flicks switches and the tanks of orange and purple settle, the yellow bulb in the popcorn machine goes out. A girl in an Army fatigue jacket comes in sopping and pays Gerald in quarters and dimes. She asks Shine for Good and Plentys, then rattles them loudly inside the box. "Lotta leg room in there," she says and grins. A boy with a bad complexion and an armful of books sheltered under his coat buys a ticket and then asks what is playing. Shine closes the back of the counter and locks it. The empty street seen through the streaming glass doors has no edges, cars and buildings appear out of focus. The theme from *The Treasure of the Sierra Madre* begins in the theater and Shine tells Gerald he can go read in the office.

A car washes up in front of the doors and Eddie Pincus — Pincus Jr. — scurries in with a large box in his arms. He passes Shine without speaking, heading for the office. Eddie is wearing a red pointy-collared shirt and plaid pants, shoes with semi-Cuban heels, and rings on all the fingers of his left hand. An Italian-hood type, thinks Shine, down low in the organization. A gunsel. A Dead End Kid pushing thirty. Pincus Jr. comes back empty-handed, goes to the car and brings in another box. Shine counts ticket stubs so their eyes won't meet. Before he leaves for good Eddie reaches over the counter and scoops himself a handful of popcorn, leaving a trail on the carpet.

Inside the theater Bogart and Tim Holt catch up with the labor contractor who has stiffed them. They argue, then fight silhouetted in stark barroom light till the contractor lies bleeding on the floor. The two winners take only what they are owed from his wallet.

Shine brings the stubs and the cashbox to the office. His swivel chair is occupied. "They never picked this up," says Gerald nodding toward two film cans on the desk, "and Mr. Pincus wants you to clear your stuff out today."

Shine leans against the desk and dials a number.

"Mr. Brandt's office, may I help you?"

"This is Mr. Shine? And I'd like to —"

"Mr. Brandt took special pains to see that you received a good print. If there's anything wrong with it then it happened on your end."

"No, see, the print —"

"In fact we're considering charging you for restoration of a few we've gotten back from you —"

"The print is fine."

"— there is also some evidence of extra screenings not provided for in our agreements. Film is a delicate medium, Mr. Shine —"

"Miss, you didn't pick up the last one."

"Pardon?"

"You didn't come and pick up last week's feature from us. *On the Town*. Gene Kelly and Frank Sinatra? I thought you might want it."

"Oh. Oh dear. Let me check something."

There is a long silence. Gerald begins to nod at his book. "Mise-en-scène," he says.

"Mr. Shine? We're very sorry, there's been a mix-up. How late will you people be open?"

"Till eleven. Have whoever you send just come in the back."

"We'll do that."

"I'd also like to confirm the cancellations."

"Cancellations?"

"There should be a letter on your desk by now."

"You realize, Mr. Shine, that there is a fee for cancellations? We take a loss on the arrangements we make. Ordering, shipping, things like that."

"Don't try to con me, Miss, you've got all our standards in stock. So put them back on the shelf."

"There is a fee for cancellations."

"You can take that up with Mr. Pincus," he says, and hangs up. "Film," he says to Gerald, "is a delicate medium."

"Time," says Gerald, deep in his book, "and space."

The two cardboard boxes Eddie Pincus brought are sitting in the corner, their tops wet. Shine can't read the smeared label and pulls one open to see. There are a couple pages of promotional literature lying on top of a boxful of tinted plastic glasses in cardboard frames. At the bottom of the promo there is a blob of pink roughly in the form of a woman. Shine puts a pair of the glasses on and the blob sharpens into a naked woman, her tits pimpling up at him from the paper. 3-D PUSSYCATS it says in mound-letters. Shine looks about him and sees that Gerald has lost all definition, the wall posters are smudged faceless, only the miniature naked lady is real anymore.

"A delicate medium."

Shine reaches around Gerald and pulls the drawers from his desk, laying them on the floor. He starts a Junk pile and a Keep pile, but keeps almost everything. Publicity photos, posters, even snippets of film — he saves them all. He sorts the posters by studio, MGM and Fox claiming the most.

"The stuff on the walls too," says Gerald. "Mr. Pincus said the stuff on the walls goes too."

Technicolor! say the posters. Cinerama! All Talking all Singing all Dancing! Brando in *The Wild One,* Dean in *Rebel,* Garfield in *The Sea Wolf* and Wayne in *Stagecoach,* all looking impossibly young and lipsticked. A picture of Shine, also impossibly young, standing with Pincus Sr., in front of the first theater. The old gentleman looking serious and dignified, his young partner grinning, out of place. Shine takes them all down and gently adds them to the pile. He imagines a cliché flashback to his youth, a slow dissolve with a harp flowing distantly on the soundtrack, till his father's face appears looking down as if to a child.

"*Our* bissness," he whispers as if sharing a great secret. "The motion-picter bissness is *our* bissness. Never forget this. Luke et Mayer," he says, "luke et Cohn. Thalberg, Selznick, Sammy Goldfish. Op front it may be American boyss, powdered meelk, Gables end Crossbys, but it's *our* bissness. We pull on the strings. Never forget this."

The camera tracks back to show a thin, middle-aged man in a faded blue usher's uniform. RIALTO it says in yellow script over the left breast.

Ridiculous casting, his father never had an accent.

Shine ties paper into bundles. The Junk pile, mostly old bills, he kicks into the corner with Eddie's 3-D glasses.

In the theater, on the screen, the three prospectors strike gold near the top of the mountain and rig a sluice to mine. There are weeks of hard, hot work. Greed creeps into the camp, and paranoia. They begin to split each day's take three ways and hide their goods from each other in the bush. Banditos attack, their leader Gold Hat braying evilly to set the standard for a generation of Mexican outlaws. An outsider tries to extort his way into the find and is killed. The gold begins to peter out and the men break camp, first putting the mountain back the way they found it. Thanks mountain, they say as they head down the trail toward civilization.

The old man, Walter Huston, is taken by Indians to be honored for saving a half-drowned native boy, leaving Bogart and bland Tim Holt to manage all the heavy-laden burros. Gold-fever and isolation begin to work on Bogart, he grapples with Holt and has his gun taken away. They sit across the fire from each other that night, Holt wary but fading with exhaustion. We'll see who falls asleep first, says Bogart. His wild, flame-lit face breaks into Satanic laughter. We'll see who falls asleep first, partner.

During slow scenes or long dissolves there is a mass creaking as the audience shifts in the old seats, like some huge animal stretching after a century's sleep. There is an occasional wet sniff and the methodical crunching of jawbreakers in the back row. The people sit deep in their seats, prop their legs before them and tilt their heads back as if being fed a long, satisfying meal. The rain outside is faintly audible, but like the glowing red EXIT signs to either side of the screen, it has long since become subliminal. The drying clothes and wet hair give off a woolly must peppered with sweat and cola and aged peppermint gum. Someone in the front has a mild case of asthma.

The phone rings in the office. Gerald listens for a moment, then offers it up to Shine.

"Hello."

"Mr. Shine?"

"Yes."

"This is Arnold Marchand of Picoso Productions? We've been informed that your theater operation is undergoing a change of policy, and we'd like to give you the chance to look over our line and see if we can do some business."

"I'm not in business anymore."

"This is Mr. Shine, isn't it?"

"Yes, but —"

"It won't be any trouble, we'll just bring down a few samples of the product for a screening. You know, trailers of the best scenes cut together —"

"I don't think you —"

"Some of our double bills have been getting very heavy traffic in your area. Did you catch *Teenage Temptress* and *Evita* at the State-Ex?"

"No."

"Ours. Played five weeks, house record. Area's been saturated with those two of course, but there's plenty more where —"

"I'm not connected with booking anymore. You'll have to speak with Mr. Pincus."

"We can supply all the promotion ourselves, it's written into the rental. Whatsay we set up a meeting Saturday, four-thirty, maybe five?"

"Talk to Pincus."

"We've got the full range, hard-core right down to Russ Meyer and the cuntless wonders, we —"

Shine hangs up. "Trash," he says to Gerald. "He's buying trash."

"So what do you call this stuff?" Gerald nods to the bundle of posters. "Art? It's pornography of the spirit, Hollywood propaganda, fluff. Different brand of trash, that's all." He returns to his book.

The phone rings again. Shine grits his teeth and lifts it. "Talk to Pincus."

"Pardon?" It is a new voice.

"Oh. Sorry. What can I do for you?"

"When are you going to have the wizard again?"

"The wizard?"

"Of Oz. When are you going to have it again?"

"I don't know," says Shine, "but I wouldn't hold my breath."

Bogart gains the upper hand and wounds Tim Holt, leaving him for dead in the brush. He tries to handle all the burros and gold himself. Not far from safety, he runs into Gold Hat and two other banditos. The two try on his hat and measure his boots as he tries to bluff them into thinking help is on its way. Gold Hat cuts him down with a machete, and not knowing unrefined gold dust from sand, slashes the bags open, leaves them lying on the desert floor and scrambles after the burros. A wind begins to pick up.

Meanwhile, Holt has been found by Indians and brought to the old man. His wounds are treated and they mount up to search for Bogart.

The phone rings again. Gerald leaves to find a spot where he can read in peace till the six-o'clock showing. "Cross-cutting," he mumbles at the door.

Shine answers. "No," he says. "*Top Hat* won't be playing tomorrow. Did you try the University? Right, bye now."

Shine puts the cans of film under his arm and goes to the lobby. The rain is heavier outside, boiling on the pavement and glass. He walks into the theater and stands at the head of the aisle. The desert wind is roaring now, Holt and the old man barely visible through the blasted sand. Shine stands with the rainstorm behind him and the dust-blow before and lets out a long, shuddering sigh. The old man and Holt find the split bags, empty now, and squat behind a crumbling adobe wall for shelter. The fortune they work months to mine and risk their lives for has blown away. Shine is shivering now and the old man begins to laugh — loud, desperate to-keep-from-crying laughter that Holt joins in, the laugh of men who have reached bottom and found it bearable. Shine is warmed for a moment, their laughter drowning out wind and rain alike, but then the movie is over and old Pudge brings the lights up before the credits are finished. There is a long, blinking silence, the audience surprised it is ended. The world is in color now, washed-out color, tufts of yellowish stuffing peek from split seat cushions, rips and seams are visible on the mottled-white screen. The people rise like roughly wakened sleepers, rubbing eyes and buckling coats, and file past Shine into the lobby. He sees a stationary head left near the front and walks up to it. It is the old tweed-lady, asleep, smiling slightly. He leaves her to rest.

In the lobby he finds them all stalled before the storm. They wriggle in their coats and stomp their feet for warmth, psyching up, they take turns pressing noses against the glass to check the downpour. No one looks eager to leave, they glance back nervously at Shine, read the wall posters, adjust clothing. No one wants to open the door and let it in.

"Listen," Shine calls to them, "would you like to stay and see a musical? *On the Town.* For free?"

They turn, smiling uncertainly, and cheat back toward the theater a bit.

"Come on," he says, "it's wet out there." They grin, conspirators with Shine, and file back in.

He tells old Pudge to go home and that the union can fuck itself, if he wants to run it himself he will. He has trouble threading the film, it has been a long time, and twice he curses and almost gives up. But he hears the rain beating outside and thinks of the teenage temptresses, the soft-core quickies that will follow him here and finally all the sprocket holes engage, the leader snakes through the guts of the machine and fastens to the take-up reel. Shine brings down the lights and the audience grows quiet. The title appears blurred at first, as if seen through a film of tears, and Shine is a technician for a moment longer, adjusting till it is sharp. There is an applause of recognition. Shine turns out all but the pilot light in the booth and waits as the clatter of the machine fades from his mind, taking the rainstorm with it. He flows onto the shaft of dancing light and is carried forward to safety, to the bright, warm colors, into the pulse and flicker of life.

I-80 Nebraska,
m. 490–m. 205

THIS IS THAT ALABAMA REBEL, this is that Alabama Rebel, do I have a copy?"

"Ahh, 10-4 on that, Alabama Rebel."

"This is that Alabama Rebel westbound on 80, ah, what's your handle, buddy, and where you comin from?"

"This is that, ah, Toby Trucker, eastbound for that big O town, round about the 445 marker."

"I copy you clear, Toby Trucker. How's about that Smokey Bear situation up by that Lincoln town?"

"Ah, you'll have to hold her back a little through there, Alabama Rebel, ah, place is crawling with Smokies like usual. Saw three of em's lights up on the overpass just after the airport there."

"And how bout that Lincoln weigh station, they got those scales open?"

"Ah, negative on that, Alabama Rebel, I went by the lights was off, probably still in business back to that North Platte town."

"They don't get you coming they get you going. How bout that you-know-who, any sign of him tonight? That Ryder P. Moses?"

"Negative on that, thank God. Guy gives me the creeps."

"Did you, ah, ever actually hear him, Toby Trucker?"

"A definite 10-4 on that one, Alabama Rebel, and I'll never forget it. Coming down from that Scottsbluff town three nights ago I copied him. First he says he's northbound, then he says he's southbound, then he's right on my tail singing 'The Wabash Cannonball.' Man blew by me outside of that Oshkosh town on 26, must of been going a hundred plus. Little two-lane blacktop and he thinks he's Parnelli Jones at the Firecracker 500."

"You see him? You see what kind of rig he had?"

"A definite shit-no negative on that, I was fighting to keep the road. The man aint human."

"Ah, maybe not, Toby Trucker, maybe not. Never copied him myself, but I talked with a dozen guys who have in the last couple weeks."

"Ahh, maybe you'll catch him tonight."

"Long as he don't catch me."

"Got a point there, Alabama Rebel. Ahhhh, I seem to be losing you here —"

"10-4. Coming up to that Lincoln town, buddy, I thank you kindly for the information and ah, I hope you stay out of trouble in that big O town and maybe we'll modulate again some night. This is that Alabama Rebel, over and out."

"This is Toby Trucker, eastbound, night now."

Westbound on 80 is a light-stream, ruby-strung big rigs rolling straight into the heart of Nebraska. Up close they are a river in breakaway flood, bouncing and pitching and yawing, while a mile distant they are slow-oozing lava. To their left is the eastbound stream, up ahead the static glare of Lincoln. Lights. The world in black and white and red, broken only by an occasional blue flasher strobing the ranger hat of a state policeman. Smokey the Bear's campfire. Westbound 80 is an insomniac world of lights passing lights to the music of the Citizens Band.

"This that Arkansas Traveler, this that Arkansas Traveler, do you copy?"

"How bout that Scorpio Ascending, how bout that Scorpio Ascending, you out there, buddy?"

"This is Chromedome at that 425 marker, who's that circus wagon up ahead? Who's that old boy in the Mrs. Smith's pie-pusher?"

They own the highway at night, the big rigs, slip-streaming in caravans, hopscotching to take turns making the draft, strutting the thousands of dollars they've paid in road taxes on their back ends. The men feel at home out here, they leave their cross-eyed headlights eating whiteline, forget their oily-aired, kidney-jamming cabs to talk out in the black air, to live on the Band.

"This is Roadrunner, westbound at 420, any you eastbound people fill me in on the Smokies up ahead?"

"Ahh, copy you, Roadrunner, she's been clean all the way from that Grand Island town, so motormotor."

(A moving van accelerates.)

"How bout that Roadrunner, this is Overload up to 424, that you behind me?"

(The van's headlights blink up and down.)

"Well come on up, buddy, let's put the hammer down on this thing."

The voices are nasal and tinny, broken by squawks, something human squeezed through wire. A decade of televised astronauts gives them their style and self-importance.

"Ahh, breaker, Overload, we got us a code blue here. There's a four-wheeler coming up fast behind me, might be a Bear wants to give us some green stamps."

"Breaker break, Roadrunner. Good to have you at the back door. We'll hold her back awhile, let you check out that four-wheeler."

(The big rigs slow and the passenger car pulls alongside of them.)

"Ahh, negative on that Bear, Overload, it's just a civilian. Fella hasn't heard bout that five-five limit."

"10-4 and motormotor."

(Up front now, the car is nearly whooshed off the road when the big rigs blow past. It wavers a moment, then accelerates to try and take them, but can only make it alongside before they speed up. The car falls back, then tries again.)

"Ah, look like we got us a problem, Roadrunner. This uh, Vega — whatever it is, some piece of Detroit shit, wants to play games."

"Looks like it, Overload."

"Don't know what a four-wheeler is doing on the Innerstate this time of night anyhow. Shunt be allowed out with us working people. You want to give me a hand on this, Roadrunner?"

"10-4. I'll be the trapper, you be the sweeper. What we got ahead?"

"There's an exit up to the 402 marker. This fucker gets off the ride at Beaver Crossing."

(The trucks slow and the car passes them, honking, cutting sharp to the inside lane. They let it cruise for a moment, then the lead rig pulls alongside of it and the second closes up behind, inches from the car's rear fender. The car tries to run but they stay with it, boxing it, then pushing it faster and faster till the sign appears ahead on the right and the lead truck bulls to the inside, forcing the car to squeal off onto the exit ramp.)

"Mission accomplished there, Roadrunner."

"Roger."

They have their own rules, the big rigs, their own road and radio etiquette that is tougher in its way than the Smokies' law. You join the club, you learn the rules, and woe to the man who breaks them.

"All you westbound! All you westbound! Keep your ears

peeled up ahead for that you-know-who! He's on the loose
again tonight! Ryder P. Moses!"

There is a crowding of channels, a buzzing on the airwaves.
Ryder P. Moses!

"Who?"

"Ryder P. Moses! Where you been, trucker?"

"Who is he?"

"Ryder —!"

"— crazy —"

"— weird —"

"— P. —!"

"— dangerous —"

"— probly a cop —"

"— Moses!"

"He's out there tonight!"

"I copied him going eastbound."

"I copied him westbound."

"I copied him standing still on an overpass."

Ryder P. Moses!

On 80 tonight. Out there somewhere. Which set of lights,
which channel, is he listening? Does he know we know?

What do we know?

Only that he's been copied on and around 80 every night
for a couple weeks now and that he's a terminal case of the
heebie-jeebs, he's an overdose of strange. He's been getting
worse and worse, wilder and wilder, breaking every trucker
commandment and getting away with it. Ryder P. Moses, he
says, no handle, no Gutslinger or Green Monster or Oklahoma Crude, just Ryder P. Moses. No games with the
Smokies, no hide-and-seek, just an open challenge. This is
Ryder P. Moses eastbound at 260, going ninety per, he says.
Catch me if you can. But the Smokies can't, and it bugs the
piss out of them, so they're thick as flies along Nebraska 80,
hunting for the crazy son, nailing poor innocent everyday
truckers poking at seventy-five. Ryder P. Moses. Memorizes

your license, your make, and your handle, then describes you
from miles away, when you can't see another light on the
entire plain, and tells you he's right behind you, watch out,
here he comes right up your ass, watch out watch out! Modu-
lating from what must be an illegal amount of wattage,
coming on sometimes with "Ici Radio Canada" and gibber-
ing phony frog over the CB, warning of ten-truck pileups and
collapsed overpasses that never appear, leading truckers to
put the hammer down right into a Smokey with a picture
machine till nobody knows who to believe over the Band
anymore. Till conversations start with "I am not now nor
have I ever been Ryder P. Moses." A truck driver's gremlin
that everyone has either heard or heard about, but no one has
ever seen.

"Who is this Ryder P. Moses? Int that name familiar?"

"Wunt he that crazy independent got hisself shot up during the Troubles?"

"Wunt he a leg-breaker for the Teamsters?"

"Dint he use to be with P.I.E.?"

"— Allied?"

"— Continental Freightways?"

"— drive a 2500-gallon oil tanker?"

"— run liquor during Prohibition?"

"— run nylons during the War?"

"— run turkeys during Christmas?"

"Int that the guy? Sure it is."

"Short fella."

"Tall guy."

"Scar on his forehead, walks with a limp, left-hand index
finger is missing."

"Sure, right, wears a leather jacket."

"— and a down vest."

"— and a lumber jacket and a Hawaiian shirt and a crucifix
round his neck."

"Sure, that's the fella, medium height, always dressed in black. Ryder P. Moses."

"Dint he die a couple years back?"

"Sheeit, they aint no such person an never was."

"Ryder P. who?"

"Moses. This is Ryder P. Moses."

"What? Who said that?!"

"I did. Good evening, gentlemen."

Fingers fumble for volume knobs and squelch controls, conversations are dropped and attention turned. The voice is deep and emphatic.

"I'm Ryder P. Moses and I can outhaul, outhonk, out-clutch any leadfoot this side of truckers' heaven. I'm half Mack, half Peterbilt, and half Sherman don't-tread-on-me tank. I drink fifty gallons of propane for breakfast and fart pure poison, I got steel-mesh teeth, a chrome-plated nose, and three feet of stick on the floor. I'm the Paul mother-lovin Bunyan of the Interstate system and I don't care who knows it. I'm Ryder P. Moses and all you people are driving on *my* goddam road. Don't you spit, don't you litter, don't you pee on the pavement. Just mind your p's and q's and we won't have any trouble."

Trucks pull alongside each other, the drivers peering across suspiciously, then both wave hands over head to deny guilt. They change channels and check each other out — handle, company, destination. They gang up on other loners and demand identification, challenge each other with trivia as if the intruder were a Martian or a Nazi spy. What's the capital of Tennessee, Tennessee Stomper? How far from Laramie to Cheyenne town, Casper Kid? Who won the '38 World Series, Truckin Poppa?

Small convoys form, grow larger, posses ranging east-bound and westbound on I-80. Only the CB can prove that

the enemy is not among them, not the neighboring pair of
taillights, the row of red up top like Orion's belt. He scares
them for a moment, this Ryder P. Moses, scares them out of
the air and back into their jarring hotboxes, back to work.
But he thrills them a little, too.

"You still there fellas? Good. It's question-and-answer
period. Answer me this: do you know where your wife or
loved one is right now? I mean *really know* for sure? You
been gone a long time fellas, and you know how they are.
Weak before Temptation. That's why we love em, that's how
we get next to em in the first place, int it, fellas? There's just
no telling *what* they're up to, is there? How bout that Alabama Rebel, you know where that little girl of yours is right
now? What she's gettin herself into? This minute? And you
there, Overload, how come the old lady's always so tired
when you pull in late at night? What's she done to be so
fagged out? She aint been haulin freight all day like you
have. Or has she? I tell you fellas, take a tip from old Ryder
P., you cain't ever be certain of a *thing* in this world. You out
here ridin the Interstate, somebody's likely back home ridin
that little girl. I mean just *think* about it, think about the
way she looks, the faces she makes, the way she starts to smell,
the things she says. The *noises* she makes. Now picture them
shoes under that bed, aint they a little too big? Since when
did you wear size twelves? Buddy, I hate to break it to you
but maybe she's right now giving it, giving those faces and
that smell and those noises, giving it all to some other guy.

"Some size twelve.

"You know how they are, those women, you see them in
the truckstops pouring coffee. All those Billie Raes and
Bobbi Sues, those Debbies and Annettes, those ass-twitching
little things you marry and try to keep in a house. You know
how they are. They're not built for one man, fellas, it's a fact
of nature. I just want you to think about that for a while,

chew on it, remember the last time you saw your woman and figure how long it'll be before you see her again. Think on it, fellas."

And, over the cursing and threats of truckers flooding his channel, he begins to sing —

> *In the phone booth — at the truckstop*
> *All alone,*
> *I listen to the constant ringing — of your phone.*
> *I'd try the bars and hangouts where*
> *You might be found,*
> *But I don't dare,*
> *You might be there,*
> *You're slippin round.*

They curse and threaten but none of them turn him off. And some do think on it. Think as they have so many times before, distrusting with or without evidence, hundred-mile stretches of loneliness and paranoia. How can they know for sure their woman is any different from what they believe all women they meet to be — willing, hot, eager for action? Game in season. What *does* she do, all that riding time?

> *I imagine — as I'm hauling*
> *Back this load,*
> *You waiting for me — at the finish*
> *Of the road.*
> *But as I wait for your hello*
> *There's not a sound.*
> *I start to weep,*
> *You're not asleep,*
> *You're slippin round.*

The truckers overcrowd the channel in their rush to copy him, producing only a squarking complaint, something like a chorus of "Old MacDonald" sung from fifty fathoms deep. Finally the voice of Sweetpea comes through the jam and the others defer to her, as they always do. They have almost all seen her at one time or another, at some table in the Truckers Only section of this or that pit stop, and know she is a regular old gal, handsome-looking in a country sort of way and able to field a joke and toss it back. Not so brassy as Colorado Hooker, not so butch as Flatbed Mama, you'd let that Sweetpea carry your load any old day.

"How bout that Ryder P. Moses, how bout that Ryder P. Moses, you out there, sugar? You like to modulate with me a little bit?"

The truckers listen, envying the crazy son for this bit of female attention.

"Ryder P.? This is that Sweetpea moving along bout that 390 mark, do you copy me?"

"Ah yes, the Grande Dame of the Open Road! How's everything with Your Highness tonight?"

"Oh, passable, Mr. Moses, passable. But you don't sound none too good yourself, if you don't mind my saying. I mean we're just worried *sick* about you. You sound a little — overstrained?"

"*Au contraire,* Madam, *au contraire.*"

She's got him, she has. You catch more flies with honey than with vinegar.

"Now tell me, honey, when's the last time you had yourself any sleep?"

"Sleep? *Sleep* she says! Who sleeps?"

"Why just *ev*rybody, Mr. Moses. It's a natural fact."

"That, Madam, is where you are mistaken. Sleep is obsolete, a thing of the bygone ages. It's been synthesized, chemically duplicated and sold at your corner apothecary. You can load up on it before a long trip —"

"Now I just don't know *what* you're talkin bout."

"Insensibility, Madam, stupor. The gift of Morpheus."

"Fun is fun, Ryder P. Moses, but you just not making *sense*. We are *not* amused. And we all getting a little bit *tired* of all your prankin around. And we —"

"Tired, did you say? Depressed? Overweight? Got that run-down feeling? Miles to go before you sleep? Friends and neighbors, I got just the thing for you, a miracle of modern pharmacology! Vim and vigor, zip and zest, bright eyes and bushy tails — all these can be *yours*, neighbors, relief is just a swallow away! A couple of Co-Pilots in the morning orange juice, Purple Hearts for lunch, a mouthful of Coast-to-Coast for the wee hours of the night, and you'll droop no more. Ladies and gents, the best cure for time and distance is Speed. And we're all familiar with that, aren't we folks? We've all popped a little pep in our day, haven't we? Puts you on top of the world and clears your sinuses to boot. Wire yourself home with a little methamphetamine sulfate, melts in your mind, not in your mouth. No chocolate mess. Step right up and get on the ride, pay no heed to that man with the eight-ball eyes! Start with a little Propadrine maybe, from the little woman's medicine cabinet? Clear up that stuffy nose? Then work your way up to the full-tilt boogie, twelve-plus grams of Crystal a day! It kind of grows on you, doesn't it, neighbor? Start eating that Sleep and you won't want to eat anything else. You know all about it, don't you, brothers and sisters of the Civilian Band, you've all been on that roller coaster. The only way to fly."

"Now, Ryder, you just calm —"

> *Benzedrine, Dexedrine,*
> *We got the stash!*

he chants like a high-school cheerleader,

> *Another thousand miles*
> *Before the crash.*

"Mr. Moses, you can't —"

> *Coffee and aspirin,*
> *No-Doz, meth.*
> *Spasms, hypertension,*
> *Narcolepsy, death.*
>
> *Alpha, methyl,*
> *Phenyl too,*
> *Ethyl-amine's good for you!*
>
> *Cause when you're up you're up,*
> *An when you're down you're down,*
> *But when you're up behind Crystal*
> *You're upside down!*

The airwaves crackle with annoyance. Singing on the CB! Sassing their woman, their Sweetpea, with drug talk and four-syllable words!

"— man's crazy —"

"— s'got to go —"

"— FCC ever hears —"

"— fix his wagon —"

"—like to catch —"

"— hophead —"

"— pill-poppin —"

"— weird-talkin —"

"— turn him *off!*"

"Now boys," modulates Sweetpea, cooing soft and smooth, "I'm sure we can talk this whole thing out. Ryder P., honey, whoever you are, you must be runnin out of *fuel.* I mean you been going at it for *days* now, flittin round this Innerstate never coming to light. Must be just all *out* by now, aren't you?"

"I'm going strong, little lady, I got a bottle full of energy left and a thermos of Maxwell House to wash them down with."

"I don't mean *that*, Mr. Moses, I mean fuel *awl*. Int your tanks a little low? Must be runnin pert near empty, aren't you?"

"Madam, you have a point."

"Well if you don't fuel up pretty soon, you just gon be out of *luck*, Mister, they isn't but one more place westbound between here and that Grand Island town. Now Imo pull in that Bosselman's up ahead, fill this old hog of mine up. Wynch you just join me, I'll buy you a cup of coffee and we'll have us a little chitchat? That truck you got, whatever it is, can't run on no *pills*."

"Madam, it's a date. I got five or six miles to do and then it's Bosselman's for me and Old Paint here. Yes indeedy."

The other channels come alive. Bosselman's, on the westbound, he's coming down! That Sweetpea could talk tears from a statue, an oyster from its shell. Ryder P. Moses in person, hotdam!

They barrel onto the off-ramp, eastbound and westbound, full tanks and empty, a steady caravan of light bleeding off the main artery, leaving only scattered four-wheelers to carry on. They line up behind the diner in rows, twin stacks belching, all ears.

"This is that Ryder P. Moses, this is that Ryder P. Moses, in the parking lot at Bosselman's. Meet you in the coffee shop, Sweetpea."

Cab doors swing open and they vault down onto the gravel, some kind of reverse Grand Prix start, with men trotting away from their machines to the diner. They stampede at the door and mill suspiciously. Is that him, is that him? Faces begin to connect with handles, remembered from some previous nighttime break. Hey, there's old Roadrunner, Roadrunner, this is Arkansas Traveler, I known him from before, he aint it, who's that over there? Overload, you say? You was up on I-29 the other night, north of Council Bluffs, wunt you? What you mean no, I had you on for pert near a half-hour! You were where? Who says? Roadrunner, how could you talk to him on Nebraska 83 when I'm talking to him on I-29? Overload, somebody been takin your name in vain. What's that? You modulated with me yesterday from Rawlins? Buddy, I'm out of that Davenport town last evening, I'm *west*bound. Clutch Cargo, the one and only, always was and always will be. You're kidding! The name-droppin snake! Fellas we got to get to the bottom of this, but quick.

It begins to be clear, as they form into groups of three or four who can vouch for each other, that this Ryder P. Moses works in mysterious ways. That his voice, strained through capacitors and diodes, can pass for any of theirs, that he knows them, handle and style. It's outrageous, it is, it's like stealing mail or wiretapping, like forgery. How long has he gotten away with it, what has he said using their identities, what secrets spilled or discovered? If Ryder P. Moses has been each of them from time to time, what is to stop him from being one of them now? Which old boy among them is running a double life, which has got a glazed look around the eyes, a guilty twitch at the mouth? They file in to find Sweetpea sitting at a booth, alone.

"Boys," she says, "I believe I just been stood up."

They grumble back to their rigs, leaving waitresses with order pads gaping. The civilians in the diner buzz and puzzle — some mass, vigilante threat? Teamster extortion? Paramilitary maneuvers? They didn't like the menu? The trucks roar from the Bosselman's abruptly as they came.

On the Interstate again, they hear the story from Axle Sally. Sally broadcasts from the Husky three miles up on the eastbound side. Seems a cattle truck is pulled up by the pumps there, left idling. The boy doesn't see the driver, all he knows is it's pretty ripe, even for a stock-hauler. Something more than the usual cowshit oozing out from the air spaces. He tries to get a look inside but it's hard to get that close with the smell and all, so he grabs his flashlight and plays it around in back. And what do you think he sees? Dead. Dead for some time from the look of them, ribs showing, legs splayed, a heap of bad meat. Between the time it takes the boy to run in to tell Sally till they get back out to the pumps, whoever it was driving the thing has pumped himself twenty gallons and taken a powder. Then comes the call to Sally's radio, put it on my tab, he says. Ryder P. Moses, westbound.

They can smell it in their minds, the men who have run cattle or have had a stock wagon park beside them in the sleeping lot of some truckstop, the thought of it makes them near sick. Crazy. Stone wild crazy.

"Hello there again, friends and neighbors, this is Ryder P. Moses, the Demon of the Dotted Line, the Houdini of the Highways. Hell on eighteen wheels. Sorry if I inconvenienced anybody with the little change of plans there, but fuel oil was going for two cents a gallon cheaper at the Husky, and I never could pass up a bargain. Funny I didn't see any of you folks there, y'ought to be a little sharper with your consumer affairs. These are hard times, people, don't see how you can afford to let that kind of savings go by. I mean us truckers of all people should see the writing on the wall, the bad news in the dollars-and-cents department. Do we 'Keep America Moving' or don't we? And you know as well as me, there aint shit moving these days. Poor honest independent don't have a Chinaman's chance, and even Union people are being unsaddled left and right. Hard times, children. Just isn't enough stuff has to get from here to there to keep us in business. Hell, the only way to make it is to carry miscellaneous freight. Get that per-item charge on a full load and you're golden. Miscellaneous —"

(The blue flashers are coming now, zipping by the west-

bound truckers, sirenless in twos and threes, breaking onto
the channel to say don't panic, boys, all we want is the cattle
truck. All the trophy we need for tonight is Moses, you just
lay back and relax. Oh those Smokies, when they set their
minds to a thing they don't hold back, they hump after it full
choke and don't spare the horse. Ryder P. Moses, your ass is
grass. Smokey the Bear on your case and he will douse your
fire. Oh yes.)

"— freight. Miscellaneous freight. Think about it, friends
and neighbors, brothers and sisters, think about what exactly
it is we haul all over God's creation here, about the goods and
what they mean. About what they actually mean to you and
me and everyone else in this great and good corporate land of
ours. Think of what you're hauling right now. Ambergris for
Amarillo? Gaskets for Gary? Oil for Ogallala, submarines for
Schenectady? Veal for Vermillion?"

(The Smokies moving up at nearly a hundred per, a shooting stream in the outside lane, for once allied to the truckers.)

"Tomato for Mankato, manna for Tarzana, stew for Kala-
mazoo, jerky for Albuquerque. Fruit for Butte."

(Outdistancing all the legitimate truckers, the Smokies are
a blue pulsing in the sky ahead, the whole night on the
blink.)

"Boise potatoes for Pittsburgh pots. Scottsbluff sugar for
Tampa tea. Forage and fertilizer. Guns and caskets. Bull
semen and hamburger. Sweet-corn, soy, stethoscopes and
slide rules. Androids and zinnias. But folks, somehow we
always come back empty. Come back less than we went.
Diminished. It's a law of nature, it is, a law —"

They come upon it at the 375 marker, a convention of
Bears flashing around a cattle truck on the shoulder of the
road. What looks to be a boy or a very young man spread-
eagled against the side of the cab, a half-dozen official hands
probing his hidden regions. The trucks slow, one by one, but

there is no room to stop. They roll down their copilot windows, but the only smell is the thick electric-blue of too many cops in one place.

"You see im? You see im? Just a kid!"

"— prolly stole it in the first place —"

"— gone crazy on drugs —"

"— fuckin hippie or somethin —"

"— got his ass but good —"

"— know who he is?"

"— know his handle?"

"— seen im before?"

"— the end of him, anyhow."

All order and etiquette gone with the excitement, they chew it over among themselves — who he might be, why he went wrong, what they'll do with him. Curiosity, and already a kind of disappointment. That soon it will be all over, all explained, held under the dull light of police classification, made into just some crackpot kid who took a few too many diet pills to help him through the night. It is hard to believe that the pale, skinny boy frisked in their headlights was who kept them turned around for weeks, who pried his way into their nightmares, who haunted the CB and outran the Smokies. That he could be the one who made the hours between Lincoln and Cheyenne melt into suspense and tension, that he could be —

"Ryder P. Moses, westbound on 80. Where *are* all you people?"

"Who?"

"What?"

"Where?"

"Ryder P. Moses, who else? Out here under that big black sky, all by his lonesome. I sure would preciate some company. Seems like you all dropped out of the running a ways back. Thought I seen some Bear tracks in my rearview, maybe that's it. Now it's just me an a couple tons of beef. Can't say these steers is much for conversation, though. Nosir, you just can't beat a little palaver with your truckin brothers and sisters on the old CB to pass the time. Do I have a copy out there? Anybody?"

They switch to the channel they agreed on at the Bosselman's, and the word goes on down the line. He's still loose! He's still out there! The strategy is agreed on quickly — silent running. Let him sweat it out alone, talk to himself for a while, and haul ass to catch him. It will be a race.

(Coyote, in an empty flatbed, takes the lead.)

"You're probably all wondering why I called you together tonight. Education. I mean to tell you some things you ought to know. Things about life, death, eternity. You know, tricks of the trade. The popular mechanics of the soul. A little exchange of ideas, communication, I-talk-you-listen, right?"

(Up ahead, far ahead, Coyote sees taillights. Taillights moving at least as fast as he, almost eighty-five in a strong crosswind. He muscles the clutch and puts the hammer down.)

"Friends, it's all a matter of wheels. Cycles. Clock hand always ends up where it started out, sun always dips back under the cornfield, people always plowed back into the ground. Take this beef chain I'm in on. We haul the semen to stud, the calves to rangeland, the one-year-olds to the feedlot, then to the slaughterhouse the packer the supermarket the corner butcher the table of J.Q. Public. J.Q. scarfs it down, puts a little body in his jizz, pumps a baby a year into the wife till his heart fattens and flops, and next thing you know he's pushing up grass on the lone pray-ree. You always end up less than what you were. The universe itself is shrinking. In cycles."

(Coyote closes to within a hundred yards. It is a cattle truck. He can smell it through his vent. When he tries to come closer it accelerates over a hundred, back end careening over two lanes. Coyote feels himself losing control, eases up. The cattle truck eases too, keeping a steady hundred yards between them. They settle back to eighty per.)

"Engines. You can grease them, oil them, clean their filters and replace their plugs, recharge them, antifreeze and STP them, treat them like a member of the family, but poppa, the miles take their toll, Time and Distance bring us all to rust. We haul engines from Plant A to Plant B to be seeded in bodies, we haul them to the dealers, buy them and waltz around a couple numbers, then drag them to the scrapyard. Junk City, U.S.A., where they break down into the iron ore of a million years from now. Some cycles take longer than others. Everything in this world is a long fall, a coming to rest, and an engine only affects where the landing will be.

"The cure for Time and Distance is Speed. Did you know that if you could travel at the speed of light you'd never age? That if you went any faster than it, you would get younger? Think about that one, friends and neighbors — a cycle reversed. What happens when you reach year zero, egg-and-tadpole time, and keep speeding along? Do you turn into your parents? Put that in your carburetor and slosh it around."

And on he goes, into Relativity, the relationship of matter and energy, into the theory of the universe as a great Möbius strip, a snake swallowing its own tail. Leaving Coyote far behind, though the hundred yards between stays constant. On he goes, into the life of a cell, gerontology, cryogenics, hibernation theory. Through the seven stages of man and beyond, through the history of aging, the literature of immortality.

(Through Grand Island and Kearney, through Lexington and Cozad and Gothenburg, with Coyote at his heels, through a hundred high-speed miles of physics and biology and lunatic-fringe theology.)

"You can beat them, though, all these cycles. Oh yes, I've

found the way. Never stop. If you never stop you can outrun them. It's when you lose your momentum that they get you.

"Take Sleep, the old whore. The seducer of the vital spark. Ever look at yourself in the mirror after Sleep has had hold of you, ever check your face out? Eyes pouched, neck lined, mouth puckered, it's all been worked on, cycled. Aged. Wrinkle City. The cycle catches you napping and carries you off a little closer to the ground. Sleep, ladies, when it has you under, those crows come tiptoeing on your face, sinking their tracks into you. Sleep, gents, you wake from her half stiff with urine, stumble out to do an old man's aimless, too-yellow pee. It bloats your prostate, pulls your paunch, plugs your ears, and gauzes your eyes. It sucks you, Sleep, sucks you dry and empty, strains the dream from your mind and the life from your body."

(Reflector posts ripping by, engine complaining, the two of them barreling into Nebraska on the far edge of control.)

"And you people let it have you, you surrender with open arms. Not me. Not Ryder P. Moses. I swallow my sleep in capsules and keep one step ahead. Rest not, rust not. Once you break from the cycle, escape that dull gravity, then, people, you travel in a straight line and there is nothing so pure in this world. The Interstate goes on forever and you never have to get off.

"And it's beautiful. Beautiful. The things a sleeper never sees open up to you. The most beautiful dream is the waking one, the one that never ends. From a straight line you see all the cycles going on without you, night fading in and out, the sun's arch, stars forming and shifting in their signs. The night especially, the blacker the better, your headlights making a ghost of color on the roadside, focusing to climb the whiteline. You feel like you can ride deeper and deeper into it, that night is a state you never cross, but only get closer and closer to its center. And in the daytime there's the static of cornfields, cornfields, cornfields, flat monotony like a hum in your eye, like you're going so fast it seems you're standing still, that the country is a still life on your windshield."

(It begins to weave gently in front of Coyote now, easing to the far right, nicking the shoulder gravel, straightening for a few miles, then drifting left. Nodding. Coyote hangs back a little farther, held at bay by a whiff of danger.)

"Do you know what metaphor is, truckin mamas and poppas? Have you ever met with it in your waking hours? Benzedrine, there's a metaphor for you, and a good one. For sleep. It serves the same purpose but makes you understand better, makes everything clearer, opens the way to more metaphor. Friends and neighbors, have you ever seen dinosaurs lumbering past you, the road sizzle like a fuse, night drip down like old blood? I have, people, I've seen things only gods and the grandfather stars have seen, I've seen dead men sit in my cab beside me and living ones melt like wax. When you break through the cycle you're beyond the laws of man, beyond CB manners or Smokies' sirens or statutes of limitations. You're beyond the laws of nature, time, gravity, friction, forget them. The only way to win is never to stop. Never to stop. Never to stop."

The sentences are strung out now, a full minute or two between them.

"The only escape from friction is a vacuum."

(Miles flying under, North Platte glowing vaguely ahead on the horizon, Coyote, dogged, hangs on.)

There is an inexplicable crackling on the wire, as if he were growing distant. There is nothing for miles to interfere between them. "The shortest distance — between two points — ahh — a straight line."

(Two alone on the plain, tunneling Nebraska darkness.)

"Even the earth — is falling. Even — the sun — is burning out."

(The side-to-side drifting more pronounced now, returns to the middle more brief. Coyote strains to pick the voice from electric jam, North Platte's display brightens. Miles pass.)

"Straight —"

There is a very loud crackling now, his speaker open but his words hung, a crackling past the Brady exit, past Maxwell. (Coyote creeping up a bit, then lagging as the stockhauler picks up speed and begins to slalom for real, Coyote tailing it like a hunter after a gut-ripped animal spilling its last, and louder crackling as it lurches, fishtails, and lurches ahead wheels screaming smoke spewing saved only by the straightness of the road and crackling back when Coyote breaks into the Band yelling Wake up! Wake up! Wake up! pulling horn and flicking lights till the truck ahead steadies, straddling half on half off the right shoulder in direct line with the upspeeding concrete support of an overpass and he speaks. Calm and clear and direct.)

"This is Ryder P. Moses," he says. "Going west. Good night and happy motoring."

(Coyote swerves through the flameout, fights for the road as the sky begins a rain of beef.)